DAVID SNATCHED UP THE PAINTED MAP OF GAMEARTH. . . .

He jumped to the fireplace with the big map in his hands. If only he could hold the others off for a few minutes, get the glass hearth doors open, and throw the map in . . .

"No!" Melanie screamed, and grabbed for it.

David wrestled with her for the map. He had gotten the fireplace door open now. He was going to do it. Gamearth would end once and for all. He stared down into the dizzying kaleidoscopic colors of terrain. He seemed to be falling down into it. A flash of light came from one of the brown hexagons of desolation terrain. A jolt of pain sliced across David's cheek, just under his eye. Gamearth was fighting back!

GAME'S END

Kevin J. Anderson

A ROC BOOK

ROC
Published by the Penguin Group
Penguin Books USA Inc., 375 Hudson Street,
New York, New York 10014, U.S.A.
Penguin Books Ltd, 27 Wrights Lane,
London W8 5TZ, England
Penguin Books Australia Ltd, Ringwood,
Victoria, Australia
Penguin Books Canada Ltd, 2801 John Street,
Markham, Ontario, Canada L3R 1B4
Penguin Books (N.Z.) Ltd, 182-190 Wairau Road,
Auckland 10, New Zealand

Penguin Books Ltd, Registered Offices:
Harmondsworth, Middlesex, England

First published by Roc, an imprint of New American Library, a
division of Penguin Books USA Inc.

First Printing, September, 1990
10 9 8 7 6 5 4 3 2 1

 ROC IS A TRADEMARK OF NEW AMERICAN LIBRARY,
A DIVISION OF PENGUIN BOOKS USA INC.

Printed in the United States of America

BOOKS ARE AVAILABLE AT QUANTITY DISCOUNTS WHEN USED TO PROMOTE PRODUCTS OR
SERVICES. FOR INFORMATION PLEASE WRITE TO PREMIUM MARKETING DIVISION, PENGUIN BOOKS
USA INC., 375 HUDSON STREET, NEW YORK, NEW YORK 10014.

For Ed Hagstrom,
who remembers Rule #1
as much as anybody

ACKNOWLEDGMENTS

Other eyes and other imaginations have helped me keep this book on a steady course. I am especially indebted to the suggestions from my writer's workshop: thanks go to Lori Ann White, Gary Shockley, M. Coleman Easton, Clare Bell, Michael C. Berch, and Dan'l Danehy-Oakes—and Linda Searle takes full responsibility for the joke.

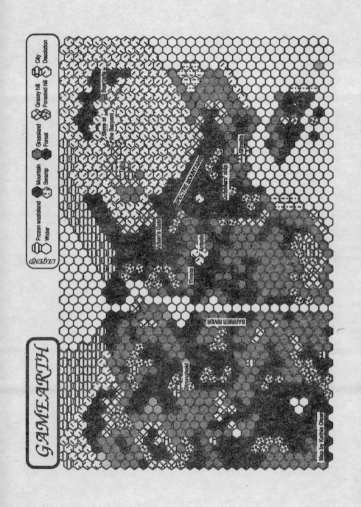

GAMEARTH

Legend: Frozen wasteland, Water, Mountain, Swamp, Grassland, Forest, Grassy hill, Forested hill, City, Desolation

Map by Kathie Olsen

PROLOGUE

David kept watching the clock. As Sunday afternoon ticked toward evening, fear grew inside him, an echo of nightmares and impossible things. Tonight they would play the Game again—or it would play them.

The empty house buzzed with silence. David opened the curtains, revealing the gray afternoon and the cold drizzle outside. Every once in a while, a gust of wind rattled the windows. The house felt fragile, as if at any moment some powerful outside being might crush the walls and sweep him away.

As he had done to characters on Gamearth.

David thought of the flat, colorful game-board that Melanie had painted. For the past two years, he, Melanie, Scott, and Tyrone had acted out their adventures on Gamearth, following rules they had created and adapted from other game systems. They enjoyed their quests for treasure, their battles, their magic. They had fun. That was the primary rule they had all agreed on—to have fun.

But as the four of them had poured their imaginations into the world, created generation after generation of characters, backstitched history and made the entire place whole and real in their minds, the players had created a synergy with their own imagination, a force that had *pushed* their made-up world into a life of its own.

And Gamearth had begun to strike back at them.

David had seen this sooner than any of the other

players. He had suggested they all stop playing before it went further, before it got out of control. But the other players outvoted him. Scott, with his technical "Mister Science" mind, simply could not believe that anything supernatural would happen. Tyrone, with his delight in the game, noticed nothing out of the ordinary.

Melanie, though, recognized the same thing David did, but she ignored what could happen if Gamearth continued to grow in power, to gain its own identity. Melanie wanted to nurture it, to watch in amazement as the Game took over their lives, breaking free from the restrictions the players placed on it. David had seen her eyes glaze over as Gamearth exerted its survival instinct on her.

David tried to create ways to squelch their creation, and Melanie fought against him with her characters. She placed them in conflict with everything he tried to do to save himself, to save them all. She refused to listen when he tried to explain it to her. David let a shudder of desperation run through him.

The house felt gloomy from the cold and wet outside. David went to the fireplace and busied himself starting a fire, using some of the fragrant wood kept in a cardboard box beside the hearth. He thought about turning the stereo on, but decided he would rather think in silence.

He lived with his dad, except for a few weeks in July when he went upstate to stay with his mother in her house trailer. Somehow he had escaped the Game last summer, but perhaps Gamearth had not grown powerful enough then.

David's parents had been separated for three years, talking coldly on the phone every few months, but they had never gone through the actual process of getting divorced. Both of his parents kept their feelings so completely shuttered off from him that David felt isolated even from the conflict. At times, he thought he might actually enjoy it if they tried to make him take sides.

But instead, his mother just engaged him in pleasant, empty conversations about girlfriends and movies, and his father just severely criticized David for his falling grades in the previous semester . . . just when the Game had started to take over. But David's father seemed to be saying those things out of a sense of obligation, not from any deep concern.

David sighed and crumpled a few sheets of old newspaper, on top of which he piled kindling and other debris from the wood box.

His dad had gone away for the weekend on a business trip, asking David if it was all right to be left alone. His tone left it clear that even if David did express an objection, his father wasn't really willing to change his plans anyway.

But David certainly didn't mind being alone this night, when they would play the Game. He felt terrified of what might happen, but he didn't want anyone else there to watch, no . . . outsiders.

He reached for the long fireplace matches, then turned on the gas lighter below the logs. Hissing blue flames swirled up to lick against the bark. He drew a deep breath and closed his eyes.

Over the past two weeks, Gamearth had gotten more vicious in its retaliation, going beyond subtle hints and turning instead to blatant displays of its growing power over the real world. Showing how it could defeat them.

Melanie's characters Delrael and Vailret had gone on a quest to create a vast river as a barrier between the east and west sides of the map. Soon thereafter, while the four outside Players were watching, a blue line had suddenly traced across the painted wooden game-board where the water would have flowed. Then, in the battle at the end of the evening, the dice had started rolling by themselves, bouncing up and down—by magic, the magic *the Players* had put into Gamearth.

During the following week, all four Players had experienced identical dreams, in which they watched other parts of the Game unfold even when they themselves were not playing. The Sorcerer Enrod had taken the Fire Stone and tried to destroy the land on the other side of the Barrier River, only to be stopped by the Deathspirits. They had never played out that scenario, yet all of them remembered it on waking up.

David had planted a creature called Scartaris on the map, a force to absorb the energy from Gamearth, to bring it back to where it was merely a role-playing game, where it was *safe*, with just a painted map and made-up characters, all put together just for fun.

But Gamearth reached out and played Melanie like a puppet. She bent and twisted the rules in ways that David had not considered. In secret, she had added a part of their real world to one of her characters, a golem named Journeyman, just as she had to another ancient character, the Stranger Unlooked-For, who had ruined David's first attempt at defeating Gamearth.

But that had been before David got serious about his own mission. And now that he understood what was going on, he could use the same tactics.

David cleared the family room floor, making an open spot where they would play that night. It was his turn to host. The fire snapped. The earth-tone carpeting seemed to absorb the warmth. A gust of wind rattled the windows again.

Gamearth was waiting. It was eager to play, to manipulate them again. And as it became real by itself, Gamearth would no doubt come out to this world, the *real* world, and begin to Play them. Gamearth would retaliate for all those things that David and the other players had done to their imaginary characters.

He could not let that happen.

David considered simply not showing up. If he didn't

play, then the others couldn't play, and Gamearth could not go on. It was the *four* of them, the synergy of the four distinct personalities that came together to play, week after week—*that* had caused Gamearth to come alive. If he didn't play, the same ingredients wouldn't be there.

David frowned, then ran his hands through his dark hair and found his fingers damp with perspiration. As chilly as it was outside, he still felt sweat from his own fear.

Simply not appearing could be more effective than all his plans to incapacitate Gamearth. His attack with Scartaris had weakened the Game greatly. The map itself was fragile now, and he sensed that Gamearth grew ready to use desperate measures.

If he stayed here, the others would somehow convince him to keep playing. He knew it. They had always done that before. But what if he canceled the game, claimed that he was sick—not too difficult, since he had been having nightmares all week.

He envisioned Gamearth characters looking more vivid and solid to him than any of the people he knew to be truly real. He couldn't face another night of that.

Before he could change his mind, David stood up and went to the telephone. He would call them all, tell them the Game was off, tell them to stay at home. If this idea worked, the Game would be off forever. A stalemate, perhaps, but better than an outright defeat . . . and the loser would lose all if they kept playing.

He picked up the phone. It felt hard and clammy against his hand. He would save Melanie for last; she would be the difficult one.

David started to dial Tyrone's number, but nothing happened. He listened but got no dial tone. He hung up again and tried punching buttons. He could hear no response; the phone was dead.

Moving stiffly, David went to the other phone in the kitchen. It, too, remained silent. He flicked the cradle up and down several times but got no sound on the line.

He felt a shiver up his spine, and he turned to stare out the kitchen window at the slick driveway and the street beyond. In the dimness, orangeish streetlights had flickered on. The storm didn't look very bad, but maybe some falling branch had shorted the phone lines.

Something inside him knew that wasn't the case.

He pulled on his black denim jacket, grabbed his car keys, and went through the garage to his old car in the driveway. Fine, then—he would forget about politeness.

He simply wouldn't be there when the others showed up. He made sure he had all the lights off in the house and all the doors locked. David would be gone, at a movie somewhere, or maybe just out driving.

When he stepped outside, drizzle spattered his face, making him squint. He grabbed the handle of the driver's-side door of the red Mustang, got in, and pulled the door shut. The hinges squeaked. But inside the car, he felt safe and comfortable. He could smell leftover scents of the rain, candy wrappers on the floor and in the ashtray, and the odor of old upholstery; it all seemed reassuring to him. A gust of wind rocked the car as if a giant invisible hand of some outside Player were trying to pick it up.

David slid the key into the ignition and turned it. The starter made a single click as it cranked, but otherwise the car made no other sound. Again and again, he twisted his wrist, jamming the key around. The keys clinked together, and the wind made noises outside. The engine remained dead.

"Come on! Start!" David hissed through his teeth.

But the Mustang refused even to try. David kept it running in perfect condition. It had *always* started for him. This was no coincidence.

With a balled fist, David pounded the cold dash and

gritted his teeth. In angry despair, he dropped his head against the steering wheel, then jerked back up as a blast from the horn startled him.

He could walk, he could go somewhere else. He had never tried hitchhiking before. But he knew Gamearth wasn't going to let him get away, no matter what he tried to do. The Game held him. He had to play.

Blinking back needle-sharp tears, David got out of the car and slammed the door again. Standing in the driveway as the drizzle came down on his cheeks, he felt the wind in his hair, cutting through the denim of his jacket. He growled under his breath, "All right then, damn you! I tried to end this. I tried to cut my losses and yours."

He sucked in another deep breath. "You'd better be prepared to win, because this time I'm playing for keeps!"

He waited for some sort of answer, but the rain only whipped up harder and colder.

1

PRISONER OF WAR

"Such monsters I have seen, Victor! It makes me doubt the Outsiders have even the slightest understanding of biological principles. But no matter how fantastical these monsters may seem, they are certainly dangerous, beyond a shadow of a doubt.

—Professor Verne,
Les Voyages Extraordinaires
(unpublished journal)

Professor Jules Verne had a difficult time maintaining his self-respect as the Slac guards hustled him forward. He stumbled, and his legs were weak and shaking. The monsters jabbed him in the ribs with their sharp knuckles. They cast him on the flagstoned floor in the main hall of Tairé.

Verne bit back a retort and allowed himself only a muffled grunt of indignation. Over the past several days, his captors had pummeled him with the polished ends of their clubs every time he became too vocal in his complaints. Now he contented himself with imagining extravagant insults instead.

Verne stood up and cleared his throat, still keeping his eyes closed. He brushed at the front of his indigo and brown plaid greatcoat, but the coat would need serious cleaning and pressing before he could feel presentable again.

In front of him in the firelight waited Siryyk the manicore, rumbling deep in his throat.

16

The leader of all the monsters towered twelve feet above the floor, though he remained seated on his haunches. His huge, maned head showed a smashed and distorted human face, with two curved horns protruding from the forehead. Siryyk's body was built like a lion's but was as massive as an elephant's. His front claws glittered like curved knives. The segmented tail curled around his legs was silvery, wider than a man's thigh, and tipped at its bulbous end with a wicked stinger like that of an enormous scorpion. Flickers of blue lightning traced the stinger and the tail, as if the manticore could barely control the power he contained.

The venomous tail flinched when Verne gazed up at Siryyk. Sparks snapped against the flagstones, highlighting other blackened spots from other times the beast had twitched his tail.

"I brought you here, human, to give you the honor of assisting me in winning the Game." Siryyk's voice was deep and liquid, as if he were gargling with some caustic substance. He reached forward with one forepaw and scraped his claws against the stone.

Verne blinked in shock and cleared his throat. "But that's not why I came here at all."

A bright light flashed and an explosion echoed from the floor as the manticore smashed his tail down. "I don't believe I asked about your preference."

Verne tried to hold his ground, but he felt overwhelmed by everything he had seen and done in the last few turns. Through dreams and guidance from the Outsider named Scott, he and his colleague Professor Frankenstein had constructed a new kind of weapon. Verne had driven a steam-engine car all the way from Sitnalta to where the growing destructive force of Scartaris appeared ready to destroy Gamearth. The Sitnaltan weapon would surely eliminate Scartaris, but it was so powerful that it might also destroy Gamearth. That thought had not occurred to Verne until long after he had invented it.

He had driven his vehicle to the desolate battlefield where Scartaris had gathered his horde. Verne had set its detectors on auto-pilot and adjusted the timer for his weapon. But a meddling ogre had appeared out of the battle, intent on something else entirely, and had tossed Verne out of the car. Taking over, the ogre rode the steam-engine vehicle toward Scartaris.

The Sitnaltan weapon had never gone off as expected.

Verne, perhaps too perplexed for his own good, but obsessed with gathering all information he could about the performance of his own device, remained behind. Before returning to Sitnalta in disgrace, he had to discover what had gone wrong.

The following day, he tried to find the steam-engine vehicle in the wreckage of the mountains. After hours of searching, he had found it intact among the broken rocks with the weapon still primed. But before Verne had been able to look at the mechanism and determine anything about the malfunction, other scavenging monsters captured him.

At times, he felt like kicking himself for his own stupidity, his own naiveté. After the giant battle, during which the Earthspirits and Deathspirits appeared and defeated Scartaris, Verne had not concerned himself with the remainder of the horde or what they might do if they found him. They had seemed of no consequence to him. He couldn't be bothered with such details when the question of the failed weapon loomed so large.

Unfortunately, the monsters didn't see it that way.

A troop of reptilian Slac, drawing weapons, had surrounded him among the deep shadows and broken rocks. One of them carried a sputtering torch, and Verne could see their slitted eyes in the light. For an instant, the professor thought they were going to execute him without even attempting to communicate.

Several Slac drew dull black arrows; one pulled out a pronged knife. They hissed and drooled and stepped toward him. Verne could only stand gaping in disbelief. He had not thought his predicament through, and he hated to die looking so stupid. The Sitnaltans admired his ideas, but some had chuckled, with good reason apparently, at their "absent-minded" professor.

But then the commander of the monster band, a powerful general named Korux, had ordered them to stop their attack and explained, "All of the other human characters have disappeared. Their army is gone. This is the only one of the enemy we have found." Korux looked at the Slac while Verne stood frozen, waiting to hear what he would say. "Take him with minimal damage."

The Slac general stood staring at Verne and narrowed his yellow eyes. "We must squeeze information out of this one. We can learn what happened here and learn how we could have been so badly defeated by an army that doesn't even exist!"

Professor Verne did not resist when they grabbed his arms and prodded his sides with the blunt ends of their weapons. He watched with great dismay as the misshapen creatures grabbed the delicate Sitnaltan weapon—so close to its detonation—and passed it among themselves as a spoil of war.

Korux ordered his underlings to take the steam-engine car. Verne twisted his head to glance back at the once-beautiful red vehicle of Sitnalta, with its cushioned seats, the tattered canopy to shade him from sunlight during long days of driving, and the great brass boiler that provided the car's power. The monsters pushed the vehicle along the blasted terrain, grunting and struggling against the rocks and broken ground.

So Verne had been taken prisoner, sweating, dirty, and hungry. Bound in rusty chains, he could barely move as his captors hustled him along, treating him like a piece of walking baggage.

The horde had gathered itself together once more under the leadership of the hulking manticore and marched westward, away from the dawn and toward the city of Tairé.

Verne spent several days in confusion and despair. His captors forced him to eat the bubbling black porridge they slopped in front of him. It tasted of sulfur and ashes; the water they gave him to drink was warm and brackish. His hands were bound, his legs shackled.

The professor's mind remained free, though—a powerful advantage to him. But he had no resources, no way he could invent a means for himself to escape.

Finally, after the monster army had reached the city of Tairé, Siryyk the manticore took time in the evening to summon Verne, his prisoner of war.

Without explanation, two hulking creatures with leathery shriveled skin and pinched faces hauled Verne from where he had been trying to sleep against a broken wall. They dragged him forward, pushing, elbowing, jabbing, forcing him to stumble as fast as his legs would move. He had given up asking questions of his captors and so just watched and waited, cooperating as little as possible, as much as necessary.

His escorts led him into what appeared to be a great banquet hall supported by stone pillars. The walls were painted full of colorful frescoes that depicted humans at work building a city. All of the pictures had been defaced with white marks from skittering claws, splatters of black tar, or smears of ash or excrement.

The hall looked empty and damaged. The vaulted ceiling left skylights open to a cold, star-studded night. Along the rafters hung glazed clay pots, some broken, some holding scraggly, dead plants.

Firepits had been dug deep in the floor for burning oil-soaked support beams from demolished buildings. Dancing orange flames shone on the painted wall, making sharp shadows. Verne blinked in the thick, smoky air, trying to clear his vision.

Siryyk the manticore growled down at him, leaning forward and showing his sharp teeth in the firelight.

Verne kept his mouth shut. He knew how delicate a line he walked as a prisoner; any time Siryyk liked, he could order Verne's head sliced off and leave the body for the other monsters to feed on. The other characters in Tairé had not been so fortunate.

The Slac general stepped out beside the manticore. Korux was clothed in a black, oily garment; tassels marked the sleeves, and glints shone from blood-red gems stitched on one breast. Verne got the impression that Korux had risen in rank because of the professor's successful capture.

Korux spoke from beside the manticore. "We know who you are: Professor Jules Verne of Sitnalta." The Slac voice sounded thin and rasping after the manticore. "We know why you came here."

Verne straightened in surprise, trying to keep his expression neutral. Was Korux bluffing? Verne had never spoken about his past; in fact, the monsters had never asked or interrogated him in any way. He thrust out his chin, making his gray beard bristle.

Korux raised his left hand and clicked the claws together. Two other Slac appeared from outside the scarred banquet hall, grunting as they carried between them the small but extraordinarily heavy weapon that he and Frankenstein had built. Verne's eyes widened as he saw the polished cylinder of whitish metal taken from the ruined Outsiders' ship, a set of red fins, and a bullet-shaped brass top with lights, dials, and gauges that might tell Verne what had gone wrong with the detonation—and also how many seconds remained on the bomb's timer.

Scrawled on the side in black grease-pencil stood the number 17/2, the patent number that Professors Verne and Frankenstein would have obtained for their awesome weapon. But they had sworn never to build another one, intending such a device to be used only once, only to destroy Scartaris.

The manticore spoke up. "We have found your

personal journals, Professor Verne. They are very interesting. *Les Voyages Extraordinaires*—is that some kind of code? Everything else is in plain language."

Korux reached into his slick black garment and removed a battered volume. The cover looked bent; some of the pages were loose and shoved back into the binding of the book, which contained Verne's own account of his extraordinary journey and the thoughts he had had while traveling across the map. It told everything about his mission and the Sitnaltan weapon.

Verne stared at the journal in astonishment. It had been pounded into him throughout all his years of education that, for the sake of the posterity of other characters, he *must* keep records of all his ideas and all the inventions that he might envision. The ideas of any Sitnaltan inventor were to benefit all Gamearth.

It had never occurred to Verne that those ideas might fall into the hands of an evil creature such as Siryyk, but even if they did, he had not imagined the possibility that the manticore could actually read and comprehend the information.

"I am a fool!" he muttered to himself.

Siryyk was the chosen commander of all the monster troops. He had to be intelligent. Scartaris had selected him to lead the most gigantic army ever to appear on Gamearth. He was not a slavering, brainless beast.

The manticore scratched his claws on the flagstones. "I understand the magnitude of power that this weapon contains. The map of Gamearth holds many things of such power. I want them all, and I will do whatever is necessary to get them." His distorted face took on a reflective expression.

"You see, when the six Spirits destroyed Scartaris and nearly obliterated themselves as well, all of Gamearth convulsed and broke. Something happened to the Rules. They may not hold as absolutely as they have in the past.

"And even if the Outsiders do indeed plan to ruin Gamearth so that it troubles them no more, I intend to get all the protection I can. I do not know what effect your weapon or any of these other things, magical things, might have on the Outside. But if the end of the Game is coming, *I* will be the one with the best chance of surviving."

Siryyk lowered his head and hunched forward, widening amber eyes that had the color of honey mixed with acid. Verne winced from the stench of the beast's breath.

"Listen to me, Professor Verne," the manticore continued. "The Outsider Scott may come to you in dreams and offer ideas, but I have dreams too. In my dreams, I can see the Outsider David. I know what he intends to do. And I can feel the anger, the desperation, he feels toward us. I also know how it is breaking him. I am no longer certain how this is happening, whether he appears in my dreams, *or if I appear in his!*"

Verne said nothing in his surprise. The other monsters seemed to be listening but made no move.

"I am doing what I can to thwart the Outsider David's own plans, though he thinks that I am his ally."

Verne cleared his throat. "Um, that is very . . . interesting, but I can't help you. That's all there is to it. Yes, I did construct the weapon, as you have learned from my own journals, but as you also know, it didn't work. It malfunctioned, and I don't know why. Obviously, my idea was wrong. The Sitnaltan weapon is no weapon at all."

Siryyk stood up, and Verne could see the ripple of muscles running down his sandy, leonine back. His huge shadow cast by opposing clusters of firelight rose in tandem against the bright frescoes on the wall, dominating them and swallowing them up.

"General Korux, would you please remove the prisoner's left shoe."

Making a husky sound deep in his throat, the Slac general moved forward, flexing his clawed fingers. Verne shrank back, but his two shrivel-skinned monster guards grabbed him by his bruised arms. Korux bent over and held Verne's black shoe in both reptilian hands. After fumbling unsuccessfully with the laces, the Slac general snorted and used one claw to rip them out of the leather. Tossing the broken laces aside, he peeled off the shoe.

Verne's foot was cramped and sweaty. He had not been able to change clothes, not even his socks, in days. But he felt no relief to be able to flex his toes now.

The manticore went to one of the firepits and, reaching into the coals with his massive hands, he pulled out a stubby, smoke-blackened dagger. Its blade glowed bright orange from the heat.

The twisted lips on Siryyk's human face bent upward, exposing overlapping fangs in his mouth. "I am going to play a game with you, Professor Verne. I think you can repair whatever went wrong with this weapon. And if that is not the case, I think you can make another weapon, something different, a giant destructive toy for me to play with. Judging by your journals, your mind is filled with useful ideas like that."

He looked down at the blade and placed his own thickly padded finger against the yellow-hot point. Verne winced as he heard the loud sizzle and smelled the wisp of smoke as the glowing metal ate its way into the manticore's finger pad. Siryyk withdrew his hand, looked at the wound, and frowned, but he showed no other sign of discomfort.

"Now then, our game." Siryyk looked around to the other monsters gathered at the entrance and standing along the walls. The manticore raised his voice.

"Shall we take bets on how many of the Professor's toes we will have to burn off before he agrees to cooperate?"

Verne swooned even as the monsters shouted out their bets.

INTERLUDE: OUTSIDE

The other three Players arrived together, keeping oddly silent, as if they could all feel the tension, too. David stared at Melanie, Scott, and Tyrone as they entered in one group; in the back of his mind, he kept imagining how they had banded together against him. Gamearth had forced them into it. He narrowed his eyes, but Tyrone stepped into the front hallway, grinning as he shucked his damp jacket and laid it on the bench.

"I got it! I passed."

David looked back at him, completely confused. "What are you talking about?"

"My driver's license! I passed, just on Friday. I borrowed my dad's car and picked up Scott and Mel."

Melanie stood beside Scott. In her hands she held the large wooden map of Gamearth wrapped in plastic to protect it from the drizzle. Her knuckles were white from her tight grip, as if she thought the map might be in danger.

"Good for you," David said to him.

"Tyrone kept babbling about it all the way over here," Scott said. He used the corner of his shirt to wipe the raindrops from his glasses. Melanie mumbled something and went straight into the family room, where she laid the map on the carpet. Her eyes were bright as she unwrapped the wet plastic and stared at the colorful patterns of Gamearth.

It looked as if a truck had run over it. Black stains showed the explosions of the great battle from the

previous week, when Melanie's golem-weapon named
Journeyman, as well as Gamearth's own Earthspirits
and Deathspirits, had destroyed David's greatest creation, Scartaris. Gamearth's destructive power, its ability to strike back at the outside world, was plain for
anyone to see.

But the map also showed cracks and jagged splinters
at the edges. A few of the hexagonal segments of
terrain had split loose, like tiles in a mosaic—which
was impossible, since they were merely a pattern painted
on a smooth surface of wood.

David stood over the map, and Melanie pointedly
refused to look at him. He felt sullen, afraid to wait,
and afraid to move on. As if mechanically, he went
into the kitchen and brought out the bags of chips he
had opened. Standing beside the stove-island, he poured
glasses of soda without asking what anyone wanted.

All their conversation felt forced. Everybody seemed
as uneasy as he was, except for Tyrone.

Tyrone went back outside to his car, leaving the
front door open. David felt a cold gust of wind and
stared, annoyed. But Tyrone reappeared, holding a
foil-wrapped platter.

"Wait until you guys taste this one! My masterpiece,
I think. It's got that imitation crab stuff, hot mustard,
Worcestershire sauce, and sour cream—goes great on
those wheat crackers."

"You sound like a commercial, Tyrone," Scott
muttered.

Tyrone didn't seem to know whether to take that as
a compliment or an insult, so he changed the subject.
"Okay, here's the joke for this week. What goes 'Ha!
Ha! Ha . . . *Thump*!'?"

David set down another bowl of chips.

"Oh, brother, Tyrone . . ."

He grinned. "A man laughing his head off!"

Melanie sat cross-legged on the carpet beside the
map, holding her soda in one hand. The firelight danced

across the room. David left the lights on in the kitchen, but the fire was the only illumination in the family room. It seemed appropriate to play in the firelight.

Melanie tucked her long brown hair behind her ears and drew a deep breath. She looked at David with a petulant expression. "We all dreamed again this week, David. We talked about it in the car. You must have, too."

"Every night," Tyrone said. "Better than watching movies."

"Tyrone, you're such a dweeb," Scott said, scowling. "This is real! Start taking it seriously. Even *I* remembered the dreams this time, and I almost never have dreams."

David bristled. He spoke in a low and serious voice. "No, Scott, this is not real. All of you—can't you understand? It's just a game! We made it up! It's not supposed to be real! And when a game goes beyond that, it gets dangerous. It's time to stop." He stifled an exasperated laugh. "You should look at yourselves. You guys are like puppets, pawns!"

Tyrone squatted on the floor and dumped their dice out of the suede pouch. They fell to the carpet, showing various numbers and glittering different colors. Two of them fell next to the wooden game map.

"Well, I'm anxious to see how it all turns out," Tyrone said. "This has been absolutely the most *intense* game I have ever imagined! My parents sure yelled at me for what happened to the kitchen table last week, though. They still can't figure out what we did."

David scowled; he could have guessed how Tyrone would react. In fact, after their years of playing together, the four of them had grown so close that they *all* knew how each other would react. They all knew the world of Gamearth and its characters and the rules of the Game inside and out. That was how they could continue playing with their own unorthodox methods, enjoying their adventures without any godlike game-master arbitrating their moves. Each of them watched over certain sections of the map. It was a strange system, developed for their own group . . . for a very unusual fantasy world— a fantasy world that was coming alive.

David decided to remain silent instead of voicing the same old arguments and objections. Gamearth had too powerful a hold on the others, and David would never convince them, at least not by arguing.

He would have to use the same tricks Melanie used. He could come up with his own twists in the rules. It was time to play dirty.

He would win the Game in his own way.

2

COMBINED FORCES

> *Combat is very important in the Game. A character's chances for victory are improved by thorough training; an army in general may increase its probability of success simply by being prepared.*
>
> —The Book of Rules

Tareah opened her eyes and uncurled her fingers. The nails had dug into her palms from the strain, and black spots of exhaustion still fluttered in her vision.

When she saw the piles of new supplies that had appeared because of her spell, Tareah let out a sigh of relief. She slumped back against the ruined wooden wall, the only part of the Stronghold still standing.

According to Rule #8, a magic-user character on Gamearth was allowed only three spells a day. But Tareah held three important magical artifacts, which increased the daily allotment of spells she could cast. She had been using all her extra spells just to replenish the stockpiles in the Stronghold and the storage sheds in the village. Delrael's growing army would need all the supplies before they could march out against the enemy; she felt glad to be doing something to help, rather than just passively observing.

Tareah possessed the sapphire Water Stone, whose powers controlled water and the weather; also, she carried the Fire Stone, an eight-sided ruby that could control fire. The Sentinel Enrod, his mind twisted by

Scartaris, had come to the Barrier River to destroy the western land with the Fire Stone's power, but the Deathspirits had stopped him, cursing him to push his raft back and forth across the river for the rest of the Game. The Spirits had stripped him of his gem and given it to Tareah, the only other full-blooded Sorcerer on all of Gamearth. These two Stones increased her spell allotment from three to five per day.

She also kept the four-sided Air Stone, the diamond that had been lost many turns before but then found by Gairoth the ogre and his runt dragon Rognoth. Gairoth had used its powers to take over the Stronghold, but Delrael defeated him in battle and took the Stone.

Later, with the Air Stone's powers of illusion, Bryl had created an imaginary army to engage the monster horde of Scartaris.

"My turn," Bryl said beside her, holding out his hand. Dressed in his blue cloak, the half-Sorcerer looked old and fragile. His gray beard had grown so bushy that it dominated his appearance. As soon as Tareah handed him the Stones, Bryl's spell allotment also would increase to six per day. She enjoyed manipulating the Rules like that; it would have made her father Sardun proud.

By the time Delrael had returned to the Stronghold from his previous quest, telling of the vast army of monsters that would soon march across the map, Tareah had already begun training the villagers. They had already seen the threat of Scartaris in their own homes.

Taking charge again, Delrael ordered the manufacture of new weapons. Derow the blacksmith worked himself to exhaustion, hammering out blade after blade; others made spears and arrowheads, bows, and shields. The forests around Steep Hill were picked clear of suitable wood.

Couriers went out to the surrounding villages, spreading the warning and calling all able characters to meet

at the Stronghold for training. Delrael meant to put
together an army, as a last defense for Gamearth, the
greatest rallying of human characters since the epic
battles of the Scouring.

War supplies came in from mining villages, smelted
iron ore in long rods, and ingots of bronze and copper.
Many characters rejoiced to see the Game mounting
toward a tremendous showdown. Some of them wanted
to have fun.

Delrael drilled all the incoming trainees. The top of
the Hill, where the Stronghold had once stood tall
and undefeated, was cleared of debris from the out-
buildings. In its place stood a training field: sword
posts and archery targets, single-combat practice
grounds, and straw dummies for spear thrusts. After
the first few days, the noise and shouting, the clang of
weapons, and the outcries of exertion or victory seemed
like an unrelenting drone on Tareah's ears.

All the while, Tareah watched Delrael grow confident, growing with his new role, as if he had been
waiting for this all his life. She thought of how his
father Drodanis must have appeared. It gave Tareah a
thrill to feel she actually knew someone like that. She
had spent so many years reading the legends.

Her father Sardun had kept her trapped in the Ice
Palace, holding her in the body of a child for thirty
years, hoping that another full-blooded Sorcerer would
be born through the vagaries of the Game. She had
been alone with the Sorcerer relics, wandering through
the rainbow corridors of blue ice, looking out at the
white wastelands of frozen terrain, the hexagons of
mountains in the distance. She had stared out at the
mosaic map of Gamearth and wondered what else was
happening across the world. She never imagined she
would see as much of it as she already had.

Sardun had at one time even earmarked her for
marriage to Enrod of Tairé. But Enrod and Sardun
had a great many differences and arguments about the

past, the future, and how the Sorcerer race fit into it
all. Tareah had never met Enrod. He never came to
the Ice Palace to see the history of the Game that
Sardun had collected since the Transition.

Now, beside the broken Stronghold wall, Tareah
stood up and brushed off her knees. The joints ached,
but not as badly as before. Her body had finally stopped
growing. When her father died and the Palace melted
into broken chunks, the spell binding her in the shape
of a little girl faded away. Her body began to catch up
rapidly with her age, growing into adulthood through
weeks of wracking pain as her joints, muscles, and
bones tried to accommodate the drastic growth.

Tareah stood tall and beautiful, with long pale hair
and fair skin of the sort meant for colder hexagons.
She knew Delrael found her attractive, and Vailret
could barely speak a coherent sentence around her in
his charming shyness. She caught sidelong glances from
several other male characters, but they were too much
in awe of Gamearth's last surviving Sorcerer female
even to approach her.

Tareah felt odd around these human characters. She
was with them, yet apart from them. For three decades, her father had forced her to study the history of
the Game. He made her learn the Rules inside and
out, with all their nuances and implications. Sardun
made her believe that the Game had something special
in store for her, that she was not an ordinary person.
So Tareah forced herself to remain aloof from the
others.

Next to her, Bryl muttered something under his
breath. She saw him sitting with his eyes squeezed
shut and his lips clamped tight, saying a spell to himself. Another pile of supplies flickered into existence
next to the others.

When Bryl leaned back with a sigh, Tareah said,
"I'm going to find Vailret." She looked up, and in the
failing light of dusk, she saw Delrael striding among

the other fighters in the training area, helping one woman with her sword stroke, showing a young man how better to hold his bow. Delrael would be busy here until there was not enough light in the sky to see by.

She left the clamor of practice battles behind and went down the hill path toward the village, moving quickly to keep her balance on the slope. The air had grown chilly already. Winter would come soon.

In the village below, tents and temporary shelters had been set up for all the new inhabitants. Inside the tent enclosures, flickering light from braziers and candles made moving shadows of the characters within.

New tents appeared every day as trainees and able-bodied helpers arrived at the Stronghold village. Word of Delrael's rekindled training spread across the western half of the map. Tareah remembered stories of Drodanis and his brother Cayon and their own legendary training sessions. Characters had come from hexagons all around to undergo instruction before setting off through catacombs and dungeons in the simple treasure-hunting adventures in the early days of the Game.

Delrael's exercises appeared frantic and desperate by comparison, with the fate of the entire map looming over their heads. Delrael brought the characters together, found what they could do, and had them practice with each other. They sharpened skills and traded hints and strategies, did anything that might help in a pitched battle or single combat against the army of Scartaris.

Tareah saw light glowing from the home of Mostem, who baked bread and fruit-pastries. Mostem was a widower and had three daughters. He constantly tried to convince either Delrael or Vailret to marry any one of them. Since the destruction of the Stronghold, Vailret and his mother, Siya, had lived with the baker's family.

One of Mostem's daughters opened the door at Tareah's knock. The three daughters each looked the same; Tareah could tell them apart only by the varying lengths of their dusty-brown hair. All three were squat, with turned-up noses and narrow, dull eyes, and kind enough, the type who would be described in their later years as "sturdy women." The girl blinked as if trying to remember what she was supposed to say when guests came to the door.

"I need to see Vailret," Tareah said. "Is he working in here?"

Mostem's daughter opened the door wider. Tareah went in, paying her no further attention. The smells of fresh bread and yeast filled the main room, along with warmth from the wall on the other side of which Mostem had his big ovens.

Vailret looked up at her and grinned, self-consciously brushing back his straw-colored hair. He had a thin nose and bright eyes that squinted too often. "Hello, Tareah!"

"Welcome, Tareah," Siya said from her seat against the wall. "While you're talking to my son, I'd appreciate a little help here." She motioned at a mound of weapons and armor in need of repair beside her.

After watching the Stronghold destroyed before her own eyes, Siya had adopted the cause wholeheartedly. She could wield none of the larger weapons, but Siya adapted her skills to help administer the growing army after Delrael's call to arms. It was Siya who kept track of the numbers of trainees and where they came from. Siya managed the food distribution and found lodging for all of them; she kept the practical matters running smoothly.

She spent the rest of her spare time repairing and cleaning the old weapons they had kept at the Stronghold and the relics brought in by trainees. Patched and restitched leather armor lay in a separate pile, cleaned and smelling of sweet oil. She polished rust off of blades, sharpening and oiling them. Now, she took a metal awl and chipped out hardened dirt and mud from the mechanism of a crossbow.

"Plenty here to do," she said, indicating the heap again.

"Mother!" Vailret turned to her, scowling. "Tareah's been using all six of her spells every day to replenish our supplies. That should be enough." He turned to look at Tareah.

"Well, I have been doing that." She smiled at him, which seemed to set Vailret all aglow. "But I can still do something while I watch what you're doing."

Without looking, Siya picked up an ornate battle-ax and untangled some fresh leather thongs from a pile on the floor. "The handle here needs to be rewrapped. The old lacings got blood on them and have started to rot."

Tareah used a knife blade to scrape the dark old leather from the ax handle and then began twisting new thongs along the wood.

Vailret leaned over his table where he had spread out the huge map of Gamearth. He seemed to be showing off to her. Other characters had constructed the big master map over generations of exploring the world and adventuring. It had once been mounted on the Stronghold wall but was damaged with the collapse of the main building. Vailret had used some of his own notes and talked to several old characters to reconstruct the details.

The flickering candles around the table made Tareah nervous that they would set the map on fire; and in fact, a few specks of wax had spattered on it. Siya always insisted that Vailret maintain enough light for his close work, especially with his weak eyesight.

Vailret squinted at two hexagons, trying to brush away smudges on a hex of forested-hill terrain. "After I get all the pieces together, I'm going to make several copies of the map for characters to have when we finally go on the march," he said. "We need to know where we're going. That'll save us lots of time."

Vailret flashed his gaze at her, as if sharing a secret. "Look here. With all the new characters coming in, we're learning about dozens of villages. Either they're new settlements, or somehow they went undiscovered during all our years of questing!"

Siya snorted at him without looking up from her work, "Characters are settling down, Vailret. Lots of them stopped questing by the time your father was killed. All those characters had to live somewhere. What did you expect?"

Vailret ignored her. "And something else strange is happening, very strange. I've only just figured it out. Our couriers were told to move as fast as they could, to explore, to find all the villages and pass along the warning about Scartaris's army. Most of the couriers traveled through their allotted number of hexagons and then stopped, out of habit. But some of them found that there's no restriction anymore! They can go farther. No matter what the *Book of Rules* says."

Tareah stopped her work with the ax handle and looked up at him. She felt a sudden rush of fear.

Vailret dropped his voice to a whisper. "With the Outsiders disrupting the Game, with the Earthspirits and Deathspirits coming back and Scartaris nearly destroying the map, and the great battle, and . . . and with the piece of *reality* that Journeyman carried, something is going very wrong with Gamearth. *Characters are breaking the Rules!* For now, it's just travel restrictions that we know about, but maybe you can use more than your number of spells each day." He raised his eyebrows. "Who knows what else can happen?"

Tareah blinked at him in shock. "That can't be! The Rules are what hold Gamearth together. Without the Rules, we . . . it would be chaos!"

"Maybe that's what we're in for, whether we win or lose."

Tareah tied the leather thongs and set the ax on top of the mound of repaired weapons. She looked up to take something else from Siya, but the old woman had packed her tools and stood up.

"Come on, Vailret, time to go," Siya said. "It's dark outside, and they'll be doing the quest-tellings again. You know how much you enjoy those."

Siya gave him what appeared to be a patronizing look, but Tareah knew that Siya enjoyed the quest-tellings as much as the rest of the villagers, especially now that she had become more interested in the battles. She always liked to hear legends about her husband, Cayon, and his quests with Drodanis.

Outside, in the center of the village, the other characters had gathered around a bonfire made from the split trunks of some of the large trees; all of the smaller branches had already been used for making spears and arrows.

To start things off, one of the characters from a mining village began telling how in her work underground she had broken into a network of catacombs that appeared ancient and well-worn by the many who had once traveled there. Marveling at her discovery, she armed herself, took supplies, and set off to explore the tunnels, where many of the early quests of the Game must have taken place. She was gone a full day, mapping her progress and moving warily, eyes open for any sort of trap or attack. In the end, she found only a few scattered gems and dusty coins, and one broken skeleton of a misshapen monster. The dungeon was dead and empty, and so she had not bothered to return there again, though some of the children of her village occasionally played there.

Accompanied by five of his students, Delrael finally came striding into the village, finished with the last details of the day's training exercises. Tareah saw him, encased in a set of armor, well-muscled, and confident in his abilities. He smiled at Tareah, Vailret, and Siya sitting together near the fire . . .

They shared food and sipped steaming cider from wooden mugs. Delrael looked very tired but charged with a new kind of energy. After some coaxing from the others, he began telling of his battle with the Cailee, the shadow-thing that was the deadly alter ego of Mindar from Tairé, a companion of theirs. As he spoke of how they had locked themselves in an underground storeroom, Tareah could picture them all waiting in darkness as the Cailee prowled just on the other side of the door, scratching at the wood with its long silver claws. Delrael told how the Cailee had attacked them out in the desert the following night, as they sat around their campfire, how it had slaughtered Mindar's horse and thrown the head into the fire . . .

Just then, a commotion among the gathered characters made Delrael pause in his story. Vailret squinted into the night. Tareah turned to see another figure approaching out of the twilight, a man dressed in dark and tattered clothes. He stumbled forward, seeming to emerge from the dark surrounding forests.

He came forward one step at a time, swaying, concentrating on his balance. Several of the trainees leaped up to steady the man, bringing him toward the firelight. His face was scratched and smeared with mud and grime. He looked gaunt and starving, his eyes sunken. Though they brought him close to the fire, the stranger continued to shiver violently.

"Well, get him some water or something!" Delrael shouted. Before he had finished his command, someone thrust a dripping ladle into his hand, and then Delrael poured its contents on the haggard man's mouth, not caring that most of it spilled down the stranger's chin.

The man gasped and turned to stare at all of them, as if suddenly realizing where he was. He seemed to melt. He looked dark of skin, with tangled black hair and strong calloused hands.

"Tell us your name," Vailret said, leaning close. "Where did you come from?"

The man's eyes flashed with alarm, and he gawked at the fire as if it would reach out and consume him. "From Tairé." He drew in a long, sucking breath, then slumped beside the fire.

3

FOUR STONES

"Yes, if all the Sorcerers depart from Gamearth, we will leave behind human fighters to defend it—but we will also leave many enemies there. We must give humans a greater advantage, a means to fight! We have much magic at our disposal. What are we going to do with it?"

—Arken, proposing that the old
Sorcerer Council create the four Stones

Delrael stood up in the firelight and spread his arms as other characters pushed forward, chattering with each other. The stranger flinched at their sudden reaction. "Stand back!" Delrael shouted to overcome their noise. "Give the man room to breathe!"

The others backed off as the stranger sat slumped and cross-legged in the dirt, shivering despite the fire's warmth. His drab clothes, dark hair and skin reminded Delrael of Tairé, the city where Scartaris had stolen the minds of all its inhabitants. Tairé was the home of Mindar, the one woman somehow immune to Scartaris's control; she alone had attacked Scartaris's installations while the other Tairans unknowingly worked at creating weapons.

But this man had escaped from Tairé. After the destruction of Scartaris, he had somehow made his way here.

Before Delrael could say anything else, Siya squatted down with a mug of steaming cider in her hands.

She looked with disdain at the unmoving spectators. "Have him drink this."

The Tairan man took the mug and held it in both hands but sat staring down at its surface. The trembling in his body caused tiny ripples to flow across the top, disturbing his reflection. He finally took a sip.

They all sat in silence. Delrael realized they were waiting for him to ask the questions, to find out what had brought the man here.

"The man needs rest," Delrael said to the other characters. "He's had a long and terrible journey. We'll find a place for him to stay. He can talk to us tomorrow."

"No!" the man said, coughing. He scowled at the cider, then took another drink. "I came this far. I can tell my story. You need to know what's happened."

Delrael dropped his voice and tried to sound gentle. "All right then, tell us your name."

The Tairan blinked, as if unable to understand the relevance of the question. He held one hand out to the fire and visibly began to let exhaustion take hold.

"I am Jathen. You . . ." And then a flash shot across the stranger's face. He turned so quickly that some of his cider sloshed out of the mug. *"Delrael!"* he said in an inhuman whisper that sent shudders down Delrael's spine.

Delrael remembered all of the Tairans massing toward him under the direction of Scartaris, ready to tear him and his companions apart with their mob frenzy. Hissing in unison, they had all uttered his name: *Delrael!*

Jathen must have been among them.

The Tairan man's expression fell. "We didn't mean to do that. None of us could help it. Now I can't help remembering."

"It's all right," Delrael said. "We know what Scartaris

did to you. What happened to your city beyond what we've already seen?"

Jathen glanced up with lost eyes. "As if that wasn't terrible enough." He shook his head.

"It happened just before dawn a few weeks ago. Scartaris was like a terrible nightmare, and we sleepwalked through it all. But then, all of a sudden, Scartaris vanished from our minds. He was gone, destroyed somehow. We in Tairé were free to face the horror of what we had done, what we had nearly helped him accomplish.

"We were stunned, but we managed to count our losses, and learn exactly who had been killed . . ." He paused, stumbling over his words, and forced himself to continue. "We learned who *we* had killed.

"Then we searched for Enrod, who had helped us build Tairé and resurrect it from the desolation. Enrod had been our strength, our guiding force, a true visionary with the best intentions for all human characters. But Enrod had left us. We couldn't understand what happened."

Jathen stared around at the faces, as if searching for some explanation. Vailret cleared his throat and turned his gaze away as he answered. "Scartaris twisted Enrod's mind as well. The Deathspirits trapped him on the Barrier River and sentenced him to shuttle his raft from one side to the other for the rest of the Game."

Jathen hung his head. "Enrod deserved better than that after all the good he did."

Delrael sighed. "The Deathspirits did not seem willing to negotiate." The bonfire continued to crackle as some of the burning logs collapsed into ashes.

Jathen remained silent, digesting the news about Enrod. Finally, he picked up his story. "We Tairans met with each other. We walked the streets. We looked at our city and saw all the frescoes, the statues—everything we had built. We saw the dried fountains, the gutters and the brittle plants. We went outside the walls and saw our dead crops.

"At first the dead grass and trees in the hills made us despair. All the terrain we had recovered was lost again. But as we continued to look at our city, it became clear to us how much we had already accomplished. We let our pride return. *We* had built this with our own hands and sweat. *We* had snatched that land from the worst blight ever seen on the map.

"The Stranger Unlooked-For came and rescued us from destruction once. Then Scartaris grew, and then someone else, another Stranger, destroyed him."

"Journeyman," Vailret muttered.

"Now we had a third chance, and we couldn't just ignore it. We felt at a loss . . . and yet the challenge made our commitment stronger. We in Tairé were stronger than the Outside forces of the Game. We would prove ourselves self-sufficient, independent of the whims of the Players. We could defend against anything. We vowed to start work immediately, to clean up the rubble and to restart the forges. To come back better than ever!"

Jathen closed his eyes and continued speaking. "We set to work with such enthusiasm as we had never felt before. We would do it this time. We Tairans have always been proud of our optimism in the face of hardship—for all the good it did us."

Jathen opened his eyes and stared into the firelight, but he seemed to be seeing something else entirely. "And then the monster army came, led by that manticore. They came without warning, and without mercy. And they *wiped us out!*"

Some of the trainees mumbled to each other. Jathen did not pause to let the noise die down.

"Because of the grassy-hill terrain to the east of the city, we couldn't see the army until it was only a hexagon away. They came in the darkness. We Tairans had been working all day and all night, taking shifts.

But we knew something was wrong at dawn, when a team of workers out repairing an irrigation system failed to return on time.

"As the sun rose and the morning grew brighter, some characters working on the top of our wall spotted the manticore's army. Not knowing what to expect, we sent out a team of emissaries, but they didn't return.

"The monster horde marched forward. For the next hour or so, we grew afraid. We had no protection. We had no weapons in Tairé. Scartaris had already taken everything we had made, stripped us of all our resources. Even our great wall had been breached."

Jathen looked at Delrael, then at Vailret. Delrael remembered how the golem Journeyman had used his immense strength to knock down a portion of the wall so that they could escape the attack of the Tairan people.

"We built barricades, we made clubs, we . . . improvised weapons. It was all we could do." He closed his eyes and made a sobbing, laughing sound.

"It was so useless. Oh, we did manage to kill some of the first creatures as they charged in, but the monsters used their own battering rams to knock down other parts of the wall. They swarmed into the city. There were so many of them, and not very many of us.

"We managed to defend ourselves for a few minutes. And then the monsters broke through and kept coming. And kept coming! We couldn't stand against them.

"We ran for our lives—all of us, not just me. Many Tairans barricaded themselves in buildings or fled to hiding places within the city. But I knew that would be useless. The manticore's army searched from building to building and slaughtered any human characters they found. They weren't quick about the killing either. Those characters who barricaded themselves lasted only a few hours. The monsters had all the advantage in this game.

"A few dozen of us fled the city out into the surrounding terrain. We ran, and there was no shelter for several hexes, just grassland or flat desolation, no place to hide.

"The monsters came fast. Most of us died out there, in the desolation. Not a good place to die. Several of us made it to the mountain terrain, where we hid among the rocks. We split up to make smaller targets. We kept running westward. I knew you were here, along with other villages of human characters. Some of us went south.

"Siryyk kept sending scouts to hunt us down; I know several others were executed that way. I might be the only one who survived. But I knew that it was no use to stay and die with the others. It wouldn't have made any difference, would it?" He looked around. "Would it? And I made it here to warn you, because the manticore's army won't stop in Tairé for long. They'll regain some of their supplies and maybe make a few more weapons."

He turned his dark gaze to the gathered characters listening around the fire. "But they will come. Oh yes, they *will* come. But will you be ready?"

The listeners gaped at Jathen and his story, at the threat of Siryyk's horde now brought closer to home.

Delrael stood up and clenched his fist. He turned to stare down the trainees. He kept his voice low but powerful. "Yes, we will be ready!"

Vailret kept trying to blink the gummy sleep from his eyes as he shuffled along in the cool dampness before dawn. Delrael had asked him, along with Tareah and Bryl, to meet in the training grounds at daybreak. They needed to discuss things before all the trainees began to work out. Everyone would be looking to

Delrael for a solution, for a grand quest they could embark upon.

Vailret appreciated that his cousin wanted advice from the others. Delrael was a better fighter than any other character; he had more experience with questing and with combat. He knew exactly how to deal with battles and strategy. But for planning and discussion, and for looking into the consequences of his actions, he needed to talk to someone else.

Vailret and Tareah had enough background in the history of the Game and in the Rules, that they could find more subtle things than Delrael would ever imagine. And Bryl, of course, kept them from doing anything too rash.

Vailret plodded up the wet dirt path on Steep Hill, kicking dew off the toes of his boots. The stripped trees in the surrounding forest looked skeletal and frightening in the strawberry-colored light of daybreak. On the training field, he saw silhouettes of three others huddled down, barely distinguishable from the scarecrow shapes of practice dummies and sword posts. He heard their low voices, but otherwise Gamearth was silent as if holding its breath.

Delrael crossed his arms and stood up, looking as if he didn't know what to do on the training field without trainees there.

Bryl saw Vailret coming and raised his voice. "Delrael, you stirred up the trainees last night, and now they're all anxious for battle. You've got the charisma to lead them anywhere, but what are we really going to do? You can't just go bumbling in and swinging swords! You know the size of the army against us."

Delrael shrugged. "We know that the monster horde has marched to the city of Tairé. They're going to come here sooner or later. So we have two options: We can either stay here and keep training and waiting, or we can go get them first."

Vailret blinked in surprise. Bryl cried out. "Go get them? Are you crazy?"

Delrael frowned. "That way we can fight on *our* terms, not theirs. The monster army knows we're here. They'll be ready for us when they get here, they'll mass at the edge of the Barrier River and figure out how to cross it. They'll take us by storm. Once they succeed, there isn't much left for us to do."

Then his eyes began to sparkle. "But think of this: if we launch our army, we can send scouts ahead and find out where the monsters are and what they're doing. We can set a trap. Even if we're outnumbered, we can win . . . if we pick the terrain and plan our attack carefully.

"Imagine a trap in the Spectre Mountains, where the horde needs to file through a narrow gorge or along a cliff face. It'll be easy, *if* we get there first. They won't know what hit them." He grinned at Tareah.

"Siryyk thinks we're just sitting here, dreading the day when he comes. We can turn the tables on him. You saw the trainees after Jathen told his story; our army is ready to fight *now*. That'll work to our advantage. We can ambush the manticore, surprise him."

He shrugged. "And if our first assault doesn't work, we can do it again and again, hounding him as we fall back. We can use the Barrier River as our last defense, not our first."

Vailret pursed his lips. "That does make sense, Del." Bryl looked terrified.

Tareah scowled, thinking about something else entirely. Delrael noticed her expression. "Speak up, Tareah. What is it?"

She fumbled for words, then finally decided what she wanted to say. "What you're planning is fine, Delrael. But doesn't it avoid the main question? You created the Barrier River, but that wasn't enough. You destroyed Scartaris, but that wasn't enough. Now the monster army is coming, and even if you defeat them, you know that still won't be enough. The Outsiders will come up with another way to attack us." She met Vailret's eyes. "Won't they?

"We have to look beyond one battle to the entire war. Siryyk seems to be our main enemy, but in truth it's the Outsiders. We need to find some way to fight them directly. They want to obliterate Gamearth. We have to escape them, to make Gamearth *real* on its own, so that we no longer need to worry."

Delrael looked disturbed. He let his hand grasp the end of his sword, and Vailret knew the reason for his uncertainty. Delrael needed to fight a tangible enemy, an opponent he could see and strike at. He needed to understand the combat, and the thought of any direct conflict with the Outsiders was alien to him.

Delrael had once stood mystified in an abandoned Slac fortress while Vailret argued with manifestations of the Outsiders David and Tyrone in their ruined half-imaginary, half-*real* ship. With assistance from blind Paenar, Bryl had struck out at the Outsiders and finally driven them back to their own world.

"I concede your point about the Outsiders, Tareah," he said, "but I don't understand what we can do about it. How can we make Gamearth *real*? What kind of weapons do we have that can fight against the Outside? It's a question with no answer."

Tareah smiled at him. "But what if I do have an answer?"

Vailret himself was interested. Bryl looked as if he knew he wasn't going to like it; he seemed too old for all this. Delrael watched her and said, "I'm listening."

Tareah cleared her throat in uncharacteristic shyness. "We've got the Air Stone, the Water Stone, and the Fire Stone. The Earth Stone is the most powerful of the four, and we know where it is, still buried in the dragon's treasure hoard on the island of Rokanun. We found it when you and Bryl came to rescue me.

Now,"—she took a deep breath—"if we bring all four Stones together—well, you remember what happens then."

Delrael frowned and turned his back to them. "Refresh my memory."

Tareah sighed at him. Vailret jumped in. "The old Sorcerers created the four Stones just before they turned themselves into the Earthspirits and Deathspirits. They knew the Transition wouldn't require all their magic, so they used the rest of it to make the Stones."

Tareah nodded vigorously. Vailret liked the way her pale hair moved in the early morning air. "Yes, and the power in the four gems exceeds the total power of the Spirits. If all four Stones are brought together, the one bearer will hold the entire magic of the Sorcerer race, enough magic to make a full Transition. This character could become the Allspirit, more powerful than even the six Spirits together. We know it'll work."

Vailret whistled. "That should be enough."

"I propose this," Tareah said. "While you march your army eastward into the mountain terrain, dispatch a second party south to Rokanun, where the dragon's treasure pile is. Get the Earth Stone and bring it back to the main army. Then one of us will put all four Stones together and create the Allspirit. It's the only way."

Vailret grinned with excitement. "The monsters will be a trivial problem then! The Allspirit should have enough power to break us away from the Outside and hold Gamearth together."

"But who's going to do such a thing?" Delrael asked.

"Our choices are rather limited," she said, "it has to be someone with Sorcerer blood to activate the Stones."

Vailret was afraid to think that Tareah might be suggesting that she do it herself. It would transform her into a supernatural being, but she would cease to be Tareah forever.

A small voice surprised them all. "It might as well

be me," Bryl said. Vailret looked at him in surprise, and Bryl sounded defensive. The wrinkles around his eyes made complicated patterns. "I used the Water Stone to call the *dayid* and stop the forest fire. I used the Air Stone to summon the illusion army for your battle against Scartaris. I have proven that I can handle that kind of power."

Bryl shrugged and huddled down into his cloak. "Besides, I'm old. I've done enough in the Game. What have I got to lose? You people will just keep dragging me on quests for the rest of my life anyway."

4

SITNALTA WITHOUT VERNE

"I don't know why it is so beneficial to us, but Jules and I will continued to work together. From this day forward, we instruct the Council to issue all of our patents jointly, under both names Verne and Frankenstein. We trust this arrangement will be satisfactory."
—Professor Frankenstein,
in a message to the
Sitnaltan Council of Patent Givers

Professor Frankenstein squinted down at the city of Sitnalta. Cool morning mist from the ocean clung to the cobblestoned streets, making the buildings appear muzzy. Off in one hexagon, he could see the lamplighters still at work, clambering up ladders to extinguish the gaslights for the morning.

Frankenstein stood atop the central ziggurat, the highest point in Sitnalta. They had once placed their powerful defense here, the Sitnaltan dragon siren, which the city used to fight against Tryos as he went across the hexagons of water to and from his island domain.

Vailret and blind Paenar had stolen the dragon siren, though, and used the *Nautilus* designed by Frankenstein and Verne to battle the dragon directly. Fortunately, they had won; otherwise Sitnalta would have been left defenseless.

Frankenstein curved his lips upward in the closest thing to a smile he had ever made. No, Sitnalta was never defenseless—not with powerful inventors like himself and Verne among its inhabitants.

Where the hexagons of ocean met the black line that delineated the shore, Frankenstein watched three pile-driving cranes that were operated with weights, counterweights, and electric generators. In the still air, he heard the sharp sounds as they worked. He also watched tiny figures of characters in suits with giant cast-metal helmets. The experimental underwater breathing apparatus would have accompanied the *Nautilus* sub-marine boat . . . but the *Nautilus* was wrecked now, and he would not want to build another one, not without Verne.

On the streets below he heard a puttering and chugging sound. Leaning over the edge of the ziggurat, he saw someone driving a steam-engine car along a main thoroughfare. Hissing sounds came from where Dirac's street-cleaning engines swirled along, scrubbing the gutters and polishing clean the cracks in the flagstones. Otherwise, Sitnalta seemed quiet and at peace.

A few weeks before, Frankenstein would have been astonished at his own lassitude. He had too many ideas, too many things to invent, too many principles to investigate. Both he and Verne had notebooks filled with sketchy ideas for inventions. He would never have enough time to patent all of them. Working in collaboration, the two professors had become legends in Sitnalta. They had used up an entire series of patent numbers and begun another set just for themselves.

But now, by himself, it didn't seem the same. With Verne gone and sending no word back, Frankenstein no longer had sufficient eagerness for the work. Looking at their stacks of ideas, he felt overwhelmed with the impossibility of it all. After completing the great and terrible weapon, he had no drive anymore.

The Sitnaltans had made a research expedition to the crashed Outsiders' ship, which was near the technological fringe, where science grew uncertain and magic reasserted itself. They had dissected the ship, looking at its controls, its molding, the contours and the engines. They had learned enough for a lifetime of analysis.

But while at the excavation site, he and Verne had shared the same dream one night, a vision inspired by the Outsider Scott himself. They learned how to remove the ship's power source, which was part *real* from the Outside, and part imaginary from within Gamearth. Frankenstein could not even hypothesize the consequences of using such a power source for destruction. Their weapon could be used to destroy the evil force of Scartaris. Verne and Frankenstein kept their weapon a secret and rolled dice to determine who would deliver and detonate it. Verne had been the one chosen.

Back in Sitnalta, Frankenstein checked his detectors and found that the force of Scartaris had vanished. But the detectors failed to record any form of detonation, and Frankenstein was sure he would have seen that. They had been afraid the weapon might destroy all of Gamearth.

Then why hadn't Verne returned?

Frankenstein squatted on top of the ziggurat, looked out over the city, and sulked. After another few days, he would propose mounting an expedition to search for his partner.

Steam rose from the stacks of the manufactories and metal-processing centers. The city began to come alive for another day of activity.

The characters below moved about in random patterns, going about their individual business and their predetermined tasks. Frankenstein thought of making a random-motion study, sitting up here all day and plotting the paths of characters. It might give him some insights into the societal structures of insect colonies, since from this height the Sitnaltans appeared similar to ants.

But as he stared, clicking his fingernails together, the randomness changed. Characters shifted in their courses and moved, as if drawn by a magnet, toward one of the large manufactory buildings by the ocean hexagons.

He squinted into the bright sunlight and saw other characters coming from different parts of the city. Many other Sitnaltans looked confused and watched those who moved with a jerky gait. Frankenstein shaded his eyes, frowning.

Below him, one man moved in a simulation of a lockstep. His arms flailed wildly. Finally, one foot crossed in front of the other—apparently intentionally—and he sprawled to the flagstoned street. "Help me!" he cried out loud.

"What the devil is going on?" Frankenstein asked himself.

But before the man below could shout again, his hand reached out and clapped across his own mouth with a sound loud enough for Frankenstein to hear from the top of the ziggurat. With awkward movements, still holding his own mouth shut, the man rolled onto his knees and jerkily made his way to his feet again; he followed the other Sitnaltans moving toward the big buildings.

"This is insane," Frankenstein said, scrambling down the ziggurat steps. His hard leather shoes slapped on the stones as he ran down. "This is beyond reason!"

Before he reached the hex-cobbled street, one of the secondary manufactories exploded in an orange fireball. The concussion made Frankenstein's ears ring. He lost his balance and fell backward onto the ziggurat steps. The tall Sitnaltan buildings obscured his view, but he watched flames and black, greasy smoke tumble into the air. From his vantage point, he could see that the explosion had been in the building where metals were stamped and cast into forms designed by the great inventors.

Several streets away, a loud alarm bell began to ring. He heard shouts as he stumbled to his feet and ran down the street, turning sideways into an alley, a shortcut to the shore. The alarm bell abruptly fell silent, as did the other shouts.

A group of Sitnaltans moved down the street in a strange arthritic shuffle. He called out to them. "What is happening? What's going on?"

The Sitnaltans continued their march. One woman in the back—he saw it was Mayer, daughter of Dirac—swiveled around and stared at him; her expression filled with relief and hope upon recognizing him. But when she saw only confusion on Frankenstein's face, she showed despair again.

"What is—" Suddenly, Frankenstein's right foot lurched out from under him, as if yanked from below the knee by an invisible hand. "What?"

He squirmed, but his leg hung at half-step in the air. His foot wavered left and right, as if testing muscles, and then the leg reached forward to step down on the pavement. His left leg yanked up, moved forward, and stepped down.

"Stop!" Frankenstein shouted to the air. He waved his arms.

An invisible grip slammed his posture straight, jerked his hips forward, and made him take four more stumbling steps. He felt absolutely helpless. "This cannot be happening! I refuse to believe—there is no explanation for this." But his words felt absurd in the situation.

His own right hand reached out in front of his face. He watched his thumb and forefinger close together several times, like snapping pincers. Then he bent forward and gave his own nose a vicious tweak.

His legs made him run to catch up with the other puppet Sitnaltans.

They strode through the streets toward the central manufactory building. Some of the characters had surrendered and moved along willingly, but others continued to make choking, gurgling sounds as they fought to resist, like good Sitnaltans. Frankenstein felt sweat breaking out all over his body, but he could do nothing.

Beside him, Mayer made her face into a stony expression of outrage, but when she tried to ask him a question, her lips clamped themselves together. He could see from her moving jaws that she was still trying to speak.

Beside the manufactory, he could see the smoking rubble from the exploded building. He heard the roar of flames, saw the bodies of several Sitnaltans among the wreckage, burned and moaning, but he could not move to help them. His head twisted around, making him stare ahead.

Under the great brick arches of the building, the doors stood wide open, knocked loose from their brass hinges. On the cornerstone of the building, engraved words seemed totally ineffectual:

BY ESTABLISHING THIS MANUFACTORY,
THE CITY OF SITNALTA DECLARES
ITS SUPERIORITY AND FREEDOM
FROM MAGIC AND THE WAYS OF THE GAME

As his body lurched, pulling him inside the manufactory, harsh chemical smells made Frankenstein's nose and eyes burn. A cacophony of banging and hissing sounds beat upon his ears.

Skylights let bright morning light into the open bay. Steam and multicolored smoke swirled in the air, making it difficult to see. Giant copper and brass vats stood in rows, studded with polished rivets; these were the processing tanks where Sitnaltans treated seawater, extracting metals and other elements. Other chambers processed or reduced raw ore taken from outlying hexagons. Pipes and valves led into a circulation system monitored by gauges and made safe by pressure-release vents.

The puppet Sitnaltans swarmed to the tanks and scrambled on the piping, using whatever tools they found to damage everything. Some characters opened valves to let chemical solutions spew onto the floor; others banged on pipes with the handles of stir-sticks.

One man struck the side of a copper vat with a heavy sledge hammer, wrestling against his own arm all the way. He managed to succeed in dropping the hammer, but then his body bent down, his hand picked it up, and he pounded again at the tank. He dropped the hammer a second time, but his hand came up and struck him across the face. He picked up the sledge one more time, heaving it back and smashing into the dented side of the vat. The polished rivets popped out, and a section of metal gave way, exposing a seam. Hot seawater gushed out, spraying him in the face and knocking him backward.

Frankenstein found himself at one of the compressors, yanking out connections and twisting a gauge. He stared at his hands as they worked of their own accord, and he snarled at them. "Stop this! You are *my* hands! Listen to me!"

But his hand only turned, waggled fingers at his face as if waving sarcastically, and then went back to unscrew the gauge. It popped off, shooting into the air and clanging against a ventilation duct. High-pressure gas hissed out with a shriek.

Mayer dumped one container of chemicals into another vat; the resultant sputtering, burning reaction knocked her stumbling away. The reaction continued to build.

Frankenstein strained until he felt his muscles ready to snap, resisting the invisible tugs on his own body. Deep in his throat he let out a disjointed animal cry. At any other time, he would have scoffed at himself for such a futile, barbaric gesture.

Then the invisible force vanished, like strings suddenly severed.

Frankenstein fell forward as his straining body suddenly snapped free from foreign control. Several characters collapsed; others screamed and fled the manufactory. As he got to his knees on the concrete floor, blinking, Frankenstein knew the controlling force had not been defeated but it had left willingly, as if it were just playing a game with them, testing its limits, taunting them.

The chemical reactions continued to bubble in the damaged tanks. Smoke poured from broken equipment. One of the skylights overhead shattered from the rising heat, sending sharp glass shards raining down to the floor.

Frankenstein realized that the fleeing Sitnaltans had the right idea. "Get out of here! Now!" He clapped his hands and shouted to the others standing in a daze. "No telling if this will explode!"

He hurried toward the door. The other characters needed no encouragement and ran for the exits, jostling each other and sloshing through spilled chemicals on the floor, stumbling, some blinded or with burned hands.

A block away from the big building, Frankenstein stopped and watched the manufactory. Colored smoke continued to pour through the broken skylights and out the windows and doors.

Mayer stood beside him wih her calloused hands balled into fists. Smoke and grease smeared her face, and her short dark hair had been singed, curled away from one ear. Her voice carried a vicious tone; she seemed to be continuing an argument with herself and spoke out loud only because Frankenstein was listening.

"That was *magic*, Professor! How dare they!"

She turned and stared at the burning wreckage, squinting her eyes. "How dare they use *magic*." She spat out the word. "Magic has no place in Sitnalta. It's not even supposed to work here. What's happening?"

Frankenstein felt weak. His muscles trembled, and

his thoughts spun with the turmoil. He only half-listened to what Mayer was saying. "What are we going to do, Professor?" she demanded.

He did not look at her, but continued to stare at the smoke. Other Sitnaltans scurried over the rubble of the adjacent manufactory, removing bodies and helping injured characters.

"Our technology is more powerful than magic," he said. "We have our minds. We have our imaginations. We have all the resources of the Rules of Science."

He took a deep breath. Verne wasn't here, and Frankenstein would have to work solo for the first time in many turns. "I vow to use all my talent and all my resources to defeat this abomination."

He moved his mouth, as if to swallow away a bad taste. "Magic in Sitnalta! The very thought of it!" Frankenstein shook his head. "This is a matter of personal pride now."

5

RIVER CROSSING

*An adventure begins when the journey begins.
Characters need not reach the end of their quest
before they encounter interesting events.*
                    —The Book of Rules

Delrael was amazed at how much effort it took to
set out with an entire army. On other quests, he and
his companions had simply packed up and departed at
dawn. Now, though, trainees asked him thousands of
questions, they argued among themselves on how to
do the same tasks; they packed and repacked, studied
maps, and worked themselves into a mixture of excitement and dread. If they delayed much longer, that
anxiety and aggression would backfire.

Delrael paced up and down, tired and hungry because he had not found enough time to sleep or take
meals. He hated to think of so many things at once, so
many meaningless details; he wanted to set off and *do*
something. Couldn't they take care of administrative
squabbles along the way? He wasn't sure he was the
right character to command such a large force.

Yellowed leaves blew through the encampment. The
weapon makers had cut down so many of the surrounding trees that debris lay scattered on the hillside,
adding dead leaves to those already falling from the
end of the season.

Finally, tired of pacing and unable to think of anything else that simply had to be done, Delrael whistled

and formed up the front ranks, directing them to start off down the quest-path toward the Barrier River. "Enough of this," he said. "Let's go!"

The fighters didn't seem to know whether they were supposed to cheer; some did anyway. Delrael stood in his leather armor, listening to the ragged mixture of sounds. The fighters talked to each other and moved about, but they seemed just as happy as he to be on the move.

Delrael watched, nodding and smiling to any charac-ter who met his eyes as the army marched by. His father Drodanis would have been at the front, waving his sword and leading all the fighters. But Delrael's army would not need a battle commander for a while, and they knew which quest-path to follow.

As the army marched into the forest, Delrael went back to take a last look at his village. In the frosty morning, it stood deserted except for those characters who could not endure the journey, a few old men and women as well as young children who had come to the Stronghold to offer their assistance in the prepara-tions. The open spaces had the marks of a sprawling encampment, scars from tent stakes and black smears of cooking fires. He saw the broad, ash-strewn circle from the central bonfire where they burned their gar-bage along with splintered and knotty wood unsuitable to be made into arrows or other weapons.

Delrael stared at the empty houses, the stripped trees, and the Steep Hill on which he could see rem-nants of the Stronghold defenses and the newly erected training area. He wondered if this was the last time he would ever see his home. Turning his back on that thought, he hurried into the forest to catch up with the rest of the troops. "Some commander!" he thought.

As the army marched throughout the morning, Delrael moved among the groups, chatting with char-acters to maintain their morale. Jorte, who operated the village gaming hall, and Mostem, the baker, kept the trainees talking about their villages and past quests. Vailret helped as well, though he seemed to spend even more time with Tareah.

Bryl seemed quiet and withdrawn. Delrael knew how worried he must be with the great responsibility he had undertaken, not to mention the aches in his old bones from the prospect of a prolonged journey. Once the army crossed the Barrier River, Bryl and Vailret would split off on their own quest. Together those two would journey south to Rokanun and secure the Earth Stone.

Delrael wanted to go with them when he remembered old quests; theirs seemed to be a more enjoyable adventure, especially with all the headaches of just keeping his army together. But Delrael was the leader of these fighters, so he had to stay with them. Besides, he could never again go near the city of Sitnalta within its technological fringe, where science worked and magic failed—his left leg was carved of magical *kennok* wood, and he could normally use it as well as his real leg. But in Sitnalta, without magic, the leg would refuse to function, perhaps permanently, and Delrael would be a cripple. No, he had to stay with his army.

From their previous expedition to Rokanun, Bryl knew exactly where to find the Earth Stone. But since Vailret and he would brave the hazards of Gamearth by themselves, Bryl would take along the Air Stone and the Fire Stone for their protection. Tareah would keep the Water Stone to aid the main army in any skirmishes.

If everything worked out as planned, Vailret and Bryl could hurry back with their prize and join Delrael's army somewhere in the Spectre Mountains. They could then use the magic in the Stones to fight Siryyk's horde, or Bryl could transform himself into the Allspirit right there. They hadn't quite decided that last part yet.

Delrael's fighters traveled over forested-hill, forest, and grassland terrain on their first day. When they bedded down on the edge of another hexagon, Delrael sensed the excitement among the army. That feeling would change as the journey grew longer, but for now they seemed caught up in the adventure. He sat on the ground and leaned back against the trunk of a tree, then reached up to touch his fingers to a knob of bark. Sighing, he bent his knees and let his eyes close in a much-appreciated moment of rest.

Siya came by and offered him a blanket, which he waved away. During the previous two days, she had proven herself invaluable, thinking of countless things they had forgotten to do, supplies to be packed, tools and equipment to be taken care of.

Jathen, the Tairan, muttered a good-night before trudging off into the shelter of trees, where he would sleep away from the main group. Jathen tossed fitfully in his sleep, in the grip of nightmares, and he chose not to disturb anyone else. From what Delrael himself had seen in Tairé, he could well imagine some of the nightmares that Jathen suffered . . .

For three days, the army continued through hexagons of forest.

Delrael had crossed this landscape before, but never with hundreds of characters marching beside him in a group much too wide for the quest-path. They forged through the trees, spreading out and scouting the area. It seemed more like a carnival than a group of fighters on a quest. The terrain remained easy, causing no troubles, at least not until they reached the Barrier River on the third day.

The vast river stood before them, rushing past with gray water channeled from the Northern Sea. The quest-path would have continued across the hex-line boundary of the river and on across the terrain had it not been submerged abruptly by the irresistible wall of water that ran down the length of the map.

The Barrier River looked uncrossable with its swift current a full hex wide. The fighters stared in expressions of awe and disbelief. Delrael stood on the bank in silence, remembering how he had persuaded Sardun to create the river, in exchange for rescuing Sardun's daughter, Tareah.

The air felt brisk against Delrael's cheeks as he rested before he faced the problem of crossing. He heard the ripple of water swirling around the sharp hex-line and listened to the rustle of leaves in tall trees above. He could smell the dampness in the air, the cloying wet stink of all the toppled trees and forest debris decomposing in the water.

Some of the exhausted characters knelt on the black line and dipped their hands in the water, splashing it on their faces, rubbing their eyes. Delrael did the same, scrubbing his sweaty, itching head.

He listened to the restless sounds of the other characters shifting packs, sitting down to rest, and tromping into the forest. He heard Siya break out their supplies, which Tareah and Vailret helped her distribute.

Delrael stood up and adjusted the chafing leather armor on his chest, when he heard a crunching sound in the trees. The army stirred off to his left; some of the fighters stood up, others looked around.

A big man came into view riding a tall black horse. Delrael used his fingers to spread dripping hair away from his eyes and forehead; he felt a trickle of water behind his ear. The man on the horse rode through the army as if looking for someone. Delrael stepped forward and introduced himself.

The stranger snapped to attention, then urged his horse forward. The man was very large and muscular, a full hand taller than Delrael. His blond hair streamed back to his shoulderblades, so pale and fine that it looked white. The black horse showed velvety purple

shadows on its hide as the muscles rippled. The horse's
hooves bore scuffed iron shoes; its saddle, bridle, and
reins looked immaculately cared for, with gleaming
silver studs.

The stranger himself wore black leather armor and a
vest with a badge carved on the right breast, which
showed a white field with the dark silhouette of a bird
of prey, wings spread and claws extended to strike. On
his back, the man carried a long bow and a quiver
bristling with arrows. At his side hung a two-handed
sword, and a dagger poked up from his belt.

Yet with all the weapons and armor and black trap-
pings, the man looked saintly, his face unblemished,
his eyebrows perfectly curved and thin. A faint flush
showed the chill on his pale skin.

"My greetings, Delrael. I've heard of your army and
your call to arms. My name is Corim. As a representa-
tive of the Black Falcon troops, I crossed the river and
came to your Stronghold to exchange information and
to offer our services. But the Stronghold was in ruins,
and some of the characters there told me you had
already departed, so I rode hard in the direction I
knew you would be taking."

"Black Falcon troops?" Delrael thought. He looked
around for Vailret, who would probably be able to
explain Corim's group.

"Black Falcons!" Vailret said in a loud voice to the
stranger. "Are you planning to do anything useful? Or
are you just here to cause havoc as you have in the
past?"

Corim surprised Delrael by ignoring Vailret entirely.
Delrael looked at his cousin, but wasn't sure what to
think. Offhand, this man appeared to be an awesome
warrior. If Corim had troops of similar fighters, how
could Delrael turn down the offer of reinforcements?
Delrael asked, "What are you talking about, Vailret?"

"The Black Falcons, Del!" Vailret seemed surprised
when Delrael gave him only a questioning gaze. Vailret

made an exasperated expression, but Tareah spoke in a patient voice. Delrael felt embarrassed as she tried not to talk down to him.

"The Black Falcons have been here since the Scouring, but at least there's not many of them. They go around killing any nonhuman character they find. They band together and use all their strength to wipe out harmless races, like the ylvans or the khelebar."

Sarcasm laced her voice. "Apparently for all their strength, they're too frightened to attack anything dangerous like the Slac or the wandering monsters across the map."

"That is a lie," Corim said in a flat voice. "The Black Falcon troops strike at any enemies we find. We've slaughtered whole regiments of Slac and defeated dozens of ogres and individual monsters. And yes, we have also struck against the khelebar, who caused great damage to human characters in the past. If you doubt that, your knowledge of the Game is . . . not accurate."

Tareah looked ready to blurt out something else, but Corim continued. "When the old Sorcerer race went on their Transition, they gave Gamearth to *human* characters, those formed in the Sorcerers' own image. That's what the Scouring was all about: the enemy character races trying to wipe each other out. Despite our defenses, the Slac nearly succeeded in conquering the entire map. Only by the efforts of the Black Falcon troops, working with other human fighters and the Sentinels, did we push the monsters back to their mountain fortresses." Corim stood silent for a moment. His lips were so pale that they looked the same color as his skin.

"The map is still infested with threats to human characters. We make no bones about it. Gamearth belongs rightfully to us. We have no wish to share it with races that have fought against us in the past. They might be peaceful now, but who's to say

they won't turn against us again? It makes no difference if they're direct threats such as the Slac, or parasites like the ylvan. They're equally bad in our eyes."

He looked at Delrael, then jerked his chin in the
direction of Tareah and Vailret. "Who are these people, Delrael?"

Keeping his voice even and his face plain so as not
to betray his anger, Delrael nodded to the two of
them. "Vailret is my close advisor. Tareah is the daughter of Sardun. She's one of the most powerful characters left on the map."

Corim's eyebrows rose, but he made no comment.

Delrael remembered the gentle but distraught khelebar, who had fought so valiantly to save their forest
from burning, and the khelebar woman Thilane who
had healed his destroyed leg; without her magic of
replacing his leg with one made of *kennok* wood, he
would have bled to death. Now, whenever he un-
dressed and ran his fingers over the soft, warm surface
of the living wood, he could see the grain from the
stunted *kennok* tree. Even more remarkable, he could
also feel his own touch and move his toes; he could do
everything with his wooden leg. He owed his life to
the khelebar, whom Corim dismissed as enemies.

He also thought of Tallin, the tough little forest man
he had rescued from Gairoth. Tallin's entire ylvan
village had been numbed by Scartaris, even from a
vast distance, so they all became easy prey for the
ogre. Tallin was a good companion, and a good friend,
until the Anteds killed him.

"What is it you're offering, Corim?" Delrael said.

The Black Falcon rider looked at Delrael's army,
but his face remained expressionless. Delrael thought
he detected a hint of scorn, though he saw nothing
obvious.

"We can offer our help in fighting this monster
army marching against Gamearth. Despite what your
. . . advisor and your Sorceress say, the Black Falcon

troops are above all else devoted fighters and have been for generations. The survival of the Game is our foremost concern."

Delrael stood, feeling inadequate with his dripping hair and unkempt appearance in front of this monolith of a man. He thought for just a moment, then answered.

"You're welcome to join us. We'd be foolish not to accept the assistance of your troops. But are you going to focus your efforts on fighting the monster horde? That's the *only* enemy that should concern us. I would forbid you to waste any time, any effort, or any resources attacking friendly character races."

Corim scowled down from his horse. Delrael could smell the horse, the leather of the saddle, and the hint of sweat on Corim's uniform. He also noted a sour, rotten smell from the bulging saddle bags and didn't want to know what they carried.

"Sometimes you must trim away small roots before you can topple a large tree," Corim said, keeping his voice low.

"Sometimes," Vailret interrupted, "you can get so busy trimming those roots that you don't see the tree about to fall on you."

Corim yanked on the reins of his horse. When the Black Falcon rider spoke, he seemed to disregard everything they had said. "I don't have time to share a meal with you, Delrael. I'll bring your terms to Annik, our leader. We'll meet again, perhaps as allies."

"I hope so," Delrael said. He wondered whether he was starting to sound more like a true commander.

Corim rode the horse directly between Delrael and where Vailret and Tareah stood. Vailret took an exaggerated step back though the horse did not pass very close. The horse charged through the trees and plunged over the black line into the river.

It sank up to the top of its saddle and began to swim across the current, tossing its head but keeping its gaze on the line of the opposite bank. Corim did not turn back. His blond hair glinted in the sunlight. The current carried the horse at a diagonal across the river, but the Black Falcon rider seemed unconcerned where they would come to shore.

Delrael refused to watch Corim's receding silhouette against the rushing water and so turned back to his army. Vailret put his hands on his hips, scowling. "Well, what are we going to do about that, Del?" The other characters were listening.

"We're not going to do anything about it," Delrael answered, realizing that his voice had grown testy. "We'll let them make their move. If they want to fight with us, they can help a lot. But we'll succeed without them, and I won't have them in my army if they go slaughtering the khelebar or the ylvans."

He sighed, then clapped his hands and raised his voice so that the characters would pay attention. "Enough of the show! We've got bigger problems to worry about . . ."

Delrael looked over his shoulder at the river as Corim, small now in the distance, worked his way around a dead tree half submerged in the current, and continued, ". . . such as crossing this river."

Normally, he would have asked Vailret's help in planning such an operation, but Delrael felt giddy with responsibility. He could do it himself. He had made it clear in his mind exactly what he wanted to do.

Delrael separated his fighters into different groups for building rafts that would carry them to the opposite bank. He selected teams to scout out nearby trees, others to work at felling them, still others to trim away the main branches and tie the trunks together. The army had enough work to keep busy for several days, but they would cross in a grand procession.

Jathen plunged into his job with enormous vigor, hacking at branches protruding from fallen trunks. His woodworking ax smacked into the wood with the solid sound of a sword connecting one of the practice posts.

Chips of bark and fragrant white wood sprayed in the air around him. Jathen puled off his tunic even in the cool air. After a while, dust and dirt smeared his chest, clinging to his sweat. Jathen's whole world seemed focused on what he was doing, as if he were distracting himself from anything else that might haunt him.

As Delrael watched them fall to their directed tasks, he felt a growing pride, because all these scattered fighter characters from villages across the map were now mobilized into a real unit, like a Sitnaltan machine in which the pieces worked together.

Delrael's idea was to construct several rafts the size of barges to haul his fighting force across the water. There, the characters would cover the rafts with brush. If his army were on the run from Siryyk's horde, if their ambushes and defensive battles had failed, they could uncover their rafts and escape down the river, leaving the manticore and all the monsters stranded behind.

As the other characters worked, Tareah wore an atypical scowl. Even in her mended clothes, she still looked beautiful to Delrael, with her long pale hair and the sapphire Water Stone hanging at her neck. He smiled at her, but she only glared at him. He felt crestfallen, wondering what he had done wrong.

Vailret finally spoke with her out of Delrael's earshot. Tareah said something to Vailret, shaking her head; Vailret looked surprised, rapping his knuckles against his forehead as if to demonstrate his own stupidity. He grabbed her arm, dragging her toward Delrael.

"Del, Tareah's got—"

"If he wants to ignore my abilities, I'll let him," she said, refusing to look at Delrael. "He's the one paying in sweat and sore muscles, after all."

Delrael still couldn't fathom what had upset her. "Tareah, what have I done to make you angry?"

She stood with her hands on her hips. For a moment

Delrael saw a reflection of furious Sardun, who had attacked when Delrael first entered the Ice Palace.

"Why do you keep stopping me from doing anything to help you? I'm one of the most powerful characters on all of Gamearth. You made a point of that to the Black Falcon rider, and so, when you have to cross this river, why doesn't it occur to you that I could make an ice bridge with the Water Stone? Would your fighters really rather spend days building rafts by brute force?"

Delrael blinked his eyes in surprise. He felt shocked and stupid. The other characters stood up beside the fallen logs and pushed sweaty hair away from their eyebrows. The forest looked churned up from their efforts; stripped logs lay scattered about.

Delrael felt his cheeks burning. Tareah was right. She could help them cross with a single spell. He had always tried to do everything he could to impress her, but in the back of his mind, he still remembered her as the little girl who had waited to be rescued on the island of Rokanun, just *waited* for some hero to come, because she thought the Game was played that way.

But she had changed much since then.

The weary characters glared at him, upset that they had done their work for nothing. Jathen stood up, blinking and looking impatient; he didn't seem to mind the work, just didn't want to stopped.

Delrael stared at the gray, fast-moving river behind them. It would be treacherous to cross even if they were on rafts. He forced himself to meet Tareah's eyes. "The rafts are a known risk, Tareah," he said. "And we'll have them there ready when we return. Can you be sure your bridge won't collapse with our army halfway across?"

"If the spell works, it works. You'll know that as soon as I roll."

"Even though the Rules are breaking?" Vailret said.

Tareah considered the question only long enough to

shrug. "If that's the case, how do you know the rafts will float?"

Delrael knew how long it would take them to complete the rafts and to work their way slowly across the current. He could well lose as many characters over the sides of the rafts as from a bridge that collapsed.

"Tareah, will you help us cross the river?" he asked.

Looking more relieved than smug, she nodded. "Yes, I will."

Tareah brushed her cheeks and arms as if preparing herself. She looked truly eager to be part of things, to be helping out. Vailret nodded to her in encouragement.

"Get the fighters ready," Tareah said. Her voice was low and husky. "My father used the Water Stone to maintain the entire Ice Palace, but I don't want to hold up a bridge any longer than I have to. I'm not quite as confident as he was."

Delrael called to the other characters. Jathen pulled his tunic on again, tugged the lacings, and stood restless, shuffling his feet. Some fighters dipped their hands into the cold river water, trying to scrub away splinters or chafed skin.

Bryl went beside Tareah. "Need any help?"

She shook her head, then stepped between the trees to stand at the black line at the edge of the Barrier River. Her brown blouse and many-colored skirt had belonged to Delrael's mother. "Fielle liked this skirt," Siya had said when she took it out of a storage trunk and gave it to the newly grown Tareah.

Delrael didn't know what to think about Tareah's fitting his mother's clothes. He rarely thought about his mother after she had died of fever years before. Because of her death, Delrael's father had gone into grief-stricken seclusion. He eventually fled the Game entirely, going in search of a legendary Pool of Peace inhabited by the Rulewoman Melanie.

Drodanis had left Delrael to run the Stronghold, although Delrael then had little training and experi-

ence. Delrael resented him for that abandonment sometimes, but at other times, he saw it as a trial by fire
that had forced him to grow into a better fighter, a
better player in the Game. Drodanis had made no
contact for years, until he sent a message stick to warn
Delrael about the threat of Scartaris. While offering
no assistance of his own, he charged Delrael with a
quest to find a way to save Gamearth. That message
stick had led Delrael to have the Barrier River made
to protect them.

And now Tareah gazed at the immense river Sardun
had created. She, too, had to live up to the greatness
of her father.

Tareah held the gleaming Water Stone in her hands.
In silence, Delrael motioned his hands backward, commanding the other fighter characters to step away. He
bumped into Vailret's elbow, startling both of them.

Tareah held her head high, and her pale hair continued to drift back in the river breeze. Delrael remembered her in her little-girl body standing up like a
great Sorcerer queen, using the power of the Stones
against the dragon.

He heard only the rippling water and the occasional
cough and shifting noise of the gathered characters.
The army seemed to be holding its breath as Tareah
knelt. She rolled the Water Stone on the ground. A
smooth sapphire face stared upward into the clear sky,
showing a chiselled "4".

Tareah, staring with half-closed eyes and acting as if
she didn't want to break her concentration, snatched
up the sapphire. She planted her feet squarely apart so
that her boots dug into the soft mud and rested high
on the black hex-line. With one of her hands crooked,
the fingers moved.

The water of the Barrier River responded, hunching
up and then squeezing forward like clay, frosting and
finally turning into ice. More water curled up under it,

lapping, freezing, and extending the curved surface out.

Tareah moved her other hand, bringing her elbows close to her ribs in a silent pushing gesture. The tongue of ice bucked, widened, and lurched farther out, suspending itself over the choppy surface of the river.

The magic flowed through Tareah now, and the water churned into froth around the base of the ice bridge. The wide white footpath looped but held firm, rippling and thrusting like someone squeezing dough through a tube.

As the arch rose up from the center of the hex-wide river, it began to curve toward the opposite shore. The base in front of Tareah's spread feet grew thicker and wider. Icicles dribbled down from its sides, growing thicker and plunging into the water as support struts.

Tareah made a coughing sound. She squeezed her eyes tightly shut; her forehead was wrinkled. Delrael wanted to place his hands on her shoulders, to comfort her or to add strength somehow, but he didn't dare break her concentration and send the ice bridge crumbling into the swirling waters.

The characters began to mutter in appreciation and awe. Jorte, the keeper of the village gaming hall, made an enthusiastic cheer. But Delrael whirled around with a glare and silenced them all.

Tareah clenched both her hands into fists around the Water Stone. She lifted her head up, and it was as if she could see even with her eyes closed. The ribbon of ice fell a hexagon away and struck the opposite shore, completing the link. She relaxed a little. Her shoulders slumped while her fingers remained curled around the sapphire.

The ice continued to thicken and widen as more water flowed up to freeze along the bridge. Its surface became stubbled and rough, with steplike projections on the steepest part of the curve.

Tareah spoke but kept her face directed across the

river. "Go across. It'll hold now. But don't take any longer than necessary."

Delrael motioned with his left arm. Some of the characters acted uneasy; Delrael as their brave leader, climbed up onto the bridge first at a brisk pace. Vailret followed behind, then Jathen. Bryl came up with Siya, and then the other fighters started to march along.

Delrael hurried. He didn't know how Tareah would come across herself, but he kept moving. The air around the narrow bridge blew bitterly cold. Its surface felt hard and slick under his feet, so he had to pay attention to where he stepped and could not allow himself to be distracted by the gurgling waters against the icicle struts below.

He did peer over the edge and see, submerged in the current, rocks and the murky shadows of toppled trees. Some distance to the south he made out a black line parallel to the bridge, which marked the boundary of the next river hexagon.

He had last crossed this river on Enrod's raft, pushed by the cursed Sentinel. Delrael wondered about Enrod now. He could sense Jathen close behind him and did not want to mention the fallen Sorcerer, who had been a hero to the Tairans.

Delrael found it difficult to keep his balance on the downward slope of the opposite side but managed to set foot on the bank again. Behind him Vailret slipped and fell on his backside into the mud. The others knew they had to be careful. Vailret managed to laugh; Delrael wondered if he had done the stunt on purpose, to make a point for them all.

Delrael reached out to take Siya's hand, but she refused. Bryl scowled at her and worked his own careful way down. "You don't get much help these days. You should take it when it's offered."

She snorted. "*You* might be an invalid, but I'm not yet."

Vailret turned and squinted toward Tareah waiting on the opposite bank. The line of fighters continued to cross over the walkway. They went into the nearby forest terrain to keep from crowding the base of the bridge.

Jathen stood beside the other characters but remained silent. He looked at the river, then gazed deep into the forest that hid their long journey toward Tairé. Delrael wondered what it had been like for the Tairan to take a log and swim across the cold river. No wonder Jathen had been sick and exhausted by the time he reached the Stronghold village.

Scattered around the riverbank, Delrael noticed the burned spots of many different campfires, as if a great number of characters had waited there. Up and down the hex-line, he saw other dead fires spaced equally apart. One still smoldered.

"Here she comes!" Vailret whispered.

The last of the fighters had crossed over. The colorful figure of Tareah climbed up and strode along the ice bridge she had made. He couldn't quite make out what she was doing until she reached the apex and began to descend toward them.

The delicate icicle bridge melted into silvery trickles of water, pouring back into the river only one step behind her as she moved along. Tareah walked with stiff legs and a shuffling step that showed just how much she concentrated to maintain her spell. As she walked closer, the melt water splashed and drummed into the river like a heavy downpour filled with chunks of ice.

Delrael caught her as she stumbled the last few steps toward the bank. He pulled her off the base of the bridge as it suddenly collapsed into a great wave that smacked back into the silty river. The big splash dumped water and mud on those who stood too close to the hex-line.

Delrael held Tareah a second longer than he abso-

lutely needed to. She pulled away, looking tired but
exhilarated. She brushed herself off and tried to wipe
some of the mud from her sleeve. She gazed back over
the river. "I did it!"

Delrael grinned back at her. "I should have known
you could." He avoided her eyes. ". . . without you
needing to remind me."

He looked at the scattered dead campfires again,
then he heard someone moving in the forest behind
him. For a moment he thought some of his fighters
had gone to gather firewood.

As he turned, Delrael saw a tall, powerfully built
man walking along the quest-path out of the trees. He
had long dark hair and a voluminous black beard; his
eyes looked red. His white robe must have once looked
magnificent, trimmed in purple, but now it was tattered and stained. Finger-smeared lines of ashes marked
a strange pattern on the cloth. The man appeared
healthy, though; powerful and confident. He cocked
his head from one side to the other, fixing a fiery glare
at random tree trunks, then at the human fighters.

Delrael recognized the Sentinel immediately.

Before he could say anything, Jathen brushed past
him and stopped two steps away from the man, blinking, his mouth open in astonishment. His usual stunned
expression now held hope and excitement. "Enrod!"
he cried. "I knew you wouldn't desert us."

Enrod the Sentinel stopped and surveyed the army.
When he saw Delrael, Vailret, and Bryl among the
gathered fighters, a flicker of confused recognition
passed across his red eyes. Delrael found himself cring-
ing inside, not knowing what would happen. This was
the Sorcerer who had tried to destroy them all with
the Fire Stone.

"I was . . . wondering when characters would come,"
Enrod said. His eyes looked up and off to the side, as
if listening to voices in his head. "Waiting for you."

6

DEPARTURES

All quest-paths lead to adventure, treasure, combat, perhaps death. Which route will you take?
—The Book of Rules

Vailret felt uneasy watching the dark-haired Sorcerer, wondering how much Enrod remembered. What if Scartaris had damaged his mind so much that he would always be a threat?

With the curious army around him, Enrod stood by the bank of the Barrier River, digging his fingernails into the bark of a tree. He sniffed, then turned his head to one of the still-smoldering fires along the bank. He smiled, then nodded toward the gray ash-clumps of other dead fires.

"I can still make fire." He bent down and smeared his hands in the cold remnants of one fire, pawing about for an ember. He held up a blackened lump of wood, but it held no spark. He dropped it with a disappointed sigh.

By the bank, Vailret looked at where Enrod's crude raft had washed up against dangling roots. Vailret remembered riding on it with Delrael and Bryl, surrounded by mist. Enrod had poled on, not seeing, only continuing his endless journey as decreed by the Deathspirits. When Vailret tried to snap him out of his trance, Enrod had moved with lightning speed, sending Vailret sprawling against the wet logs. The Sentinel had never spoken a word.

79

Now Enrod splashed his ash-coated hands in the rushing water, confused by all the characters watching him.

"How long have you been . . . awake again, Enrod?" Vailret asked. Despite Vailret's misgivings, Enrod of Tairé would be a great ally if he fought with them against the enemy horde. Delrael stood watching, as if he had not yet made up his mind about the Sentinel.

Enrod continued to stare at his broken raft hung up on the black hex-line. Mud and silt had clogged up under one corner of the crude craft. A broken blade of grass drifted by, bobbing on a ripple, and then continued out of sight downstream.

"Days. Not sure." He rubbed his hand over his mouth. Some of the wet ashes stained his lips.

"Like a dream. The Deathspirits . . . held me. Couldn't think. Couldn't move. Back and forth across the river." He stared out at the hexagon-wide current. "Until now. Scartaris is dead, Deathspirits gone. I'm left here on this side. Where do I go?"

He looked at them, turning his head so he might see all the characters there. But his eyes remained unfocused. "Something happened in my city. Scartaris." He closed his eyes and pushed a hand against the side of his head. "Made me think things. Do things. It still echoes in my head!" His expression snapped into clarity and the words came out with sudden focus. "I always wanted to rebuild Tairé—that was my goal, but I could only think of burning." He fixed his stare on Delrael, but it seemed to carry no antagonism. "Because you created this river."

"We destroyed Scartaris," Delrael said. "You shouldn't want to hurt us."

"Not . . . anymore," Enrod said.

Vailret bent forward. "The Earthspirits came to fight Scartaris. So did the Deathspirits. But they vanished from Gamearth again, went to rest. Maybe they forgot about you, loosened your curse."

"Forgot about me." Enrod made a thin smile. "But I can still make fire." He kicked at the ashes in a circle by his feet.

"The Deathspirits could have gone off to their other realms, to play Games of their own creation," Tareah said. "That's why they made the Transition in the first place."

"I don't know. But they're gone." Delrael sounded impatient with the discussion. "It's a good thing you didn't stop trying to fight against them." He hesitated. "Are you all right?"

"Never stop trying. Never." Enrod turned his gaze back to the washed-up raft. "This is no longer part of me. Gone."

He planted his foot on a corner of the raft and, bracing himself against a tree, shoved the log. The raft lurched out into the current, leaving a cloud of mud in the water. The raft swerved one way and then curled around in the other direction as it was sucked into the current.

". . . That's why I stayed in Tairé for so many turns. In the desolation."

Enrod stared away from the river, back to the east. "Never stop trying."

Jathen, his heavy eyebrows and dark hair hanging about him, came up beside Enrod. Jathen's eyes glinted bright against the nightmares behind them. "Enrod, you and I are the last survivors of Tairé. When Scartaris sent you away, he made the rest of us Tairans do his work. We had to create weapons and shields for him!"

"Weapons—from Tairé?" Enrod sounded astonished.

"We furnished supplies to his horde of monsters. We sweated and worked . . ." Jathen swallowed and turned his face away. "We gave ourselves. Hundreds of us were skinned for leather, butchered and dried for meat to feed his army . . ." Jathen looked as if he were about to gag, then whirled back. All the nightmares had resurfaced.

"That's the worst part, isn't it, Enrod?" In his anger, he stood up straight. "Yes, we're free of the control. We can do what we want now. But we're not free of the memories. Scartaris made us do what he wanted. But he didn't hold our minds tightly enough to make us unaware of our actions. And now that I can remember what we were doing, it's burning me up inside, because if I can remember so clearly, why couldn't I refuse?"

"It's not your fault, Jathen," Delrael said.

But the Tairan turned to him and snapped. "It isn't? I worked in the tannery. Didn't I know what I was doing? Was Scartaris so powerful that he could direct every finger? Every step I took? Every . . . cut with the knife? I can see it all in front of me. I spent days there skinning people, characters that I had known and grown up with, fought with and worked with. But none of that stopped me. Maybe if I'd tried harder I could have resisted. But I didn't. I took the knife. They stood before me—their eyes were pupilless, focused ahead, unseeing.

"But if I can remember what I was doing, surely they knew what was about to happen to them! Scartaris wouldn't let them do anything more than stand there and wait as I drove a knife into their throats. Did he at the last minute release them, letting them feel their own dying? I wouldn't doubt it. Why should he bother to waste energy controlling them as they bled out on the floor of the tannery? While I stood waiting for them to stop jerking and writhing so I could skin them more easily and not waste a bit of their leather."

Enrod interrupted him and spoke in a quiet but piercing voice. Jathen's words seemed to intensify Enrod, forcing back the maze of shadows in his mind. "If you're responsible for all that, then I must be responsible for everything that I did." He paused. "And that's not a burden I can bear right now. Look ahead, not back."

"And forget about Tairé?" Jathen asked. He looked dumbfounded that his hero, the great Sentinel Enrod, would suggest such a thing.

"No, never forget," Enrod said. He looked behind him to the clustered trees and the quest-path that wound eastward away from the river. "Go back there."

Jathen held his breath in anticipation. Vailret could feel the tension in the air. Enrod brought his attention back to Delrael. "I will follow your army. Fight for Tairé."

Delrael's voice was gruff. Vailret could see that his cousin wasn't sure how much to say about their plans. "That's where we're going."

Enrod drew himself up, didn't quite smile, but tugged a lock of black hair away from his face. Vailret noticed for the first time a thin streaking of white hairs in his beard. "I still have many powers. Spells." Enrod looked down at his own hands and tattered robe, as if embarrassed at the level to which he had sunk. "I have lost the Fire Stone."

Delrael appeared about to say something, but Bryl suddenly broke in. Vailret realized that Bryl had covered up his own two Stones as soon as they had seen Enrod again. Since Scartaris had used the eight-sided Fire Stone as a means to corrupt Enrod, Vailret silently agreed with Bryl's decision.

"The Fire Stone is . . . safe," Bryl said.

The following morning, Vailret and Bryl prepared to go down their own quest-path as the remainder of the army broke camp.

"Time to go," Vailret said, clapping Bryl's shoulder. He had not been looking forward to this moment, but they had no time to waste. "The Earth Stone is waiting for us."

"I'll be sad to see you leave," Tareah said, smiling at him. Her words made Vailret's skin tingle with delight. He shuffled his feet.

His mother, Siya, gave him a brief hug, hesitated, then, to his embarrassment, gave him a much larger one. Siya turned with tears in her eyes and snapped at the characters around them. "What are you looking at!"

Vailret felt uncomfortable with the entire ritual. He did not look forward to leaving the protection of the large army. As he stood there, wishing he could just be on his way, he had to wait as Delrael and Jathen bade them luck on their quest, as did other fighters he had come to know during training. It seemed to take forever.

"With all the luck we're being offered, we shouldn't have any troubles at all," Bryl muttered to him.

"No," Vailret said, "none at all."

INTERLUDE: OUTSIDE

The sheen in Melanie's eyes made David want to slap
her face in order to shake her out of it. But she would
be completely beyond reason; Gamearth held her mind
too firmly. David could only hope that the others were
not as weak—or everything was already lost.

"It's all or nothing tonight, David." Melanie's voice
was like the growl of a small dog that wanted to sound
threatening. It didn't seem like her own voice anymore, and it probably wasn't.

She had won the dice roll when David contested her
use of the character Enrod. Enrod had been David's
own character, raised in Tairé, which was *his* city. He
had had Scartaris use Enrod to attack the Stronghold,
to weaken Melanie and stop her desperate schemes to
keep the Game going. But Melanie claimed that since
David had abandoned Enrod, the character was up for
grabs. So she took him. She beat David by one point
in the dice roll.

Something about the way the dice fell made David
more concerned. If the powers of the Game could
reach out and manipulate them, if it could stop the
phone from working, make his car engine refuse to
start . . . couldn't it also alter dice rolls? Couldn't
Gamearth play itself if it wanted and make sure it
won?

But David could not accept that. The very founda-
tion of Gamearth was built on the Rules. The Rules
could not be tossed aside so easily. If Gamearth were

85

willing to break those Rules, then the map would go about destroying itself without any help from him.

Tyrone squinted at the map, pressing his face close to the painted hexagons. "I thought we might be able to see it. The ice bridge, you know? Like we could see the Barrier River when we created it."

David fought back his resentment. Tyrone was so focused on how much *fun* he had with the growing Game that he couldn't conceive of any danger.

"It would have melted already, Tyrone. You should have looked before the round ended," Scott said. Nothing else, no censure about "being ridiculous." He seemed to accept that the Game could do something so unnatural. David had won an important victory with Scott, who always insisted on a rational explanation. At least Scott now realized the seriousness of the Game and how it was affecting their lives.

The flames continued to crackle in the fireplace. The room got so warm that David pulled off his sweater. As the dusk grew into night, he could still hear the storm outside the house.

"Are you going to bring out any other old characters, Mel?" Tyrone asked.

David wanted to shake Tyrone and shout at him to face the reality of their situation. But Tyrone just didn't *understand*.

Melanie glanced at Tyrone, reflecting, then her eyes lit up. "Any character we've introduced before is fair game. David's not going to pull any punches." She refused to look at him. "So I'm going to use everything I can think of. David has captured Jules Verne and the Sitnaltan weapon. We have to find weapons of our own."

David resented how she automatically included Scott and Tyrone in her conflict with him—unless Melanie was speaking of her own characters when she said "we." David couldn't tell.

"I . . ." Scott said, then paused. He took off his

glasses; his eyes looked small without the thick lenses. He seemed vulnerable and uncertain of what he wanted to say.

"I've been thinking about this mixup with the Game and our world. There's really no way we can deny it. Not after the Barrier River and the explosion last week."

He nodded toward the blue hexagons on the map and the blasted parts around Scartaris's battlefield. The force released from that struggle had damaged Tyrone's kitchen table and burned David's hands.

"So if *this* is really going on—," Scott said the word "this" as if it encompassed everything—"then I have to worry about something else. The Sitnaltan weapon that Verne and Frankenstein built, that *I* directed them to build . . . was made from the ship that David and Tyrone created out of their imaginations. The power source they took couldn't have been totally real, and yet it couldn't have been totally imaginary, either."

He stopped for a moment, as if waiting for the others to understand the implications.

"If it's part real and part imaginary, the Sitnaltan weapon may be a lot more devastating than we know." He swallowed. David could see him struggling with the concept. "What if it's *more* than enough to destroy Gamearth? What if it can backlash outside the map? What if it's enough to destroy *us* too?"

Tyrone groaned comically. "This is boggling my mind!"

David ignored him and felt a shiver up his spine. That fear had been tickling the back of his mind, but he had not faced it until now. He remembered times when he didn't seem to have complete control over his own characters. If Siryyk the manticore wanted to detonate the weapon now that he had Verne captive, David wasn't sure he could stop him.

He let his voice fall to a whisper. "I'm beginning to wonder just who created who."

Melanie looked at him in a rare moment of rapport, but then the defiance returned to her eyes. "Or is it mutual now? Are we and the Game so intertwined that we can't survive without each other?"

7

MAYER'S RESEARCH EXPEDITION

"Once we have finished gathering data, we are by no means finished with our research. In fact, the work has only begun, because then we must discover how to apply that information for our own benefit."

—Dirac, Charter of the
Sitnaltan Council of Patent Givers

Mayer felt sore from riding the bicycle. She wobbled along the path, unsteady on the hard tires but impressed by the distance she had already covered. She still had several hexagons to go before she reached the Outsiders' ship.

Only a few hours after leaving Sitnalta, Mayer's legs already ached from the effort of pedaling over the bumpy terrain. Her dark hair streamed with sweat in the sunshine. She had spent too many hours in her tower workroom, pacing back and forth, thinking, scrawling designs in chalk on the dark wall, and not enough time exercising her body.

With determination, Mayer pushed her legs down, applied force to the pedals, which turned the gear, pulling the chain and rotating the wheels, and carried her forward. Simple exhaustion wasn't going to stop her.

The black bicycle had been welded together from scrap piping. It was one of several prototypes developed by her father Dirac in his younger days; but the invention had never caught on in Sitnalta, probably, Mayer now thought, because the thing had never been designed with the comfort of its rider in mind. The seat was a flat metal triangle with rounded corners and two rigid springs that made each bump feel like a blow to her buttocks. The minimal padding did little to ease the ride.

But it would take a team of engineers to get a steam-engine car up the winding paths that Mayer knew she would be traveling. The initial Sitnaltan research team to the Outsiders' ship had needed strong characters to hoist and lift their vehicles around sharp corners in the mountain terrain. Mayer could never do that by herself, and so she was left to her own resources. She could travel faster with the bicycle than by walking.

She rolled across a hex-line from flat grassland into abrupt mountain terrain. Mayer began to puff as the quest-path took a steep upward turn. After only a short while of this, she stopped, dismounted and let the bicycle fall to the dry grass and rocky earth.

Mayer patted her thighs, stamped her feet, and flexed her hands to keep the blood circulating. She blinked and turned to look behind her across two flat hexagons of grassland sprawling toward the intricate city of Sitnalta.

A bird flew up from the grass, and Mayer squinted, studying the shape of its wings and the color of its markings. She tried to recall the proper genus and species name, though biology had never been her strongest subject. Professor Frankenstein would have known the name instantly.

Mayer's face shrank into a sour expression at the thought of the dark-eyed professor. He had disappointed and angered her at the same time. After the cruel force seeped up through the Sitnaltan streets and destroyed the manufactories, Frankenstein had vowed to find a way of combating the invisible enemy.

Straight-backed and on fire with determination, Mayer went to the professors' workshop. Here Frankenstein and Verne had created so many inventions that even the Council of Patent Givers could not keep up with them all. She burst through the door without knocking and stood watching the dark inventor.

He continued pacing around the cluttered room without even looking up at her. Mayer saw a thousand different inventions, some disassembled to be repaired, some half-constructed and then abandoned, not because they would not work but because the professors had grown more interested in something else.

Frankenstein had knocked half-finished gadgets to the floor, ignoring any damage he might do to them. He simply needed more table space. Diagrams of human anatomy and large drawings of muscles and joints were pinned up on the walls and lying on the table in stacks. Scattered dissection reports of nervous systems poked out from other piles beside scrawled treatises on how different parts of the body worked.

Professor Frankenstein had always been fascinated with living things and how they functioned. He had spent much of his early solo effort in creating mechanical automatons, imitations of living things, such as metal fish that swam in the fountain pools, moving mechanical arms that assembled items in the hazardous areas of the manufactories, and claws that picked up castings too hot to handle.

In the jumbled workroom, Mayer's dark eyes were wide and fascinated as she drank in all the details. "I've come to help you, Professor."

He turned, startled into annoyance by the distraction. "I don't need any help. I didn't ask for any."

Mayer leaned with both hands on the edge of Frankenstein's work table. The sharp windings of a screw stung her palm; she brushed it aside. "You work better with a partner. I know I can help you. Haven't I proven I can do it? Look at all my own inventions. I'm as angry about this . . . this intrusion as you are. Let me contribute."

Frankenstein's shoulders slumped, and his face took on a weary expression. "Yes, I did work well with Verne. With *Verne*. But he's gone. Now I work alone."

Anger welled up inside Mayer. She drove herself as hard as any character. She would be a good match for Professor Frankenstein, if only he would let her. "Professor, I must insist—"

Frankenstein picked up a metal plate and tossed it to the floor among the scattered debris there. The crash and clatter startled Mayer; she heard something break, the tinkle of glass shards falling to the floor. The professor glared at her, and she saw how angry he was, how absorbed he had been in his own work.

"Please leave!"

"You vowed to rescue Sitnalta from this invisible force. It's been happening four times a day to different buildings and different parts of the city. We've got to find a way to stop it."

"I will," Frankenstein said, "if you stop bothering me. Don't you see how difficult this is going to be?"

"Let me help!" Her head pounded with the intensity of her desire, but she felt that she had already lost.

"You can help by going away. If you have a brilliant idea, put it into practice yourself. You're a good inventor. Right now I've got my own idea."

Pointedly ignoring her further, he sat down on a stool and dragged papers in front of him, rearranging them on the table. He let his face show exhaustion and anguish deeper than anything Mayer expected. "I need to do it this way. This time. Now please let me work."

Mayer felt her lips trembling as she tried to contain her disappointment. "It's something to do with what you and Verne learned at the Outsiders' ship, isn't it? The information that you won't reveal to anyone."

He shook his head but continued to stare at his drawings. "No. It isn't that."

Mayer knew otherwise. She thought she could tell when he was lying. She stormed out of the professor's workroom without another word, but in her mind she made promises to herself. She knew where to go. She would have to do it alone. She would have to hurry, before the invisible force continued to make the Sitnaltans destroy themselves. . . .

It had been chilly that morning when she set out on the bicycle. The sluggish sea mist still crept through the hex-cobbled streets until the dawn grew strong enough to burn it off. Mayer pedaled out through the main gates as Sitnalta began to stir for the morning. Many characters had left their own research projects to help clean up destroyed buildings from the previous day's manipulations and to begin rebuilding. They did not say to each other that the evil compulsion could make it all wasted effort at any time.

Mayer pedaled off along the quest-path, pushing herself to get to the Outsiders' ship as fast as possible. She didn't know how the travel restrictions spelled out in Rule #5 would affect her progress on a bicycle, so she would need to keep track and contribute more data to the Sitnaltan collection of information.

As she rested beside her bicycle on the mountain terrain, Mayer felt her leg muscles shaking and her body prickling from sweat. She took a drink from a small water flask and then shrugged the pack off her shoulders.

Crawling out of her warm outer clothing, Mayer felt the breeze cool the sweat on her skin, raising a few goosebumps. Once she started riding uphill again, the effort would keep her warm enough. She crammed the clothing inside her pack. With a deep breath, she shouldered the pack again and righted her clumsy bicycle.

Mayer set off again, puffing and pedaling up the steep slope but making steady progress.

She had marked on her own small map exactly where to find the ruins of the ship, which lay crashed next to an abandoned Slac fortress. The first Sitnaltan expedition left the excavation site the morning after Professor Verne had ridden off alone. Frankenstein had declared their mission over and ordered them to pack up and depart immediately, giving no explanation. Not until later, through hints, did the professor tell about his and Verne's dream from the Outsider Scott, which showed them how to create a devastating weapon from the ship's wreckage.

After they had finished, Frankenstein used a firepit in the old Slac fortress to burn all their plans and notes, so that no other character might know about the weapon they had developed. Mayer and many others in Sitnalta found this attitude appalling. Professors Verne and Frankenstein had created enormous numbers of inventions and had always shared every detail. Just the thought of the two destroying information that was by law common property of all characters caused friction with the other inventors.

Frankenstein remained firm, though. He and Verne had made a vow that this was one invention they would not share. Not ever.

By returning to the ship, Mayer would find a way to learn what they had learned, or some other means to fight for Sitnalta. She remembered the words the Vailret had said as he confronted her on the docks at night, just before he and blind Paenar had stolen Verne's *Nautilus* sub-marine boat.

"You tinker with your calculating machines and street-cleaning engines, but when faced with a problem your technology may not be able to solve, you dismiss it as something not to be considered." Vailret had said. "Scrap your frivolous gadgets and invent something to stop this thing! If we fail, all of Gamearth could *depend on you.*"

Mayer had no idea whether Vailret had been successful on his journey to the island, though the dragon Tryos had not been seen again. She didn't know what had happened to their greater enemy, Scartaris, but Verne had disappeared with his secret weapon, and even Frankenstein didn't know what had gone wrong.

The force corrupting Sitnalta might have something to do with Scartaris, or the Outsiders, or the rumored end of the Game. Their own detectors showed nothing, and Mayer had no idea. But she would take up Vailret's challenge and try to invent something to counteract the danger.

Her dark eyes glazed with the effort to keep pushing uphill, focusing only on the quest-path before her. Her skin was flushed, her face set in the obsessive expression she thought might be like the one she saw so often on Professor Frankenstein's face. He was one of the greatest inventors since Maxwell, but he apparently did not have the same admiration for her, since he spurned her assistance.

In late afternoon she crested a peak and abruptly crossed another hex-line of mountain terrain where the slope changed and the crags spread out before her in a different pattern. The quest-path zigzagged ahead like a white line carved into the cliffs. The air felt cold, like rough cloth against her face, but so far she had not encountered enough ice and snow to make for treacherous riding.

Some of the peaks on Mayer's left blocked the setting sun, filling the valleys with shadows. As she looked ahead, she could discern the stark parapets of the crumbling Slac fortress, with its tiny black window slits and jagged, forbidding spikes. She stopped for a moment, drawing a deep breath.

As the fading light glinted around the cliffs, she saw gleams and reflections of the collapsed metal from the

Outsiders' ship, excavated girders that the Sitnaltan expedition had left exposed.

Mayer pedaled furiously, picking up speed as the quest-path plunged downhill. The narrow tires were awkward on the rough trail, letting her skid among loose rocks as she tried to stop herself. The ship seemed to be waiting for her, a box filled with wonders and ideas that she could discover. With this incentive burning in her, Mayer felt the need to discover something of tremendous significance to the entire Game. The answer lay buried somewhere in the ruins ahead.

"I'll show you, Professor Frankenstein," she muttered between teeth clenched with effort and the cold, "and I'll show you, Vailret."

8

POOL OF PEACE

*"I shall never return. I am done with the
Game, and the Game is done with me."*
—Drodanis, on his departure from
the Stronghold

The great still Pool, as smooth and flat as a puddle
of quicksilver, began to drain away. It seemed as if a
hole had cracked open at the bottom of the map,
letting it all pour to the Outside, into nothingness.

Drodanis stood beside the trees, staring down at his
reflection. His face looked back at him, but he also
saw through the placid water to the depths of the
Rulewoman's Pool.

Near the bottom, he glimpsed the boy Lellyn, frozen in a block of forever-ice. The Rulewoman Melanie
had encased Lellyn there to protect him from his own
destructive doubts. But now as the level of water in
the Pool fell visibly and without a sound, Drodanis
realized that even her protection could not last.

The Rulewoman had not shown herself to him in
many turns. She had come occasionally to speak with
Drodanis, to talk of the rest of Gamearth and how it
continued without him. Drodanis had been one of her
favorite characters, she said. When the Outsider David began his work to destroy the map, she had allowed Drodanis to send a warning to his son Delrael,
but then she had departed and never returned.

The Rulewoman Melanie would be occupied with
other concerns, more serious adventures with a bear-

ing on the entire Game, he thought. Drodanis remained in the silent forest, resting . . . existing, but doing nothing else. The past had left its crippling scars on him. His mind had replayed the tragic events of his life so many times that the memories had exhausted themselves—

The death throes of his beloved Fielle, sweating, her skin warm and damp to the touch as Drodanis knelt over her and watched the fever course through her system like a serpent's venom. He felt weak, barely recovered from the fever himself . . . the fever he had passed on to her while she tended him back to health. Fielle died as he stood there. He watched the milky glaze grow on her eyes when the delirium faded into a thicker glaze of death. . . .

He saw again the last cocky grin on the face of his brother Cayon while he fought the deadly ogre out in the forests. Cayon: always trying to compete with him, to outdo his older brother, to prove that he could tackle this monster on his own. But he was desperately mismatched, and didn't even realize it until it was too late. . . .

Again and again those memories had flooded Drodanis's mind, focusing his thoughts. They had made Drodanis leave his life behind, to come here in search of forgetting and avoid the responsibilities of questing and amusing the Outsiders.

Here in this peaceful place the bad memories had replayed themselves many times, but with each recollection, they grew smaller and weaker, like a giant wall of rock being eaten away by a river. By now those memories were withered ghosts, still part of his past, but powerless.

Drodanis stood by the trees, feeling empty. Now that the pain from his past had faded away, it left him only numb. He had nothing else to do and no companions, not the Rulewoman, not young Lellyn who had followed him on his long journey here.

And now the Pool of Peace was draining away before his eyes.

Drodanis stared at the reflection of the old fighter looking up at him from the Pool's surface, and he asked himself if he really had changed that much. In his own mind, he still pictured himself as the brash young quester, the fighter character who had gone out with Cayon on adventures, who had found piles of treasure and slain dozens of monsters.

But now he saw a man whose face looked drawn and slack; his eyes appeared hollow, his expression vacant. This man frightened Drodanis. His rich brown hair, long moustache, and beard were now streaked with gray. He hadn't cared for his appearance for a long time; he had seen no point to it.

Drodanis remembered when Fielle had combed his hair for him and he had braided hers, when he strutted around wearing the jewels, weapons, and fine armor that he had won through his quests. Now he recognized only a once-brave character who had been badly used and then discarded.

Drodanis drew a deep breath and felt a strange emotion stirring in him, resentment and anger—not directed toward himself, but focused outward at the Game.

A ripple in the Pool of Peace startled him. The very thought of something marring the surface was so puzzling that he took a moment to realize that the water level had dropped enough that the motionless, encased figure of Lellyn was beginning to protrude. The Pool drained around him, exposing the young boy's head and shoulders.

Beneath the milky ice, Drodanis could see Lellyn's expression locked in astonishment, disbelief, and terror at what the boy had just realized. "Ah, Lellyn, what is going to happen to us?" Drodanis said.

But he heard no noise, not even a trickle from the draining water. Tall black pines and oaks and willows shielded the Rulewoman's Pool from curious characters. No quest-paths led here, and Drodanis had found the place only after long searching.

When Lellyn was still beside him, they had debated with the Rulewoman about the Rules and *reality*. Lellyn seemed too perceptive for his own good. Lellyn himself was a Rulebreaker, a self-contradiction in that he was a human character with powerful magical abilities. Lellyn became obsessed with the contradictions. He had queried the Rulewoman too much about *reality*, and about Gamearth's place and how it had been created.

When in his mind he had so firmly grasped the idea that Gamearth was not *real*, that he was not *real* . . . when he had locked onto the concept and refused to let go, and in his heart he completely disbelieved in his own existence—at that point the Rulewoman had stopped him. She froze him in forever-ice and submerged him in the Pool a moment before he could have vanished into nothingness.

Now the Pool had nearly drained away, and Drodanis could see the forever-ice melting.

Lellyn's body stood exposed up to his shins, and the water drained even faster. The boy apprentice had his arms locked in a warding gesture, trying to wave away the realization that was forcing itself upon him. His legs were taking a step backward, as if trying to flee.

The remaining water stood out in glistening puddles, like frozen mirrors. The bottom of the Pool showed dark and lumpy rocks where no plant could take hold in the magical water.

"Rulewoman! What do you want me to do?" Drodanis shouted into the air, breaking the silence. His voice sounded like a roar, and he expected to hear disturbed cries of birds in the forest, but nothing answered him, not even a breeze among the trees. The air felt perfectly warm and still, too comfortable.

The spark of anger in him grew a little brighter.

He heard a crack and saw a chunk of the forever-ice fall from Lellyn's shoulders. Other spidery lines appeared along the filmy coating that covered the boy's entire body. The forever-ice split and fell off, part melting, part vanishing into sparkles of light in the air.

"Lellyn!" Drodanis cried.

The boy moved and turned his head, keeping his eyes wide. He took one more step backward and waved his hands. "No!" he said—but he was answering a question asked many turns ago. He could not change his thoughts fast enough. "How can I get this out of my mind?" he cried, but his voice turned high and distorted.

Lellyn rippled and faded. "Where am I going?" he managed to say, and just for an instant before he flowed into an uncertain image, Drodanis watched the boy's expression change to one of wonder.

Lellyn dissolved into the air, leaving behind no more trace than had the water in the Pool.

Drodanis hung his head and squatted down at the rim of the basin. Everything was gone now, his memories, the Pool, Lellyn, the Rulewoman . . . his reasons for existing.

If the map survived, these battles for the survival of Gamearth itself, not the simple quests, would be remembered as the greatest times of the entire Game. Drodanis had stepped away from all that, bowing out to let other characters shoulder the burden.

The only small part he had offered to the Game was to send a message—a warning—to Delrael about the need for stopping Scartaris. Delrael had taken the quest, and the younger generation of characters now determined the events of the Game. Drodanis was proud of his son.

He blinked his eyes, and the tears burned there. It felt strange to him. Living too long with comfort and peace had drained him, like the waters from the Pool;

it made his life gray instead of filled with the bright colors of happiness and sadness.

He could not compete anymore, this old empty fighter who had not used his training for many turns. He felt useless. He wondered if he had made the right decision so long ago to leave everything behind.

Drodanis concentrated on the small flame of anger inside, and it seemed to be the only living part in his entire body, the only spot of color in his world. As he thought about what he had done—and what he had failed to do by running away from it all—he watched the spark grow brighter. He felt his senses reawaken.

"No, I am not useless," he said to himself. "I can still remember how to fight. How to change things."

Perhaps the Pool had gone away to punish *him* for going away, to kick him out of his numb surrender and show him that Gamearth still needed Drodanis.

He stood up and went to one of the few remaining puddles at the bottom of the Pool of Peace. He bent over and scooped up the cool water in his hands, splashing it on his face and trying to wash away some of his weariness. But now it was just water after all, and the refreshing strength he gathered came from within himself.

Drodanis stood again, took a deep breath, and felt his body: arms that could still swing a sword and eyes that could still spot an enemy and aim an arrow.

Leaving the empty Pool of Peace behind, Drodanis walked out to the trees without turning back, searching for a quest-path that would take him back into the Game. Back into life again.

9

BLACK FALCON

"Few characters have a mission as clear as ours. Few characters have a responsiblity as great as ours. If humans are to win this Game, then we must be pure in our motivations and we must be decisive in our actions. We answer to no one but ourselves and to the Outsiders."

—Annik, chief of the
Black Falcon troops

When Delrael's army arrived at the ylvan settlement, the Black Falcon troops had already slaughtered most of the forest people.

The trees stood too dense for Delrael to see the smoke rising up until he could smell it. He heard distant sounds of shouting, some kind of struggle, screams. Delrael sent three characters to run ahead and investigate as he swung the rest of the army toward the disturbance.

He broke into a trot off the quest-path directly through the forest, urging his fighters on. He wrestled with his own impatience to strike against a tangible enemy rather than to continue a long, tedious journey.

"Prepare for a fight," he said to Jathen behind him. The other characters passed the message along so that Delrael did not have to raise his voice and alert an enemy. Delrael elbowed branches out of the way and kicked at brambles by his ankles. He drew his own sword. He heard shouts, the crackling of flames, scattered painful screams.

The three scout characters hurried back to Delrael. They looked shaken and gray, their eyes wide with terror. "They're being slaughtered," said young Romm, a farmer from the village.

"I can hear what's happening," Delrael said, then he broke into a run. When he burst into the clearing, the appalling violence of the scene stunned him enough that he stopped for a moment and had to concentrate to keep from dropping his sword.

Three of the camouflaged ylvan nest dwellings crackled with orange flames that licked up the matted brush. The air smelled of oily smoke and blood. The towering trees all around were stained with soot and disfigured with white gashes from axes and swords. Ruins of a campfire lay on the ground, stomped and scattered.

One of the blazing dwellings split open at the bottom, dumping smoldering debris. Sticks and ylvan possessions tumbled onto the ground. When the anchor rope burned through, the entire nest-dwelling toppled to the ground.

Around the clearing rode a dozen burly Black Falcon fighters on dark horses, outfitted as Corim had been. One towering woman rested a bloodstained two-handed sword on her shoulder as she pointed and shouted orders. The others charged around in circles, shooting arrows at a few surviving ylvans who tried to flee in the trees above.

In a snapshot moment, Delrael saw the splashed blood and the broken bodies of little forest people who had dressed in greens and browns to camouflage themselves in the trees. A handful of others lay tied up in a net, struggling to break free.

Several more dangled from trees with their necks in poorly made nooses. Three still squirmed and kicked on the ends of their ropes, though their faces had turned blackish from lack of air. Their tongues stuck out and their eyes rolled up. The ylvans clawed at their throats, trying to tear the nooses apart with bleeding fingernails.

One Black Falcon rider lay motionless with several arrows in his throat, chest, and back. He had been propped against a tree trunk but was obviously dead. A riderless horse, apparently belonging to the dead fighter, wandered about.

Delrael made a wordless cry as he crashed into the clearing. His other fighters, still running to keep up with him, paused to gawk at what they saw. Delrael finally managed to form words, shouting, "Stop! Stop!"

The Black Falcon troops whirled toward the new characters. After a moment of surprise, they appeared relieved to see humans coming out of the forest and not some other character race.

"Archers! Find your mark!" Delrael shouted. "All of you Black Falcon troops, stop!" Delrael's other fighters nocked arrows and aimed at the black riders, who appeared dumbfounded.

Jathen ran ahead of Delrael, got to the central tree in the settlement and severed the ropes hanging the squirming ylvans. They dropped to the ground. He ripped at the ropes and tried to open the ylvans' air passages. The skin on their necks was gnarled and puckered from the bite of the rope. One of these ylvans had aready died. Another, unconscious, broke her ankle upon falling to the ground; the pain woke her up, and she gasped in air as Jathen pulled off the noose. The third, a powerful-looking ylvan with a drawn face, dark hair, and pinched mouth, was still alive and aware. As Jathen cut the first woman free, the ylvan man pulled his own noose off. He rolled over to his knees and vomited, trying at the same time to wheeze in lungfuls of air and to retch.

The Black Falcon woman on horseback turned her mount and glared at Delrael with a half-bemused expression. "What are you doing? Only enemies of Gamearth would interfere with us." She turned to her troops. "Ignore them. Go ahead and execute the rest of the parasites."

Delrael snapped at his own fighters, "If another ylvan dies, kill all the Black Falcon troops. All of them. I'm sick of this."

One of the Black Falcon riders cried out, and they all whirled to look at him. A small arrow protruded from his shoulder. Several barely seen ylvans scurried through the branches above, concealed by the smoke and fire.

The Black Falcon woman bellowed at the top of her lungs. "Get them! We're not winners until they're all killed."

"I said no!" Delrael stormed forward with his sword in front of him. He stood blocking the woman on her tall horse.

She stared down at him with an icy, amused smile. "Oh, I'm tired of your whining." She looked behind her. "Corim!"

Out of the forest terrain on the other side of the village emerged a full dozen more Black Falcon riders, each holding a long bow in hand with the string drawn fully back. They aimed their long arrows directly at Delrael. Corim led the group. His face remained dispassionate, with no sign of pity or recognition.

"Your army might outnumber us," the woman said, "but I guarantee that each Black Falcon will take out ten of your fighters before he falls."

Jathen, red with anger, stood up beside the still-choking ylvans. As Delrael's army continued to emerge into the clearing, old Siya, Enrod, and Tareah appeared. "Enrod, do something!" Jathen said.

As the Sentinel from Tairé cocked his head without understanding, Delrael felt all twelve arrows pointing at his heart. The Game paused for a moment. He sensed his heart beating, and he wanted it to continue beating. Tareah took out her Water Stone, but looked uneasy about whether to take the risk.

"No," Delrael said. His voice sounded small to him. "You can't do anything in time."

The hanged ylvan man crawled to his feet and screamed in a voice hoarse from a damaged throat. "How dare you! What have we ever done to humans?"

He gaped at the bloodshed, the slaughtered ylvans. Though barely able to stand, the little man carried murder in his eyes. He started to lunge forward with his hands extended, claws ready to tear the Black Falcon woman's eyes out. Jathen grabbed him by the elbows and held him back.

Delrael stared into the Black Falcon woman's face. He wished Vailret had stayed with them, because Vailret was the talker. He could smooth things over between hostile characters. Delrael swallowed and tried his best, keeping his eyes on the riders. Occasionally he caught the gaze of Corim on the edge of the clearing.

"We're wasting time here, and wasting effort," Delrael said to the woman. "Didn't Corim bring you my message? We wanted you to join us. There's an enemy worth fighting. You're just throwing away your talent here. We can't afford to waste characters at this point in the Game, when everyone is needed to defend Gamearth."

The Black Falcon woman lowered the two-handed sword to her side and climbed off her horse. Even standing in front of Delrael, she towered a head taller than him. Her hair hung in ponytails, long, pale and shot with gray. She had tied each clump of hair with leather thongs and iron ball-bearings that had turned brownish-red from exposure to the damp and rain. Her face looked rough, not beautiful, with a haughty expression of distaste. Her arms emerged bare from a leather vest that protruded because of her enormous breasts. She did not look at all clumsy, but like a juggernaut.

"I brought your message, Delrael," Corim said from his position, without relaxing the bowstring or wavering with the pointed tip of his arrow. "But Annik had thoughts of her own."

The woman, Annik, looked at Corim, scowling for just a moment as if angry at having another character answer for her. She glared at Delrael again, now that she knew who he was. "Corim conveyed your preposterous suggestions."

Delrael bristled, but Annik launched into her speech, raising her voice among the other sounds of the burning trees, stamping horses, and the moaning of injured ylvans. "Why would we ever want to listen to you, an amateur? We've been fighting this battle for generations! Since the Scouring, the Black Falcon troops have been making Gamearth suitable for human characters.

"So, after all this time, you get an idea to go marching and decide that every one of us should drop our own missions and listen to you? We should ignore a lifetime of training, of struggle against parasites, wandering monsters, anything that's made Gamearth unsafe! All of a sudden, you want us to become friends with them? You are a child."

Delrael drew himself up as tall as he could. His hands trembled on the hilt of his sword, but not from fear. "And you, Annik," he said, "are so stupid that I can't believe you survived in the Game this long."

The other Black Falcon riders stiffened, rattling their weapons, but Annik looked angry for only a moment. Then she began to laugh and continued laughing, which made Delrael even angrier.

He continued, "We need your assistance. All of us have to fight together. These ylvans were enough to bring down one of your own fighters," he said, indicating the dead man propped against the tree. "They could just as easily bring down one of the monster fighters. But instead you'd rather fight simple, defenseless opponents. Are they worthy adversaries for you?"

He looked at each of the bowmen still aiming at him. "If you kill me, then my fighters will wipe you out, no matter what it takes. Yes, I'm sure your Black Falcon troops will be great in battle, and I'm sure they'll succeed in murdering some of my fighters before they fall. But they will fall. You'll all die—for what? What do we gain if all of your troops are slain? What do you gain if my characters are injured or killed while fighting against you?"

He rested the tip of his own sword on the ground. "Only Siryyk and his army would win. They suffer no losses if you and I fight. We'll all be losers: you, my army, and the ylvans. Let them go and join forces with us." Delrael kept his tone even, though the thought of joining the Black Falcons galled him now.

Annik shook her head with a disturbed smile on her face. The ponytails and ball-bearings swung from side to side like weapons. "You don't understand very well how the Game is played. Once we get to this situation, we cannot let it just end like that. It's not in our nature."

The ylvan man coughed again and struggled to break from Jathen's grip. He spoke in his harsh voice, snapping at Delrael. "Don't bargain for us, human. This is our battle, and if we lose, then let it be because of our own failings, not because one human is stronger than another."

Delrael pursed his lips. "I propose this solution." His voice sounded much more reasonable than he felt. He drew a deep breath. "Rule #10 encourages single combat to solve disputes. Annik, have the Black Falcon troops pick their champion. Then the ylvans will choose theirs." He raised his eyebrows at Annik. "That method of settling problems is most certainly in our nature."

Annik looked around at the tiny ylvan, shot a glance at the survivors still hiding somewhere in the trees, and smiled again at Delrael, showing the tips of her teeth.

"Maybe you're not a fool after all, Delrael. That does sound much more reasonable than wasting our lives. What would be the terms of victory and surrender?"

Delrael frowned, pretending to be thinking, though he had decided already. "Well, if the Black Falcon champion wins, then my army departs and you go do as you like, without any interference from me. If the ylvan champion wins, you cease harassing them and join my army against the real enemy."

Annik stroked the side of her great horse as she flashed her eyes at the struggling ylvan man again. Some of the other ylvans bound beside the trees moaned in fear at Delrael's terms.

"That sounds interesting," she said, resting the massive sword blade on the ground, where its tip dug into the ashes of a scattered ylvan firepit. She held the horn of her saddle. "I'm the champion of the Black Falcon troops. That's how I gained my position here. But who would the ylvans pick?" She stared at the little dark-haired man, who finally shook off Jathen's grip and stood tall.

"I am Kellos. This is . . . this *was* my village. I will choose my champion."

The Black Falcon riders chuckled to themselves. Delrael's army seemed uneasy and confused, not knowing what they should do.

Annik smiled disparagingly at Kellos. "Take your time, little parasite. We're not in any hurry, and the battle certainly won't take long."

Kellos stared at the wreckage of his settlement. One of the hanging nests continued to burn, and clusters of mud and branches split off and fell to the ground. He looked at the blood of the others and at the ylvan woman groaning beside him from the pain of her broken ankle. The strangled ylvan man sprawled on the ground with a black and swollen face, his eyes bulging. A flush came to Kellos's face, and he glared at the Black Falcons, then at Delrael's army. His expression became pinched with a sudden idea.

He pointed his finger at Delrael himself. "You are the champion I choose, human. You will fight for the lives of the ylvans as well as for your own life."

The fighters in Delrael's army cried foul, and the Black Falcon troops reacted in surprise. But Delrael remained motionless. He felt relieved inside. He had hoped Kellos would think of this.

He drew himself up, lifted his chin and narrowed his eyes. He looked first at Annik and then back at Kellos. He remembered little Tallin, the ylvan man who had followed them away from his village, who had befriended Delrael . . . and who had died in front of Delrael's eyes as the Anteds attacked. Delrael hadn't been able to help the little ylvan then.

"I am honored to be your champion," he said.

When Annik looked at him, she seemed even more pleased. She shifted the giant two-handed sword with her massive arms. Delrael wondered if the single-combat challenge had been such a good idea after all. He did not feel a much better match for her than one of the ylvans would have been.

But Delrael had undergone all the training his father could give him; he had gone on numerous quests; he had fought Gairoth the ogre, the colony of Anteds, Tryos the dragon, the shadow-creature Cailee, and the entire horde of Scartaris's creatures.

"Well, Delrael." She let out a small chuckle. "Make your first move." She raised the sword and held it close to her shoulder.

Delrael turned to Kellos. "I'll do my best for you."

The moment he was distracted, Annik lunged forward, sweeping her great sword with both hands. Delrael saw the sudden change of expression on Kellos's face. At the same moment Jathen spat out a warning.

But he was already diving to the ground. The edge of Annik's blade made a moaning sound as it scythed across the air. Delrael rolled and sprang to his feet, watching her recover from the stroke. She twisted her face with concentrated effort to wield the heavy weapon. She had intended to lop his head off before he could even strike.

Delrael leaped to his feet. The Black Falcon troops snickered among themselves. Corim sat stony-faced on his horse.

Delrael charged in with his sword up to guard himself. His fighting fury seethed through his veins even more intensely now than when he felt only outrage at what the Black Falcons had done to the ylvan village.

He swung and ducked, trying to get close to Annik, where she could not use her two-handed sword. But she swept low with the point of the blade this time and would have disemboweled him if he had not skipped back.

Delrael's ears roared with the cheers and cries of ylvans, his own army and the Black Falcons. He thought he heard Tareah wishing him luck. He knew old Siya would be watching in horror, remembering another battle in which her husband had been slain.

Delrael felt his muscles sing with the energy. This was fighting, this was doing something, *this* was the way the Game should be played. But it should be fought against a worthy enemy, not a misguided fool.

Delrael forced himself to pause for one heartbeat as he recentered his thoughts. He looked at Annik, trying to drive back the emotion, focusing on how to defeat her rather than on how to get revenge. Revenge would only distort his thoughts.

Delrael gripped the hilt of his sword with both hands and reached up to block Annik's swing. When the blades struck, the clang of metal rang out in the forest air. Delrael felt his arms shake in their sockets, just as in the battle against Gairoth, with his spiked club. But Gairoth had been stupid; Annik and the Black Falcon troops were not.

He kept his eyes on her blade locked against his, but a movement of her arm distracted him. Annik took one hand from her sword and moved it to her waist, where she slid out a long dagger. The massive sword in her right hand dipped toward the ground as she concentrated on the dagger, thrusting it forward and up.

Delrael squirmed away, but the edge sliced along his leather armor, gashing it open in a stinging line along his ribcage.

He struck up with his sword, trying to knock Annik's knife hand away. Then he noticed, too late for him to act, that even with only one hand, Annik brought her great sword around, low to the ground because she couldn't lift it high enough for a lethal blow. Her face grimaced with the effort.

The wide blade smashed into Delrael's unprotected left leg below the knee. He heard a loud *thwock*.

White lights and thunderous pain exploded up his leg and into his brain. Delrael screamed and fell over backward, unable to think or move.

He heard vague echoes of his army crying out in dismay. He thought he heard ylvan voices among them. He tried to blink the swimming black blotches out of his vision. As his sight finally cleared, he attempted to defend himself somehow, but a sickening feeling greater than the pain told him he had lost, that he would never fight against Siryyk's army and save Gamearth. He would fall here, the victim of another human fighter.

Annik stood over him, broadsword upraised in two hands. Her dagger lay behind her on the ground where she had dropped it. Annik obviously intended to chop off his head on the forest floor among the ashes of old ylvan campfires.

But her expression transformed itself into one of horror. Her ponytails, weighted with the iron balls, hung in front of her face like reaching tentacles. She gawked down at the wound at his leg, at the lack of blood.

He squirmed up, seeing only a white gash, the chewed notch in the *kennok* wood that had been carved into the shape of a human leg by the khelebar.

Delrael felt the pain, but the injury would not be crippling. Thilane Healer had shown him how to repair the magic leg.

The Black Falcon troops stood around with astounded expressions. Annik looked appalled. "You're not even human!" she said, working the words out of her mouth one at a time.

Delrael, still holding onto his sword, gathered up his own energy, ignoring the artificial pain in his leg. He croaked, "Are you?"

He moved his body, coiling at his waist and bunching his shoulders. He lunged upward at Annik. The tip of his sword pierced her stomach, struck something hard and deep—her spine—slid sideways, and then poked out between the ribs of her back. The black leather vest rose like puckering lips around the protruding blade.

Blood gushed out and ran down her dark leather armor. Annik's eyes bulged, filling with red as they hemorrhaged from inside. She choked, coughing blood, and hung balanced on Delrael's sword until her weight drove his arms down. She slumped farther onto the blade, collapsing on top of him.

Annik lay over him like a smothering weight. Delrael couldn't hear anything but her dying gasps and gurgles. Her body spasmed as she tried to move. But it was just reflex. Annik had already died.

Delrael pulled himself out. Jathen helped him up. "You won," he said.

Delrael took a deep breath. "Wonderful, isn't it? Help me stand."

The Tairan pulled Delrael's arm over his shoulder and hauled him to his feet. Delrael left his sword in

Annik's body and used his free hand to wipe at the blood on his chest. He succeeded only in smearing it into dark streaks that soaked into his leather armor. He looked down at his injured leg and saw that a large chunk of the wood had been hacked out, as if a woodsman had struck him with an ax. Delrael ignored the wound. The pain still surged through him, but he could endure it. Trying to keep his breathing in check, he looked at the upset and confused Black Falcon riders.

"I've won in single combat," he gasped, "according to the Rules. You must now leave the ylvans alone and join us in our fight against the manticore."

Anger flared in the Black Falcon riders, but Corim held up his hand. He urged his mount to take two steps forward, then turned his dispassionate expression toward the dead form of Annik lying face-down in the dirt. Blood pooled under her. The end of Delrael's sword protruded from her back, gleaming bright as the stain ran off of it.

"Annik fought you," Corim said, "but I never heard her agree to your terms." The other riders grunted their assent. One laughed.

"Therefore, you had no agreement. We don't feel bound by any bargain."

Delrael's army made sounds of their own anger, and the ylvans shouted.

Corim continued, "However, if you offer protection to the ylvans, I don't think it's very wise for the Black Falcons to keep preying on them. But we will never join your army; there are too many differences between us."

Corim swung his bow and mounted it back on his shoulder. "Though you might not agree, Gamearth's enemies are our enemies, too. We may fight together with you someday if we see you battling a worthy enemy and you need our assistance."

Corim motioned at two of the Black Falcon riders.

"We'll take our dead, Delrael, and let you do as you wish."

Other riders dismounted and went to the dead fighter against the tree. Lifting him, they spread his body across the back of his horse, sideways on the saddle. The Black Falcons plucked the ylvan arrows from the corpse and threw them to the ground in disgust.

Corim himself rolled Annik's body over and removed Delrael's sword. With no expression on his face, he handed the blade back to Delrael. Jathen took it and glared at the Black Falcon man, but Delrael kept staring at Corim.

The Black Falcon troops completed their preparations without speaking a word to Delrael, his army, or the ylvans. Delrael motioned for his fighters not to interfere. Corim bent under the horse and tied Annik's hands beneath the saddle so her body would not slide off. The horses appeared upset by the blood and dead bodies. The Black Falcon riders mounted up again.

Kellos stared at them like a bomb ready to explode. Delrael had trouble keeping his voice steady as the pain pounded in his leg. He turned to the little man. "Gather your survivors. Free the others and go find the rest of your people. The ylvans will come with us."

Corim looked back once at Delrael and met his gaze but said nothing. Without a word, the Black Falcon troops rode into the forest.

Then Delrael allowed himself to pass out.

10

UNWELCOME GUESTS IN SITNALTA

> *"We cannot blame the Outsiders for every-*
> *thing that happens to us. Characters are respon-*
> *sible for their own actions. No one can take that*
> *burden away from us."*
> —Dirac, city leader of Sitnalta

The quest-path traced a pale line across the flat grassy terrain. Vailret squinted ahead. The walls of Sitnalta rose tall, visible from far off.

"I'm actually relieved to see that place," Bryl said, "though we didn't have much fun there last time." Vailret murmured his agreement. It was the first settlement of human characters they had seen since splitting off from the main army.

Vailret's feet felt sore and his body ached, but he walked with exhilaration as well as exhaustion. Though Bryl complained about aching joints, the cold of sleeping outside, and how he was too old to keep doing this, he managed to keep pace with Vailret.

"Are you letting your beard grow bushier?" Vailret asked.

"Maybe it's just my face getting smaller," Bryl muttered. He seemed in no mood for conversation.

Their journey had been smooth and uneventful, but Vailret felt anxious to get the Earth Stone and return to the protection of the main army. He had spent too much time studying legends instead of swinging swords; he could not defeat many opponents if it came to a battle. Vailret didn't know how well Bryl could defend them even when using the Stones as weapons.

The observation parapets on the Sitnaltan walls looked out over the surrounding terrain. Vailret shaded his eyes and threw his hair back. He could see no human faces in the tiny windows.

Vailret remembered approaching the city the first time, with Delrael limping on his *kennok* leg, which was stiffening because its khelebar magic had begun to fade inside the technological fringe. Delrael could never return to Sitnalta, because it would leave him crippled again. Mayer had come out to meet them from the tower.

"Hello the tower!" Bryl shouted, then lowered his voice. "At least they'll give us hot food."

Vailret waited for an answer, but no one came to the dark windows. "We need the Sitnaltans to help us cross the ocean hexagons with a boat, or another balloon, or something. That's more important than food."

"I am not riding in a balloon again!" Bryl said. "I prefer keeping my feet on the ground." He stamped on the quest-path for emphasis.

"Well, unless you can find some way to walk across the water hexagons to Rokanun, you're going to have to put up with it."

Bryl huffed and looked toward the city. "The gate's open. Let's just walk inside."

They entered Sitnalta, and Vailret looked around, puzzling at how it had changed. The sky remained clear of belching smoke and steam from the large manufactories. The air carried only normal noises: people and activities, not the bustle and frantic pace that Sitnalta had shown before. Vailret and Bryl stopped and stared, standing on the clean streets cobbled with hexagon-shaped tiles.

A little old man hurried out of an annex building beside the observation tower. "You don't want to stay here!" the old man said, waving his hands to shoo them back out the gate.

"Yes we do," Bryl said. "We've been here before."

"No, no!" the old man insisted. He had dark brown eyes deep within sockets haloed by wrinkles. His gray-flecked eyebrows protruded from his forehead like bottlebrushes. He looked older and more intense than Bryl. "Get away before it notices you! If you wait too long, you might never be able to leave."

Vailret bent down to the old man's height. "We need your help. We don't have any choice."

The old man appeared distressed, and Vailret spread his hands to look as diplomatic as possible. "Can you call Mayer, or Professor Verne, or even Dirac? One of them'll speak for us."

Bryl frowned at the mention of Dirac, the bureaucratic city leader who had created many inventions—seventy of them, as his daughter Mayer had said over and over—but Dirac had refused them any assistance on their first quest.

"Do you have some way of communicating with them?" Bryl said.

The old man's eyes lit up. "But of course! The best communication system on all of Gamearth. I'm Professor Morse—I developed it myself, installed it in all the streets of the city for direct and instantaneous communication via electrical impulse. Amazing, amazing—I wonder at it myself sometimes, and I invented the thing! Amazing, indeed."

He paused and put a finger to his shriveled lips. "But some of the lines are down. The wires snapped, you know, when the buildings toppled. I'm . . . who was it you wanted to contact again?"

"Mayer, or Professor Verne, or Professor Frankenstein even, or Dirac." Vailret ticked off the names, hoping Morse could reach at least one of them.

Morse counted on his fingers. "Well, Professor Verne left a long time ago. Something to do with the destruc-

tion of the world, I believe. I didn't pay much attention. Mayer's gone too. She disappeared just a day or
two ago, went back to that Outsider ship. Got it into
her head that she'd find some way to rescue the city of
Sitnalta from its dreadful plight." Professor Morse
flashed another broad smile. "When you sit by the
communications systems, you get to hear all sorts of
little tidbits." He chuckled.

"Professor Frankenstein is very busy, I'm afraid,
and I'd rather not disturb him." Then he held up one
finger by itself. "Ah, but Dirac! He'll find the time.
We have lots of work rebuilding what we've destroyed,
but I don't think he bothers with any of it."

Morse ducked inside his small building. Vailret and
Bryl peered inside as the old man flipped switches on
an apparatus. He began tapping on a gadget that sent
clicks along a wire. After a moment, he scowled down
at it, frowned, and adjusted a dial.

"No, that won't work." He tapped his fingernails
against the desk. "Alternate routes, alternate routes.
With the complexity of our system here, there are
always alternate routes."

Morse began tapping and clicking again, and this
time he beamed. "Ah yes, that's done it. Now, we just
wait." He flicked the machine again.

"What are we waiting for?" Bryl asked.

Two thick prongs of a metallic gadget began wob-
bling together like chattering teeth. "That!" Professor
Morse cocked his ear, slitting his eyes half closed. He
seemed to be keeping track of something on his fingers.

"What are you—" Vailret began.

"Shhh!" Morse continued to mark invisible letters
on the palm of his hand, then sat up. "It's a code, you
know. I have to pay attention. Yes, Dirac is coming
right over."

"What is this dreadful plight you keep talking about?"
Vailret asked. "What's happened in Sitnalta?"

Morse turned red with contained anger. "It's a curse,

I say! But that's not very scientific, so I don't say it often. But until proven otherwise, I'll continue to call it a curse."

"So what is it?" Bryl asked.

Morse pursed his lips and hummed, as if trying to construct an acceptable explanation. "You know how the Outsiders supposedly Play us? Make their characters do whatever they want? The Outsiders do it well, because we all operate under the illusion that our actions are our own. When you move your arm up and down"—Morse waved his arm from side to side—"it doesn't seem to be any idea but your own. Although we know otherwise."

Vailret tapped his fingers against the wall.

"Some force has suddenly taken on the role of controlling us more directly, yanking our arms and legs like little automatons, forcing us to do things that aren't in our own heads. Four times a day, every day! It's made us demolish the manufactories and wreck some of our other facilities. Why, we even lacked street lights for a while because the gas conduits had been broken."

"What's causing it?" Vailret asked. He cocked his head, listening for the approach of Dirac's vehicle.

Morse shook his head. "None of us has formulated an acceptable hypothesis, although Dirac has offered a prize for the character who does it—a genuine patent certificate and an engraved metal plaque on a building."

"Oh boy," Bryl muttered.

Morse turned toward the open door. Vailret heard a faint chugging noise. "That must be Dirac himself." Morse glanced at a timepiece propped against the wall, then tilted his head so he could see the correct time. "Yes, it's been long enough."

They stepped outside and saw a blue steam-engine car coming around the corner. Pennants and flags poked up from either side, red, gold and green, each bearing the stylized crest of Sitnalta. The colors waved

in the breeze as the vehicle rattled over the cobblestones. The pennants flipped away from the clouds of
steam gushing out the stack.

The car rolled along, grinding its own gears. In
front, Dirac sat alone in the seat, a portly man with
reddish-brown hair curled around ears that looked like
tiny plates. His lower lip protruded pink from his
florid skin. Dirac's fingers were short, like sausages
wrapped around the steering levers.

His eyes looked wide and wild, though. As he approached, Dirac drew back his lips and clenched his
teeth. A line of spittle trickled into his puffy beard.

"What's wrong with him?" Vailret asked, looking to
Professor Morse.

"Oh no!" Morse said. "How does it always know?"

The boiler in the back of the steam-engine car glowed
a cherry red, much hotter than it should have been.
The rivets holding the metal seams together appeared
even hotter, a whitish yellow.

Dirac stopped at the far end of the street, pointing
the car directly at them. His arm moved, jerking, then
gripped the acceleration lever; he engaged the clutch.
The blue car sprang forward on its narrow wheels.
Dirac waved his other arm, trying to frighten them
away.

"What's he doing!" Vailret said.

He and Bryl ran to one side of the street. Morse
backed against the door of his communications annex.
As Vailret and Bryl dashed toward a side alley, Dirac
yanked the steering lever to one side to steam after
them. A strange sound came from his throat.

"Split up!" Vailret shouted.

Bryl ran one way, and he dodged the other. Dirac
yanked the steering lever back and forth, as if wrestling with himself. The car weaved, kicking up the
cobblestones and leaving streaks of black tire on the
street.

The car continued to pick up speed, faster than it

should have gone. The bottom of the boiler flared orange. Black smoke mixed with the gushing steam. Dirac squeezed his eyes shut. The car charged toward the end of the street.

Morse stood by the communications building and waved his arms. "No! Not here—no!"

Dirac tried to roll off the seat. But his arm moved of its own accord to grab one of the handles and pushed his body back, forcing him to remain in the car.

Vailret turned to shield his eyes as Professor Morse leaped away from the door of the communications annex.

The steam-engine car crashed into the side of the building. Dirac gave the first note of a scream, then the car struck the walls.

The boiler exploded in gouts of flame and steam and chunks of flying metal. One of the towers teetered and crumbled. The side wall sloughed away from the explosion, burying the car, Dirac, and Professor Morse's communications center.

Morse scrambled to the rubble. He hunkered down to his knees and began to sob. "Do you see what I told you? Do you see? If this isn't a curse, then I'm no scientist!" He sat up, blinking at the contradiction of what he had just said.

Vailret stood horrified. Bryl came up to him, greenish and ready to gag. Other Sitnaltans ran over to the scene, looking distraught and angry. They didn't need to ask questions.

Morse stared at them. "Now all our communications are down," he said. "And I suppose we'll need to pick a new city leader, too."

He pursed his lips. "Did you two have any . . . suggestions when you came here? We're always interested in new ideas. Maybe you have a solution to our problem."

Vailret gaped at him. No one seemed even distressed at Dirac's death. He felt deep grief, if only because Mayer had lost her father. Bryl gave him an elbow in the ribs.

"Uh, we'll offer any ideas we can think of," Vailret said. "But we were hoping to ask *you* for help. We need passage across the water."

Morse stood up and brushed dust from his hands. Blood ran down one palm. The other Sitnaltans cleared rocks and bricks away from the main pile.

Vailret didn't want to be there when they uncovered Dirac's smashed body.

"Go to the center of the city, then," Morse said, pointing. "We've got plenty of construction projects going on. We need to rebuild faster than the curse makes us tear things down. See Professor Frankenstein. Yes, new ideas. Perhaps that's the only thing that can save us."

Vailret and Bryl hurried through the streets, feeling a strange oppression on them. Vailret squinted up at the tall buildings, but didn't understand what he had seen happen. "It's like Tairé and Scartaris all over again," Bryl said, "mindless characters being manipulated."

Vailret stared at one of the chugging street-cleaning gadgets that scoured the gutters; he remembered Mayer telling him that Dirac had first patented it. He shook his head. "No, not like Scartaris. These characters know what they're doing, but they just can't control their own bodies. It seems more limited than Scartaris."

Bryl blinked his eyes. "Like a spell of some kind."

Vailret stopped at the thought. "A *spell* in Sitnalta? But we're inside the technological fringe."

"Do you think the Rules have weakened that much?"

Sounds from around the corner led them into a broad square. Characters gathered in front of a tall building with all the windows smashed and columns of the facade yanked out. Yet the Sitnaltans had rigged up scaffolding, ropes, and pulleys. New construction materials lay around: pallets of bricks and mortar, wood hauled from forest terrain and stone blocks. Foundations were being poured, too. The characters swarmed over the front of the building. From the bright newness of one entire wall, Vailret could see how much they had rebuilt already, and it all appeared to have been done in a single day.

Some of the characters looked down at him, but most of them moved too quickly, were too wrapped in their own business for any such distraction. They seemed afraid to stop for even a moment.

A rope creaked, and a new pane of glass swung up, dangling sideways, then hung down straight as four characters cranking a winch hauled it up to the second story, where a large window had been smashed out.

"Excuse us!" Vailret called. "This is very important."

Every single one of the characters working on the reconstruction stopped, like Sitnaltan automatons that had been switched off. Vailret couldn't imagine how he had commanded such instant response, but then the Sitnaltans groaned in unison, crying out in anger. Some muttered, "Stop! Not again!"

Two women cranking the winch that raised the pane of glass stepped back. One kicked the release, and the rope hummed as the winch twirled. The glass hurtled down to the cobblestones and exploded in sharp fragments.

All the while cursing and growling in disbelief, the Sitnaltans yanked at the scaffolding, especially at the support struts. Metal crowbars came out and smashed into the new brick and the still-soft mortar. Characters threw wooden boards through glass panes while watching themselves with horrified expressions.

One man sawed the rope of a scaffold, sending himself and four others tumbling head first down to the street. The heavy scaffold and its load of bricks and stone landed on top of them.

Nine Sitnaltans used levers and pulleys to rig up a complex system with heavy grappling hooks; using it, they ripped off half of the entire facade. In a group, they moaned in dismay as the front of the building crumbled to the ground.

Vailret now realized where they stood. In the center of the square stood a stagnant fountain. In the greenish water, slime-covered mechanical fish puttered around in slow circles; several had sunk to the bottom, where algae grew on them.

Across the plaza stood the rebuilt shrine building, the museum that contained original writings of the great inventor Maxwell, whom Sitnaltans revered as the founder of their city. The first time Vailret had stayed in Sitnalta, the shrine building had caught on fire. He had charged inside to rescue their precious documents when none of the Sitnaltans proved willing to take the risk.

Now the struggling characters scrambled over the wreckage of the other building they had just demolished. Lining up in straight lines, they marched across the square, curling around the dead fountain, where Bryl and Vailret stared at them. The Sitnaltans aimed straight for the rebuilt shrine building.

The Sitnaltans themselves saw what the controlling force was driving them to do, and they fought back with redoubled urgency. One stout woman managed to trip herself and tumble in front of two columns of the other Sitnaltans. The next three tripped over her, and then the others kept walking, stepping on her body. She cried out, but she could not roll away.

Vailret ran forward, using his shoulders to knock characters aside. He pulled the woman away; Bryl grabbed her other arm and helped drag her across the cobblestones. She gasped but seemed unconcerned with her own pain.

"Not me! If you can move, stop them! They'll destroy the Charter of Sitnalta."

More than a score of Sitnaltans went toward their target. Vailret looked at Bryl. The two of them couldn't possibly fight against so many. Even if the Sitnaltans themselves didn't wish them any harm, the controlling force would have no such qualms.

"Bryl, use the Air Stone!" Vailret said. "Confuse them."

Bryl pulled out the four-sided diamond and stared at it. "But this is Sitnalta. Magic won't work here."

"Try it anyway," Vailret said. "There's a chance."

Bryl closed his eyes and tossed the pointed diamond to the ground. A "3" appeared. Vailret smacked his fist into his palm.

"How did that happen?" Bryl gaped. "I'm not supposed to roll anything but a '1' here." But after a moment, he snatched up the diamond and concentrated on his illusion.

Around the scrolled and columned building, a maze of brambles, each as wide as a man's thigh, sprang up. They twirled and tangled, with needle-sharp thorns as long as daggers.

Bryl held the Air Stone with both hands, closing his eyes. The Sitnaltans stopped, gawking in amazement. A few moved around the edges of the brambles but could see no way in. They stopped and looked as if they were gathering strength. Vailret feared what they would do.

Then one column plunged forward face-first into the brambles.

Vailret did not know if they simply disregarded the illusion and pushed ahead, denying what their eyes told them, or if the controlling force had accepted the sacrifice of a few characters and compelled them to go forward anyway.

The illusion could not maintain solidity. The Sitnaltan column marched through the brambles unscathed. As they succeeded, the other Sitnaltans mobilized and pushed forward.

"It isn't working," Bryl mumbled. He let go of the diamond, and the illusion dissolved.

"Time to be more decisive then," Vailret said. "You've got the Fire Stone. See what that does."

Bryl took out the ruby. "If the Air Stone was just a fluke, there's no chance this one will work. The odds are . . ."

"Just try it!"

Bryl rolled the eight-sided ruby, and it landed with the "5" showing up—another success.

This time a tall ring of fire surrounded the building, feeding off nothing but the cobblestones. The Sitnaltans gathered around, pushing close enough to the fire that the hair singed away from their foreheads and eyebrows. Smoke smudged their faces. If they tried to plunge through the fire, they would die.

"You'd better watch out, Bryl. I don't want to slaughter them. I'd rather let them rip up their damned documents."

But then the Sitnaltans wavered in their step, paused, and finally collapsed, set free from an invisible grip.

The moment the characters struck the ground, most scrambled back to their feet, tense and ready to pounce on any enemy they could see. Some remained crosslegged on the ground, sobbing and shaking.

"It *is* like a spell," Vailret said. "You were right."

The Sitnaltans appeared baffled as they turned. Some stared in relief at the intact, though smoke-stained, museum. Others gawked at the building they had just torn down.

"Maybe we should just swim across the water terrain," Bryl said. "I'll even give up a hot meal and a good bed to get out of here. Professor Morse was right." He shivered, tucking his hands into the folds of his blue cloak. He looked very old. "If that controller gets hold of us, we might never be able to get away."

"If that controller makes you use the Fire Stone against your will, you could bring down this entire city in a single day." Vailret looked around. He didn't particularly want to speak with the stunned Sitnaltans.

"Let's go find Professor Frankenstein before anything else happens."

Bryl had never been to the workroom of Professors Verne and Frankenstein, but Vailret remembered asking the professors to invent a new pair of mechanical eyes for Paenar, whose magical eye-staff refused to function in Sitnalta.

Oriented by the fountain and Maxwell's museum, Vailret recalled the other places Mayer had shown him in his tour of the city, the thinking lounges and the great room where characters rolled dice and kept track of the scores to discern some pattern to the Rules of Probability.

"Frankenstein is just down this street," he said, trudging ahead. With each step, he feared that the invisible manipulation would sink claws into his mind and drive his body to do terrible things, especially now that they had called attention to themselves by using the Stones. If the force indeed used magic to control characters, maybe it would want the Stones for itself.

A confused jumble of doorways and facades marked the Sitnaltan homes and research establishments. Mayer had pointed out details as they walked, and now Vailret tried to remember the important parts. Mayer had been upset when he and Paenar asked to see the professors, rather than continuing their tour with her. She had stopped at the appropriate doorway, then stalked off, leaving them to fend for themselves.

Vailret stopped. "This one."

An engraved plaque on the door announced:

Profs. Frankenstein and Verne
Inventors at Large
PLEASE DO NOT DISTURB

It looked as if a piece of tape had once obscured Verne's name, but someone had peeled it away again. "We're going inside," Vailret said. He pounded on the door, wincing as he struck the ornate carving with the side of his hand.

Loud curses and a clatter of toppling books and equipment came from inside. Footsteps moved toward the door, accompanied by continued mutterings. Vailret took a half step backward and put himself behind Bryl. "You can stand in front."

Someone yanked the door open from inside, and a gaunt man thrust his head out. His dark hair had been mussed, grease stains were smeared across his cheeks, and his eyes looked glazed. His voice carried a thick overtone of anger.

"I'm doing important work here! If you want . . ." He stopped, blinking at Vailret and then turned down at Bryl. After a moment of confusion, Frankenstein recognized them and, surprising them both, his face lit up with delight.

"Ah, magic!" He grabbed Bryl's arm and yanked him inside. "I need you to tell me some things!"

Vailret had to hurry through the door before Frankenstein slammed it and then threw the bolt from inside.

11

VERNE'S CANNON

RULE #9. Weapons on Gamearth can range from simple improvised sticks and rocks to complicated seige machines. Clever characters will find weapons anywhere. The character with the best and most weapons has the greatest chance of winning the Game.

—The Book of Rules

Two hairy, misshapen creatures grunted and strained at the giant handles, turning an enormous crucible to pour whitish-orange iron into its mold. Droplets of fire gushed into the air.

Jules Verne shielded his eyes, blinking tears and sweat away from his raw face. He wiped soot across his cheek. His lips were chapped, his mouth dry. His body felt weak.

"Enough, enough!" the Slac general Korux cried as the hairy creatures kept pouring even after the mold brimmed. Splatters of molten metal flew into the air, scorching one of the creatures. Its matted hair smoldered, sending greasy smoke into the stifling air. The creature shrieked, released its end of the handle, and beat at its smoldering back.

Tilted, the crucible sloshed sideways, letting liquid metal drool over its rim. The second creature planted both feet and grimaced as it tried to keep the crucible from overturning.

Verne, feeling dizzy, stumbled back on his painful

131

bandaged foot. He leaned against the smoke-blackened wall. One burly Slac continued to pump the bellows, keeping the fire hot enough to maintain the iron at its melting temperature.

"Don't stop now!" Korux bellowed into the rumbling background noises. "We need to fill the other half of the mold!"

Several of Siryyk's monster fighters slinked toward the door. Korux pointed a clawed hand at one. "You! Take the place of that idiot! And get him out of here. Tend to his injury, ease the pain, and then kill him."

The burned creature snarled and scrambled to his feet, hunching into a defensive posture as several armed beasts came toward him. Korux paid little attention. Out of the corner of his brittle mouth, Korux said, "Or just kill him first if he doesn't want the medical attention."

Three squat gray-skinned monsters lifted and slid the first mold out of the way, scooping ashes around it to even out the cooling. They pushed the second mold under the crucible.

"If this new weapon of yours doesn't work, human . . ." Korux jerked his angled head at the glowing crucible. "We'll give you a bath in that."

Verne looked but felt no increase in his constant state of terror. "No you won't," he muttered under his breath, but made sure the Slac general couldn't hear him over the hissing of the forges. "Siryyk needs me to make more weapons."

The most difficult part had been fabricating anything at all complicated under the primitive conditions of Tairé. The old city had raw materials, some facilities, and a few tools, but none of the advanced technology Verne used in Sitnalta. Tairé depended on manual labor and hand tools.

To stall for time, he had redesigned parts of the existing Tairan forges and casting furnaces. He delayed as long as he could, but he knew Siryyk had to see some results, or Verne would lose more toes.

The professor had drawn up a sketch of his new cannon, with several parts deliberately designed wrong so that the weapon would fail, requiring that Verne take more time to fix it. But the manticore, whose paw was as massive as the sheet of plans, stared down with his slitted eyes. He curled his lips back and extended one claw to poke a hole through the paper.

"This part will not work." The manticore looked up with his squarish, distorted face. The curved horns protruding from the forehead looked deadly. His bestial eyes met Verne's. "You seem to have made a mistake, Professor. See that it does not happen again."

So Verne had redesigned the cannon, fixing his deliberate errors and beginning production of a prototype model. In his own mind, he knew it would work. He could no longer depend on defects that he introduced himself. Of course, he never had any guarantee that his inventions would work anyway, because other faults occurred through legitimate misunderstandings of the Rules of Physics, flaws in construction, or problems with engineering that he could never anticipate.

But a sick feeling in his stomach told him this invention would work just as intended.

At least the cannon would be far less devastating than the Sitnaltan weapon. By giving Siryyk a new toy, perhaps Verne could prevent other catastrophes. He wondered what Frankenstein would think of his decision.

A gurgling howl broke through the background noises. Verne turned to watch the burned hairy creature stabbed from three sides with barbed spears.

Beside Verne, General Korux smiled as best he could with hard, reptilian lips.

Siryyk the manticore rumbled in his sleep, churned by nightmares of the Outside.

An explosion of power and falling rocks brought him away from his dreams. He raised his massive shaggy head, clearing his throat with a liquid cough. His scorpion tail still throbbed from the detonation.

In his nightmare, he must have tossed and lashed out, striking one of the rock columns in the open amphitheater. Blocks of stone collapsed on his lion's body, each of them large enough to squash a human character into a smear of blood and meat, but only bruising his monster body. The smack of the stones on him reminded Siryyk of the blow the treacherous stone gargoyle Arken had struck against him during the battle on the threshold of Scartaris.

Smoldering blazes in the firepits lit everything with an orange glow. Siryyk blinked his eyes as he sat up. Slac guards stood around shivering, fearing what the manticore had seen in his nightmares.

Siryyk heaved himself to his four feet and shook his head. He looked again at the broken column and the swath of stars overhead that he had exposed by bringing down part of the criss-crossed ceiling.

He had dreamed of the Players again. Outside, sitting in their cozy dwelling, they looked down at the map and manipulated Gamearth. Siryyk felt himself moving within the Outsider David's mind. David was young and weak, with trivial thoughts and concerns overlapping with images of giant hands and puppet strings. In the Outsider's mind were also whimsical decisions—and growing fear.

Siryyk knew he was merely a creation of these weaklings. But the Outsider David had begun to suspect how powerful an opponent he had created. The manticore was supposed to be David's ally, but Siryyk had thoughts of his own.

Siryyk had fun with the battles on Gamearth, as the Outsiders expected all monsters to do, gathering forces and striking across the map. Scartaris had intended that. The Outsider David meant to devastate Gamearth, leaving nothing for the others to Play.

And when Siryyk marched with his armies, David would think the manticore warlord was cooperating with him. But Sirryk had Verne's Sitnaltan weapon now, and the professor would create other gadgets for him. The army would strike at the human Stronghold and get back the great Fire Stone lost by Enrod when he went to attack the other side of the map. Siryyk had learned of other Stones; a total of four, three of which were already held by the human character Delrael.

Siryyk would strike against Delrael's forces. But not because the Rules of Gamearth demanded it. Not because the Outsider David wanted that to happen. But because Sirryk desired the Stones. With the Stones, and with the Sitnaltan weapon, he would have enough power to strike back against the Outsiders. He would make them notice.

The morning sky hung blue and transparent enough that when Verne stared up, he thought he might be able to see the edge of Outside.

Off to the west, dust clouds churned in the ruins of the map near the final battlefield against Scartaris. No one dared venture there anymore since hexagons had fallen away into nothingness. The map itself had been damaged all the way through, leaving a great void, jagged edges, and broken Rules.

No one knew what happened there. No one dared to go near.

Twenty-three muscular Slac, garbed in clinging black robes, worked together as they hauled Verne's cannon through the collapsed section of Tairan wall and out into the desolation terrain where they would test-fire it.

The cannon would have been functional two days before, but Verne had insisted on polishing the exte-

rior and mounting bronze handles; "support struts" he
called them, but they served no purpose other than
decoration. Korux had melted down one of the bronze
Tairan statues for the metal.

The great cylinder rode on metal-rimmed wheels as
tall as Verne himself. The cannon was long, the bore
smooth on the inside, and black and shiny on its
barrel. Several goblins kept busy using pumice daily to
remove any oxidation.

The wheels of the cannon left deep grooves in the
ashen desolation as the team of Slac rolled it away
from the city. Their own footprints left puckered in-
dentations on the ground.

Verne limped along, accompanied—no, guarded—by
Korux and two other Slac. The manticore strode into
the daylight, taking ponderous yet agile steps. He
looked as big as a small dwelling. Siryyk turned his
slitted eyes toward the sky, then down toward the
cannon. He appeared pleased, which meant Verne
would survive a little longer.

Siryyk carried the huge cannonball himself; both
Verne and Frankenstein together could barely have
lifted it. The manticore's scorpion tail stood erect behind him and ready to strike. All the monsters knew
to stay well away from him, in case he had an acciden-
tal twitch.

Verne had commandeered dozens of the exploding
firepots from the monster army, scraping out all the
firepowder, which he would use to propel the projec-
tile from the cannon. General Korux had objected to
losing some of his valuable bombs, but Siryyk ordered
the firepowder to be released. If the professor's cannon worked properly, he said, it would outperform
any number of exploding pots.

The twenty-three Slac stopped hauling the cannon
out and then turned it around, aiming it back toward
Tairé. They had used ash and grease to paint a broad
target on the side of a tall building. Standing behind

the cannon, one of the Slac swiveled and cranked the device so that the barrel pointed toward the bullseye.

Verne had no doubt the cannonball would smash any building it struck.

Korux carried a torch and stood at attention as the monsters dumped firepowder into the cannon and took the ball from Siryyk's paws. Verne watched them do everything properly. He knew it would work. This time he did not feel the joy he always experienced upon watching an invention tested for the first time.

"Now we shall see, Professor Verne," Siryyk said, taking the torch from Korux.

But as the manticore stepped behind the cannon and stared toward the target on the building, he hesitated and looked up again. His face twisted in what seemed to be either a grimace or a smile.

Siryyk used his other front paw to push down on the back end of the cannon. The handle of the altitude-adjustment crank spun around as the gears turned. The manticore kept pushing until the end of the barrel pointed toward the sky.

"We can destroy buildings ourselves any time we wish," he said. "Let's show the Outsiders just what we can do."

With a deep bass growl, Siryyk touched the torch to the fuse of the cannon. The Slac, Professor Verne, and the other monsters took a step backward. But the manticore remained behind the weapon, without flinching.

The fuse hissed for just a second, then an enormous explosion rang through the still air. Verne cringed and then looked up.

Belching smoke curled from the end of the cannon, as expected. But the metal cannonball sailed high into the air, where it disappeared against the glass-blue sky.

Verne squeezed his eyes shut and refused to watch where it landed.

INTERLUDE: OUTSIDE

The Game continued without apparent complications.

David sat back, tight lipped, and watched as the adventures went ahead, the characters moving on their quests. Tyrone looked just as possessed as Melanie, but in a different way. To him the Game seemed like a drug, and his eyes shone with the depth of his smile. Scott had relaxed. They were all playing together, which reminded them of old times, when Gamearth had been just a simple game.

But it was more than that now. And David couldn't keep pretending.

Between turns, Scott went into the kitchen and pulled open a new bag of chips. With a rattling sound he dumped them into a bowl. "You guys want anything else to drink?"

David stared into the fire, watching the flames dance like broken edges of heat. He heard the crackle. He felt a sharp claw tickle his spine.

As his eyes blanked, he saw not the fire in the family room but a smoky blaze in the firepits of a dark amphitheater. He saw soot stains on the wall, defaced paintings and friezes chiseled into stone columns.

David blinked his eyes, and he felt huge lids come down and up again. His chest filled with rumbling breaths. As he moved, he sensed something incredibly massive, bunched muscles like steel rope, an enormous body. He turned his head, expecting to see claws the size of pencils. He squeezed his eyes shut.

138

"Go away!" He said the words in the back of his throat, keeping his mouth shut so no one would hear. The alien thoughts poked around in his head, playing, exploring.

It was Siryyk. David had set up his own schemes to destroy Gamearth, adventures to be played out to the end. The monsters would devastate the map or just wipe out Melanie's characters; he didn't care which. And the thing he had planted in the southeast—in much the same way that Melanie had created her golem character Journeyman—would keep her other team of questers from helping. Together, his forces would be enough to stop Gamearth.

But his own characters were no longer willing puppets. He had given too much power to the manticore, too sharp a mind, and now the monster had crawled outside the Game and into David's thoughts. He didn't know if he could resist long enough for his complicated plans to come together. He wondered if this possession had happened with the other players as well.

He saw how they were paying little attention to him.

The fire continued to burn, warming the room.

It struck him that it would be so simple to end the Game. Enough of this weekly arguing and suffering through nightmares and trying to fight in subtle ways against the Game. Gamearth was never subtle.

David would take his own action.

"What are you going to do next, Mel?" Tyrone asked, hunkering down beside her.

When she had her head turned away, David rolled to his knees and snatched the painted map from the floor. He lunged to his feet. Dice clattered off the hard surface of the map and plopped to the carpet. He twisted, yanking the map away as Melanie reached out to grab it.

"Hey, Dave!" Tyrone said.

Scott came out of the kitchen.

David jumped to the fireplace with the big map in his hands. He had to get the glass hearth doors open; if only he could shove the map into the flames, the wood would burn and the paint would bubble and blacken, destroying the hexagons. He had to hold the others off for only a few seconds.

"No!" Melanie screamed.

She grabbed his arm. He shoved an elbow into her jaw and heard her teeth click together. But she grabbed onto the map and pulled. He heard a splintering sound, and a handful of bright blue hexagons fell off, pattering to the stones around the fireplace.

David kept silent, wrestling with her for the map. Tyrone pulled on his shoulder. David squirmed.

He had gotten the fireplace door open now. The flames seemed to flare up, eager for new food. The heat blasted him. He was going to do it.

Gamearth would end once and for all.

In the kitchen the telephone began to ring in one long steady bell, like an alarm. But David knew the phone was dead; Gamearth was just trying to distract him.

"David, what are you doing!" Scott stopped, holding glasses of soda in his hands.

David's eyes glistened with tears from the strain as he fought. He stared down into the dizzying kaleidoscopic colors of terrain on the map. He seemed to be falling down into it. He let out a cry of terror as the map tilted.

With one last push, he attempted to hurl it into the flames, but Melanie and Tyrone both had their hands on it now.

A flash of light came from one of the brown hexagons of desolation terrain, a puff of smoke and a barely heard sound. A jolt of pain sliced across David's cheek just under his eye.

Crying out, he cast himself away from the map. He

stumbled aside, holding his hand to his face. Blood dribbled between his fingers.

Melanie grabbed the map to herself, hugged it, and took it back to where the dice lay on the floor.

Stunned and defeated, David bowed over. Scott and Tyrone both saw the blood. "Hey man, what happened?" Tyrone said. "Are you nuts or something?"

David glared up at him. Blood dripped from his fingers.

"You got a bad cut there, David," Scott said. "What did you hit?"

"I didn't hit anything," he answered. "Gamearth shot back at me."

"You mean Verne's cannon! Wow!" Tyrone came close to look at David's wound.

Scott gave him a wadded handful of napkins, which David pressed under his eye. Blood seeped into it, but he held it there. The stinging pain made him focus his anger. He had failed.

"That's cheating, David, if you're trying to end the Game," Scott said to him. "I thought you knew better by now."

He stared into David's eyes. Scott's glasses had slid down on his nose. "I don't even want to *think* what might happen if we throw away the rules, because when you start breaking them yourself, Gamearth can, too. It's bad enough when we know what the Game's limitations are."

David stared at him and understood what Scott meant.

Down by the fireplace, he saw a dozen broken hexagons scattered like colored tiles on the floor.

12
NIGHT RECONNAISSANCE

"I cannot imagine how I would ever grow weary of seeing the streets of Tairé or the characters standing high and proud, defying the desolation on which it sits. Tairé is a monument of all that is hopeful on Gamearth."
—Enrod the Sentinel

Jathen squatted down, resting his back against the sharp edges of rock. He drew his knees up and folded his numb hands around them, staring down the eastern side of the Spectre Mountains.

He sat apart from the others in Delrael's army, but he felt comfortable with his separateness now. As night deepened in the mountain terrain, he gazed across the sprawling map.

The rest of Delrael's army made exhausted noises as they set up camp, handing around blankets and building small fires in the shelter of rocks. Old Siya wandered about, muttering that they should have brought more blankets and warmer clothing.

Jathen shivered once, but he clenched his teeth together. He cleared his mind, washing the cold from his thoughts. He had survived worse than this—much worse.

The army had trudged across the map for days, crossing hexagon after hexagon, through forest and hills, and the last two days, over difficult winding mountain paths. They traversed snow and narrow tracks

142

through the ice, but the fighters had crossed the pass and looked down on the opposite side, where Scartaris had reigned only a short time ago, and where Siryyk's monster army still lay encamped.

Jathen remembered crossing that distance with other survivors who had fled Tairé, running from the monsters, closing their ears to the echoing screams of all the characters trapped there.

Jathen squeezed his eyes shut, then shook his head slightly, feeling the pain against the stiff muscles in his neck. He tried to find the blank spot in his thoughts again, the place he had emptied of memories.

Delrael came up beside him and then crossed his arms over his chest. His brown hair blew back in the brisk wind; it had already tangled at one side, and his cheeks looked spotted with a red flush from the cold. Steam came out of his mouth as he spoke. "We can see the fires of Tairé from here." He pointed with his chin. "Siryyk is still encamped in the city."

Jathen had already seen the orange glow marking the city. Cooking fires, encampments, perhaps even a burning building or two. He didn't know. They didn't know why the monsters had remained in Tairé for so long.

Jathen said nothing, nor did he stand up. He felt just uncomfortable enough where he was.

Delrael continued, "We thought the manticore would only pause there before marching across the map. But if they have made a permanent settlement in Tairé, maybe we've got more time. Maybe they have decided not to march against us."

Jathen scowled at the thought. Delrael kept talking.

"Now I don't know what to do. We don't have enough characters to fight them all down there. I've sent scouts to look for likely ambush places in the passes we crossed in the last few days."

Jathen continued to stare at the dull glow of his city. Off to the side, he saw Enrod standing on a rock, not even chilled in his thin white robe. His dark, bushy hair lay matted and unmoving in the breeze as he also gazed down at Tairé. Jathen had no idea what confused images passed through Enrod's mind.

"Then send scouts into Tairé to see what's happening." Jathen kept his voice low, but he knew Delrael heard him.

Delrael frowned. "Too dangerous. I wouldn't ask any character to do that."

Jathen couldn't tell if Delrael was simply being coy, or if the idea truly hadn't occurred to him. "I'll go, of course. And I wouldn't doubt that Enrod will want to come with me." He finally stood and turned to face the distant firelit hexagons. "That was our home."

In Jathen's mind, the mountain wind hooting around the rocks sounded like the moans of all those Tairans who had died because of Scartaris, those who had fallen by Jathen's own hand in the tannery. He tried to find the empty, peaceful spot in his thoughts again, but somehow it was all filled up.

Enrod responded with as much enthusiasm as Jathen had expected. The Sentinel stood by one of the large campfires, fixing his gaze on the bright flames. He didn't even blink his eyes. "He and I can survive there. We know Tairé. We will learn . . ." The fire popped, apparently breaking his train of thought. After a moment of silence, Enrod finished his sentence, ". . . what Siryyk is doing."

He lowered his voice and turned his dark eyes toward the distant heaxagons of Tairé. "I built that city."

Jathen stood next to Enrod. "If we leave now, we can cover the first hexagons, lie low during the day, and reach the hills by nightfall tomorrow. We can get into the city after dark and look around when we'd be least likely to be spotted."

Enrod nodded, and kept nodding. Jathen felt thrilled

to be a partner to the Sorcerer who had created the city where Jathen grew up. The Sentinel would strike a blow for Tairé. Enrod could win. Enrod could make it right again.

Delrael nodded. "Go when you're ready."

Siya prepared packages of food for them, from which Jathen and Enrod ate sparingly through the rest of the night. They stumbled down the winding quest-path into the growing dawn.

The two moved in silence for the most part. Enrod seemed swallowed by his own thoughts; at times he rubbed his hands together and stared at the skin. Jathen felt too much in awe of him to start small conversation.

Finally, as the morning grew bright and a line of grassy hills blocked their view of the city, Enrod turned to him and said, "Your last memory of Tairé. After Scartaris. Tell me what I should expect."

"Imagine the worst you possibly can," Jathen answered. His throat felt thick, clogged with too many screams he had never dared to utter. He closed his eyes. "And then double it."

He thought of his own work in the tannery, with the gray-skinned and gray-clad Tairans shuffling up and down the streets, mindless because of Scartaris.

"Tairans were put to work making weapons. Our blacksmiths forged swords and spearheads. Our tannery made shields and armor. You knew that already. We emptied our storage bins to provide supplies to Scartaris. He took all our horses."

Jathen took a deep breath. "Scartaris didn't slaughter characters just to amuse himself, though. He killed them when he needed their bodies more than he needed their lives. Siryyk the manticore killed everyone just because they were in his way."

Enrod shook his head and kept walking. "Wish I could remember."

Jathen turned away. "I wish I could forget."

*   *   *

When darkness had fallen and the orange flames glowed behind the city walls, Enrod and Jathen stared at a Tairé that had become a complete stranger, a dark and broken whisper of itself.

Several of the side gates stood unguarded; other parts of the wall had been torn down, with broken stones strewn on the barren ground. The two of them slipped through the narrow Tairan streets, making no noise.

Keeping their backs to the walls and sinking into the shadows of deep-cut friezes, they moved into Tairé. The buildings showed black windows filled with shadows on the inside. Jathen had never thought his city looked so sinister before.

Enrod appeared too appalled even to utter a comment. His dark eyes looked like wide black holes in his face. He seemed most disturbed by the malicious defacing of buildings and artwork. "Why?" he muttered. "Why?"

They stood in front of the broad fresco showing the powerful but faceless image of the Stranger Unlooked-For who had once rescued the land around Tairé. Some of the monsters had drawn a cruel, distorted visage on it; Jathen took a moment to recognize that the scrawled mane and horns were meant to indicate Siryyk the manticore. Siryyk, replacing the savior of Tairé.

Around another corner they stumbled upon a pile of bones, some picked clean, others glistening with gelatinous lines of red and yellow. Skulls poked out of the refuse. Jathen slapped a grimy hand over his nose to prevent the smell from making him retch.

Moving ahead, they came as close as they dared to a group of monsters around a blazing bonfire. The creatures ate shapeless lumps of meat or scooped steaming black gruel out of bowls with their fingers. Others talked and roared and made strange sounds. Many of the gathered creatures appeared relaxed. Weapons lay next to discarded and uncomfortable-looking pieces of armor.

Siryyk's soldiers played dice games and threw sticks at a target on the wall. In the center of a ring of spectators, two hunchbacked beasts with great curling tusks crouched down and glared at each other, weaving back and forth until, at some invisible signal, they lunged forward into each other, butting heads with a sound like two bricks clacking together. The other monsters roared and threw down wagers.

"They don't seem to be mobilizing," Jathen said.

Enrod shook his head. "Can't let them stay. Not in my city."

"We have to get back and tell Delrael," Jathen said. "This will change his plans."

But when they turned, they saw seven tall Slac, each carrying a spiked mace. The Slac stood in silence, glaring at them, battle ready, and blocking their way.

Jathen had never seen the manticore up close until the Slac guards dragged him into the amphitheater. The Slac clutched his arms so tightly that their claws tore into his skin. Struggling only deepened the wounds, so he stopped.

This amphitheater had once been used as a meeting place for characters to discuss the future of Tairé. Jathen remembered from the time he was a little boy how Enrod had stood on the platform, speaking about his great visions for a reborn land. Enrod had been full of charismatic words then, calling for a flourishing Tairé, for all the human characters to heal the scars that the Sorcerer Wars had left across the map. Enrod himself had made the first strokes on the large mural on the amphitheater wall. The mural was now chipped away by thrown stones and smeared by soot and filth. Enrod stood beside him, another helpless captive.

The manticore arched his lumpy eyebrows as he

drew in a long breath of surprise. "What are these? More guests?" With a low growl, he looked at the monster soldiers. "I thought we had evicted all humans from the city and surrounding hexagons."

"We captured them," one of the Slac said. "But we have not yet interrogated them. We thought you might like that pleasure."

The manticore padded three steps closer, crouched down to glare at the two captives, and then suddenly he slashed across the air with a paw filled with razor claws. Siryyk missed Jathen's chest by the thickness of a piece of cloth. Jathen stumbled backward, but the Slac guards stood like trees, still holding onto his arms.

"Now," Siryyk said, "tell me who you are. I don't want to play games just yet."

Jathen saw no point in refusing this information at least, especially when he could make a reasonable lie. "My name is Jathen. I ran into the mountains when you attacked Tairé and killed all my people. I managed to escape the monsters you sent to hunt us down. They were clumsy, and they didn't try very hard. Many of us escaped."

Jathen tried to keep himself from smiling as Siryyk raised himself up, bristling from the shoulders down. He snarled at the gathered Slac.

"Find who was in charge of that operation! I want to hear from him. Briefly."

Then Siryyk swiveled his huge head. Jathen thought he could hear the muscles creaking. The manticore let his torchlike yellow eyes fall on Enrod.

"You are Enrod the Sentinel, a powerful magic user. Scartaris sent you with the Fire Stone to destroy Delrael. And, because you failed, Scartaris didn't succeed in conquering Gamearth!"

Jathen saw Enrod concentrating on the words. He made no answer. Jathen wondered if Siryyk would just kill them for Enrod's failure. Then the manticore laughed. "I'm glad Scartaris didn't succeed. Otherwise we'd all be annihilated now." He raised his voice to a roar. "But you lost the Fire Stone! Now Delrael has it to fight against me. And he has two other Stones, each as great as the weapon I possess."

Siryyk hunkered down again. "Tell me, Enrod, what do you know of the end of the Game? You're a great Sentinel. Explain to me what the Outsiders intend to do when they stop Playing. How can we protect ourselves?"

Enrod tilted his head, as if listening to the distant voices again. His lips curved upward in a secret smile, but he said nothing.

The manticore continued. "Is it true that if I gather all the Stones I can create my own Transition? Where is the fourth Stone? I want them all. If I have that power, along with the Sitnaltan weapon, that might be enough for me to escape the map and continue an existence of my own, even when the Rules have expired and Gamearth is no longer part of any universe. The Outsiders will certainly notice such a concentration of power."

Siryyk leaned forward. His eyes blazed. "Tell me, Enrod, what can I do to save myself from the end of the Game?"

Enrod asked, "Do the Outsiders speak to me?" He seemed to be asking a serious question. His eyebrows raised. Jathen couldn't understand what Enrod was doing. He hoped the Sentinel had some kind of plan.

Siryyk let out a long, bubbling sigh, and closed his eyes, as if knowing that further discussion would be useless. "Then it's time to play a game of our own. The moment you decide to answer my questions, we can stop."

The manticore grunted at the troops crouched around a firepit. "Bring me my little pins," he said. "The ones I put in vials."

Two of the creatures grumbled to themselves and

then elbowed a smooth-skinned goblin, who scurried
out a low door in a side wall. Jathen wondered what
amusements a manticore would enjoy.

Then a large Slac in a finer uniform than the others
strode into the amphitheater. The nails on his squarish
feet clicked on the flagstones. "Siryyk! Professor Verne
has escaped!"

"What!" the manticore roared. Blue lightning played
on the tip of his scorpion tail as he held it erect.
"How?"

"He created some sort of mechanism that chewed
through the stone wall. He must have palmed a caustic
substance that ate through his manacles. He is not
there."

"Find him again! He must be inside the city somewhere. And Korux, do a better job than you did
capturing the Tairan escapees!"

Korux didn't seem to know what the manticore was
talking about until he noticed the captives. Siryyk
continued before the general could ask a question.
"See that no harm comes to him. Verne has much
more work to do for me."

"Bring out the car!" Korux turned around and
shouted into the night. His flowing black robes flapped
behind him. He clapped his scaled hands like the crack
of a stick against a stone wall.

Jathen watched through the open archway as four
other Slac pushed a battered red vehicle of some sort.
He had never seen anything like it before: it had four
wheels and a torn canopy, protruding levers, with
seats for several characters. Steam poured out of a
stack on the top. Acting very excited, Korux climbed
into the seat and played with the levers.

The other Slac turned the vehicle around, pushing it
from behind. Great puffs of steam belched from the
stack, and the car began to move by itself. Korux
played with the steering levers, making the vehicle

veer left and then right as it chugged off into the
shadows.

The goblin returned to the amphitheater, cradling
vials filled with different-colored liquids. The goblin
hunched in front of Siryyk and placed the vials by the
manticore's paws. One of the vials tipped over with a
clink, but the goblin snatched and righted it before
Siryyk could react. Then he scurried away.

The manticore reached forward to hold one of the
vials up to the light. "These vials contain liquids.
Three are harmless, three are slow-acting poisons. Two
contain a venom that I squeezed from the jaws of one
of our deadliest monster fighters. Though this poison
kills instantly, the pain appears to be excruciating
enough to make it seem like a long, long time."

Siryyk used the tips of his huge fingers to claw
at a jewel-studded golden needle that rested inside
the vial. "These are hair pins. We plucked them from
some of the dead Tairan women who weren't burned
too badly."

Jathen felt his insides squirm as his mind brought
him too-vivid pictures of the slaughter.

"Now, you will select one of the vials, and we will
pierce you with the needle."

Siryyk pulled the golden pin out so that one droplet
hung at the end like a tiny blue sapphire, dancing and
reflecting the light from firepits.

"I refuse!" Jathen snapped.

Siryyk gave a minimal shrug. "Then I'll be forced to
choose the first needle for you."

"Pick," Enrod said to him. "No choice."

Jathen felt astonished, betrayed—or did Enrod have
a trick up his sleeve? Enrod, the great Sentinel, certainly would fight somehow. Jathen had to have faith
in Enrod.

"Give me the amber-colored one," he said, then
closed his eyes. He drew a deep breath between his
teeth.

One of the Slac came forward to pick up the indicated vial, then withdrew a long pin with an emerald mounted at the top. Jathen remembered seeing similar pins in the piled hair of women at celebration dances marking the anniversary of Tairé.

The Slac shuffled forward, holding the needle in front of him so that Jathen could see the thick golden droplet hanging from its tip. Jathen didn't know how to read the fire in the narrow green eyes that stared at him. The Slac stood in front of him and raised the sharp pin. It slowly moved to the left, then to the right, like some serpent trying to lull its prey.

Jathen tried to calculate his chances. Three of the liquids were harmless, out of eight vials. Less than one in two, but still not terrible odds.

"If you have anything to say to me, you could interrupt this game," Siryyk said.

"I have nothing to say to you," Jathen said. "Nothing you'd want to hear."

Siryyk was not impressed. He nodded to the Slac.

The creature moved behind Jathen. Jathen didn't turn. He kept staring ahead, staring at the manticore, waiting. At any moment he expected the sting.

Beside him, Enrod squeezed his eyes shut and mumbled incoherently. Jathen couldn't tell if the Sentinel was just talking to himself. He turned his eyes as far to the side as he could, attempting to see the Slac.

He heard a quick rustle of fabric, then felt a stab as the needle plunged into his shoulder. Jathen made only a tiny sound before he cut off his cry of pain. The gold needle felt like fire, and then the Slac jerked it back out again.

Jathen waited for venomous lava to eat him from inside. But after a moment he still felt nothing more than the sharp sting.

"Enrod, it is your turn."

As if distracted, Enrod selected the blue liquid that Siryyk had used as his example. Jathen wondered if the monster's corrupt touch alone could be enough to transmute an innocuous liquid into poison.

Enrod winced when the needle stuck his arm, but he survived as well. "It burns," he said.

Six vials remained.

Trying to stall, wondering what Enrod intended to do with his magic, Jathen took a long time to make his next choice. "The orange one," he said, then swallowed as his throat became dry. This time he had only one chance in six, assuming that they had both chosen a harmless liquid the first time around.

The Slac wasted no time withdrawing the needle and jabbing him in the arm. Jathen felt a greater stinging, but nothing more. In Jathen's mind, he considered himself already dead from the moment the monsters had captured him.

"Choose, Enrod."

Enrod stared at the glowing firepits next to the wall. He didn't seem to be paying attention.

Just when the manticore reached for one of the vials of his own choosing, Jathen interrupted. He couldn't just stand by any longer.

"All right, Siryyk! Let me tell you this much. Delrael carries all four Stones now. He has already found the Earth Stone. But he can't use them, because he's a human character. He needs a strong magic user."

Enrod shook his head, then nodded instead. He picked up Jathen's story. "Doesn't trust me. I came to destroy his land."

Jathen raised his voice. "Delrael will never let you take the Stones. His army may be untrained, but they'll fight to the death."

Siryyk made a grunting chuckle deep in his chest. "That's how I like it. He can't keep the Stones from me if I want them."

Enrod continued to glare at Siryyk. At his side, his hands clenched and unclenched. His lips trembled, and his eyes had a vacant look, as if he were only partially distracted by the manticore.

"Very well," Siryyk said, "For that information . . ." He picked up one bottle filled with a diamond-clear liquid. "We'll remove this one. It contains one of the deadly venoms. Your odds are slightly better. Now choose."

"Green," Enrod said. His body went rigid. If only three vials had contained harmless liquids, then even with the best of luck, the next one contained poison.

The Slac soldier moved forward, extending the long needle. One droplet fell to the flagstone. Jathen looked to see if the liquid sizzled on the floor; it left only a wet spot.

When the creature tried to prick the base of Enrod's neck, the metal of the needle hissed and dripped molten down the white robe. Enrod clenched his eyes shut, and his entire body shuddered, turning red. Tears streamed down his cheeks and puffed into steam as his skin glowed more brightly.

Enrod drew his lips back away from his teeth. Waves of heat baked off of his body. The Slac stumbled back with a grunt of astonishment. The manticore rose up. "What is this?"

With an outcry from the effort, Enrod smashed his fists together. His entire form blazed with heat and light, shimmering so that Jathen could see only the Sentinel's blazing silhouette.

"Eyes and mouth!" Enrod hissed to Jathen. "Cover them!"

As if hurling something heavy but invisible, Enrod motioned his arms to the vials on the floor. All the bottles shattered in the gust of heat. The mixed liquids erupted in flames. Two of the vials burst into greenish-black smoke that rose thick into the air; the other poisons sizzled on the floor.

The manticore roared and clawed at his eyes as the corrosive vapors billowed into his misshapen face.

Smoke filled the amphitheater. The monsters choked and coughed.

"Run!" Enrod hissed and hurried out the front of the amphitheater. Jathen stumbled after, holding his breath and covering his stinging eyes.

Slac guards rushed to assist the manticore. Five of them lay already dead from the poison. The other monsters ran around, making inhuman sounds of anger and surprise.

Jathen burst into the cool night air. Enrod remained standing for a moment at the entrance of Siryyk's headquarters. Jathen saw an expression of pained dismay through the shimmering blaze around Enrod's body. Then the Sentinel smashed his arm into the archway. Stone columns crumbled with a roar, blocking off the main entrance.

Then all the heat ran out of Enrod, pouring down and out of his body like warm oil, until he stood panting.

"We have to run," Jathen said, afraid to touch his arm and pull Enrod along. "We have to get out of the city."

Enrod followed, and Jathen continued jabbering. "I knew you were going to do something! I was waiting. They'll be scattered now. The monsters won't know what to do, since Siryyk is injured and their Slac general is out hunting down that professor."

Enrod heaved a deep breath, but couldn't make words come out.

Jathen blinked his eyes. "What took you so long? I was worried!" Jathen talked fast. "I waited for you to do something. I was afraid you really had surrendered."

Enrod leaned against a building deep in the shadows. In the distance, they could hear monsters running pell-mell around the city, but Jathen had no doubt the two of them would be able to escape now.

"First spell failed." Enrod sighed and looked up at

Jathen. "First spell. To turn poison into water. It didn't work."

Jathen felt his heart thump, rising up and then falling. Enrod had tried to protect him from the poison, but it had failed. "We'll just have to trust to luck, then. That neither of us got the slow poison."

"Yes," Enrod said. "Luck."

Jathen began to stumble midway through the following morning as they crept behind the grassy hills west of Tairé. At first Enrod thought it was merely weariness, because he was greatly tired, too. But the unhealthy flush in Jathen's skin and the strange lack of focus in his eyes led Enrod to believe otherwise.

The sun pounded down on them, and Enrod felt the rays heating his skin. It seemed much weaker than the heat he had made the night before. His own confusion was getting worse.

They were both parched. The monsters had stripped Siya's food from them, so they had nothing to eat, nothing to drink. Enrod had no way to ease Jathen's growing misery as the slow poison ate its way into his body.

"Keep going," Enrod said. "Back to army by night."

Jathen broke out in a clammy sweat, but he said nothing and kept moving with Enrod. They plodded through the grass, avoiding the direct quest-path.

They had escaped the monsters indeed, for all the good it would do Jathen. Enrod had used his fire. They crossed the hex-line into mountain terrain in the mid-afternoon, but as the path became steeper, Jathen worsened rapidly.

"I wonder which one it was," Jathen said. His lips seemed loose, and he mumbled his words. "The first needle, or the second one. It seems you were lucky."

Enrod shook his head. "Burned any poison from my body. Fire inside my skin." He turned ahead, not wanting to pursue the conversation. "Come on."

He moved ahead, but Jathen stumbled so much on the rugged path that rocks skittered behind him and rolled down the slope. Enrod paused and put one of Jathen's arms over his shoulder to help him along. Even that help wasn't enough.

When Jathen finally collapsed an hour later, Enrod took him to an overhang of rock. The setting sun cast long shadows from the mountains, like black hands reaching across the hexagons toward Tairé.

Jathen's legs started to twitch spasmodically, and his feet jittered against the ground. His teeth chattered. He had retched several times, bringing up nothing from his empty stomach.

Enrod positioned him comfortably, where Jathen could look across the landscape, toward the great desolation and the distant city walls.

"If I'm going to die here anyway," Jathen said, wheezing great breaths of mountain air, "then I wish I had died in Tairé."

Enrod sat next to him and placed a broad hand on his shoulder. His mind became sharp and clear for a moment. "Can't choose when and where we die. Not part of the Game."

"I don't care about the Game anymore," Jathen said. Enrod could think of no way to answer him.

Enrod looked out, and with his sharp eyes he could see Tairé. Masses of figures poured out from the ruined gates. He sat up straight. As he hoped, Enrod had provoked the manticore to march out before he was ready.

Jathen coughed, but he couldn't see. "Do you think we defeated them?"

"Sure of it," Enrod answered. Without further words, he stared down at the desolation, where he could see Siryyk's immense army pouring out, mobilized and heading toward them. . . .

Enrod waited there until full darkness had come. By that time, Jathen died.

Enrod did the best he could to pile scrub wood around the body, a mound of brush, twigs, and stunted branches. "I can still make fire," he said.

With a simple, powerful spell, he turned the pile into a blazing funeral pyre for Jathen. He stood, holding his hands up to the flames and feeling the heat.

With a last glance behind him at the advancing monster horde, Enrod moved upward to rejoin Delrael's army. Jathen's funeral pyre crackled in the night.

13

FRANKENSTEIN'S DRONE

> *"As our enemies find better ways of fighting us, so we must develop better ways of striking back. Is there any character in Sitnalta who is not willing to meet this challenge?"*
>
> —Professor Frankenstein, in
> a guest lecture
> to beginning inventors

Frankenstein pulled Bryl toward the back of the cluttered workroom. The professor's fingers left greasy marks on his cloak.

Vailret blinked in the dim light shining through cobweb-covered skylights. If anything, the workroom looked more chaotic than he remembered it from the first time he had visited there. He tripped over a stack of half-opened books, sheaves of paper, and scrawled drawings.

"Hurry, if you please," Frankenstein said over his shoulder. "It's most disquieting to be so vulnerable out here."

In the back of the room, the professor heaved open a trapdoor, then let it thud onto the floor. Bright chips of wood showed where the heavy door had gouged marks from repeated openings.

"Down you go!" Frankenstein practically stuffed Bryl into the hole.

"Wait! I—" Bryl said, but the professor lifted his foot and pushed down on the half-Sorcerer's shoulder.

"Professor, why don't you just explain yourself?" Vailret said.

Frankenstein climbed into the trapdoor as well. He turned with his shoulders above the floor. "Follow us if you like. I can't stay out where the invisible force might get me; I have too much at stake."

He continued to descend. Vailret could hear Bryl's footsteps clicking on a metal staircase. Frankenstein reached up to grasp the handle of the trapdoor. "Are you coming or not?"

Vailret squeezed past the professor and worked his way down the twisting stairs. Frankenstein used both hands to swing the trapdoor over his head and ducked as the heavy door crashed into place. "Ah, much better," he said. Frankenstein closed his eyes and sighed.

The bottom of the trapdoor, along with the walls, ceiling, and floor of the entire underground room, had been covered with plates of dull, dark metal.

Bryl stood at the bottom, waiting for them. Frankenstein descended the narrow stairs while Vailret squinted around the broad chamber. Serving trays, dirty plates, and half-eaten food lay piled near the stairs. The professor had obviously spent a great deal of time down here.

"Professor Verne and I constructed this underground workroom years ago. Every inch of it is lined with lead shielding." He ran his fingers along the wall. "The lead prevents even the Outsiders from detecting what we do down here. We use this place for our most secret investigations into certain topics. We didn't want the Outsiders to know that such ideas had even occurred to us."

He made a thin-lipped smile. "With that invisible force attacking four times a day, I have taken permanent refuge here. The force can't penetrate the lead. *That* has been proven time and again." Frankenstein strode into the chamber. "Here I can work alone and undisturbed to develop some means of rescuing Sitnalta."

The entire chamber was piled with tools and raw materials: metal piping, pulleys, gears, glass spheres, switches, wiring, sheet metal. Boxes crammed full of rivets and screws lay stacked on top of each other. Wrenches, screwdrivers, and soldering irons rested beside half-assembled pieces of machinery.

Vailret could recognize almost nothing in the chaos. Bryl poked among the coiled wires on a table.

"Don't touch anything," Frankenstein said.

In the center of the room, propped up on solid blocks, stood a large squarish frame in which Frankenstein had hung a network of cables and pulleys. Wires protruded from the corners of the frame.

Vailret stepped forward to peer at another object on one of the long worktables. Five curved cylinders as long and as thick as his leg protruded upward and bent in the middle. Vailret cocked his head, then stopped as the skewed perspective finally came into focus. The metal framework and the five cylinders looked like a hand as large as his own body.

"What is all this?" he said, staring at the enormous central frame and the other scattered cylinders and gears. In his mind, a picture began to come clear.

Frankenstein patted the "thumb" of the metal hand and picked up a long roll of paper. He tacked the top against a cork board he had mounted on the wall, unrolled the paper, then pinned down the bottom. The corners curled up, and the professor swiped at them with his hand, trying to get them to lie flat. Finally, he stuck the corners down with two other pins.

He stepped back to display a sketch of a burly manlike machine, an automaton the size of ten characters. "I will call it my Drone," Frankenstein said. "My servant, like a worker bee." He paused a moment, as if for them to appreciate his work.

"I have analyzed that magical force coming from below. It Plays living characters just as a Game-master does, but it has no effect on Sitnaltan machines. If the controller could manipulate our machines, the entire city would have been leveled long ago."

Frankenstein turned away from the sketch to look at Vailret and Bryl. "I have spent my life discovering the way living creatures work. Professor Verne and I constructed small automatons, playthings like the mechanical fish in the fountains or character-sized robots that played games against solitary characters." Frankenstein's eyes looked wistful. "A tremendous success, that. Our automated dicing companion never cheats, you know."

Then he dismissed his nostalgia. "But those were just practice inventions. This is my crowning achievement. Drone will seek out and destroy the perpetrator of this vile force." He paused, turning his gaze away. "I just studied the life forms, explained them to him, and Verne was always able to invent similar machines. Unfortunately, Drone has been an entirely solo effort."

He pointed to the top of the drawing, snapping out of his distraction. "The human brain is far too complex for me to understand, much less imitate. I have dissected several brains and tried to discover how they work, but such organs are fairly difficult to come by these days."

Frankenstein sighed, as if distressed at having to admit his failure. "So, since I'm unable to construct an adequate mechanical substitute, *I* will act as the brain of Drone. I'll construct a control chamber, also lined with lead, so that I can ride along with the machine to hunt out our enemy."

Vailret watched him, listened to the speech, and had the odd impression that Frankenstein had taken on this task as a challenge to his problem-solving ability, rather than to stop the terrible manipulations from happening.

"Dirac is dead," Vailret said. Maybe that would shake him out of it. "We thought you should know."

Frankenstein continued to stare at his drawing, tracing a finger along a diagram of nested gears. Old oil and grease left a dark curve under his fingernail. "What?" He looked up.

"I said Dirac is dead. The invisible force made him come after us in a steam-engine car. Dirac tried to kill us, but he crashed into your communications facility instead."

"Oh, no," Frankenstein said. "Is it destroyed?"

"Dirac is dead. There was a big explosion."

Frankenstein made an impatient wave. "No, the communications facility. All of Morse's wires."

Bryl blinked. "Aren't you listening? Your city leader is dead."

Frankenstein frowned, and his voice grew hard-edged. "Plenty of greater characters than Dirac have already fallen. I choose not to tear my hair out in grief. I've got too much to do." He looked at them in defiance. "Jules never returned from his mission—he's probably dead, and I'd certainly mourn *him* sooner than I would shed a tear for Dirac."

He plucked the bottom pins out of the drawing, which rolled back up into a loose cylinder. "If Dirac hadn't quashed the idea years ago that we Sitnaltans should attempt our own Transition through technology, we wouldn't be in this trouble right now. We might all be in a far better state. Dirac's own daughter, Mayer was very disappointed with him about that."

"Mayer?" Vailret interrupted. "How is she?"

"Rather high tempered about this whole mess. Her heart is in the right place, but she's too bullheaded about the challenge. She will charge and meet it head-on, no doubt. But it doesn't help to charge into a brick wall. It's better to find a door. Fewer headaches that way."

Bryl picked among the scattered dishes on the floor,

as if looking for something still worth eating. "But what do you want with *me*, Professor? You dragged me in here."

Frankenstein put a finger to his lips and raised his eyes. "Ah, yes! I can't find any explanation for this force other than that it must be caused by some evil sorcery. So I've been thinking a lot about magic. If the Rules have indeed been damaged, and magic can operate even here in Sitnalta, then I'd better learn about it. You see, I was able to discover exactly how the old Sorcerers succeeded in their Transition spell. Oh, it took a while to track down the records and everything, but when I did, I found something amazing."

He looked to Vailret, who suddenly felt a keen interest. The stone gargoyle Arken had told his own memories of the grand event, but Frankenstein, with his strange technical perspective, would have a different assessment.

"The probability of the exact dice roll the old Sorcerers needed—even though it took them day after day of constantly rolling the dice in the attempt—defies common sense. To get five '20s' in the same roll should happen only once in three million two hundred thousand times! Some sort of magic must have had its hand in that.

"Therefore, if Sitnalta is relying on me to combat a magic-driven enemy, I need to understand how best to strike back." He turned to Bryl. "Spend a few hours here with me, explaining spells and magic. Tell me what are the limitations, tell me how a spell works, what you say to invoke the magic. It's very important."

"We have a favor to ask as well, Professor," Vailret said, but Frankenstein waved his hand in dismissal, as if that were a trivial problem.

Bryl finally found a half-eaten piece of cake. He

brushed off part of it, flicked crumbs from his fingertips, then pushed the piece into his mouth. He spoke
as he chewed.

"At least it's safe here."

14

ROLE PLAYING

*The merit of any sacrifice, small or large, can
be judged by no one but the character who
makes it. Small sacrifices gravely made may out-
weigh great deeds that are done without fore-
thought.*

—The Book of Rules

By the time General Korux and the marauding creatures had scoured the ruins of Tairé for the escaped
professor, Verne had already crossed his second hexagon of desolation terrain at a dead run.

The night was cool and clear. He wheezed in the
dry air but continued to forge eastward. Wherever
possible, he stepped on rocks to hide his trail. It
would probably be mid-morning before Korux began
to investigate beyond the city walls.

Before dawn, though, Verne wanted to be on the
other side of the forested-hill terrain. The hills stood
tall and covered with grasping, skeletal trees. The thin
branches had been dead so long that they looked
fossilized in the baking climate.

While languishing in his miserable cell, Verne had
calculated that eastward would be the least-expected
direction for his escape. He could have gone south,
back toward Sitnalta. He could have gone west, where
the mountains and the forest terrain would make it
easier for him to hide, but Verne had no hunting or
forest skills, and any of Siryyk's creatures would no

doubt succeed in tracking him down. If they looked in the right place.

His best chance lay in making them guess the wrong direction of his flight. He aimed for the awful forbidden zone of terrain where the climactic battle with Scartaris had broken the map.

Everything would be strange there—or so he had heard. The monsters were terrified of that place. No character would go there intentionally, which was why Verne considered it a safe bet. And, though he didn't want to admit it, the sheer anomaly of the bizarre area had piqued his natural curiosity.

Verne felt weak. He had nothing to drink with him and had eaten little for weeks. But after Siryyk forced him to create the cannon, Verne knew he could not remain a captive any longer. Knowing the manticore also possessed the Sitnaltan weapon made things even worse.

The weapon contained the power source from the Outsiders' ship—a power source that was a hybrid of *reality* and the imagination. If it was deadly to Gamearth, it might be just as deadly to the Players. The Outsider Scott had created a bigger stick than he bargained for. And the manticore wanted to use it.

Verne cursed himself for not being able to dismantle the weapon or sabotage it in some way before his flight. But Siryyk kept the weapon under very close guard.

He had verified that the device itself remained undamaged, and he hoped that the manticore would not discover how to reset its timing mechanism. But Verne held little hope of that; Siryyk had already shown himself to be highly intelligent.

He wondered what Frankenstein would have done. He wondered what Frankenstein was doing now. Detectors would have shown that the weapon never detonated. Did Frankenstein think him dead? What did Victor think of him and his failure?

Verne had no way to send a message. He had no way to fight. Simply by taking all his undeveloped inventions away from Siryyk's army, he had struck a severe blow.

Verne limped across a hex-line where the desolation abutted a section of forested-hill. Verne chose to continue through the desolation, heading northward to steer away from the sharp eyes of any pursuers.

Though he stood low on the desolation, by late afternoon he saw the first distorted hexagons of broken terrain. The hexes had been pried up from the map and tilted at the wrong angles. In the center, he discerned a misty void, shapeless and colorless, like a death wound for Gamearth, growing larger.

Scouring dust gusted up from the desolation, staining the sky. Verne's throat felt as if he had swallowed hot rags rolled in sand. His legs shook. His woolen greatcoat felt hot and sticky, but he could not leave it as a flag for any following creatures.

He plowed ahead. He didn't know what he would do in the destroyed zone, but his mind had focused on that one goal, and he continued in that direction.

Behind him, Verne heard a faint puttering sound that grew louder. He turned and saw a tiny black form. The sun lowered toward the distant mountain terrain and shone in his eyes. Verne squinted, wishing he had brought an optick tube. But even without enhancements, he could make out a Sitnaltan steam-engine car coming toward him.

He thought he had become delirious. Professor Frankenstein had come to rescue him, somehow knowing where Verne would be. His heart lifted with elation. Finally, signs of civilization! Yes, Frankenstein's detectors must have seen the terrible anomaly on this portion of the map, and he had come to investigate.

Two large figures accompanied the steam-engine car, much taller than any human character could be. They loped along with great strides that allowed them to match speed with the vehicle.

Verne waved his arms, trying to draw their attention. His voice came out hoarse and raspy. "I'm over here, Victor!"

The vehicle veered and came toward him. Gouts of steam showed that the driver had jammed the acceleration lever all the way forward. Verne dropped his arms down to his side. He blinked his red and sore eyes. "Oh, dear," he said.

He recognized the hulking monsters bounding beside the car. The reptilian form of Korux sat behind the steering levers. "Oh, dear!" he said again.

Somehow pulling new energy from the marrow of his bones, Verne ran blindly toward the broken hexagons. He didn't know what he would find there, but he did know what would happen if Korux captured him. Siryyk wanted Verne alive, but the Slac general could cause a great deal of pain and maiming before he endangered the professor's life.

Verne stumbled on the rocky soil and kept running. The steam-engine car grew louder, chugging and puttering. Up ahead he saw the first broken hex-line, a lip half as high as a man, where the terrain had shifted.

Verne pushed himself toward it. The car could not go over the boundary. They would have to leave their vehicle behind. They would be on foot, just as he was. But the giant creatures could catch him in no time.

He chose not to think of that and fell to his knees when he reached the uplifted hex-line. It felt hard and glossy, thrust up from the surface of the desolation terrain. He scrambled over it and rolled.

The desolation lay canted at an angle, as if the entire hexagon were ready to collapse. He ran, tripping faster as the slope increased. Ahead he saw the gray maw of static, mist, and black stars from the other side of the map, a void—the Outside. Verne knew it would be certain death to fall in there.

The giant monsters scrambled over the line and plunged after him, shouting. They would capture him, or he would die.

A calmness welled up from the core of Verne's body. What better way for a great inventor to die than this? What more perfect end for one of the most profound thinkers of Sitnalta than to perish while plunging headfirst into the greatest mystery of all?

A swirling stormcloud of dust rushed by as the wind picked up. His cheeks and eyes stung from the sand flying at him. Verne lurched forward, his mind firmly made up.

He heard a loud whuffing from behind, and a ten-foot-tall shaggy creature grabbed him by the coat, clutching his shoulders.

Verne cried out and strained ahead. He popped out of his greatcoat, letting the inside-out sleeves dangle behind him. He fell to the ground. The monster ripped the coat to shreds, yanking the sleeves off, and bounded forward again to grab Verne.

Then the ground started to shake and lurch beneath the map. The surface of the desolation terrain bucked and tilted first one way, then the other. The entire hexagon wobbled loose, creaking. A rumbling roar seemed to split the sky itself.

As the angle of the terrain steepened, the giant beast holding Verne threw itself back toward the hex-line, scrambling and grunting. It tucked the professor under its arm like a heavy log. Verne struggled. The monster smelled rank, like all the bile of all the sickness in the world boiled down to a thick jelly.

Ahead, on the other side of the black line, Korux waited beside the Sitnaltan car. The second hairy creature bounded down to take Verne from its companion. The first giant took a large step just as the hexagon rumbled and bucked again.

The second monster sprawled flat, facing uphill. The other creature tripped face-first into the sand. It rolled, kicking dust and rocks, picking up speed as it plunged downward. Its roars became shrill with fear; ahead, it could see the great void.

Verne scrambled out of the second giant's grip and crawled toward the stable black hex-line. At the front of his mind, he tried to convince himself to stop. Intellectually, he kept insisting that he wanted to die, that he wanted to fall down there, that he didn't dare be recaptured, but his traitorous body moved with its own survival instinct.

He reached the line just as he felt the ground sink like a rug snatched out from under his feet. He grabbed out with elbows and hands, snatching the edge as he heard a tremendous *snap*. Then strange-smelling air gushed up. The hexagon fell away.

He turned for just a glance as the section of terrain— flat brown, with the hairy giants looking like two specks—fell away, growing smaller. All around it swirled a cosmic nothingness.

He gritted his teeth, jamming his elbows and hands into the rough surface of the desolation. His feet dangled below him, touching nothing. He wanted to let go, to drop, to see—even if only for the tiniest instant— what awaited him down there.

But instead, he worked his shoulder muscles to get up. He heard a grating hiss and tilted his head, grinding his beard among the rocks and dirt on the edge of the world.

Verne saw the silhouetted form of General Korux bending over. He thought that the Slac would kick him over the side—and even hoped for that in the back of his mind, but he knew it would never happen. Korux would forfeit his own life if he lost the captive.

"I hope you've learned not to play games with us." The Slac reached down, grabbed his arm, and dragged

Verne up over the edge, sending him sprawling onto the stable terrain.

Far below, off in the void, Verne heard a long rumble like distant thunder.

Korux tossed him into the still-chugging car and released the braking lock after he climbed in beside his captive.

"Siryyk has ordered all the monster armies to march. We're on the attack now," Korux said. "We have no time for this."

15

ALLIES

*"We played our games. We had our fun. But
the Rules have changed, and now we face a
different game—one of survival."*
—Tayron Tribeleader of the khelebar

Delrael's army had found its stride. Over the days
of marching, they learned how to work with each
other, how to function as one vast unit.

After traveling this far, they had passed through
the stages Delrael had expected to see: initial excitement at approaching unknown adventures, which gave
way to sore weariness from walking across hexagon
after hexagon, then the misery of camping under poor
conditions and eating bland food for too many days.
Finally, as they retreated northward along the spine of
the Spectre Mountains, they had hardened under the
routine.

Delrael sent scouts ahead and to the side to seek
possible obstacles and likely places for ambushing
Siryyk's horde; rear scouts reported regularly on the
progress of the monsters.

The manticore's troops had spread out on the rugged mountain terrain, with a long vanguard of foot-
soldiers marching ahead of the main group. Siryyk
still didn't know that an entire human army remained
only one step ahead in the mountain terrain.

Delrael gave permission for teams to dig traps and
to set obstacles. These proved a nuisance to Siryyk but

caused no real damage, nor did they suggest to the manticore that anything more than a few isolated characters were harassing them. But Delrael knew that such annoyance would keep the horde angry and marching.

Delrael sent his fighters marching well before dawn. In the darkness, they tramped along the quest-path, bearing torches when the terrain proved too treacherous in the dark.

By the time sunrise lit their way, the young man Romm came back from ahead to report. "The next hexagon is forested hills, as we knew from the map. I went with two other scouts." He seemed uneasy. "We sensed other characters around us. You know how it gets when you're alone in a dense forest. You can feel when someone's watching you."

Delrael nodded, but let a smile creep across his face. He knew exactly where they were. "I don't think we'll have any trouble with the khelebar. Don't worry."

Romm looked at him as if to ask a question, but he decided not to. He went back through the lines to get some food from the supply packs.

Delrael took out one of the small maps Vailret had copied back in the Stronghold village. It would be interesting to see how Ledaygen had fared after the forest fire.

Upon approaching the forested-hill terrain, the surviving ylvans seemed elated. Delrael knew from his memories of Tallin how much they hated to be away from the trees. The ylvans grew up in the protection of the forest, camouflaged, learning their woodcraft so they could become deadly fighters.

But when the army crossed the hex-line to leave the bleak mountain terrain behind, the ylvans became uneasy again.

Delrael himself stood astonished among the close-packed trees, sure that he had misjudged their position. Ledaygen, an entire hexagon of trees, had burned to the ground. He had expected, even with the meticulous work of all the panther-people, to find no more than barren hillsides cleared of dead tree hulks, fertile ash sifted across the soil, and possibly rows of dusty-green seedlings of oaks and pines. It had been only a few turns.

But Ledaygen stood *tall* and bristling with thick branches. Delrael wondered if the reforestation could have resulted from some backwash of magic from the *dayid*, the congregation of spirits that had lived in the forest. Bryl had worked with the *dayid* to quench the forest fire, but Ledaygen had died, leaving little to salvage.

Now the forest stood lush . . . but *wrong* somehow.

Kellos, the ylvan leader, came up to him. Kellos squeezed his mouth into a tight shape. Dark circles under his flinty eyes made him look exhausted from the burden of bearing so much anger inside himself. The purple bruise from the noose looked like a bandanna at his throat; when he spoke, his voice remained scratchy and harsh. In the days since their rescue from the Black Falcons, Kellos had never once called Delrael by name.

"Something's wrong with this forest." Kellos jerked his head up at the trees. "It's like a blow to the stomach. Can't you feel it? They're all screaming. This forest is in pain."

Delrael continued to lead his fighters ahead anyway. "I can see that."

Scowling, Kellos dropped back.

The trees themselves were thin and unbalanced. Their branches reached up like claws. Each joint swelled with large knobs, like the fingers of a starving man. The force of the trees stretching upward, trying to grow as fast as they could, made the air taut with energy.

It reminded Delrael of the blackened tree planta-

tions on the hills outside of Tairé. He wondered if
Jathen would have made that comparison. Enrod stumbled along, looking disturbed. He had acted even more
disoriented since Jathen's death.

The human army continued through the trees. The
forest seemed close and oppressive. Delrael knew they
should stop for a meal and a rest, but none of the
fighters seemed eager for that.

Kellos came up to him again. "Characters are watching us from out there in the trees. They're very good
woodsmen. Even I can barely detect them. But they're
here, now, very close to us." He looked around, ready
to pull his crossbow and arm it.

Delrael signaled his fighters to stop. A few moments later, when all the characters had come to a
halt, he stepped in front, alone and vulnerable. He
looked out into the trees.

"I know you're there, khelebar. I am Delrael, called
*kennok*limb. Your Healer Thilane gave me a new leg.
Noldir Woodcarver made it for me."

He peeled up his trouser leg to expose the grain of
the golden wood and the choppy white gash from
where Annik had struck him. "Call Tayron Tribeleader.
He knows who I am."

The silence bothered Delrael; suspicion and uneasiness did not fit with his memories of the khelebar at
all. But he had been injured that first time, followed
by only two companions. Now he brought an entire
army.

Delrael waited and blinked his eyes. In that moment
a khelebar man emerged from the trees directly in
front of him.

His hair was dark and cropped close to his head. His
broad shoulders remained bare. His chest showed no
ornament. The bottom half of his body was that of a
panther, with four powerful clawed legs, dusty fur,
and rippling muscles. His panther tail twitched as he
stepped forward.

"We remember you, *kennok*limb. I see that much
has changed." The khelebar man looked around the
thick forest. "Much has changed here as well. Do you
remember me?"

Delrael looked at him, but he recalled a man with
long hair hanging in black braids down his back and an
ornate pinecone pendant at his throat.

"Of course I remember you, Ydaim Trailwalker."

The khelebar man smiled at him. "Since you remember me, I have no choice but to welcome you."

Tayron Tribeleader padded about in the council clearing where the khelebar made bonfires and told tales.
Delrael remembered the war councils the panther-
people had held during the forest fire and in planning
their assault against the Cyclops.

Delrael sat cross-legged on the ash-covered clearing,
waiting for Tayron to continue. He looked over at the
hex-discontinuity, where the forested-hill terrain met
the adjacent hexagon of mountains; the terrains did
not match up correctly and left a sheer cliff. Many
khelebar had thrown themselves over the edge in the
last moments of the fire.

Near the center of the clearing stood a pine seedling
about as tall as Delrael's knee. This, he remembered,
was the one pine tree that had survived from the old
Ledaygen, protected from the flames by the fall of the
towering Father Pine in the clearing. The seedling
looked normal and alive, the only truly healthy tree
Delrael had seen in the entire hexagon. Somewhere
deep in the hex should be an oak tree similarly healthy
brought back to life through the sacrifice of Thilane
Healer.

Beside the pine seedling stood a complex symbolic
monument to the forest. Noldir Woodcarver had fashioned it from the scorched hulk of the Father Pine.

Tayron's dusty blond hair had also been cut short,
as had the hair of all of the khelebar Delrael had seen.

Ydaim explained to him, "We will not allow our hair to grow until Ledaygen has grown to its former glory."

Tayron stopped his pacing, and the sunlight played across his back. He finally spoke again. "Few khelebar remain here. Most could not face the enormous task of resurrecting the forest. They could not bear the scars they saw, and they have gone to lesser forests to form their own groups. Only I, Ydaim, and a few dozen others do all this work.

"But the blood of Ledaygen has made the soil magic. You see how fast the trees have returned. Our work has paid off. We will never leave our home."

Delrael turned his gaze away and pursed his lips. Until now, Tayron had not asked about the human army or its purpose; but Delrael could no longer avoid the issue.

"Tayron, I have to tell you why we're here. A gigantic monster horde follows us only a day or two behind. Their purpose is to destroy the map. They will flood through here like a storm, and they'll cause as much destruction as the fire did. I know of no way you can avoid them."

Ydaim melted out of the forest to stand by the clearing. His face bore a shocked expression. Delrael thought he saw shadows of other khelebar between the trees. Tayron stared at him with wide, devastated eyes.

"You are bringing the evil creatures here! To destroy our work? How could you do this?" His voice cracked as it grew shrill. "You know what Ledaygen has already suffered—why couldn't you choose another route and protect us?"

This time frustration began to bubble up within Delrael. He thought of Vailret and Bryl taking their risk as they went alone to get the Earth Stone. He thought of how Jathen had been murdered by the manticore and of all the Tairan characters slaughtered in Siryyk's attack. He drew himself to his feet and felt his hands trembling.

"The end of the Game is near, Tayron, and this could be the final battle. All characters are in play. We can't afford to shelter one place or one group. Everything counts now." He scowled. "I'm sorry for your forest, but we are fighting for all of Gamearth. If we win this one struggle, then we—not the Outsiders— determine our fate. We will always have peace."

"A war to end all wars?" Ydaim said, interrupting from where he stood. His face wore a cynical expression. "I'm not sure I believe in the idea."

Delrael turned to him, but just then three human figures appeared among the trees. "Delrael!" Romm shouted as all three marched into the clearing.

Between Romm and another scout stood a tall human fighter, heavily muscled and wearing old but well-tended armor. He moved with a slow grace that disregarded his two escorts. Each step was careful and precise. His hair hung long, streaked with gray, and thin on top. A full beard made his massive face look larger. His eyes were narrow and dark.

Despite his apparent determination, he seemed to have an aura of calmness about him. He carried an unsheathed broadsword in his right hand. When he stepped forward, the fighter looked as if he would make no compromises.

"He came right through the army," Romm said. "He won't tell anyone who he is. Just wanted to see you."

Tayron and Ydaim fell silent in the clearing, as if sensing the import of the moment.

Delrael felt amazement stab through him like blue-cold steel. Part of him grew surprised that Romm hadn't recognized the fighter, but it had been many years.

"Father!" Delrael's voice came out in a whisper.

Drodanis took two steps forward and rested the flat

of his sword on his shoulder. "I've come to help. Could you use another fighter?"

Delrael stood stricken for a moment and then ran forward as both of them burst into huge grins.

The campfire crackled, shedding warmth into the night. Above, stars showed through patchy clouds and the tangled ceiling of branches.

Delrael and Drodanis sat near each other. The remainder of the army rested by their own fires with strict instructions not to harm any trees or to wander from the well-marked paths. They left Delrael and his father to catch up on years of conversation.

"I was very angry when you left," Delrael said. "I wasn't ready for the responsibility you gave me. I had my training, but you suddenly placed me in command of the Stronghold when you ran off. You gave up! A great fighter like you shouldn't surrender!"

Drodanis stared into the flames and made no comment.

"I have had companions die too . . ." Their faces welled up in Delrael's memory, but he blinked them away. "But I continued the Game. I didn't let my grief poison me. You ran away and left me."

Delrael took a deep breath. "And then you sent that message stick from the Rulewoman, giving *me* the responsibility of saving Gamearth. You told me to find a way to stop Scartaris, while you sat and wallowed in self-pity for turn after turn!"

Drodanis accepted all the comments Delrael flung at him, and then turned tired eyes to his son. Delrael saw the firelight reflected in them. "Everything you say is true. I did give up. I was wrong—that's the loser's way out. We weren't created for that kind of response. That's why I came back to rejoin the Game, to make amends."

"I wish you'd come back sooner," Delrael said. The campfire snapped and popped over his words.

"Yes," Drodanis said. "We forgot our purpose here on Gamearth. We allowed ourselves to get too wrapped up in dull activities and day-to-day life. Our whole purpose on Gamearth is to amuse the Outsiders. We are here to have adventures, and the Outsiders are not at all interested in our chores, in our bland home lives.

"When we stopped questing, when we stopped searching for treasure and exploring catacombs, and battling monsters solely for the sake of *having fun*, we lost the Outsiders. We can only hope that this struggle against Siryyk is exciting enough that we rekindle the Outsiders' interests. They can save us all."

Delrael frowned with distaste. He poked a branch into the fire, stirring the flames. "My purpose in life is not to amuse someone else. I'm responsible for this army, for the characters in the Stronghold village. I'm working to save the map from destruction. And I'm doing that because it must be done, not because I hope the Outsiders are going to enjoy watching my efforts. If they find my tasks entertaining, then so be it. But that is not the only reason I'm here."

Drodanis looked at his son as if he had just uttered blasphemy. "Are you forgetting Rule #1, Delrael? With the end of the Game, our purpose in life goes away. If that happens, it doesn't matter if the map survives. If the Outsiders no longer play, then we have no reason to be here at all."

Delrael shook his head. "Rule #1 has taken on a whole different meaning. Rule #1 is to *survive*, not just to have fun."

Drodanis closed his eyes with a disturbed sigh. He lay back on the ground, ready to sleep. "So much has changed, Delrael. So much has changed. This isn't my Gamearth anymore."

Delrael tried to sleep, though his mind continued to swim with conflicting thoughts. "But that's the Gamearth we're fighting for," he muttered.

*   *   *

Tayron Tribeleader walked among the dark passages in the regrown Ledaygen. The trees rose tall around him. The branches appeared black and oily, lit by the gleams of stars.

His pawed feet moved silently among the ashes on the ground. He let his fingertips touch the trunks as he passed them.

Tayron tried to remember what Ledaygen had been like before, but that had been so long ago now. He had spent many turns convincing himself that this was natural, that the forest had suffered no fundamental change. He had forced himself to ignore the pain in the trees. He remembered the horror of the fire. He remembered his father Fiolin crushed under a great slab of rock hurled by the Cyclops. His death had left Tayron as Tribeleader.

Tayron passed two sleeping human fighters curled up near the base of a tree. They didn't move as he passed.

The decision weighed heavily on him, caused by the fear and uneasiness at admitting his basic failure.

Tayron wondered if he would ever be considered a great leader of the khelebar. Would he ever be compared to Jorig Falselimb and his great courage as he faced the slavering wolves and drove them from Ledaygen?

He plucked a curved twig from the end of a branch and held it up. The twig looked like a long, sharp hook. When he brought the broken end to his nose, the sap smelled sour and rotten.

Tayron squeezed his eyes shut, forcing the tears to run sideways down his cheeks.

This was not Ledaygen. It would never be Ledaygen. He had fooled himself, as had all the khelebar. All their effort had merely been to distract them from grief. They should have accepted the loss, healed, and moved on. Ledaygen was gone; it had been gone since the fire.

*   *   *

Delrael's army completed their preparations several hours before the vanguard of Siryyk's horde arrived. Most of the fighters had moved into position on the far side of the hexagon.

Many fighters walked about, eager for battle. They had marched long and trained hard; knowing that the monsters were so near made them enthusiastic for a fight. But Delrael refused, telling them that they had no need to tip their hand yet, or to risk lives.

Tayron Tribeleader's ambush plan required none of that.

Kellos and seventeen ylvans waited on the leading edge of Ledaygen, watching as the vanguard approached. They hid behind trees, camouflaged in their splotched uniforms. Kellos crouched close to one of the trunks, but avoided touching the bark. The wrongness of all the trees made his skin crawl.

He looked behind him, making sure he could find the tiny marks on the ash-strewn forest floor. The other ylvans also noted their positions, making sure they could locate the subtle signs even in the frenzy of retreat.

The front line of monsters approached under the hot afternoon sun. They plodded along at a steady pace. The creatures on the flanks seemed uneasy; they had been harried enough by scattered attacks and traps that they walked with heightened awareness.

A regiment of Slac formed the rigid front lines with locked shields made of greenish-tan leather. They held various pointed weapons, spiked balls, barbed spears, and jagged swords. Behind them followed ranks of demons with exaggerated claws, fangs, and spined armor. They did not slow as they reached the hex-line bordering the forest terrain.

Kellos made a crackling noise with saliva in his mouth. It sounded like branches clicking together overhead, but the ylvans took out their crossbows. As soon

as Kellos coughed, all seventeen leaped away from
their hiding places, shouting as they launched a full
attack with crossbows. They fired over and over again.
The tiny bolts made whistling sounds in the air.

As the monster army reacted with a roar, fourteen
of the front Slac toppled with crossbow bolts in their
eyes and throats. Predictably, the rest of the army
lunged forward, brandishing weapons and charging into
the trees.

Kellos paused for two seconds longer and let off
another pair of crossbow bolts, bringing down one
more enemy. Then he gave the signal for retreat, and
the ylvans turned and fled deeper into the trees, stepping only on their marks.

When the front wave of the vanguard crashed into
the forest terrain, suddenly the ground vanished beneath their feet with a puff of gray ash. Twenty monster fighters plunged face-first into long trenches filled
with spikes.

The second wave of booby-traps sprang as the ylvans
brushed past them, and a line of trees toppled backward into the monster army. All the topmost branches
had been sharpened into wooden stakes.

Laughing, Kellos and his ylvans continued to flee,
careful not to touch any of the warped trees of
Ledaygen.

Siryyk's vanguard howled behind them, negotiating
the obstacles and struggling deeper into the forest,
deeper into the trap.

Delrael waited as the ylvans burst back to the hex-
line where his own army stood prepared. The little
forest people looked flushed, smeared with ashes and
scratched from their rapid flight. Even Kellos bore an
expression of stormy delight at the destruction he had
caused.

Tayron clapped his hands for the attention of the

other khelebar. "You know your positions. You know what you must do."

The panther-people stood uneasy. Ydaim turned to the Tribeleader. "Are you certain, Tayron? You can't change your mind once we go."

"My decision has already been set in motion," Tayron answered. "We must hold the memory of Ledaygen true, not waste our efforts with a distorted imitation. We've worked hard, and that is nothing to be ashamed of. But now we must do what the Game calls for. The true Ledaygen vanished in the first fire."

One of the khelebar groaned, but Tayron whirled. "We will have no more despairing! We are strong. Now go . . ." Despite his words, his own voice caught as he spoke the command. "Go and burn Ledaygen."

The khelebar, bearing torches, loped off to their positions around the hexagon, where they would flank the monster vanguard. Their torches flickered as they vanished among the doomed trees.

A sharp breeze whipped up and over the hex-discontinuity, whistling around Noldir's carving. The hole where Tayron Tribeleader had dug up the pine seedling looked like a dark wound.

Tareah waited in the trees on the far side of the council clearing. She heard the sounds of the approaching enemy army long before the monsters actually arrived. She got ready.

Across from her, Enrod stood in his tattered robes, preparing his own spells. He held his hands out under the bright sunshine, staring at the warm light on his skin.

Delrael had at first forbidden them to take part in the attack. "Not necessary," he said, "and I don't want to risk you." But Tareah had looked at him with a thread of anger behind her eyes, and Delrael stumbled on his words. "Well, only if you think it's safe. And I mean that!"

Tareah had smiled. He seemed afraid of repeating his own mistakes over again. "We can strike from a distance and cause some damage, then we'll leave before they can find us."

Delrael had dispatched several scouts to keep an eye on her. But that didn't bother Tareah; she found his concern touching, as long as he let her participate in the adventure.

The vanguard of the monster horde had lost all semblance of rank and order when they charged into the clearing. Tareah wasted no time and rolled the Water Stone. She grabbed it up again; power surged into her.

Thick storm clouds congealed in the sky, swirling and scraping masses of air and sending many-pronged spears of lightning. The bolts struck, blasting chunks of dirt and monster fighters into the air. The creatures screamed at the sudden attack.

Tareah rolled the sapphire again, using more than a single spell at once. This time she summoned an enormous wind that caused the running monsters to stagger. She caught a group of demons near the edge of the hex-discontinuity and, jutting her chin with an imaginary push, flung them over the edge. Then she struck again with the lightning.

The vanguard swirled about, not knowing where to run or where the attack was coming from.

Enrod made a fist and looked up with glazed eyes. The weapons held by the creatures suddenly turned cherry red. They dropped their steel, their burned hands sizzling. Four black-robed Slac erupted into flames from the insides of their bodies; blue fire spurted from their eyeballs and ears with a popping sound. They didn't even scream. Enrod let out a shuddering sigh of ecstasy.

"Enough!" Tareah called among the screams of battle. She wanted to roll the sapphire again, but she had agreed. Together, they turned and ran back through the forest before the monsters could find them.

Delrael watched the smoke from the advancing fires. The khelebar had laid out careful kindling paths so that the inferno would move inward, leaving the monsters with no escape.

"Let's get out of here," Delrael said.

"That soil is thirsty for blood," Tayron said. "It has acquired a taste for it."

The Tribeleader carried a deep wooden container that bore the seedling of the one healthy pine. "We are not destroying Ledaygen. Ledaygen died long ago. We are merely making it impossible for an abomination to thrive."

As they drew farther away from the hexagon, Ydaim and the other khelebar returned. Tareah and Enrod stared behind him, toward the edges of the forest.

Great curls of smoke poured up from the entire hexagon. Dozens of individual blazes reached out and encircled the trapped monsters.

Ledaygen burned.

16

THE VIEW FROM THE VOLCANO

What lies beyond the edge of Gamearth? An ancient map fragment bore the notation Here Be Monsters. *But we have monsters aplenty on Gamearth itself. Is something even worse beyond the edge?*

—The Book of Rules

Professor Frankenstein walked with his back hunched from the enormous weight of the lead helmet on his head. He plodded with each step, grimacing as his legs hauled their extra burden.

"How do you know that helmet will even work?" Vailret asked.

Frankenstein shrugged, but the gesture made his head tip forward off balance, about to roll off his shoulders. "I don't *know* that it'll work. But I must do anything I can to decrease the risk. If the invisible force is controlling our minds, then I must shield my brain."

"Whatever you say," Vailret said.

They kept up with Frankenstein's quick, tiny steps. They reached a tall building near the ocean hexagons.

"We destroyed the manufactories up and down this thoroughfare with our own hands, under the direction of the evil controller," the professor said, "but this warehouse hasn't been a target yet. We use it only for storage." From his belt, Frankenstein removed a ring that jingled with many keys. He started to bend over, but propped himself against the brick wall. "Please look down at the bottom brick," he said. "There should be a code number chiseled in it."

Bryl knelt down. "It's a long one—R124C 41 + ."

Careful not to tilt his head, Frankenstein held the key ring up to his eye level and flipped through the keys until he found an identical number stamped along one shaft. He opened the padlock on the door and then, wavering on his feet, stepped back to let Vailret and Bryl pull the doors open.

The warehouse proved to be one large hangar. Light shone from cracks in the roof slats, and dust motes fell like gold flecks through the sunlight. Inside, near the front, Vailret saw a leather-trimmed basket, the gondola of a balloon just like the one they had taken from Sitnalta. Tucked inside it and draped along the back lay the voluminous folds of the balloon itself, with bright splashes of red and white.

Frankenstein stood with his elbow against the wall. His hand propped up the back of his head to take the weight of the lead helmet from his neck.

"You recall that when we first gave you experimental balloon number VI, we weren't sure it would work. We had never found a Sitnaltan volunteer to test it.

"But after you proved it to be a complete success, Jules and I enlisted the aid of other inventors to construct this larger model, which can comfortably carry several passengers. Otherwise, all the details are the same, even down to the red-and-white pattern, on the chance that the heat-absorption properties of specific colors made some small but significant change in its performance." He ran his fingers along the folds of the bright balloon lying limp in the basket.

"But we grew engrossed in other things. Investigating the Outsiders' ship, which you told us about, occupied most of our time." Frankenstein turned his head and winced at the strain on his neck muscles. "We never got a chance to go exploring with this balloon."

Vailret looked off to one side, deeper in the dusty shadows, and saw another large machine. This one was bright green with a wooden framework and several stretched batlike wings extending from the sides of a waspish body. Two propellers protruded, one from the rear and one from its top. Other wires and rudders were connected to steering levers, and two fragile seats sat just behind sets of pedals.

"What's this?" Vailret said.

"We're not interested," Bryl said.

Frankenstein turned to look, and his dark eyes took on a distant expression. "Oh, that's another flying contraption, called a 'pedal-kite,' I believe. It was invented by Professor Wright and his brother, Professor Wright. It's got a very light construction, good for updrafts once you reach a certain height. By pedaling with your feet, the propellers turn and provide lift for the entire vehicle, which then can glide a short distance. It's aerodynamically sound and based on solid scientific Rules, just as a good invention should be. But it does have one drawback. You see, if you stop pedaling, the entire vehicle crashes." He frowned. "Not good for long journeys, I'm afraid."

"We'll take the balloon," Vailret said.

"I thought you would."

Bryl helped Vailret drag the gondola across the concrete floor of the hangar and out into the middle of the street. Frankenstein watched them, breathing heavily. "Blast this helmet!" he muttered to himself.

Vailret and Bryl pulled out the balloon and spread it on the cobblestones. Other Sitnaltan characters watched what they were doing. Vailret began to feel a sense of urgency, afraid the invisible force might decide to make the Sitnaltans attack them.

Vailret and Bryl used the ropes to attach the balloon to its basket, straightening tangles and double checking fastenings. Frankenstein muttered encouragement and offered instructions when they became confused.

Inside the warehouse, Vailret found four canisters of the lighter-than-air gas extracted through electrolysis from seawater in the Sitnaltan manufactories. He and Bryl linked two canisters to the open end of the balloon and twisted the valves to bleed out the gas.

They tucked the folds, watching the great sack fill sluggishly. It seemed to take a long time for any noticeable change. Vailret cranked the valves farther open; the hissing gas sounded like the roar of a fire.

When the balloon finally swelled like a limp, overripe fruit, Vailret and Bryl climbed into the gondola. Bryl moved slowly on his stiff, old legs. Frankenstein waved at them. They called farewell to him, but the professor turned and staggered away, holding onto his helmet with both hands.

The gondola skipped and bounced on the hex-cobbled streets, dragged forward by the half-inflated balloon as the intermittent breezes through the alleys picked up and slacked off. They moved again, rising, this time skimming a hand's-width off the ground.

"Isn't there any way we can steer this?" Vailret said.

"Just push against buildings."

Then the invisible controller struck again. The Sitnaltans began to approach, moving in a lockstep that Vailret had seen before. They carried sharp fragments of brick, sticks, and pointed shards of glass that cut their fingers.

"Uh oh," Vailret said.

The balloon skipped against a building and rose higher, picking up speed as a breeze gusted. The Sitnaltans unsuccessfully tried to counteract their own actions but continued to stumble forward, brandishing their weapons.

"Should I use the Fire Stone to blast them away?" Bryl said. "An illusion won't do us any good."

"No!" Vailret said. "Remember what Verne told us

before. The gas is flammable. One spark and this whole thing goes up in a giant fireball.''

They rose another foot off the ground as the canisters continued to hiss into the balloon sack.

"Pull in the ropes, quick! We don't want them to grab hold.'' They yanked up the ropes, but the balloon still rode low enough that the Sitnaltans could clutch the bottom of the basket itself.

Vailret could see their anguished expressions as they tried to resist. But the invisible role player directed their actions. One of the pointed sticks jabbed through the bottom of the gondola, snagging on Bryl's blue cloak.

"We've got to make this lighter!'' Vailret cried.

"We have nothing to spare,'' Bryl said, putting his hands on his cheeks.

"Here, help me throw one of these half-empty canisters over.'' He disconnected the nozzle from the end of the balloon.

"We won't have enough gas to get back!''

"If we never get there in the first place, we won't have to worry about getting back.''

Bryl didn't argue. Together, they heaved the bulky canister over the side. It clanged and thudded to the cobblestones, gouging the street.

Immediately, the balloon lurched another ten feet into the air. They began to drift away from the city. The Sitnaltans gathered below, growing smaller, with loud shouts that sounded more like cheers than cries of anger.

Vailret stared down at the receding city terrain. In the late afternoon, they soared out toward the broad hexagons of water. Off in the distance lay the murky island of Rokanun.

The balloon floated along in the darkness. They heard no sounds other than the ripple of waves far below. Not even the wind made noise as they drifted along. They felt no rocking, no gentle motion, just a constant peace that made Vailret sleepy.

Vailret leaned back against the criss-crossed wicker of the gondola, trying to get comfortable. Bryl seemed uneasy and afraid to doze. "We should get the Earth Stone in another day or two," Vailret said. "Are you afraid about what you're going to do? The Allspirit, I mean. It's not a trivial task."

Bryl took a long time to answer. "Vailret, I'm old. I remember Delrael running the Stronghold, and before that Drodanis, and all the way back to your great-great grandfather Jarriel.

"Every day my joints hurt, and my body feels stiffer than it should be. When I had a warm room at the Stronghold, I could hide it, but this constant traveling makes everything worse. My hair is falling out, I'm tired all the time, and I always feel cold.

"And then I remember how I felt when I used the Water Stone to link up the the *dayid* in Ledaygen. It was so . . . wonderful. The power gave me an entirely new perspective. I can't describe it to you. I remember how Sardun looked when he used all his magic to create the Barrier River.

"I've touched that much power before, enough to know that I'm not afraid of it. I'm anxious for it. I'm eager to do what I can." He stopped and swallowed.

"Crashing in this balloon, though—now *that* frightens me!"

They landed just after dawn on the western side of Rokanun.

Vailret let the buoyant gas out of the balloon, and they dropped. This time, at least, they did not have to worry about hiding from the dragon Tryos.

As they came down, the wind currents eddying around the island brushed them with updrafts and downdrafts, swirling them around. Vailret readied the tie ropes.

"When we get close enough, I'm going to drop over the side and hang on with the rope. If we get where I can tie off the balloon without letting out all the gas, our one canister may be enough to get us back across the water."

"You've been to Sitnalta so many times," Bryl said, "that you're coming up with hare-brained solutions to problems."

"Look, do you want to get back or not?" Vailret asked.

The balloon dropped low over forest terrain. He hoped they wouldn't crash into the jagged treetops. Then they passed over the next hexagon, sweeping closer to the rocks of the volcano.

Vailret crawled over the edge of the gondola and let himself down as the rope dragged along the ground and caught among chunks of hardened lava. A large boulder blocked his path, ready to smash his knees; but Vailret bent his legs, kicked up over the top, and dropped down again.

Above, in the basket, Bryl called down, "Well do something! Tie it somewhere."

Vailret let his feet touch the ground and stumble-ran after the balloon, refusing to let go. Finally, he managed to jam the rope into the crack between two large boulders. The balloon's own motion wedged it tight.

"Throw down the other ropes!" he called. A moment later they came snaking down, one after the other. As he tied a second rope around the rocks, a third struck him on the back of the neck.

"That's all of them," Bryl said.

"Thanks a lot." Vailret flexed his stiff fingers and his raw palms. Then he looked at the steep side of the volcano. "This is going to be easy. We're already halfway up."

A few hours later, when the lava rocks still held pockets of frost in the mountain's shadow, they were trudging up the steep quest-path, panting. Vailret stopped counting switchbacks just to keep his sanity. He remembered doing the same climb with blind Paenar, guiding him around corners because the technological Sitnaltan eyes no longer functioned.

The climb took Vailret and Bryl all day. In the hot afternoon sun, they began to wish for the morning chill. Sweat drenched the back of Vailret's tunic. Bryl pulled out a cap and placed it on his head to shield himself from the sun.

"It didn't seem this bad when I climbed up here with Delrael," Bryl said.

"You're older now. You've said that yourself."

"That's part of it." Then Bryl stepped around a corner by a rockfall and let out a groan of despair. Vailret looked at the jumbled rocks and couldn't see what the half-Sorcerer meant.

"There," Bryl said. "That was the passage Delrael and I took to get inside the volcano. A short-cut. It must have collapsed in the eruption when Tryos died."

Vailret kept plodding up the path, not wanting to lose his momentum. "That means we'll just have to go all the way to the top."

"If the Outsiders think this is fun," Bryl muttered, "I'd like to drag one of them up here."

The sky had taken on a purple pallor of dusk by the time they hauled themselves over the lip of the volcano and rested at the highest point. Vailret remembered standing here when he used the Sitnaltan dragon siren to summon Tryos.

The air remained silent except for the wind. The western sky was shot with red and gold fingers of cloud extending from the sunset. Far below, he could see the small, colorful sack of their balloon, partially deflated like a squashed ball.

Bryl stopped and put his hands on his hips. His cloak blew behind him. Vailret heard his sharp indrawn gasp of breath. Instead of gazing down into the

mouth of the crater they would descend, Vailret turned
to follow Bryl's line of sight out across the ocean.

Far out across the flat panorama of the map, giant
blue hexagons of water terrain lay spread out, abutting
each other and delineated by a webwork of black
hex-lines. But off in the distance toward the edge of
the world, he saw something that struck terror through
his heart.

The black hex-lines had widened, and the most distant sections showed great cracks as the map itself
broke apart. Between the fissures, he could see an
enormous gulf of blackness spattered with stars from a
sky that did not mirror Gamearth's.

Off to his right, at the nearer edge of the map, he
saw places where entire hexagons had broken away
and fallen into the void, leaving a jagged nothingness.

Even from this great distance, they could hear a
cosmic rumble as the farthest section of ocean snapped
and drifted away, lifting up and floating off to vanish
into the maw of emptiness.

"It's true!" Bryl said. "It's really true! The map is
falling apart."

"We don't have any time to lose," Vailret said.
"We have to get the Earth Stone and take it back to
Delrael. We need the Allspirit *now* to hold the map
together before we lose any more hexagons."

He turned toward the sloping inner wall of the crater. Rough black splotches showed where lava had
spattered. "We can't wait until morning to get down
into the crater."

Bryl stared at the inky shadows in the mouth of the
volcano, but even those seemed less frightening to him
than to watch Gamearth fall apart.

Vailret's boots echoed off the rock walls of the
dragon's treasure vault. The fireball in Bryl's hand lit
the grotto with jittering flashes of light, while simmer-

ing lava in the center of the volcano cast a steady
orange glow and waves of baking heat.

Splatters of gold covered the walls of the treasure
grotto, which Tryos destroyed in rage on learning that
the human characters had betrayed him. Heat from
the volcano's eruption had caused golden chalices and
silver figurines to slump and droop. Some gold coins
had baked together into lumps.

"I don't like it in here," Vailret said. "It's too
quiet."

Contradicting him, the lava lake bubbled and hissed
as it belched out exhaust gases into a flickering lobe of
flame that died away. "Relatively speaking, I mean."
He looked around. "Can you find the Earth Stone?"

Bryl walked among the treasure heaps with a puzzled expression that turned to distress. He pawed among
the piles of gold, casting metal coins aside.

"What's wrong, Bryl?"

"Look around here," he said. "Do you see any
jewels at all? Any gems? Look at all this gold and
silver. Back in the alcove, you'll even find some blackened statues and ruined tapestries from the height of
the old Sorcerer days. But no gems! There used to be
rubies and diamonds, emeralds and sapphires."

"I don't care about them. What about the Earth
Stone?"

Bryl looked at him with panicked eyes. He set his
fireball hovering in the air above his shoulder, and he
bent to dig his fingers deep into the piled gold. He
closed his eyes in concentration. He remained silent
for a long time, but his lips trembled. When he stopped,
his jaw hung open.

He turned back to Vailret. "That's what I mean!
The Earth Stone is not here. It's gone!"

17

SIRYYK'S GAME

"Single combat against a talented opponent requires skill and speed. However, a large-scale battle is choreography of vast groups of characters, requiring much effort, planning, and strategy. It is perhaps the most difficult game any of us will ever attempt."

—Drodanis, to trainees at the Stronghold

Delrael's army moved at a rapid pace northward, charged with elation from their victory in Ledaygen. Rear scouts estimated that a third of the horde had been killed in the fire. Siryyk's remaining army had drawn together and so now was not spread so thinly over the terrain. But the monsters still outnumbered Delrael's troops four to one.

When Romm and the other scouts returned that afternoon to report, Delrael sat back and listened. They knew from the maps that mountain terrain lay along their path. But they did not know the characteristics of each hexagon or how they could use them to advantage.

"The mountains are particularly rugged in the next hex," Romm said. He sat down on a lichen-spattered boulder and brushed a few sweat-clumped strands of hair away from his forehead. His long face had been sunburned from the altitude, and his lips were chapped. Delrael gave him a flask of water, and Romm dutifully took a sip, but he seemed more preoccupied with making his report.

"We found a few places where we might set up an effective attack. In particular, there's one path along a cliff in a narrow canyon. Our numbers would not be a disadvantage there."

"One other thing," the second scout said. She was a wiry woman with short brown hair who came from one of the mining villages northwest of the Stronghold. Delrael could not remember her name. "We saw Black Falcon riders in the mountains, but they didn't notice us."

Delrael frowned. "Corim said they might shadow us. We can only hope he chooses a more appropriate enemy than Annik did."

He saw his father sitting by himself and sharpening his sword. Drodanis had watched and complimented his son's work on the ambush in Ledaygen. Most of the other characters, in awe of all they had heard about the legendary quests and adventures of the old war leader, shied away from him.

"Father!" Delrael called. Drodanis looked up and tossed his flat stone to the ground. "Come here. I'd like you to help plan strategy for our next attack."

Delrael felt warm as he saw his father's face light up with sudden interest. "I would be honored to offer my thoughts."

Tayron Tribeleader went alone off the quest-path into the steep rocks. The rest of the army didn't see him leave. A few of the khelebar watched; they made solemn nods.

Using his agile panther body, Tayron climbed into a sheltered place, a kind of amphitheater he had found. Shallow soil and some grass stood in the middle of a ring of rocks, a place where water trickled down, where the winds did not blast too fiercely—and where the new Father Pine could have a home.

He placed the wooden pot beside him on a flat rock and bent down to scoop a depression in the soil.

"It will be a hard life for you here," he said to the tree, "but a hard life makes us strong. You are the last survivor of Ledaygen. I know you have the power within you."

He planted the tree and patted the damp soil back into place. The tree would live.

"No one knows you are here," he said. "That may protect you."

Tayron climbed out of the amphitheater of rocks and stood looking down at the tiny pine. "Perhaps one day we shall return and find that this entire hex has become a great forest."

Drodanis waited until Siya and the older characters from the village had finished serving the midday meal before he came up to her to get his own rations.

He remembered some characters from his days at the Stronghold: Sitael, the thin, grumpy tanner and Mostem, the overweight baker. It pained him to see how much they had changed, and it made Drodanis wonder if he had changed as much in their eyes.

Siya seemed worst of all. She had always been somewhat stern and humorless. Drodanis couldn't understand what Cayon had found so endearing about her, but Cayon had probably considered it a challenge to win the heart of someone so totally unlike himself. Siya had always disliked Drodanis, or so he thought, and she had not spoken to him since he had returned to Delrael's army.

"Are you avoiding me, Siya?" he asked as she gave him a plateful of potatoes and stewed dried meat. She plopped a hard biscuit on top.

Siya took a deep breath and faced him squarely. Her gaze looked very sharp. "Drodanis, you remind me of things I'd rather not think about. When Cayon and Fielle both died, you ran away from it all. Some of us chose to accept our lives and move ahead as best we could." She put her hands on her narrow hips.

"When I see Vailret march out on quests and adventures, I can't help but remember how Cayon died on that foolish errand with you. Why couldn't you have gone ogre hunting by yourself?"

Drodanis could understand her attitude. He had thought similar things himself. "Siya, I've found it's better to remember the good times and hold them close to your heart rather than to relive the pain over and over. It took me a long time to understand that."

Siya served herself from the remaining food but did not taste any of it. She kept watching Drodanis. The other characters had backed away, leaving them to their discussion.

"Thinking of the good times only intensifies the pain of what I have lost."

But Drodanis couldn't help himself from smiling. "Oh, Siya! Don't you remember that archery tournament we held when Cayon was courting you? He and I had equal scores, and in the last round he lost by a single point because he was busy showing off to you rather than paying attention to his aim? Or how about the time when we explored the abandoned mine shafts in the western hills? And that Slac treasure pit Cayon found, and that special emerald brooch he gave you—it might have been from an old Sorcerer queen, Lady Maire perhaps."

Drodanis laughed at his memories. "Remember that cursed opal he found! It turned his skin bright blue and the color didn't go away for more than a month! Just think of all the treasure we brought back, all the monsters we slew, and all the adventures we had." He drew a deep breath and felt his eyes sparkling. He seemed so alive just remembering these things. "Ah, those were the good days."

She took her plate and went off by herself. "No," she said over her shoulder, "they were not."

*   *   *

Before the army could break camp and march ahead, hoofbeats rang out on the mountain path. A Black Falcon rider came around the overhang of rocks and approached Delrael.

He stood up, waiting to see what the rider wanted. The nearby fighters tensed. Some put their hands on weapons, but Delrael waved them down.

As the rider came near, Delrael recognized Corim. The large blond man looked weary, scraped and bruised. His armor was nicked and tattered. His scabbard was gone, leaving only frayed leather thongs on the saddle of his black horse. The sword's blade was notched and stained with dried blood, as if Corim had made no effort to clean it. The horse itself bore many wounds; foam flecked back from its lips.

"Delrael, I must speak with you," he said.

Before Delrael could say anything, he heard a *click* and then a whistle of something flying through the air.

A crossbow bolt suddenly sprouted in the base of Corim's throat, just below the larynx. The rider's eyes widened. He kept one hand on the reins of his horse as he reached up to claw at his neck. Blood gushed from his skin, dribbling down into the black armor.

With his fingers still clenched around the reins, Corim opened his mouth wide and tried to suck in a breath. His horse snorted and bucked backward.

Corim tilted sideways and slid off the saddle like melting wax. He coughed as he struck the rocks on the ground. His horse backed away.

Delrael ran toward him, as did several other fighters.

Three men grabbed Kellos and pulled him into the air, yanking his crossbow away. The ylvan flailed. "Who denies me the right? Who denies me!" Kellos shouted. His voice remained hoarse and high pitched.

Corim coughed, and blood came out of his mouth. His eyes stared upward without seeing, but apparently he knew Delrael stood beside him.

"Was coming to offer help," the Black Falcon man whispered without using his voice. "Join forces."

The fighters brought the struggling Kellos over to Delrael. The black horse backed away farther until it stood against the rock wall. Delrael snarled at the ylvan leader, "I should throw you over a cliff!"

Kellos broke free of the fighters' grip. "He killed fifty of my people!"

"And Siryyk's army just might kill the rest of them," Delrael snapped back. "We could have used help from the Black Falcons."

Corim's hand snatched out to grab the ylvan's thin arm in a death spasm. The Black Falcon clenched his hand. Kellos tried to squirm away, but he could not break the man's grasp. Corim shuddered. The blood pouring from his throat slowed and glistened in the sun.

Kellos struggled and then drew a dagger from his belt and used the blade to pry up Corim's dead fingers.

Delrael turned to see that other Black Falcon riders had arrived and stared at their dead leader in anger. They muttered and drew their weapons. One man pointed at the ylvan. "We claim vengeance!"

Delrael balled his fists, feeling as if he had lost control of everything. His own army tensed, drawing their weapons but not certain which side to take. The other Black Falcon riders looked as battered and injured as Corim had; one woman carried her arm bound in a sling, and a man had blood-soaked rags tied over one eye.

"No," he said, "I've had enough of this. Kellos claimed his own vengeance. This feud is now over. We have a real enemy to worry about."

He glared at the Black Falcon riders, daring them to question him. "Corim's last words to me were about joining forces, not about getting revenge. Will you listen to him or not?"

The Black Falcon Troops sat rigid on their mounts,

waiting for someone to make the first move. Finally, the woman with the injured arm said, "Only twenty of us remain. You were right when you described the threat of this demon army. The Black Falcon troops attacked them." She hung her head, then fell silent.

The man with the bloody eyepatch continued for her. "They defeated us. We had to flee. We took a great toll on them, but they were too many. An enemy like that demands different tactics than the Black Falcons generally use. We argued among ourselves, but Corim insisted that we join forces with you, because your army is large enough to have a significant impact on the horde."

Kellos bristled. "How do we know they won't just cut the throats of my people at night? And of the khelebar, too?"

Delrael looked at the ylvan man. "How do we know you won't do the same to them? I said *enough of this!* We have a battle to worry about."

"We have no leader," said the woman with the sling.

"Delrael," Drodanis spoke softly, but the words carried even without his raising his voice. When he stood, the massive fighter looked the match of any of the Black Falcon riders. "I command no troops of my own. If these brave fighters will have me, I swear I'll lead them to a victory greater than any of my other quests."

The Black Falcon riders looked at Drodanis with unreadable expressions. Drodanis snatched the mane of Corim's black horse. Delrael knew his father would make good on the promise.

In the deep night, the horses of the Black Falcon troops grew restless after waiting in the same spot. They snorted and stamped their feet in the cold mountain air.

"Keep them quiet!" Drodanis hissed.

Other Black Falcon riders tried to shush their animals. Drodanis sat back against the rough granite and stared up at the stars, waiting. He always hated this part of battle, the waiting in ambush.

The narrow quest-path wound along a treacherous ledge. The sheer cliff dropped into a jagged canyon where, during the day, they had watched a frothy mountain stream churning over boulders and rockfalls. Now, in the darkness, they could only hear the whisper of distant water echoing up through the canyon.

At the mouth of the gorge, on a wide plateau, Drodanis could see fires burning in Siryyk's encampment. Many of the monsters who had survived the trap in Ledaygen probably never wanted to see fire again. They would shiver in the cold instead, demoralized from their defeat in the forest.

Drodanis stood up to flex his legs and fingers. He felt cold to the bone, but he had endured much worse in other campaigns. "Everybody get ready," he said. The Black Falcon riders snapped to their positions. These fighters impressed Drodanis. They would be a good team for his quick, vicious assault.

"We'll charge in, light our arrows from their own fires, and ride through, setting the tents and their food ablaze. Kill whoever stands in your way, but remember: our object is to destroy their supplies, not to engage the monsters." He paused. "In case you don't think that's a worthy target, remember they have a large army, but no magic users to replenish their supplies, as we do. They can't find enough other food in mountain terrain. This will be a very severe blow to them. Finally . . ." He smiled, but in the starlight he realized that few of them could see anything other than his silhouette. "The point is to lure them out where the rest of our army can take care of them."

He mounted up on Corim's horse. He made sure that he had securely fastened his rag-wrapped spears to the side of his saddle. He withdrew his long sword

from its scabbard and held it in his right hand. Steady-
ing himself on the horse, he looked back and saw that
all twenty of the Black Falcon riders waited for him to
signal.

"Remember Rule #1!" he said, then urged his horse
into motion. "Go!"

The twenty-one horses thundered along in single file
on the quest-path. They split up at their designated
branches on the trail, then rode hard along the sides of
the plateau, appearing over the lip just as the monsters heard them approach.

Drodanis and the three riders behind him galloped
past the first line of scrambling monsters, directly
toward a small campfire. Drodanis kept the horse on
track with pressure from his knees as he swung with
the sword in one hand and pulled out the two spears in
his other.

The creatures shouted among themselves, not certain what was happening.

Drodanis jammed the ends of his two cloth-wrapped
spears into the fire and circled the blaze, keeping the
tips buried in the embers until the spears flared up like
torches. He jerked both shafts high. In a reflex, he
slashed with his sword at a Slac who staggered toward
him with reptilian claws extended. The tip of Drodanis's
blade caught the hollow under its scaled chin and
ripped the bottom of the monster's jaw off.

Without slowing, Drodanis turned his horse toward
the supply tents. He heard shouts and saw other Black
Falcon riders appearing on different parts of the plateau. They charged up, yelling their own cries of challenge and victory.

Flaming arrows thunked into some of the piled sacks.
Drodanis threw his own spears into a patched, oil-
stained tent. Flames crackled and ate up the side of
the enclosure; the stains on the cloth flared more
brightly than the rest.

He saw five Slac converge on one Black Falcon

rider, the woman with her arm in a sling. She bore a flaming spear and jabbed it at them. Without both arms, she could not use a bow. She flailed the torch in the creatures' faces.

Drodanis urged his horse to come to her aid, but before he could close half the distance, the Slac had grabbed her. They hacked the legs of her horse, causing it to tumble. She fell on the ground, and they surrounded her. All Drodanis could see was a blur of Slac weapons, blood, and nothing of the fallen rider.

The tents blazed more brightly. He saw in the center of the camp a gigantic form, the manticore stirring. Drodanis felt fear crawl down his spine. The monster stood immense, ten times the size of the ogre that had killed his brother Cayon. To destroy such an opponent, Drodanis thought, would be the greatest challenge any fighter could have.

But he had no hope of doing that now. Battling Siryyk himself would have to wait for another time.

"Riders, turn about!" Drodanis cried. "Back!" He charged toward the edge of the plateau, to the quest-paths marking their route back. He looked at the sky and saw a tinge of dawn just breaking there. He had timed it perfectly.

One of the smaller pavilions burned and then exploded with an enormous concussion. Flames belched out, knocking the nearby monsters flat. Others ran about, beating at fire on their garments. The Black Falcons had destroyed part of the supply of firepowder as well. Drodanis grinned—an unexpected plus.

"Ride!" he shouted again.

His horse, deafened by the explosions, obeyed easily and charged toward the rocky path. Drodanis let the horse lead itself, because the flames had dazzled his own eyes.

The other attackers also rode back out of the camp, striking and slashing as the monster horde scurried into motion. The creatures gathered their weapons and ran after the humans.

Drodanis didn't look back. He saw four Black Falcons ahead of him galloping down the quest-path. He heard other riders behind, mixed with the snarls and shouts of pursuing monsters. They rode long and hard, knowing their horses could easily outdistance most of Siryyk's fighters.

The dawn grew brighter, but the narrow trail forced them to pick their path with care. Below, still in deep shadow, gurgled the rushing stream; the sheer cliffs forced them to continue in single file. The monsters might be able to catch up, but the riders could battle well on this narrow path.

Drodanis didn't gain distance too rapidly. He wanted Siryyk to see exactly where they had come from. Seeing only a few riders, the manticore would suspect vengeance-seeking survivors from their earlier skirmish with the Black Falcons and would follow straight into Delrael's army hidden on top of the bluffs.

Drodanis looked ahead and behind as they moved along. He counted eighteen. "We have lost two, then," he said.

The rider ahead turned back and nodded. "Acceptable losses."

Drodanis watched the still-burning fires in Siryyk's encampment. Not many of the monsters seemed to be following them. They were probably getting together for a massive march, just as Drodanis had hoped.

He felt exuberant. He wondered how he could have stayed away from the Game for so long. He felt more important now than since before Fielle and Cayon had died. He'd forgotten why he was a character on Gamearth. Now he remembered what it was all about.

Blood spattered his face, and his arms ached from the effort of the fight, but Drodanis grinned. He would not have traded this night for anything.

* * *

Siryyk the manticore stood with his lips peeled back. Anger made a deep gurgle in his throat as he tried, but failed, to find words that expressed his outrage. Whoever kept attacking them seemed to have only a few fighters, but still Siryyk's army continued to fail.

A third of his fighters were burned to death in a forest fire, then seventy-three monsters were killed by a group of black-clad human riders. After the human riders had fled, Siryyk himself had counted the fallen enemy. Ten humans! They had killed seventy-three monsters and lost only ten of their own!

Now all of Siryyk's supplies were burning after yet another attack.

His scorpion tail sparked blue. He padded forward to a blazing tent and clawed away the fabric that sheltered their meat and grain. The fire burned his fingers, but he didn't feel it. He winced as he attempted to hurl smoking sacks away from the blaze.

His head ached and burned, and the vision in one eye seemed milky. Siryyk knew that his entire face swelled and festered from the venomous smoke Enrod had blasted into his eyes. Another twenty of Siryyk's fighters had died then.

Scartaris had controlled all their minds when he assembled the tremendous horde, but Scartaris had apparently not deemed it necessary to create an army of fighters with more than minimal skills and intelligence.

General Korux came up to him. "Siryyk, we have located the ones who attacked us. We can see them on a quest-path going across the cliff. Do you wish us to follow them?"

The manticore whirled. Other monsters leaped out of the way of his swinging electric tail. "Of course!" But then he stopped. "No, show me."

Korux led him to the edge of the plateau, where he

looked into the growing dawn to see tiny figures working their way along the sheer rock wall. "Bring me Professor Verne instead. Have a Slac team bring the cannon around to the edge. Do we have any firepowder left?"

"We have lost half of it, but just in case of such an incident I made sure it was not all stored together." He rubbed his rough hands together as if congratulating himself. "We still have enough to fire the cannon several times."

"Do it, then."

Siryyk paced and watched as the huge black cylinder trimmed with frilly bronze "stabilizing struts" rolled forward on its tall wheels. The Slac steered it and tilted its barrel toward the black figures fleeing along the cliff wall.

Korux came up with his scaled hand wrapped into the folds of Professor Verne's torn shirt. The professor shivered and struggled. His hands were tied behind him and bled at the wrists. Since his escape attempt, they had kept Verne bound and hidden most of the time. Siryyk flared his nostrils. How ironic it would have been if the human fighters had burned the professor's tent and killed the captive.

"I thought you might like to watch," the manticore said. "We're going to test your cannon on a real target."

Verne saw the escaping riders and stammered, but he apparently could think of nothing to say.

"Why are they moving so slowly?" Siryyk asked. He felt suspicion growing in him.

"Gives us time to load the cannon," Korux said. He gestured at the Slac who were already pouring firepowder into the breech and hoisting up one of the huge cannonballs.

"Aim high," Siryyk said. "It's far away, and we must strike the right place to cause the most damage."

The Slac team took turns sighting along the barrel, adjusting and readjusting. Korux finally stood behind the cannon, nodded, and went back to one of the scattered campfires. He returned carrying a burning stick in his hand.

"It's ready, Siryyk."

"Any advice, Professor?" the manticore asked.

Verne mumbled, and then shrugged. "Fire the cannon if you like, but it will fail. Your powder is damp and cold. You could damage the cannon by using it now."

Siryyk laughed. "A nice try, Professor. But ridiculous. Korux, you may fire!"

The Slac general brought the end of his stick to the touchhole, then dropped it and leaped backward, covering his ears. A huge explosion knocked the cannon backward a full ten feet, rolling over one of the Slac and crushing his legs.

Siryyk decided he would have to remember to chock the wheels with stones next time.

He stared across the gorge with his one good eye. It would take a second or two for the ball to find its target. The time stretched out longer and longer. He saw the distant explosion well before he heard the crack and rumble.

Directly above the line of human fighters, the cannonball struck the overhanging rock. The rock splintered and, with a slow rumble, an entire side of the cliff came down in an avalanche.

Some of the monsters cheered. Korux clapped his hands. The smoke and rock continued to slide downward into the gorge below. The entire ledge broke away, sloughing down as it gathered momentum. The grinding avalanche knocked away every single character on the path, crushing them, sweeping them toward the foaming river far below. Dust clouds swirled and sank downward.

The manticore turned, grinning a twisted smile at Professor Verne. Verne stood with his jaw hanging open, eyes wide, and his face completely ashen.

"Your cannon is not very sporting, Professor," Siryyk said. "But it's quite fun nevertheless."

INTERLUDE: OUTSIDE

Tyrone rattled the knob on the front door, then fiddled with the lock and tried again. "Your door's stuck, David."

David remained sitting on the floor with his back against the easy chair. He drew his knees up against his chest. Even with his sweater back on, he felt cold, and the fire did nothing to warm him. He didn't look at Tyrone.

Tyrone tugged at the door and banged it with his fist. "I just wanted to get some cookies out of the car. What did you do, David?"

"I didn't do anything." His voice remained low enough to vanish in the noise from the fire.

Scott looked at him strangely, then stood up from the carpet. He walked through the kitchen to the door that led into the garage. "Yes," David thought, "Scott knows. He's figured it out."

Melanie remained hunched protectively by the map, making sure David stayed away from it. He sat off to the side like a pariah. His cheek still stung, though the bandage had stanched the bleeding.

Scott rattled the door to the garage, but it, too, was locked. He hurried to the patio door but couldn't open the latch.

"The Game won't let you out of here until it's finished," David said. But Scott went through all the motions anyway. David felt tired and defeated, still angry at the Game and at his companions.

"We're locked in!" Scott finally said.

Tyrone appeared astonished but not quite afraid. "How did the doors get locked? We were all sitting right here."

Scott went to pick up the phone. He hesitated with it in his hand, as if afraid to lift it to his ear.

"The line's dead," David said.

Scott listened into the phone, shook the receiver and put it to his ear a second time. He refused to hang it up. His eyes grew wider.

"Tyrone," he suggested, "why don't you turn on the TV?"

"What for? Shouldn't we get back to the Game?"

"Just turn on the television!"

Tyrone shrugged and walked across the family room. He found the remote control and stepped back, looking to find the power switch. He pushed it. With a buzz, the television came on, but they heard no sound. In a moment, a colorful picture appeared, a test pattern made up of bright hexagons.

"This is really getting wild!" Tyrone whispered.

Melanie glanced at the television, then looked back at the map.

"What did you expect?" David asked.

"Shut it off, Tyrone."

Instead, Tyrone flicked through the channels, but the same pattern showed on each one.

On the last channel, though, the pattern dissolved into static. As they watched, a vague figure of a young man snapped in and out of focus, as if from a signal very far away. Through the roaring distortion, David heard faint words. "Where am I? Let me go back! Is all this *real*?"

Melanie crept forward on her knees, but seemed afraid to touch the picture. "Oh no," she whispered.

"Are you the Rulewoman?" the image said and then vanished, leaving only featureless, multicolored electrical snow.

Scott put the phone to his ear again and listened, and his eyes fairly bugged out of their sockets. "My god, it's Lellyn!" Scott slammed the phone back down and unclipped the cord from the wall.

Then he grabbed the TV remote out of Tyrone's hands and punched the power button off.

David let his eyes fall closed and tried to remember other times when he had been away from the Game. When he had gone to stay with his mother in the summer, the group had had to postpone their weekly adventures. His mom always wanted to play cards or cribbage with him. He had spent time with his father on the beach, going into the city, or tagging along at some of his dad's business picnics.

His dad, trying to make him into the stereotypical version of the all-American boy, insisted that he play baseball or football or just plain catch. His father disliked David's obsession with role-playing games, as if they weren't "acceptable" things to play.

But this Game had gone far beyond any of that.

Tyrone held up his half-empty plate of dip, extending it toward Scott. "You want some more dip while we figure this out?"

"No, dammit!" Scott smacked the plate out of Tyrone's hands, and it toppled onto the carpet. "Can't you get it through your thick head what's going on here? This is serious, man!"

Tyrone looked shocked and upset. His big brown eyes swam with a turmoil of emotions, fighting back tears.

David got to his knees and crawled toward the map. Melanie stiffened into a defensive position. She splayed her hands out like protective claws, but David ignored her.

Tyrone got some paper towels from the kitchen and started cleaning up the mess on the carpet, glaring at Scott. "Just leave it," David said. "We've got more important things to do."

Scott and Tyrone both stared at him. David brought his voice back to a normal level. "We have to play this through to the end."

He picked up the dice from the carpet and extended them toward Scott. "Now it's clear *exactly* what the stakes are."

18

BROKEN RULES

*We all carry the greatest power on Gamearth.
We have our minds. We have our imaginations.
With these tools, we can accomplish anything.*
         —handwritten note found
           in abandoned quarters of
           Mayer, daughter of Dirac

Throughout the night, the gusty mountain wind lifted a metal flange and let it fall against the Outsiders' ship, sending echoes and screeches through the corridors. Mayer attempted to track down the source, furious at the annoyance. But the sound traveled through the bulkheads, distorted and magnified by the thin walls, and she could not find where the noise came from.

Finally, without the energy to go farther, she curled up in a sheltered corner where the air remained still but cold. Her nose was red and numb. She tried to rest with her fingers curled together and fists under her chest to keep warm. The air inside the ship seemed frigid enough to be brittle.

Mayer sniffled and closed her eyes. She concentrated on keeping her teeth from chattering. "I can endure this," she said. "Other characters do it."

She cursed herself for not having worn warmer clothes and for not having brought some sort of heater (which might or might not have worked here anyway). She hadn't the slightest idea how to start a fire from scratch, without matches or a galvanic igniter. She had been so wrapped up in the problem of solving Sitnalta's crisis that she had ignored the mundane matters of preparation and survival.

After a long time, her body warmed the floor enough that she did not feel completely uncomfortable. Mayer fell asleep.

For several nights, she had done the same, while during the day she continued her excavation work. Each time the sun set and darkness fell like a dropped curtain over the mountains, the warmth leaked away into the night.

The brooding Slac citadel loomed over the ruined ship. Mayer could have found shelter there, but she felt more comfortable away from the claustrophobic chambers with spikes on the doors and windows. Not that stories of ancient Slac and their torturings of human characters frightened her. But she preferred the tarnished metal, the indecipherable controls, and the winding corridors of the ship. It seemed more like Sitnalta.

When daylight leaked through the cracks of the hull, Mayer blinked her eyes and felt the stiff aches of her body. The wind outside had died down with dawn, and the persistent flange ceased its rhythmic squeaking.

She stood up, cracking the stiffness from her joints and spine. Her eyes had gummed shut, and she blinked several times, pawing at her face. Mayer didn't admit to herself how miserable she felt. None of that mattered. She had work to do.

The first Sitnaltan team had left the ship before finishing their work. Though Mayer was only one character with one pair of hands and one set of crude tools that she had managed to improvise from among the debris, she would find the answer in here somewhere. She could still save her city.

Sitnalta held the future for all of Gamearth. In this city, human characters imagined progressive ways to solve their problems without relying on magic and superstition. Mayer knew their ultimate destiny, though many Sitnaltans did not understand it yet, not even her own father.

Several years before, Mayer had proposed an idea that she felt would mark Sitnalta's mission on Gamearth. She was young but had several inventions already to her credit. Because she was the daughter of Dirac, he succeeded in getting her a hearing before the Council of Patent Givers.

When she stood before the gathered professors, she felt nervousness slink into her stomach. Seated men and women carried storming ideas behind their eyes; just the sight of them filled her with awe. She had always imagined that she herself would someday be part of this auspicious body. Now she had to make a good first impression.

Dirac stood at his podium and smiled, fluttering his hands. He looked foolish, but that was his personality and his manner. Everyone understood that.

"My daughter proposes a topic for debate," Dirac said. "I don't know what it is myself, but she assures me it is of great importance." He smiled and drummed his short fingers on the podium. "Very well, Mayer, let us hear it."

Mayer drew herself up and tossed her head. Her short, dark hair fell neatly into place. She maintained a serious expression, controlling her emotions. She wanted to emulate the fire she saw in Professor Frankenstein's eyes, the passion he had for his ideas. She stepped forward.

"Remember to clear your throat," Dirac whispered as he brushed past her, "or they won't take you seriously!"

She cleared her throat, then began her speech. She had rehearsed it a dozen times already.

"Distinguished inventors of Sitnalta, let me begin by telling you a story you already know. The race of old Sorcerers ruled Gamearth with magic's iron hand. After they had brought destruction to the map, they gathered their remaining magic together and forced themselves to . . . to evolve. They transformed their collective consciousness into a set of enormous gestalt beings, the Earthspirits and Deathspirits. They called this magical process the 'Transition'—a rather technical term for a very unscientific process."

She stopped and looked around the tiered chamber. Some of the professors shifted restlessly. Sitnaltans rarely paid heed to tales of uninteresting events of the past. Magical deeds, whether failures or successes, simply did not pertain to their lives.

"Now," Mayer continued, "we Sitnaltans pride ourselves that anything the primitive magic users could accomplish, we can do equally well or better with our own inventions. No need for hands waving and gibberish-mumbling spells. We can do better with science.

"I believe that we of Sitnalta should focus our efforts into finding a way, through the Rules of science, to create such a 'Transition' for *us*, for human characters. It will free our minds from the bonds of the map and launch us forward into the future. It is a destiny on which all human characters should take pride. Imagine the challenge!"

Mayer raised her head a little and half closed her eyes in reverence as she finished. The other professors murmured among themselves. She felt relieved for that at least: her greatest fear had been that the Council of Patent Givers would greet her proposal with total silence. She had at least sparked a debate.

Professor Darwin rapped his palm on the polished railing in front of him, signaling that he wished to comment. "What Mayer suggests is interesting. The characters best equipped to survive on Gamearth will indeed survive. But I am a bit skeptical about this sudden shift, since evolution must be a gradual process of adaptation and change. This sudden 'Transition' may be too rapid for any of us to endure."

Mayer looked to see her father's reaction, and in surprise she saw that he knitted his eyebrows, trying to fight back a scowl.

"Mayer, you must remember," he said, "that we know nearly nothing about this 'Transition' that the old Sorcerers inflicted upon themselves. In order for us to create an improved technological substitute, we must know all the details about the process we are trying to emulate. None of us has wasted our time studying the way mumbo jumbo spells operate on the rest of the map. Our efforts are focused toward driving the stain of magic away! What you suggest smacks a little too much of sorcery and gobbledygook to me. I'm not sure our technology is fitted to this purpose."

Professor Clarke cleared his throat and stood up. He was a tall man with a broad face and thick, black spectacles. "You are splitting hairs, Dirac," he said. "Any sufficiently advanced technology is indistinguishable from magic."

The other Council members broke into a hubbub of discussion. Dirac allowed this to continue for a few moments, then rapped his hands on the podium again.

"My daughter has given us an interesting theoretical idea to ponder. At the moment it is eminently impractical, for we do not know enough about the Rules or about magic to implement it." Then he smiled at her, and she hated him for it. "But it does show good imagination, and many of us had worse ideas as our first experience with the Council. She is still young, but I think she shows promise."

He began to clap for her. Mayer's skin flushed as she turned away. The scattered applause in the Council of Patent Givers seemed like mocking laughter to her ears.

She is still young.

She would show them.

Mayer spent that day digging out a half-buried corridor deep beneath the ground where the ship had come

to rest. The other cabins that she excavated yielded
nothing but small items of furniture and seemingly
nonfunctional gadgets she could not understand. As
she worked, she hummed and mumbled to herself.

Gamearth had begun to fall apart. If she found a
way for the characters of Sitnalta to emulate the Transition, Mayer could free them from much more than
just the invisible manipulator beneath the city.

She thought of the Outsiders playing their games,
creating a race of characters, the old Sorcerers, who
used their magic in the Transition. The Spirits then
supposedly went off to create their own worlds and
play their own games.

Something about that idea disturbed Mayer, tickled
the back of her mind. But then she drove down into
the caked dust with her digging implement and heard
a *clang* where no wall should have been.

Mayer stopped as the echo died away because it was
muffled in the dirt and debris. She smiled, suspecting
she had encountered something significant . . . exactly
what she had been hoping to find. Mayer wanted to
use both hands and claw the dirt away as fast as she
could, but she forced herself to be calm and patient.
She didn't want to damage what she found. The anticipation felt delicious.

Mayer uncovered the great hinge of a heavy bulk-
head door with a round locking valve set in the center
like a steering wheel. As she brushed the dirt away,
she saw that the door was a dull brownish red; it had
probably been bright as an alarm once. Her thrill
grew.

During the first expedition, she had uncovered the
ship's control room. Professors Frankenstein and Verne
had dismantled it to construct their mysterious weapon.
Now she had found something else.

Mayer used both hands to grip the locking valve and
attempted to turn it. She had to use her digging implement as a lever to crack the seal. She cranked the

round wheel until a hissing sound burst from the door as it unseated from its airseal.

Had she perhaps found the living quarters of the Outsiders? That didn't make sense, for the Outsiders had not truly come here but only sent manifestations of themselves because they were *real*. And the Game was not.

Somehow this ship sat on not just the technological fringe between science and magic, but also in some sort of zone between Gamearth and *reality*. Perhaps the Rules lay bent and twisted here.

Maybe she was about to see what the old Sorcerers had seen when they suddenly became the great Spirits.

Mayer pulled open the heavy metal door, closed her eyes, then stepped into the darkness. Silvery light shimmered around her as she entered the chamber.

Mayer stood in a hall of mirrors.

Each angled facet of the wall carried its own crystalline reflection. Mayer stepped further in and saw thousands of images of herself unfold. Each of the mirrors had angled the reflections on top of each other, overlapping, extending into an infinite kaleidoscope of images within images within images. Though she stood alone, Mayer felt surrounded by an enormous crowd of herself. Her dark eyes widened in awe as she turned around, staring.

Then she noticed that the images were not all the same. Some appeared subtly different in her bodily position, her motions, the clothes she wore. In one she saw long dark hair, in another she saw a scar on her face. In some, her expression appeared lined with deep sadness and trauma; in others, filled with delight.

Mayer blinked with shock, as did most of her images. She couldn't tell which image truly reflected herself. These were all images of her, all Mayer, but all different, an unending series of Mayer characters.

"Is this some sort of game?" she said out loud. Her voice echoed much more than it should have, as if a thousand overlapping Mayer images had each spoken the same thing.

She considered a cruel trick the Outsiders might play, toying with their own creations. However, one set of their creations had evolved and gone on to play their own games, to create their own characters.

As Mayer stopped and looked into the endless versions of herself, she felt an intuition exploding in her mind. One of her other images expressed it before she could form the words.

"It goes on and on. In both directions!"

Another image interrupted. "The Outsiders create the old Sorcerers. The old Sorcerers go on the Transition, and then they create their own games, their own characters . . . who then go on to create their games."

"And on and on," said a new Mayer. "We're seeing only a few links in an endless chain."

"The Outsiders themselves must have some sort of gods, some external Players that manipulate their actions. And those gods in turn have *their* versions of the Outsiders."

"It never ends!" said several Mayers at the same moment.

"The only thing that remains throughout," Mayer said herself, and the other images stopped to listen to her, "is the Game! It's all a Game, the whole universe, no matter who we are or what level we play in. The Game moves through—a game within a game."

"Within a game."

"Within a game."

The phrase repeated and echoed, growing stronger and louder as if each version of Mayer had to say the same thing.

One of the mirrors shattered, sending shards of glass spilling outward, falling to the floor as the image of that Mayer vanished, leaving only a flat black spot on the wall.

"Within a game."

Another mirror shattered, and another. Flying glass filled the air. The explosions grew louder as the mirrors crumbled. Images of Mayer disappeared.

She turned, covering her ears, trying to duck to keep the glass away from her eyes. The door behind her had vanished. She saw nothing, only the mirrors as they exploded again and again. Mayer tried to run, but she had no place to go.

"Within a game."

A mirror beside her broke, and a long dagger of glass bounced next to her feet, but somehow she didn't cut herself. One reflection of Mayer—with long hair braided in green ribbons—shrank back with a shocked expression on her face, and then she, too, shattered.

In the black void behind the mirror stood a young man, his form wavering as if he could barely remember himself. His clothes appeared wet. His eyes were wide and shining, as if they knew too much from within. "Only you and I understand," he said to her. "Not even the Outsiders can see this."

Mayer froze in utter terror, completely without understanding—or perhaps understanding too much. She opened her mouth to scream.

"Let me show you the way out," Lellyn said and extended a hand to her. "Out of the Game."

And then Mayer felt the razor of pain bursting through her entire body, as she herself shattered.

19

ICE FORTRESS

"I won't care about the Game after I am gone, as long as I have fun while I'm here. I want to die a hero."

—Cayon, in a quest-telling
at the village gaming hall

The Game held no interest for Delrael anymore. He sat listlessly polishing and sharpening his sword. The rest of his army bustled about, preparing for their surprise attack on Siryyk's approaching horde.

Now that the avalanche had destroyed the quest-path along the side of the cliff, the monster army would have to ascend the steep bluffs overlooking the canyon. Delrael's army waited out of sight. Siryyk would walk right into the trap.

Normally, Delrael would have been excited at the prospect of such an easy, surprise blow. But all he could think of was the distant cannon explosion; all he could see was the sliding rock, the scrambling Black Falcon figures helpless on the narrow ledge, the avalanche crushing and sweeping them all away.

Now he had lost his father twice.

Romm came up to him. "The monster army is moving. They're already climbing the slope. I'm sure they don't know we're here." He paused, as if waiting for Delrael to say something else, but Delrael only looked at him.

Romm continued. "We've got the first line of defenses set up. All the archers are ready. The other fighters are anxious—this is the first battle for most of them, you know."

"Good," Delrael made himself say.

"It shouldn't be too long now," Romm said again. "The monsters are halfway up the slope."

Delrael realized that the scout wanted him to get up and inspect the fighters, to encourage them, to lead them in the attack. "They know what to do," he said instead. "Wish them luck."

Romm looked crestfallen and turned to go. He stopped and said over his shoulder, "I'm sorry about your father, Delrael. I'm also sorry I didn't recognize him at first."

"Thank you, Romm."

The scout left to join the others. Delrael stared at his own clean sword. As a commander, he had no right to act this way. He had destroyed far more of Siryyk's soldiers in the fire in Ledaygen; Drodanis and the Black Falcon riders alone had probably killed at least an enemy apiece in their little skirmish. Delrael's losses had been minimal.

Losses were never minimal.

The wind whipped cold around the rocks, and he stood up. Gray clouds dotted the sky, growing thicker. He seemed to have lost all sense of time.

He realized Siya stood beside him, frowning with a pinched expression. She had looked mortally stunned as Drodanis fell, as if reliving her nightmares, reminded of Cayon's death all over again. But that first sorrow had hardened her, tempered her somehow.

"It was Drodanis's way of life," she said, displeased with Delrael. "It's how he wanted to die. A hero. He wanted to do something that characters would tell legends about." Delrael kept gazing at his soldiers in line near the edge of the bluff.

"Delrael," she continued, "heroes count only if they're on the winning side."

"I know," he said.

He watched his fighters pause and tense. He thought he could hear the movements of the horde below, climbing closer. Suddenly all his human fighters lunged to their feet, shouting and banging their weapons.

They pushed against the line of large boulders they had positioned at the edge of the slope. Some characters shoved with their hands, others pried with sticks. Dozens of rocks crashed down like battering rams onto the approaching army.

He heard the echoing uproar as the monsters discovered the surprise. The boulders rolled down, bouncing, smashing and kicking up stones.

Siryyk's horde gathered itself for an angry surge up the slope now that they had an enemy they could see. Delrael knew that the boulders would have crushed scores of the monsters. With this one blow, he had avenged the death of Drodanis.

But it was not enough.

The front line of fighters dropped their sticks and ran behind the second line of Delrael's fighters. They pushed to the edge of the slope, all armed with bows. They shot arrow after arrow into the helpless horde. Kellos and the surviving ylvans fired with their small crossbows.

The monsters shouted and screamed, scrambling to lift their shields. Many of them turned and tried to run back down the slope. They tripped and fell, taking others with them.

Delrael's archers kept firing. The thrum of their bowstrings sounded like an enraged hive of bees.

But then some of the other human fighters, over-anxious, drew their own weapons and charged howling down to meet the monsters. Delrael muttered to himself, upset that they placed themselves in danger before the archers had caused all the damage they could. If he had been in better control of his army . . .

"Don't give up like your father did, Delrael," Siya

interrupted him. "For all those years. And look how he paid for it."

Tayron Tribeleader, holding his polished, wooden sword in hand and leading Ydaim Trailwalker and the other khelebar, plunged over the edge and down the rocky slope. Kellos and his ylvans surged after them. The rest of the archers stopped firing, secured their bows, and joined the attack with their blades.

Delrael took his own sword, looked at its new sharpened edge, and strode toward the fighting. His characters were falling now, his fighters were being torn apart by Siryyk's monsters.

He saw the manticore seething and bounding around on the slope, striking with the blue lightning of his scorpion tail. Many of Delrael's fighters already lay scattered and dead. The monster army rallied itself and pushed upward. Ranks of Slac had lined up, using their shields as an impenetrable wall and pushing up the hill.

Delrael's fighters lost their advantage in only a few moments. They had used their surprise and sprung their traps. But the monster army greatly outnumbered the humans. Delrael had already struck his blow; they would gain nothing by remaining.

Delrael stood at the crest of the bluff and shouted orders to retreat. He stopped the rest of his eager fighters from marching over the side. Romm and several of the other fighters had already held them back, keeping them in their strategic position on top where they could strike at the monsters coming up.

"We've done our job for now!" Delrael shouted. "Retreat!"

Lightning bolts blasted into some of the monster soldiers. He looked up to see Tareah standing on a rock, holding the sapphire Water Stone in her hand.

Delrael turned to the fighters still standing on the top of the bluff. "Move! March northward along the quest-path! We must split up. We have to find time to set up another attack." He grabbed Romm by the arm. "Go to Tareah. Tell her that we need to stall the monster advance. Have her use the Water Stone to delay them. She can think of something."

Romm ran off across the rocky ground. Delrael stood on the edge and urged his fighters to get to the top and run. Many had already fallen and lay wounded. Some characters helped the injured back to the top of the slope. Little goblins swarmed over the terrain, slashing the throats of characters who lay wounded.

The monsters cried out in surprise again as water gushed from cracks in the rocks and burst out to pour down the slope, drenching them all.

Tareah stood above with her hair flying in the air. She twisted the Stone, and the pouring water crackled and froze into a slick, silvery sheet of ice. Delrael allowed himself a smile. The monsters would find it impossible to make progress up the steep bluff.

Most of the human army had made it to the top and marched away. "We have to run! Move."

Below, the horde continued to shout curses and clawed at the treacherous slope. Delrael turned and followed as his army moved. It would take some time to tally their losses.

Now Siryyk knew about the entire human army waiting to fight him.

While the monsters killed off the severely wounded left on the battlefield—their own wounded as well as the humans—Siryyk paced and thought. Much of the ice had melted. He glowered at Professor Verne, then swished his scorpion tail back and forth; the air seemed charged with the energy radiating from it. Verne appeared terrified, but tried to stand tall.

The manticore raised his right paw to swat Verne on the chest. The professor flew backward to the rocky ground with a torn shirt and long red gashes across his skin. "That was just a scratch," said Siryyk.

Verne lay sprawled next to the bloody corpse of a young human fighter who had been stabbed and then decapitated. The fighter's open-eyed head lay near his shoulder, mouth gaping dark and empty toward the sky. Verne stammered but could say nothing.

"We have only enough powder to fire the cannon a few more times, Professor."

Among the rocks and bodies on the twisted slope, General Korux and his other Slac grunted and strained as they hauled the cannon up to the top of the bluff. The tall wheels were set too wide for any path, and Korux had to push it up the smoothest part of the cliff face. Siryyk wondered if Verne had done that deliberately when he designed the cannon.

"I want you to fix the Sitnaltan weapon."

Professor Verne propped himself up with his bleeding elbows and tried to back away. "You can't use it, Siryyk! Don't you understand that it's a *doomsday device*? If the Sitnaltan weapon is triggered, then all of Gamearth and maybe even all of the Outside will be destroyed."

With a snarl, Siryyk brought his scorpion tail down to strike the headless corpse beside the professor. Blood and smoking flesh blasted out, spattering Verne.

"I will hear none of that! The weapon is mine. I want it to work. Whether I use it will be my decision. Now tell me *what* is mechanically wrong with it?"

Verne began to say something complicated and nonsensical, but Siryyk drew himself up to glare at him. The professor stopped. "The timer switch is broken. That's all. The weapon itself is undamaged. It will be trivial to fix."

"Then do it," the manticore said and swiped at him again with his paw, keeping his claws sheathed. The blow knocked Verne sideways to his knees. The professor scrambled to his feet, and two Slac grabbed his elbows, escorting him over to where the weapon waited, strapped into the battered steam-engine car.

The monsters had taken some prisoners, and Siryyk stalked about before finally gesturing at one of the Slac. The Slac snatched up a tiny, struggling man whose face looked battered; blood caked his mouth from broken teeth. The little man wore forest greens and browns that provided no camouflage at all in the stark mountain terrain. The little man's jaw dropped as he stared at the immense manticore.

"Now, captive," Siryyk said, "I want to know about this army that just attacked my troops. Where did it come from? Who is its leader? Who are you?"

"I have nothing to say to you," the little man snapped.

Siryyk glared at the Slac holding the captive. The monster grabbed the little man's hand and shoved it into his jagged reptilian mouth. The Slac bit down, twisted his chin, and snapped his head back. He spat out two of the captive's twitching fingers.

The little man screamed as blood poured from his hand.

"Who are you?" Siryyk said again. "Who leads the army?"

"I am Kellos!" the little man said, shaking either with anger or with terror; Siryyk could not tell which.

The Slac grabbed Kellos's arm again. Blood glistened from his pointed teeth. The little man snarled and struggled.

"Delrael leads the army! He commands them all. We struck at you in the forest. We ambushed you along the quest-path. We've been carving away at your army, and we will defeat you yet!"

The Slac released him, and Kellos stood, holding the bleeding stumps of his fingers against his chest to cut off the flow of blood.

Siryyk paced and turned around. "Delrael!" he muttered. His black lips twisted upward in a smile. It all became clear: the storms and the lightning and the forest fire and the ambushes. Delrael had been using his powerful Stones all along. "So, the prisoner Jathen lied to me. This is the human army, closer than we thought."

The Slac hissed, and suddenly Kellos broke into a run, trying to dodge between his captors and Siryyk's great bulk. He ran toward an opening on the slope, as if he actually had a chance to escape.

Moving faster than his enormous size would seem to allow, the manticore whirled and lashed with his coiled scorpion tail.

Kellos screamed for only a moment before the flash of blue lightning incinerated him. His blackened and sizzling body flew ten feet in the air before striking the jumbled rocks and leaving a wet black stain as it slid sideways and stopped next to a clean patch of ice.

Siryyk turned to watch Korux and the others straining to get the cannon over the lip of the slope. Most of the other monsters had managed to negotiate the ice and the treacherous rocks.

Delrael's army waited up there for him. Their surprise was over. "The Stones are in my grasp now."

Tareah pointed at the map Vailret had drawn. Delrael held it against a flat rock surface with the sun shining on it; the corners kept flapping in the cold breeze. Delrael squinted, trying to see what she meant. "It's only a couple of hexagons away," Tareah said. "We can return to the site of my father's Ice Palace."

She turned and looked at him. "*Listen* to me, Delrael! There's mountain terrain blocking us off on one side, the Northern Sea, frozen wasteland, and the Barrier River on the other side. It'll be hard on the monsters, especially since Drodanis has destroyed most of their supplies."

Delrael pondered. The rebuilt Palace would provide a defensible fortress for his army. All his fighters needed a rest after their first taste of battle, not to mention the injured characters among his troops. It seemed reasonable, but he felt uneasy; he would be trapping his own army in a place like that. He wanted room to move, to strike and run. But they had been doing that all along.

Tareah stood up. "If I go now, and hurry, and your army follows behind, I can have the Ice Palace rebuilt by the time the fighters get there."

Enrod stood beside her, intense but silent until he said, "I can use the Water Stone. I can help." Tareah stiffened, looking defensive, but then she shrugged.

Old Siya waited nearby again, listening in. She had gathered swords from several of the fallen soldiers; while the army rested, she polished them for any character who might need a new weapon.

"That's what Drodanis would suggest," she said.

Delrael had no answer to that.

Though only a distortion remained on the smooth field of ice and snow, the site of the Ice Palace shone clear in Tareah's mind. She had spent three decades there.

Her life had changed a great deal since the Palace last stood tall. She had been bound in the body of a small child, while Sardun waited for some other full-blooded Sorcerer to manifest himself. Enrod was the only other Sentinel still alive on Gamearth, but Sardun did not approve of Enrod's philosophy.

Then Tryos the dragon had blasted his way into the Ice Palace to steal Tareah. In the dragon's treasure grotto she had waited for some heroic character to rescue her, because that's what she thought she was supposed to do. All those years with Sardun had taught her the old ways of the Game. She had never questioned what he said.

And Delrael did rescue her, but she returned only to find the Ice Palace melted and collapsed. Her father had succumbed to the half-Transition, adding his spirit to the *dayid* beneath the Palace.

Now that Tareah had spent time with Vailret, Delrael, and other human characters, she had a new perspective on the Game. No longer did she merely read and chronicle the legends about other characters. She participated in the adventures herself—whenever Delrael allowed her.

She and Enrod trudged across the flat snow in the light of sunrise. They had walked the rest of the afternoon over the mountains, pushing ahead of Delrael's army, and through the night, resting for only a few hours in the coldest and darkest time before dawn.

Tareah didn't feel tired at all, but eager. She would rebuild her old home.

She stepped over the boundary of the site, noting where the great ice pillars had collapsed and where the towers had melted and fallen to crumbling blocks. When she had returned here with Delrael and the others in the Sitnaltan balloon, Sardun had left a farewell message for her.

He would be greatly surprised if he could see her now. She had grown to her full height, and her joints had stopped aching. Tareah had become her own character.

The world hung silent around them. The cold made Tareah's fingers numb, but the breeze had died away. The jagged hexagons of mountain terrain stood behind them, bounded by the black hex-line. The blue expanse of the Northern Sea channeled into the rushing hex-wide Barrier River. The air smelled clean, with other scents dampened by the snow.

"This is probably going to take all day," Tareah said.

Enrod squeezed a handful of snow until it melted through his fingers. He looked at the water dripping down.

She held the glistening sapphire cube in her hand. In the sunlight, it reflected the white ice. Holding just one of the Stones, she could use only three spells, as would Enrod when she passed the Stone to him. However, Tareah hoped she could awaken the *dayid* that lived at the site and would focus and intensify her spells far beyond anything she could do herself. With such help, Sardun had created the Barrier River.

She rolled the six-sided sapphire on the snow. The number "6" showed up, the highest she could roll. Tareah knew the *dayid* was already there helping her.

When the magic surged within her, she forced it through the facets of the Stone. She channeled the power to shape the surrounding water, ice, and snow, sculpting, pushing the towers and the parapets, making them rise tall and monolithic. She swirled the ice around into solid blue bricks.

She sucked all of the snow, mud, and debris away from the underground vaults where Sardun had kept his old Sorcerer treasures. She scoured the area clean.

Tareah rolled a "6" with each of her three spells.

For hours, she kept herself submerged in the power, building up the walls, fashioning passages, opening rooms and adapting the structure to make it more appropriate for protecting Delrael's army.

When her last spell ended and Enrod took the Water Stone from her fingers, Tareah saw him trembling. Enrod had not used a Stone since the Deathspirits stripped the Fire Stone from him. She wondered whether he felt afraid of handling that power again, that it might open up some scar within him, something that had caused him to turn evil.

She wanted to snatch the sapphire cube back. She had nearly finished the Ice Palace herself, so she didn't really need his help. Perhaps by midnight, when she would get three more spells, she could finish the construction. Delrael's army would arrive by then, but maybe the monsters would not be too close behind.

Before she could say anything, Enrod rolled the Stone. Tareah watched him become strong again as he grabbed the sapphire and turned toward the new Palace.

Numbed by her own exhaustion, Tareah leaned back, not even feeling the cold. She sat in the snow and watched the dark-haired Sentinel build the outer walls taller, make a slippery mound on all sides of the fortress, and add other defenses against the monsters. He thickened the fragile towers. He made hidden places where parts of the human army could march out and attack the unsuspecting monsters.

Enrod rolled again, and Tareah drifted into sleep . . .

When the vanguard of Delrael's army arrived, stumbling and weary, she and Enrod stood in the tallest tower and watched the army approach. The first fighters passed through the wide gap in the first wall.

Enrod gazed out at the mountains, the northern sea, the rushing Barrier River. He seemed pleased with his work. "I prepared Tairé's defenses, too," he said.

Tareah paused to hide her initial skepticism. "It looks like a blocky fortress now. Not what I remembered at all." She tried to keep a sour tone out of her words. "But I suppose it can't be a fragile monument to the Sorcerer race anymore, not for our purpose."

Enrod murmured his agreement. "A place to make a final stand."

Tareah went down to meet Delrael and the others as they came marching into the courtyard and the main lodging rooms of the rebuilt fortress. Delrael seemed extremely tired, but his eyes glistened. She could tell he felt proud of her. He stared around at the blue ice walls and grinned.

"There, Tareah," he said, "see how I'm using your abilities? I'm giving you tasks to do, just like any other fighter in my army."

He smiled, but Tareah scowled, feeling stung. What Delrael thought he was doing had not even occurred to her. "You just ruined it by pointing that out to me, Delrael, rather than just making it seem like a natural decision."

He blinked, confused by her reaction.

She went outside into the courtyard and watched
the last of the human fighters come in. She waited a
few minutes, but the hexagon of wasteland remained
empty behind them, marred only by a wide, slushy
trail where the army had marched.

Tareah raised her arms and motioned toward the
central gap in the wall where the soldiers had passed
through. By closing her eyes and letting the back of
her mind touch the magic still in the ice, she imagined
the two separated ends of the outer wall. They flowed
together into an unbroken barrier, sealing the army
safely inside the ice fortress.

At sunset, several sentries called Delrael to the watch-
towers. As they stared eastward in the long shadows
of the fading light, they could see the massive crowds
of dark figures pouring out of the mountain hexagon,
crossing the black line, and swarming over the frozen
wasteland.

Seen on the flat terrain rather than hidden by the
mountains, Siryyk's army appeared huge. They had
arrived to lay seige.

20

TUNNELS OF THE
WORM-MEN

> *"I wish the Game challenged us with only one
> enemy at a time, but the Outsiders are not so
> simplistic. As soon as we defeat one adversary,
> another takes its place."*
> —Stilvess Peacemaker

Gold stood in puddles, still soft from the heat blasting out of the nearby lava lake. The seething inferno baked Bryl's face and made his blue cloak hot to the touch. He used one hand to shield his eyes as he took another step closer. His knuckles stung from the searing air. His eyes filled with tears.

At the top of the crater high above, he could see the hole where the orange-dappled volcano walls opened to the night. But the bubbling lava heated up any cool breezes that swirled around the island.

"We don't even know that there's a *dayid* here!" Bryl said. His throat felt raw; when he sucked in a breath, his nostrils seemed on fire. His nose hairs curled. He fought back the urge to cough, because that would mean gulping in more of the heat.

"There must be!" Vailret shouted back. He stood in the shade, behind one of the large boulders. "Try anyway!"

Bryl squeezed his eyes shut and felt tears ooze down his cheek in cool lines that rapidly evaporated. "Easy for you," Bryl muttered. "You're not standing out here."

Bryl had sensed the *dayid* at the heart of the volcano. It seemed likely that he would find one here, knowing what he did about the Sentinel spirits. But the volcano's *dayid* felt small and weak, perhaps even dormant.

Bryl had to call it up and somehow speak with it.

He didn't know if he could. Bryl's parents had killed themselves in their half-Transition when he was just a boy, and he had grown up without magical training, always feeling inferior. His heritage as a Sorcerer had been denied expression for so long that he wanted to make up for it, to show all of Gamearth that he could indeed use the magic that was meant for him. He could do that if he got all four Stones and so became the Allspirit.

He thought of the *dayid* and clenched his hands around the folds of his cloak to cover the exposed skin. He squeezed his eyes shut and recalled how he had touched the *dayid* in Ledaygen by working through the Water Stone. He had to feel that power now, seek it out, and pull it into his presence.

The Earth Stone had vanished. If the *dayid* remained here, the *dayid* would know about it. The perfect ten-sided emerald was the most powerful of the four Stones.

The lava glowed orange, belched and sputtered. The air reeked of sulfur like a handful of rotten eggs smashed all at once.

"*Dayid*, show yourself!" Bryl said in the loudest voice he could manage. He didn't know what else to say. He knew no summoning spells, no binding he could place on the *dayid*. Either it would appear to him, or it wouldn't.

He felt a warm presence like melted honey reaching within him from the depths of his stomach and back, creeping up along the inside of his spine.

"Bryl, look!" Vailret said, peeping his head around the rock.

Bryl tried to shade his eyes from the oven heat. As he looked, he felt the searing temperature drop, softening and spreading out so that Bryl could stare at the center of the lava lake.

With a *pop*, a lava bubble burst, shooting a tall flame upward like an orange, feathery pillar that grew brighter, shining into the gullet of the volcano.

Bryl felt his skin tingle. The raw burns faded away; his singed hair no longer felt stiff and crumbly. "*Dayid*, I am Bryl," he said. His voice pinged off the rock wall, tiny in the vast roaring chamber. Realizing that the name would have no significance, he added, "I am son of the Sentinels Qonnar and Tristane. If you can recall some portion of your past, you must remember them."

The flame brightened and wobbled, bending toward Bryl. Images shimmered up from deep within him:

He saw flashes of his mother, his father, and a flickering series of other Sentinel faces. He recognized some of them, but most remained strangers. He saw his father and mother accused by Jarriel's widow, Galleri, of poisoning him. Bryl felt their despair, and confusion at how their good works had twisted around to strike at them. He felt other memories of the *dayid*'s components as they acknowledged Bryl's presence.

"*Dayid*, we have come for the Earth Stone. We know it was here. We must have it, or Gamearth will crumble apart. The Outsiders will put an end to the Game. You must be able to sense that hexagons are already flying off into space. It won't be long before this entire island is destroyed. With the Earth Stone, though, we can bring enough magic together to create an Allspirit."

He clamped his lips together to keep himself from babbling. He trembled with fear and awe of the presence in front of him. "Help us find the Earth Stone," he said again.

Images filled him again and congealed into an understandable message. Though his eyes still saw the fire and the lava in front of him, in another layer of vision he also watched Tryos's treasure, piles of gold coins, strings of pearls, and carvings of onyx and jade studded with sapphires, rubies, and garnets. Bryl's vision melted through layers until he saw the potent Earth Stone, as green as the heart of a leaf in the middle of summer, ten-sided, the greatest Stone of the four. Bryl felt elated to glimpse it even in this second-hand sight.

Then the *dayid* showed him other creatures, twisted forms with grayish skin, manlike torsos on bloated, serpentine bodies. The creatures had blank saucer eyes, smooth heads, and clawlike hands protruding at the wrong angles from their shoulders. He saw swarms of the worm-men, werem, tunneling up from below and breaking into the treasure vault. He watched grasping hands pluck away all the gems. They snatched the Earth Stone as well, intending to deliver it to their Master.

The visions faded. Bryl remained standing as the waves of heat returned, only this time, they felt like the heat of anger. The worm-men had stolen the Earth Stone. The *dayid* felt outrage, but had no way of fighting. Not until Bryl and Vailret had arrived.

They needed the Earth Stone back.

"But where is it? How do we find it?" he said. His throat felt dry enough to snap if he raised his voice.

The flame of the *dayid* bunched up and flickered, breaking away from the lava. It shot through the air to blast at the inner wall of the crater. Among the jagged blobs of hardened lava, the flames struck and illuminated a blotch of shadow, a passage descending into the rock.

Then the *dayid*'s flame petered out. The melted-honey sensation dissolved inside of Bryl, and he found himself unprotected in the searing heat again.

He pushed his face into the folds of cloth on his

elbows and staggered backward. He felt Vailret grab
him and pull him to the cooler sections of the grotto.

"What happened?" Vailret said. "I saw the fire and
I heard you talking, but it didn't make any sense. Did
you learn anything?"

Bryl's eyes felt red, and his entire face seemed stiff
and prickling from the shallow burns. "Yes," he said.
"I know what happened to the Earth Stone."

To Bryl, the tunnel felt dank and claustrophobic,
closing around them with stifling shadows. It plunged
down, away from the volcano and its heat. He and
Vailret stumbled along until the passage finally leveled
out, then they continued at a more normal pace.

The smooth catacombs had no branch tunnels. Bryl's
hand-held flame lasted a long time, but he lost all
sense of the passing hours. They had been too long
without seeing the stars overhead.

"Do you think it's daylight yet?" Vailret asked.

"Of which day?" Bryl said.

Vailret fell silent, walking behind his stretching
shadow. He broke the silence again. "If the werem
took all the gems, were they really interested in the
Earth Stone in the first place? I seem to recall that
they believe all gemstones belong to them."

"Seeds of the earth," Bryl said, "planted in the
rock, from which all life springs. They took the gems
to return them deep underground. But I think they
had a special purpose for the Earth Stone. The *dayid*
made me sense something that the werem call their
Master."

They continued ahead. "We have just passed another hex-line," Bryl pointed out.

Vailret turned to squint, then plodded along the
tunnel. "Is that four now?"

"I can't remember. We must be under the water
hexes already."

"We're heading in that direction."

Bryl followed him, maintaining the same pace. "Have I ever told you about Delrael's training in the old weapons storehouse?"

Vailret did not look back. Of course Vailret would remember his own storehouse training, when he had to imagine being captured by Slac, who made him fight an invisible monster in their arena.

Vailret stopped. "Del fought the worm-men, didn't he? Did he win?"

Bryl remained silent for a few moments. "Nobody wins the storehouse training," he said. "Drodanis and I set it up that way. But everyone learns."

"What did Del learn, then?" Vailret asked. Bryl could tell he just wanted to keep the conversation going, to break the tedium of their long, dark journey.

"He learned never to get captured by werem."

"It figures," Vailret said. He moved on as Bryl followed behind him with the ball of clean fire in his hand. Their shadows lurched ahead, dancing on the tunnel walls.

Bryl and Drodanis had planned young Delrael's training meticulously, using all the details they could find from legends about encounters with the werem. When they brought young Delrael into the weapons storehouse, closed the shutters, and barricaded the door, Bryl asked him, "Are you ready?"

Delrael had nodded. He looked confused, but even then he seemed ready to confront whatever problem they threw at him. Bryl blew out the candle.

"Delrael, you are camped alone beside the shore of a lake," Drodanis said from a dark corner of the room. "You have a small fire burning on the shore, and you have just finished eating. You're relaxed. Your senses are dull. You're about to go to sleep."

"Then," Bryl said, "the ground bubbles at the lake shore. Dirt spatters in the air as three worm-men tunnel out of the ground and lurch up into the moonlight. They're caked with slimy mud. They have thin arms with sharp elbows and powerful claws. Their eyes are wide and white, but the creatures are blind because they live under the ground. Their bodies are long and segmented, trailing in their holes as they lunge forward."

"What am I supposed to do?" Delrael said. Bryl could hear the alarm in his voice.

"What would you like to do?" Drodanis asked. "They come toward you from three different sides."

"I've got my sword, right? And my armor? I'm going to fight."

"Of course you are." Drodanis's voice carried a lilt of amusement.

"Pick a number between one and seven," Bryl said. "Guess right, and we'll let you defeat them."

And so Delrael had fought several rounds against the worm-men, killing one of them, but then the battle became tedious, so Drodanis had the other two werem overpower Delrael's character and drag him underground. They pulled him through the wet tunnels where dirt fell on him and mud caked his face, and he could hardly breathe. Though he continued to struggle, Drodanis wouldn't let him break free.

The werem took him through their tunnels under the lake to a large central chamber. Their emperor sat atop his bulbous coils of segments wound in a high mound beneath him.

"The emperor grows one segment for every human character he kills," Bryl said. He thought that was a nice detail.

When the werem hauled Delrael before him, the folds of the emperor's segments split. Fat, white grubs spilled from the cracks, wet and oozing mucous. They flopped along the emperor's segments and left sticky trails.

"They are the larvae of the werem," Drodanis said. "Like maggots, without the human arms and heads of full-grown worm-men. They have only a mouth filled with teeth—and the instinct to chew into a human body, to devour a character from the inside out. Only through the taste of human flesh can the larvae mature."

Though Delrael's character did break away and kill two more of the worm-men, they overpowered him again and dragged him in front of the werem emperor. Delrael struggled when they planted the larvae on his body. As he writhed and screamed and squirmed, Delrael could feel the grubs chewing into his arms, into his stomach, into his back.

Then the werem backed off and stood with their blind faces cocked toward him. Their nostril slits flared as they smelled his fear and pain.

Delrael lay on the floor and felt the larvae inside him, eating, snapping his muscles. Blood poured from his wounds.

"Once the larvae get to your heart, you will be dead," Drodanis said.

Bryl kept his voice cold. "You are dead already. You have only a few moments left of the pain as you feel the grubs devour your body."

"Can I get to my sword?" Delrael said.

Bryl hesitated, letting Drodanis decide.

"Yes. But the werem are backing away from you. You've already killed three of them. They won't stand near, and you don't have much control over your body."

"I'm going to take the blade and hack at the hardened mud pillar in the center of the chamber. The one holding up the ceiling and the water of the lake above."

"Good, Delrael!" Drodanis said. "You're weak, but the werem don't know what you're doing. You can take a few strikes at the pillar."

"Pick a number between one and five," Bryl said.

"Two."

"The pillar is starting to crack."

"I'm still swinging."

"You can feel the grubs moving inside you. They're chewing at your spine. Soon you're going to collapse," Drodanis said.

"I'm swinging again. And again!"

"Pick another number. Between one and four this time."

"Three."

"Oh, let him have it, Bryl."

"The pillar cracks more. The ceiling is starting to fissure. Water is trickling down. By now the worm-men know what you're doing, and they hurry forward. You have another strike, maybe two, with your sword before it's too late."

"I'm swinging again."

Bryl laughed. "The pillar breaks. The ceiling is crumbling. Water gushes down. The worm-men are running about, frantic."

"Do I have time for—"

"You have no time. The grubs have just eaten your heart. The last thing your eyes see is the ceiling collapsing, and the great explosion of water thundering down."

The storehouse training always disturbed Bryl. It seemed so real to the characters, this role-playing game. He was glad it remained just a game. Vailret continued to walk in silence.

But suddenly the side walls of the catacombs flaked outward, and Bryl heard scratching, clawing noises.

"What's going on?" Vailret said. Bryl's hand-light bobbed against the ceiling.

The packed-earth walls split open. Mud-covered, smooth-skinned werem burst out on either side, reaching out. Bryl stepped back, stifling a scream.

He felt a lump on the floor, and a clawed hand snapped out to grab his thin ankle. He kicked and squealed, stomping down on the worm-man's wrist.

The whole creature emerged, rising higher and flinging mud off its chest and limbs.

The worm-men trapped them, front and back.

"Use the Stones, Bryl! The Fire Stone—now!"

Bryl grabbed both Stones out of his cloak. He held the diamond and ruby in his hand, gripping the sharp corners.

But his hand refused to drop the Stones. His arm remained locked into place. He strained as much as he could, but it didn't seem to be his own hand at all.

"Roll them!" Vailret said.

The worm-men made wet clicking sounds as they slithered forward, not in any hurry at all. Their sightless eyes turned toward the captives.

"I can't! I can't move my arm!" Bryl said.

Vailret tried to turn toward him, but he froze as well. His legs locked. Vailret's neck muscles twitched and jerked as he strained, but something else held onto him, controlled his every action.

"It's the same thing that's attacking Sitnalta!" Vailret said through clenched teeth. "The invisible force, it's got us now!"

As they remained motionless, with legs together, Vailret and Bryl could offer no resistance as the werem picked them up. They glided down the tunnels, moving with a caterpillarlike motion that made Bryl feel sick. He found that his body cooperated just enough to let him shiver.

Ahead, they saw two other werem widening a hole in the side of the passage. Bryl's fireball bobbed along behind them.

As their captors reached the other worm-men, they stopped and plucked Vailret and Bryl from their segmented backs. They placed their captives on the dirt floor inside a grave-sized hole they had dug. The werem seemed to be clicking and chattering among themselves.

One of them turned, bent down with a liquid motion, and snatched up Vailret and Bryl, stuffing them into the hole.

Paralyzed, Bryl could do nothing but slump against Vailret and watch as the hideous blank-eyed figure of one werem leaned forward, filling the opening with his silhouette. He reached forward with one four-fingered hand.

"The Master will make good use of these," the werem said in a scratchy, hollow voice. He snatched the Air Stone and the Fire Stone out of Bryl's locked grasp.

The fireball illuminating the tunnels winked out, leaving them in complete blackness.

Bryl could only hear the worm-men moving and chittering. They slathered dirt as they built up the tunnel wall again, piling it back inside the cell. They walled Vailret and Bryl into the chamber, without food, without light, without air.

21
SARDUN'S VAULTS

*"She is our future! Tareah is the last full-blooded
Sorcerer woman. Our race will rise again. She
will shepherd them back to us, to make things the
way they were."*

—Sardun the Sentinel

Delrael's army exhibited an odd mixture of horror
remembered from their first battle and nervous frivol-
ity from considering themselves safe in the ice fortress.
Many characters slumped against the ice blocks, tucked
a blanket behind them, and fell deep into a numb
sleep.

Siya took great pains to provide an extra large and
well-prepared meal for them all. She moved about as
if in a daze, staring at the fighters, especially the
wounded ones; something seemed to be working in
the back of her mind since she had watched Drodanis
die.

Tareah did what she could to help. The Ice Palace
felt so different with a human army inside. She remembered Sardun's little touches, his pennants and
ice intaglios along the walls. Neither she nor Enrod
had been able to add embellishments, so the great
banquet chamber seemed larger and colder than it
should have.

Enrod came up to her and stood by, wanting to say
something. She noticed him, but did not encourage
conversation. She felt uncomfortable around him and

his disjointed madness. He looked up at the vaulted ceilings and around the ice fortress.

"Tareah," he said. His voice sounded calm, but his face appeared harder. "Sardun said harsh things." He stared down a corridor, then flinched at something she couldn't see. "Unfair to me."

Tareah tried to keep any emotion out of her answer. "My father didn't like you. Apparently he never considered the feud finished. He was upset because you abandoned your heritage."

Enrod's heavy eyebrows knitted together. "Not abandoned! I stayed! After the Transition, after all the Sorcerers ran away, I stayed! I used my abilities to help human characters. Help them! Sardun . . . lived too much in the past. More important work to do."

Enrod drew a deep breath and ran his fingernails along the ice blocks of the wall, shaving off a thin line of white. "I used my power. I offered my assistance. We built Tairé."

He lowered his gaze. The ice shaving melted on his fingertips. "We owed humans that much. We created their character race for *our* wars. We gave them Gamearth already broken. I helped fix it."

Though Enrod's hair remained dark and his beard bushy, Tareah could see how truly old the Sentinel was. He had lived nearly as many years as Sardun, a full generation more than Bryl, and for several generations of human characters.

"I should become the Allspirit," he said, surprising her. "Me."

Tareah looked at Enrod, wondering how he had reached that conclusion.

"I would lose nothing, and *I* . . ." He paused, and she saw the deep pain on his face. "I know how power can hurt. What kind of Allspirit would Bryl make? Not even a pure Sorcerer. Tainted! Tainted!" He took a deep breath, then blew it out and saw vapor in the cold air wafting upward like smoke. "A full-blooded

Sorcerer should make the last Transition. I am the only one left."

Enrod seemed to be speaking to himself. Tareah shook her head and felt her hair flowing behind her neck. "So am I, Enrod. Why does everyone always forget about me?"

Enrod blinked at her. "Sardun kept you locked away."

Tareah felt angry now. No matter how much she did, they all continued to take her lightly, even the people on her own side.

"My father had his own reasons for protecting me, regardless of whether you or I agree with them. He isn't here now, and I make my own decisions."

Enrod shrugged.

In the large hall, Siya continued cleaning weapons, sitting by herself. The other non-fighter human characters tended the wounded soldiers and helped the army bed down.

"Do me one thing, for the sake of the memory of my father," Tareah said. She pointed at Enrod. "He was upset because you never once came here to see the history he had compiled. Go to the vaults yourself. Look at what he kept from past turns. You insist on looking toward the future, and that's good. But the past might hold some surprises for you, too. Go to the vaults. You might be impressed."

Enrod drew himself up and looked at her with his ageless eyes. "I will." With a slight bow, he stepped backward and walked away. As he moved, he drew his fingernail along the wall.

Tareah held the Water Stone in her hands, thinking about what else Enrod had said. She already knew what she had to do.

Tareah tried to sleep. She lay in a re-creation of her old chambers. She had rebuilt the room exactly as she remembered it, making the same polished furnishings, the same frost-intaglios in the walls, even the single, narrow window that now looked out upon the massed and huddling monster army on the ice-packed desolation. She could see only three or four small fires out there, apparently made with their limited supply of wood.

Delrael's army would be asleep by now, except for a few sentries she could easily avoid.

Tareah wandered through the blue-ice corridors again, just as she had always done when she couldn't sleep. During the day the walls shimmered with rainbows from the sunlight; at night she saw only dark and refracted starshine. As a girl, sometimes she listened to her father tell legends that she already knew by heart.

The memory of her father reminded her of the way she and Vailret had swapped stories back in the Stronghold village. She thought of Vailret and Bryl and how far away they must be. Surely by now they had managed to get the Earth Stone—but how would they know to come all the way up here to the Ice Palace? They were supposed to locate the human army somewhere in the mountains. Originally, Delrael had planned to send regular scouts to search for them when they returned. Now, though, even if Vailret and Bryl did happen to come up here, how could they ever get past the tight cordon of monsters?

They could do enormous damage with the three Stones, blasting their way in, but Bryl was only one magic user . . . and spells could fail.

Tareah stopped and shivered from a cold that didn't come from the ice corridors. What if Bryl didn't succeed? What if all three Stones passed into the hands of the manticore? Normally, she would have doubted that any monster could have a trace of Sorcerer blood in his veins, but the ogre Gairoth had proven otherwise.

In the last days of the old Sorcerers, their race had been weak. They mated with the humans, trying to regain their fading magic; some of them, more desperate, had interbred with a few of their own more horrendous creations. Who could say that in all of Siryyk's horde not one monster could bring magic from the Stones?

It was a foolish risk to take, she knew. Delrael, with his constant overprotection of her, had certainly lectured enough about senseless risks.

She descended a narrow staircase and got to the ground level of the ice fortress. The human army could survive a long seige within the battlements. They had many supplies, and Enrod could always replenish them.

Winter had fallen on the northern hexes, and even without the Water Stone's magic, the fortress would remain frozen for months. Tareah had done all she could here.

The need was greater elsewhere.

She slipped out a low side arch, one of the doorways Enrod had added for brief surprise strikes and retreats. He hadn't expected her to be the first character to use it.

Under a few stars that hung in black patches of night around clumps of clouds, Tareah approached the western wall of the defenses. Most of Siryyk's horde lay camped along the opposite side, but that didn't mean other sentries wouldn't be stationed all around the fortress.

At midnight, her allotment of spells had been replenished, and now Tareah took out the Water Stone. She rolled the sapphire on the ground but got only a "3". Though she felt the magic surging through her, the *dayid* must not be helping her this time. It did not want her to take the Water Stone away.

She walked forward into the wall.

The ice clarified and puddled around her hands, turning into water as she stepped through the blocks. The water shimmered and sealed behind her, refreezing as she stepped through. The ice trickled away in front of her, and she emerged on the other side.

Cold water dripped from her garments and her long hair, but a thought through the Water Stone left her warm again. Tareah called up a thick night fog to hide her movements from any monsters that might be patrolling the area.

She hurried across the snow, following her ears to the Barrier River, which lay only half a hex away. Her body felt refreshed and tingling from touching so much magic in so little time. But this would be only the beginning. She covered the distance in less than an hour.

At last, after all her studying of the Game and its legends, she had embarked on her own adventure.

Tareah stood on the hex-line where the rushing water poured through from the Northern Sea, gushing among the rocks and frothing with chunks of ice. Tareah fashioned a wide, flat raft of solid, transparent ice that showed the water foaming beneath it in large bubbles. She stepped onto her raft, squatted down in its center, and detached it from the black hex-line of the shore.

With a lurch, her raft pushed southward, reeling away at the speed of the current, bouncing and twisting. She dug her fingers into the ice, melting handholds for herself. The raft swirled, and as the Water Stone spell continued, she called up waves in the current.

Giant blue hands of froth and spray rose up, one after another in a flurry, pushing the raft and then dissolving into the water again. A constant stream of the watery hands shoved her faster and faster, doubling the speed of the current so that the raft skipped and bounced over the river surface.

Tareah's hair whipped behind her, and she couldn't stop herself from laughing. The dim hexes of the shore

sped past, blurry and dizzying at her rate of movement.

She had two more spells to last the rest of the night.
By morning she would be many, many hexagons away.

Enrod carried a flickering torch—a *torch*, because
he had used all his spells that day in rebuilding the
fortress. The flames hissed and crackled. He held his
hand near the fire to feel its warmth. The light glinted
and flared along the ice stalactites.

He wandered around in the museum for which Sardun
had spent his lifetime collecting. Tareah's father had
sent out human Scavengers, paying them for any relic
of the old Sorcerers they could uncover: jewels, manu-
scripts, weapons, or tiny keepsakes—anything that en-
hanced his collection.

Sardun had annotated each object. Enrod found the
blackened swords of two old Sorcerer generals, apparently the actual pair that the commanders had thrown
into Stilvess Peacemaker's death pyre. Or was it some
other pyre? Enrod couldn't remember.

Even before the fall of the old Ice Palace, Sardun
had seemed to know that his museum would collapse,
and he had taken great pains to preserve everything.
Glowing protection wards and shielding fields hovered
around all the relics. Though Enrod was the first to set
foot in these restored vaults, everything seemed pristine.

The vault spread out to the edges of the torchlight.
Under a low ceiling in the far end, he saw ranks of
bodies positioned side by side with great reverence.
These were the empty, dormant bodies of the old
Sorcerers.

After most of the race had gathered together in the
broad valley, Stilvess and other Sorcerer commanders
sat in their tent, rolling and rolling dice until they
achieved a seemingly impossible, perfect roll that would
set off the Transition. All the old Sorcerers had waited

there, except those who had chosen to remain behind like Enrod and Sardun.

When the Transition worked and the lives of all the old Sorcerers were forged together into the Earthspirits and the Deathspirits, they had left their physical bodies behind, empty and dormant—not dead, but not alive, either.

Sardun and the others had carried all of the bodies here and erected the Ice Palace as their monument. Over the years, Sardun arranged the figures, labeling it with the name they had carried in life.

Enrod stood in the oppressive closeness of the vaults. He could imagine the long, slow intake of breath, perhaps only once every minute or two as the old Sorcerers inhaled in unison, then let out an equally interminable exhale. Their heartbeats seemed to echo like distant, widely spaced drumbeats: a faint thump, a long, long pause, and then a smaller thump.

Enrod thought about Sardun's demise. He could feel the *dayid*, he could feel all the lives of the Sentinels who had vanished in the intervening years, calling upon the half-Transition to destroy themselves when they could no longer tolerate their lives. The voices whispered more loudly in his head.

Enrod looked out at the tomb of the nondead Sorcerers and wondered if this was what they really wanted.

He turned away then and poked among the relics for a last few moments. In a small, unimpressive container he found the spell for invoking and commanding a gargoyle, one of the stone creatures formed by a single Sentinel's wandering spirit.

Enrod looked at the spell, realizing that it could be useful. Below it he found written a single name for the gargoyle to be summoned: Arken.

The next morning Delrael awoke refreshed and tingling with a new energy. The Game had turned in his favor, and he felt eager for it now.

His father had fallen in the battle, but Delrael could make it up to him if he won the war and saved Gamearth, just as Drodanis had charged him to do long ago in the Rulewoman's message-stick.

His army could rest and recuperate here in the Ice Palace. The fighters could strike at the horde whenever the monsters approached too close. Delrael had only to wait. Vailret and Bryl held the key to the next step, the End Game.

Delrael arose at first light and, before his fighters could stir, he walked along the ice corridors and climbed one of the tall turrets to look out over the frozen desolation. The last scraps of an unusual morning fog blew away with the dawn.

On top, he met one shivering sentry, a woman whose hair had blown about and tangled in the night breezes; she looked as if she had reached the limits of what she could endure. The cold air snapped the last of Delrael's weariness away as he stood beside the sentry.

"They're just starting to move now," she said. He listened to her teeth chattering.

He watched the forms of Siryyk's army. The horde moved around their main encampment like ants from a stirred-up colony. A few creatures had surrounded the ice fortress at strategic positions. But as the morning fog burned off, Delrael knew that the monster sentries had done little or no good in the darkness.

He watched a detachment of Slac march across the flat snow to reach higher ground, a hilly jumbled terrain of broken ice blocks and brown-stained snow. Plumes of steam poured up, like fumaroles from some underground volcanic chamber.

But as the Slac detachment moved onto the hummocks, they suddenly scurried away. The ground began to move around them. The lumps cracked, and powdery snow blasted into the air. The steam thickened and gushed upward. A dark form burst out from beneath the blanket of snow and ice.

The Slac ran for their lives, dropping weapons and shields. Their black cloaks flapped behind them as they fled.

Great pointed wings snapped free of the ice. A long serpentine neck rose up that supported a pointed head filled with jagged fangs. Snorts of flame gushed out of the beast's mouth, blasting two of the Slac. The enormous wings beat, lifting the entire form.

A huge, metallic-looking dragon rose into the air, sweeping cold gusts around it and craning its head. The morning sun glinted on blue and tarnished-silver scales. The dragon turned its head to stare down at the monsters that had disturbed it.

The dragon looked formidable, though relatively small for such a creature. Seen in comparison to the little Slac, though, it appeared immense indeed. The monsters mobilized against the new threat. Delrael could make out the giant form of Siryyk striding out to direct his horde.

But the dragon flew up, circling around and shrieking down at the monsters as if greatly annoyed. It circled and then flapped its wings again. Ice and snow flaked off, dropping to the ground in a jagged rain. The dragon let out another shriek and then swooped toward the ice fortress.

Delrael ducked back inside and started to charge down the tower steps four at a time, stumbling and leaping, shouting as he went. He heard other sentries sounding the alarm. A dragon had destroyed the Ice Palace the first time, when Sardun had tried to defend it; Delrael didn't know what *he* could do that Sardun hadn't tried. His words echoed throughout the corridors.

"Rouse everyone! We're under attack! A dragon! All characters to arms!"

The human fighters stirred as he burst into the main room below. Several grabbed weapons; others scrambled to get into armor; a few blinked groggily, fighting off a deep sleep. A handful of fighters followed Delrael out into the courtyard just as the dragon stirred up snow and ice crystals where it landed in an open spot within the protection of the walls.

The dragon strutted around in the courtyard, blinking its eyes with audible clicks and breathing with the sound of wind moaning through a cave. "Bad monsters!" the dragon hissed in a broken, rumbling voice. The words sounded distorted from echoing out of such a long throat.

Delrael stopped, gawking up at it. The dragon seemed to have no hostile intent. He wondered if it merely sought refuge from further disturbance.

"No sleep! Bah!"

Then Delrael recognized a rubbed-raw scar on the dragon's throat where the scales had been worn away long ago and never grown back. The reptilian skin was discolored and hard, but Delrael remembered the thick iron collar.

"Rognoth!" he said.

The dragon stopped, swished its long tail and smacked it into an ice wall. It curled the tail around its haunches with a startled hiss. "Rognoth," it said.

This had been the companion of Gairoth the ogre, who had originally captured Bryl and held him in the swamps before taking over the Stronghold. Gairoth had let the runt dragon gorge himself on all the Stronghold's supplies, until Delrael brought back Tryos. The larger dragon, furious at his little brother, had chased Rognoth far to the north and lost him.

Rognoth had been in the frozen wasteland all this time, maturing and toughening.

Rognoth looked down at Delrael, then craned his neck forward to push his monstrous head close to the man's face. Delrael stood firm.

The other fighters rushed out, saw their commander face-to-face with the dragon, and backed up. Many drew their bows; others held swords and spears but didn't know what to do.

Delrael felt the thick stench of the dragon's breath pouring over him. Rognoth blinked his eyes again and reared back, as if finally recognizing him. "Delroth! Haw! Now I kill you!" he roared in a very good approximation of Gairoth's voice.

Delrael thought at that moment that he was doomed, that Rognoth carried the ogre's grudge as well. Gairoth had followed Delrael across the entire map, trying to catch him, and had finally died on the threshold of Scartaris. Now Rognoth would finish the job.

The dragon shook his enormous head and spat-sputtered flame and smoke into the air. "Stupid Gairoth! Haw! Haw! Hope I never see him again!"

Delrael wanted to laugh with relief. "Gairoth will never come," he said. "We've taken care of him. We also took care of Tryos. They'll never bother you. They are all dead. You're safe."

Rognoth flapped his wings and made a rumbling sound in his throat that sounded like a purr. "Then you are my friend, Delroth."

Delrael felt relief wash over him like warm bathwater. He called to all his gathered fighters to stand down and sheathe their weapons. "It's all right now, it's all right!"

But later, when he went to Tareah's chambers to tell her the news, he found only her note.

She had taken the Water Stone and left.

22

TECHNOLOGICAL FRINGE

"I told you how Enrod turned his back on his Sorcerer heritage, but others have done far worse. I have even heard of one human city where all the characters have forsaken magic! How can this be? Without magic, Gamearth cannot function. All of these characters must be insane."

—Sardun the Sentinel

Tareah stopped and stared at the enormous city of Sitnalta; though exhausted from her long journey, she ran forward. Its size amazed her.

Tareah had never before encountered such a large city so close. After growing up with only Sardun for company in the entire Ice Palace, she found it difficult to conceive of so many characters packed together in buildings. All the noise and activity overwhelmed her.

Entering Sitnalta, she strained her neck to gawk up at the tall buildings and at the machinery puttering along the alleys. Her astonishment felt so unusual to her. These buildings and characters and clanking devices seemed as amazing as the grandest legends of old Sorcerer battles.

Sardun had warned her of this place. A terrible city where the characters had turned away from all magic, he said. But her father had told Tareah many things she now questioned.

Sardun had convinced her that Delrael, like the great Game heroes, was the type of character she should most admire. But though Tareah respected Delrael for what he could do, for his bravery and his drive to win . . . she just didn't find him interesting enough for her. Vailret was the one who captured her attention, even if she had never told him that. She wondered what he would have to tell her about his quest for the Earth Stone. She needed to find him first.

Vailret and Bryl had gone to Rokanun, but they had to pass through here first. She would ask about them in the city and find out when they had departed for the island. If Vailret and Bryl had already returned, then she would have to catch them on their way back to Delrael's army.

Somewhere far away—it seemed to be deep beneath her, shielded perhaps by rock—Tareah could feel the tingling pull of the other Stones. The three remaining Stones together contained enough magic that she could sense it even here. The tingling grew stronger and then vanished.

She couldn't understand it, but it was heartening to know that the Air, Fire, and Earth Stones had indeed come together. Vailret and Bryl had succeeded in that much at least.

"Excuse me, please," Tareah said to a muscular woman in a grease-stained jumpsuit. The woman tinkered with some kind of monitoring box connected to pipes and tubes that ran under the streets. She looked up, distracted, and turned, finally setting her eyes on Tareah. She blinked. "Yes, what is it?" Tareah saw a smudge of dark oil across the weathered wrinkles on her cheeks.

"I'm looking for two companions. Their names are Vailret and Bryl—Bryl is a magic user, Vailret a scholar."

"Oh, I don't think I know them," the woman said and then frowned. "A magic user? In Sitnalta? My!"

She bent back to her work and continued tinkering with the metal box.

Tareah caught the attention of another man who strode purposefully along. He wore dark clothes beneath a white lab smock. He didn't slow as she spoke to him, forcing her to turn and hurry along beside him.

"—a magic user, old, and he wears a blue cloak. He's with a young man with blond hair."

The Sitnaltan man didn't turn to her as he hurried off. "No, neither of those sound familiar to me. Too much is happening in Sitnalta these days. I can't keep track of all the characters who come and go. I'm busy now. We don't have much time left."

He grabbed a door and walked inside a tall building with low ceilings. Tareah followed after him. Her multi-colored skirt swished as she moved. "What do you mean you don't have much time? Why won't anybody talk to me?"

The man paced down a corridor. On either side Tareah could see rooms and tables strewn with glass tubes and bottles, experiments cooking, and complicated notations scrawled on chalkboards. In one room, several men and women sat by a table, throwing dice and chalking scores on a board; by the grim feverishness on their faces, she could tell they didn't consider their efforts a mere game.

The man proceeded to the opposite side of the building, where a door led back out to the streets again. He shrugged out of his dirty lab coat, grabbed a clean one from a hamper, and pulled it on. He straightened his sleeves, then flashed a glance at her.

"The invisible force, of course. It controls a handful of characters at a time, and it knows how to cause great destruction. It seems random, chaotic. Despite concerted efforts of our greatest teams and our most brilliant solo inventors, we haven't found a way to stop it."

He stepped into the street. His black shoes slapped the steps.

"It used to happen four times a day, like clockwork. We charted it on a graph." He turned and made squiggling motions with his fingers against the brick wall.

Tareah didn't know what a graph was.

"But then two days ago it suddenly jumped to *six times* a day. How are we supposed to resist that? We can't even understand what makes it work once. So . . ." He stopped and slipped his hands into the wide pockets of his lab coat.

"I apologize for our attitude. Welcome to Sitnalta . . . but perhaps you could come back some other time when we're not quite so busy? Hmmm?"

He turned and walked off again. This time Tareah didn't follow him.

"An invisible force," Tareah thought. Controlling characters? Attacking Sitnalta? That made no sense. When the man had said the force struck four times a day, then suddenly increased to six times . . . something clicked inside her head, but she couldn't be sure what it meant.

While she stood pondering, Tareah leaned against a stone bench that ran along the side of the building. Scrawled in black and red markings on the smooth seat were nonsensical equations, numbers, and half-finished drawings of preposterous inventions. She imagined characters sitting there, doodling ideas while waiting for someone.

From a nearby alley, Tareah heard a loud clanking, mixed with the din of ratcheting and chugging, like the slow approach of a weary behemoth. She stood up. Other characters also looked around; they seemed excited. Whatever made the noise, it moved out of

sight behind the tall buildings. Above one rooftop, she
saw a misshapen dome move forward with a lurch.

Several characters hurried toward it, not afraid but
curious. Tareah had seen so many wonders in the city
that she followed, eager to see what could be so spectacular that it amazed even the Sitnaltans.

Rounding the corner, Tareah came upon other characters staring up at a colossal metal giant fully as tall
as any construction in Sitnalta. Its hands each looked
as large as Tareah's entire body. The mechanical man
had bulky legs of different alloys and was draped with
wires, cables, and pulleys. Bolts held all the pieces
together. Steam chugged up from an exhaust vent at
the robot's shoulder. Polished brass rivets glinted in
the light. Blinking indicator lights flashed on its square
metal chest.

Tareah heard the gears grind and the cables strain.
The towering automaton lifted its left leg, bending at
the knee and heaving its foot off the ground. The
robot, feeling its way, pointed its toe and extended it
forward for the next step, learning how to walk.

The automaton had been armored with iron spikes
at its joints, formidable enough to ward off any
attacker.

The automaton's head looked like a square bucket
huge enough to hold food for an entire army. Its
unblinking eyes were great paned windows, one larger
than the other. Behind the eye-windows, she saw the
shadowy figure of a human character moving about,
pulling at controls.

The automaton shuffled forward one more step,
then raised its right arm as if flexing a muscle. It
stepped toward the corner with a ponderous gait, its
steps so enormous that it moved along at a respectable
pace.

As the robot reached the corner, it swiveled on one
foot to turn sideways and then stepped forward again.
It cut the corner too close and walked into the wall,

slamming its shoulder into the bricks with a clang and a thud. Tareah watched shards of mortar tumble down.

The automaton stepped backward, prying one of its long shoulder spikes free of the wall. It shuffled sideways, then advanced again, but it still could not clear the corner. Striking the edge with its metal arm, the automaton spun partway around to face the wrong direction.

The robot repeated its back step and forward march one more time before it finally cleared the corner. By this time, it had knocked down part of the building, leaving piles of brick on the ground.

The automaton swiveled at its waist to aim the eye-windows down at the ground. The right metal hand extended toward a pile of brick in the street.

The spectators observed all this maneuvering with delight. Tareah glanced at them, then watched the robot again.

Its right hand struck the ground to the right of the bricks. In a separate motion, its fingers curled together but missed the target.

The automaton stood up again, straightened both arms to its sides, then bent over a second time, extending the right arm. The curling metal fingers missed the bricks again. Even moving with meticulous care, the huge fingers could not grasp a simple object. The automaton bent over and stopped where it guessed the bricks lay. Steam burped and bubbled out of the exhaust slit, but the robot halted.

Tareah saw the shadow moving behind the eye-windows, in and out of focus. A metal hatch opened in the metal figure's back, swinging upward. A single character emerged, a man wearing a dark helmet that appeared so heavy it nearly stopped him from moving. He worked his way down steps and rungs on the outer surface of the automaton until he reached the ground.

Several of the Sitnaltans cheered and applauded. "Hooray for Professor Frankenstein!" someone shouted. Tareah looked at the man with sudden attention; Vailret had told her about the brilliant Frankenstein. The professor seemed to ignore the attention of the spectators.

Frankenstein went to where the metal hand lay a full two feet away from the bricks. He stared at the automaton, swaying backward from the weight of the helmet on his head.

He went to the wide foot of the robot, muttering and grumbling to himself. Out of spite, he kicked the metal leg, then let out a disgusted sigh. "None of this ever happened when Jules was here." He stopped beside the mechanical hand resting on the hex-cobbled streets.

Frankenstein bent over, putting his back underneath the broad cables and pipes of the automaton's wrist. He heaved and strained with all his might, lifting the hand up, shuffling sideways and dropping it down on top of the bricks.

"There!" He pulled a shining ratchet from his pocket and used it to tighten and readjust nuts and cables in the wrist. Straining upward, he tweaked something in the automaton's elbow. "How many times do I have to calibrate you?" he shouted up at it. "And why am I talking to *you*? You're just a machine!"

Several Sitnaltans had dropped out of sight, having gone back to their work. Tareah saw from their expressions that they were embarrassed to watch Frankenstein's difficulty with his own invention.

Tareah went toward the professor, though, conscious of the menacing bulk of the automaton. "Are you Professor Frankenstein?" she asked.

He stood up and swiveled his body at the waist to look at her. The heavy helmet made it difficult for him to turn his neck. He gazed at her with no recognition.

"Who are you?" Then he frowned, because, judging by her sapphire Water Stone and her handmade clothes, Tareah obviously did not belong in Sitnalta.

She took two more steps toward him. The giant automaton looked even more awesome. She stared at the countless connections and adjusting nuts, the pulleys, all the tiny systems Frankenstein had installed.

"My name is Tareah," she said. "I'm a friend of Vailret and Bryl. Vailret has told me about you and about the last time he came here to Sitnalta. They rescued me from the dragon."

Frankenstein looked at her, pursing his lips. "Yes. They thought you were someone important, I seem to recall."

"My father was Sardun." She paused and, with some astonishment, realized that he did not recognize the name. "Sardun the Sentinel."

"Was he a magic user?" Frankenstein asked.

She couldn't believe what she heard. "Of course he was a magic user. He was a Sentinel. My father built the Ice Palace. He was one of the most powerful characters on Gamearth!"

"Not here he wasn't," Frankenstein said. "He wouldn't have been able to make an ice *cube* this side of the technological fringe. Magic doesn't work here, or at least it didn't. Does that mean you're a magic user, too? A good one?"

She drew herself up, trying to look impressive. "One of the last two on the whole map who carries full Sorcerer blood."

Frankenstein's dark eyes lit up with enthusiasm. "Ah! That could be most useful, then, cover some of the contingencies in my plan."

Before the professor could elaborate further, they heard shouts and mutterings. Tareah looked around. A broken brick struck the cobblestones at her feet, throwing shards in a star-shaped pattern.

Frankenstein held onto the side of his mechanical man and craned backward to look up. Characters had gone out on the crumbling rooftop of the building broken by the automaton. They shouted and moved stiffly, picking at the bricks and hurling them down.

Two shards clanged on the broad back of the robot. "Stop that!" Frankenstein yelled. Then the Sitnaltans started throwing bricks at him.

Other characters came down the street, but Tareah saw from their contorted expressions and bizarre, synchronous movements that they were all being guided, driven by something she could not see. "What is this?" she asked.

"Oh, bother—they're doing it again!" Frankenstein groaned. "I'm protected by my helmet, but you'd better come with me inside Drone. I wouldn't want the controller to get hold of a magic user.

A rain of bricks pattered down on the street and bounced off the metal hull of the mechanical man. One ricocheted and struck Frankenstein's shoulder. "Ow! Time to go. Come on!"

The professor grabbed her arm and pulled her toward the nearest metal leg. He scrambled up the footholds and handholds to the hatch, swaying with exaggerated movements because of his helmet. Tareah slipped once, then climbed up after him. She stumbled through the hatch.

Frankenstein had seated himself in the cramped control compartment. "This was never meant for two characters, but we'll make do. You're shielded in here. Close that hatch!"

Tareah reached up and pulled the metal lid down. Rocks and bricks continued to strike the automaton, making dull echoes inside.

"You can lock it down with those flanges on the side." She fumbled with the metal strips and soon had the hatch secured.

"Hang on." Frankenstein pulled controls and steer-

ing levers. "No more time for practice." He leaned
back in his seat, and Tareah grabbed onto a support
handle as the bulky automaton straightened at the waist.
The professor played with the panel in front of him,
turning dials, punching buttons, and engaging gears.

The compartment moved and shuddered. She heard
the hiss of steam. Drone lifted one foot and set it
down again. It began to walk.

All around her she saw a cluttered chaos of controls
and wires. The entire pilot compartment felt warm
from the great steam-engine boiler.

She could smell oil, grease and stuffy air in the
chamber.

"Why did they start attacking you?" she asked.
"What's wrong with them?"

"Six times a day. I certainly hope I can find the
source and stop it. I am beginning to lose patience."

Tareah looked through the two eye-windows installed
directly in front of where Frankenstein sat. She stared
from one to the other down at the street; the view
jumped, and Tareah saw that the panes of the left
eye-window had been set at angles and curved into
lenses so that the view out of one eye was magnified in
comparison with what she saw through the other.

Drone jerked and bounced as it moved away. Outside, the Sitnaltan characters converged, and blows
continued to patter on the hull. Lines of characters
stood on the rooftops, throwing things.

"Where are we going? How can we get away from
this?" she said.

But Frankenstein jerked the levers feverishly and
tried to do dozens of things at once. He spoke to her
in a clipped voice through lips that barely moved.
"Don't bother me! This is taking all my concentration."

Tareah stared at the controlled characters around
them. Every day, this had happened four times, forcing the Sitnaltans to destroy their own buildings; re-
cently the attacks had increased to six times a day.

Then her jaw slowly opened. A magic user with one Stone would have four spells a day. If that same magic user somehow obained two more Stones—say, the Fire Stone and the Air Stone—the spell allotment would increase to six.

"Oh, no!" she said. The professor didn't seem to hear her, but he glanced up when she spoke again. "That invisible force—it's the Earth Stone! Someone is using the Earth Stone to do this."

23

THE LAST MARCH OF
THE OLD SORCERERS

*"Commanding an army is much more com-
plex than leading a small group of questers. A
good commander must play all his forces as a
unit, much as the Outsiders Play the characters
on Gamearth."*
—General Doril, Memoirs of the Scouring

After only a few days inside the ice fortress, Delrael's
army grew restless, angry to go out and fight again.
But Delrael bided his time, safe inside the high
walls.

The manticore led three separate assaults against
the fortress. Delrael's fighters took great glee in shooting arrows or throwing spears at the approaching monsters. Siryyk's troops could not scale or penetrate the
ice walls.

The humans suffered only a single loss, one man
who stood carelessly away from any of the defenses,
laughing down at the impotent monsters. A stray arrow caught him in the chest, and he toppled over the
wall. If the wound did not kill him instantly, the fall
broke at least his legs, and the monsters rushed up to
grab their symbolic captive. They dragged him away
and made a great show of plunging their spears and
swords into his form.

Delrael's fighters grew angrier.

In the days since Tareah had taken the Water Stone
away, their morale had initially dropped and then

returned to its former high. The characters felt invincible within the ice fortress and were tired of waiting.

The fighters sat down against ice walls or hunched cross-legged on the floor. Many kept blankets around them, most wore their armor. Small groups amused themselves with dice games or tic-tac-toe scratched into the ice with knife points. Delrael spoke with them at least once a day, asking for their suggestions.

One woman with short brownish hair and wide-set dark eyes stood up and waved her hand. Delrael nodded for her to speak.

"I think we should strike a quick blow. A quick one. March out, attack, use our element of surprise, and then hurry back in! Our losses should be minimal. Just think of what damage we could do to the monsters."

"Minimal losses," Delrael thought. Drodanis and the remaining Black Falcon troops had been "minimal losses." The other fighters in the chamber murmured their agreement. One man who remained seated, huddled in his blanket, said, "At least we'd be moving around. It's always so cold in this place."

"It would be foolish to go out and attack!" Delrael raised his voice. They had been through this before, and his decision still stood. "There's no reason for more of our characters to die. The horde still outnumbers us."

Romm stood up. A flush passed across his pale skin. "If you don't think each of us can kill at least two monsters, Delrael, then we're not suitable fighters. What difference does it make if they outnumber us?"

Delrael frowned. "Look, Siryyk is getting desperate. He's already lost half of his fighters, and he has no more supplies. They only have enough wood to make one or two campfires every night. We can just wait him out and laugh at him in here."

"Some commander," one character mumbled, but Delrael couldn't see who it was.

"What if Tareah and Bryl don't come back with the

Stones?'' someone else shouted. Delrael chose to ignore that possibility.

Old Siya turned her head toward Delrael and kept
her voice low, speaking to him alone, but her words
carried well in the cold air of the broad chamber.
"Fighting monsters is what the Game is all about,
Delrael. Isn't that what you always said? You can't
win by sitting and waiting. What would Drodanis think
of you?''

Delrael scowled. "That's uncalled for, Siya.''

She scowled right back at him.

"Wait!'' Enrod said from the wall. He had held his
hand against the ice block for so long that water trickled down; when the Sentinel removed his palm, Delrael
could see a dark indentation where his body heat had
melted its way into the wall. Enrod's hair remained
wild, and his eyes clicked back and forth, as if tracking
and trying to focus on something.

He paused at inappropriate times in his sentence. "I
know how . . .we can win this game.'' Enrod drew
several deep breaths; just when Delrael thought he
had completely lost his train of thought, the Sentinel
swiveled his head. He met Delrael with a piercing
gaze.

"Kill Siryyk. That alone . . .'' He paused again,
then locked his eyes on Siya, and then on Romm out in
the audience as if he were playing a kind of staring game.
"Will do a lot of damage. Siryyk commands them. Kill
Siryyk. The monsters won't know what to do then.''

The other fighters muttered agreement or questions.
Enrod laughed. Delrael said, "But how would you kill
him?''

The Sentinel nodded, but answered a different question. "A Slac general will lead after Siryyk falls.''
Enrod grinned. "Then the Slac will feel favored in the
army. The other monsters won't like that. There'll be
infighting before . . .''

He stopped, stretched out his hand to the wall again

and carefully lined up his fingers and his palm with the indentation he had already melted into the ice. "You see? I still have fire!"

"How would you kill the manticore?" Delrael asked again, raising his voice this time.

Enrod looked at his fingers and the ice; then with his other hand he reached inside his tattered robe to pull out a small scroll. Delrael could see words written on its surface.

Enrod nodded. "Arken."

Siya stepped into the courtyard and felt the biting cold on her hands and arms. She had not bothered to bundle up. Standing next to the dragon would keep her warm.

She carried a large cauldron, swinging it to keep her balance. She stepped out under the muffled sky. The metal pot remained warm from the noon meal.

Rognoth the dragon beat his tarnished-silver wings and craned his neck, already waiting for her. As the dragon moved, Siya smelled a rank warmth that overwhelmed the cold.

Rognoth bowed his long neck and hissed as he stuck his head into the cauldron and began lapping out the leftovers. His breaths sounded like a blacksmith's bellows echoing within the pot. She heard the sound of his tongue scraping against the inner surface.

She had been bringing food, scraps, and garbage to the dragon since he had arrived. Rognoth distracted her from the haunting images in her head of Drodanis, an insignificant black figure falling in a rain of rock down the infinite cliff slope, or of her husband Cayon battling to the death someplace in the forest without her.

What had those two characters known that she did not? What had Siya failed to understand? It seemed so clear how her life should be lived; and yet these questers who went out for adventure, swordplay and bloodshed . . .they seemed to know something. Siya looked around herself every day. She watched Delrael. She tried to understand.

"More?" Rognoth said, sticking his head into the cauldron again and plucking it back out. Globs of porridge stuck around his nostrils and pointed chin.

"No more," she said. "Later." They went through this ritual every day.

"More?" Rognoth said in a quieter voice, then turned his head away, as if in deep disappointment.

Siya reached into her cloak and took out five biscuits. "Here," she said and tossed them to him. Delighted, the dragon snapped them up and seemed satisfied.

Rognoth appeared strong and happy, vibrant with energy. She looked at him and felt a pang inside herself. Even this dragon knew his place in Gamearth. He knew something she didn't know.

The dragon lowered his head, and Siya felt warmth radiating from his nose and throat. He spoke again, starting the longest conversation he had ever had with her.

"Gairoth bad to me. Tryos bad to me." He raised his head.

"Yes, they were bad to you," she said.

"But you nice." He drew the last sound out into a long hiss, and then said it again. "Nice!"

Not sure she could stand any more of this, Siya hurried back inside, leaving the empty cauldron with the dragon.

Long after darkness, when Enrod had summoned up the magic to call Arken forth, he heard the whispering voices of the *dayid* within his mind. Any time he had worked magic inside the fortress, the voices had tugged at him, distracted him, called to him. But Enrod didn't mind. He was accustomed to hearing voices in his head. They kept him company.

Enrod watched the lump of rock protruding from the packed snow in the courtyard within the ice walls. Moonlight shone down, making the rock dark with exaggerated shadows. Two characters arrived, holding torches under the tall arches and lighting the area with reflected orange. Trickles of water ran down the ice walls next to the flames, then refroze before they reached the ground.

"Arken!" Enrod said again under his breath.

The boulder shifted and elongated, until it formed itself into a bulky body. The bottom half split vertically and thinned into two pillars that became legs. Arm columns lifted up. Protrusions from the back of the stone torso extended into wings. The forehead shoved forward and cracked open to show a single crystalline eye. Clumps of snow clung to rough spots on the gargoyle but fell off as Arken moved and took a single step. "I am called again?" he asked in a gravelly voice.

Delrael went forward to take charge. Enrod watched, flicking his gaze to the gargoyle then to Delrael, back and forth, trying to see everything at once.

"We need to ask your help, Arken. Do you remember us?"

The blocky stone head turned, but all expression was lost on the rough features. "Of course, traveler. But is Scartaris not destroyed? I could feel that when it happened. I was free."

Delrael nodded. "We need you to fight against the manticore who now leads his army."

"Manticore?" Arken said. His stiff stone wings pried open and then closed again with a crunching sound. "Ah! It will be good to fight him again. He destroyed me last time."

"Go out at night and wander among the creatures encamped around the ice fortress," Delrael said. "In the morning, when the other monsters can see, challenge Siryyk to single combat. We hope you can kill him."

After a moment, the gargoyle spoke. "The manticore has already defeated me once."

Enrod spoke up, clutching the scroll he had found in Sardun's vaults. "Then we will summon you again! And again!"

Arken swung his head from side to side in a stiff motion. "No, fashioning this body grows more difficult each time. When Scartaris forced me to return and serve him—twice—I lost much of my strength. You see . . ." He held out one arm; the hand was just a blocky lump of stone without fingers. "I have done a poor job this time. It will get worse."

Enrod crumpled the scroll in his hand. "Kill Siryyk the first time."

The manticore strode out of his tent, slashing at the flaps with his claws. The sores on his face, continuing to burn from the venom Enrod had blasted at him, felt worse.

Siryyk heard preparations among his troops, but he ignored them. He shook his maned head to clear away the last muddled nightmares, the backwash of fear and the Outsider David's loss of control.

The Game would end soon, one way or another.

Siryyk had to capture the Stones before the time came. He didn't know what he would do with them, but somehow their enormous magic could shield him. And if that strategy didn't work, and they were all going to die anyway, then Siryyk would use the Sitnaltan weapon to destroy everything, the Outsiders along with Gamearth.

The horde had trampled most of the snow and ice in the area, leaving only bare rocks and frozen footprints. General Korux watched as two Slac scooped snow into the boiler of the steam-engine car, making it ready. On its front seat sat the Sitnaltan weapon that

Professor Verne had repaired. Other monsters wandered about, none of them knowing what to do. They were growing hungry, Siryyk knew. The human riders had ruined most of their supplies.

Three small goblins used pumice to scour off oxidation from the surface of Verne's cannon. Today, Siryyk decided, he would blast the ice walls down.

Out of a nearby group of demons, a bulky stone figure plodded forward. Siryyk turned toward him. A gargoyle . . . he did not recall having seen this creature in his army before.

Then the manticore remembered him—it was Arken, the gargoyle who had broken from Scartaris's control and attacked *him* instead. Siryyk had blasted him into shards of broken stone.

"Siryyk, I bring you a message from Delrael," the gargoyle said.

Siryyk let out a rumbling roar, not knowing what Arken wanted. The other monsters stopped what they were doing and turned to watch. The manticore raised his scorpion tail, feeling the angry energy just behind the stinger. He wanted to destroy the messenger, but first he wanted to hear what Arken had to say.

"What is this message?" Siryyk said, rearing up to glare down at the blocky gargoyle.

In response, Arken bunched up one mammoth arm and put his entire body behind an enormous roundhouse punch, striking upward and cracking into Siryyk's jaw.

The manticore stumbled one step backward with an astonished grunt, swayed, then fell into a sitting position. He tried to clear the black explosions of pain from his head. The world spun.

He must have lost consciousness for a few seconds, plunged into distorted dreams of the Outside. Vaguely, he realized that the other monsters were firing arrows and throwing spears at the gargoyle. Some left little white nicks on the stone, but otherwise caused no damage.

Siryyk shook his head. Blood dribbled down the side of his black lips, and he could feel a splintering ache in his mouth. The instant his vision cleared, he spat out a roar mixed with flying droplets of blood. He lurched to his feet again and, throwing all his energy into the attack, struck out with his scorpion tail.

But Arken had already stepped out of the way. When the flying mud and dazzling light cleared, Siryyk turned, still dizzy, and faced the clumsy gargoyle again. Other monster fighters had gathered around to watch the duel.

Siryyk struck a second time, but the moment before his stinger touched the slow-moving gargoyle, Arken's stone arms and legs flowed back into a shapeless boulder. The manticore's tail exploded the rock into flying, sharp shards.

Then Arken emerged from another boulder by Siryyk's side, fashioning stone arms and legs and striding forward out of the rock. Before Siryyk could turn, Arken slammed his fist into the manticore's leonine body, cracking ribs.

Siryyk reared up, bringing both paws together in a hammering blow. He caught the gargoyle's two wings between them and snapped off the sheets of stone. He struck with the stinger once more, but again the gargoyle vanished into the rock. The manticore felt drained, propped up only by the anger and the pain in his body. He had already expended most of his power.

Behind him, Arken strode forward out of another rock, but this time he seemed thicker, more clumsily formed. He moved much more slowly.

Siryyk turned to attack with his weakened stinger, and the gargoyle slid out of the boulder, escaping into yet another rock. The manticore's small bolt of power only splintered pieces of the stone's surface.

Siryyk turned around and around, looking for the

gargoyle to reappear. His head still screamed from the pain of the first punch from Arken's fist, while his cracked ribs sent stabs through his chest. But he could not show weakness in front of the other monsters.

He found one boulder slowly moving. Its outline pushed and reformed into a vague silhouette of Arken. But the figure seemed only half-completed, and then it stopped all motion, looking like a statue that had weathered away over the centuries. Siryyk panted and stared, wondering what the gargoyle's trick was.

But nothing happened. The gargoyle, all his energy expended, did not move farther.

The monsters began to whisper; some cheered.

Siryyk strode forward, trying not to limp, and used his left paw to topple the petrified gargoyle. Arken broke in half among the other rocks.

Delrael stood atop the ice fortress, shading his eyes to make out Arken's duel as well as he could. The gargoyle failed in the end.

Delrael clenched his fist, seeing the knuckles turn white in the cold. He looked around at the other towers, where the sentries observed in silence. The wind whipped around the battlements, where more characters watched the duel. He heard their mutterings of disappointment.

Enrod had not even stayed to watch Arken's contest. Instead, the Sentinel wandered through the ice fortress, speaking out loud to no one, stopping, and turning back the way he had come. He seemed to be debating with himself.

Arken's fight stirred up the monster horde, though. The Slac general stood beside the wounded manticore as the other creatures waved weapons and yelled curses at the ice walls.

One of the sentries on another tower called out and pointed. Several characters on the battlements looked down, craning their necks to see.

Across the snow ran a single figure dressed in armor and carrying a sword. Faint words drifted back in the cold air as the character shouted a challenge at the monsters. "Will no one fight me in single combat?" The figure stopped some distance from the monsters, planted feet squarely in the snow, and held the sword high.

"What!" Delrael blinked his eyes in astonishment. "Who is that?"

The creatures shouted and rushed forward, clattering their weapons. The single human figure did not move from the battle stance.

"Who is that?" Delrael shouted again, turning around.

Romm scrambled up the tower stairs and stood out of breath. "It's Siya!" he said. He gulped in a breath. "She took a sword and some armor."

"What?" Delrael grabbed onto the balcony wall. "Siya!" he bellowed as loud as he could into the wind. She couldn't hear him. He whirled back at Romm. "What the hell is she doing?"

Reeling and angry, the manticore stormed toward her. Siryyk snarled at the other monsters readying their arrows and spears. "The human is mine!"

Romm beat a fist against the ice wall. "We have to march now, Delrael! Get every fighter out there. We can save her."

But Delrael saw the monsters only seconds away from her. They could never even get down the stairs in time. "It wouldn't do any good," he whispered.

Siya looked ridiculously puny in front of the enormous manticore. Her sword looked too small to cause damage even if Siryyk did nothing at all to defend himself.

"Delrael!" Romm cried. "We have to go now!"

Delrael whirled to snap at him. "It'll take at least half an hour to get our army out there. Think! She's going to die in the next few minutes!"

With a flurry of smoke and fire, Rognoth burst into the air from within the ice fortress. The sunlight glinted off his silvery-blue scales; his wings made the snow swirl as he swooped down over the monster army.

"Leave her alone!" the dragon shrilled.

Siya craned her head upward, pointing her sword in the air. Rognoth coughed out short bursts of fire, torching four of the nearest creatures. The downdraft from his wings demolished a pavilion set up on the packed ground.

The manticore reared back at his true enemy. Rognoth flew down, attempting to land in front of Siryyk, but instead he crashed right into the monster commander.

Siya stumbled backward, away from the battle between dragon and manticore. Delrael, thinking fast, shouted down to the other gathered fighters. "Send Ydaim Trailwalker and Tayron Tribeleader! They're our fastest runners! Go fetch Siya! Take her away from there."

Siryyk reached up with both powerful forepaws and wrapped them around Rognoth's neck. The curved lion's claws scraped on silver scales, sending up a shower of sparks.

Rognoth threw his weight forward, using his leverage. His wings flapped, driving him ahead. His own forelegs were weak, but he spat fire onto the manticore's back and neck.

Siryyk twisted around to bring his scorpion tail up. Its end flickered with a skittering, blue glow. The stinger struck and struck again into Rognoth's armored side. Weakened from the recent battle with Arken, the manticore could not summon much power. But each blow blasted a dark hole in the dragon's tarnished scales.

Delrael watched two khelebar streak out from the ice fortress walls, moving like reflections on the snow.

Most of the monster army watched the titanic duel between Siryyk and the dragon, as did Siya.

"Why doesn't she run away from of there?" Delrael muttered to himself. His jaw hurt from the angry clenching of his teeth.

Ydaim and Tayron dashed up to her and, without pausing, snatched Siya off the ground. She struggled, but Ydaim grabbed her sword and Tayron forced her onto Ydaim's back.

Rognoth hissed and craned his neck, snapping with sharp teeth at the manticore's back. Siryyk stung again with his tail but did little serious damage.

General Korux took up a jagged-tipped spear and rushed forward to stab at the dragon's body. The scaled armor deflected the first blow, but when Korux recovered, he plunged the blade into one of the blackened wounds Siryyk had already made. The spear tip sank into an exposed area on Rognoth's flank.

The dragon yowled and belched a scattered ball of fire at Korux. The spear shaft snapped out of his hand, and the Slac general fled, taking some of the flames on his shoulder. He rolled in the snow to extinguish the fire on his clothing.

Rognoth bent down to snap at the spear shaft embedded in his side.

Siryyk shifted his grip with his claws and tore at the wide band of scarred skin on the dragon's throat, the patch where Gairoth's iron collar had long ago worn away all scales.

Rognoth squawked and choked, flapping his wings to get away. Siryyk dug his long claws into the unprotected flesh and sheared sideways, then lunged forward and sank his own fangs into Rognoth's exposed throat.

Blood spurted, and the dragon no longer made any noise except a long whistle of air hissing down the gurgling tunnel of his throat. The manticore reached

more deeply with his claws, tearing, roaring and stinging repeatedly with the scorpion tail.

The dragon's spine snapped.

Siryyk tossed the dragon's limp neck on the ground,
smashing Rognoth's head into an exposed outcropping
of rock. Stepping away from the carcass, the manticore roared his victory.

The other monsters picked up the cry.

"Come to us."

"Join us."

"You are the last."

Enrod stood with his hands at his sides, deep in
Sardun's vaults. The voices of the *dayid* spoke to him.
He could see little light here, only a faint glow trickling through the thick ice. He had brought no torch
with him this time; that would have shamed him in the
company of his race.

"You belong here."

Enrod had resisted this call for centuries. He had
watched Gamearth continue after the Transition, when
only a few Sentinels remained. During the generations
of the horrible Scouring, the Sentinels had assisted
human characters in fighting off ogres and Slac and
helped the humans establish a stable society. As time
passed, more of the Sentinels, seeing their work either
finished or pointless, had annihilated themselves in a
half-Transition that liberated their spirits and destroyed
their bodies.

"You are the last one!"

But Enrod had never given up. He had turned all of
his enthusiasm into helping human characters. That
battle would never be over, but he felt so old and tired
now. He had played the Game for more turns than
any other character. He had avoided this for so long,
and now it seemed the only way.

It was the last thing he could do, a proper sacrifice
and a fitting end. It would cleanse everything else

from his mind. He would go through the half-Transition himself. Now. It would liberate enough energy to resurrect all the old Sorcerer bodies. He stood in the dimness and walked toward the sloping ceilings where, in shadow, lay all the frozen bodies that had not moved since the Transition.

"You will help now," he said to them. "Yes, help. *You* will march out and fight. Fight until you drop. Feel no pain because you are not alive." He made a fist. "Real soldiers. Not just players like before, with other characters to do your fighting."

He bent down and looked at the motionless face of a middle-aged woman. Somewhere in the back pockets of his mind he should know her name, but it had been too long. He saw the frost in her hair, on her eyelids, and on her cheeks.

He kept smiling in the dimness. "Do this for your human inheritors."

He moved to another man, whose gray-streaked hair hung braided over his left ear. Enrod placed his hand on the man's frozen cheek, letting his own body heat soften the frozen flesh. Enrod bent so close that his breath warmed the man's face.

"You can make up for abandoning the humans. I think you owe it to them, don't you?"

He bent over the next motionless body. "Don't you?"

Enrod stood, still crouching under the low ceiling. "Like an old Sorcerer council!" He raised his voice, letting his words echo from the ice. "Does any of you object?" He laughed. "I thought not!"

He stepped back to the center of the vaults where he could stand tall again. "All right, then, *dayid*. Take me now. I'm ready."

He closed his eyes and hissed a long breath through his teeth. Deep within himself, he concentrated, weaving together threads of power into a pattern he had always known but had never dared to attempt. When

he made the last connection, he squeezed his fiery
eyes shut. A single tear oozed down his cheek.

And then he released it all in one exhale. All the
magic he had learned throughout his long life-span
surged out, gushing through his veins, and his muscle
fibers, exploding out of every cell in his body. He saw
behind his eyelids an incredible light brighter than a
thousand suns. His body twisted, spiraled, spun into a
cyclone of his own making.

He tapped into the vortex of the *dayid* below the ice
fortress. Enrod felt it join him, help him along, increase his power. He knew what he wanted, and the
dayid had already agreed.

All the power shot outward, melting the walls of the
vault so that water gushed down the bricks and then
refroze into stalactites. Steam swirled in the room as
the magic spilled into the bodies of every one of the
old Sorcerers lying there.

When nothing remained of Enrod the individual,
silence hung for just a moment in the devastated vaults.

Then the bodies began to stir. The old Sorcerers sat
up without blinking their eyes, staring straight ahead.
They began to march.

Delrael ran down to the courtyard as Tayron and
Ydaim hurried through the low gate, bearing a dazed
Siya between them. Though she could not hear him,
Delrael was livid and shouted at her. "What do you
think you're doing? I'm in command here! No one
goes out without my permission!"

At that moment, lights shot through the ice of the
fortress, and steam poured out the windows.

"What's going on now!" Delrael held his arms up in
exasperation as well as fear. He looked around but
nobody could answer him. He guessed what it was.
"Where's Enrod?" He stormed back toward the main
entrance to the ice fortress.

Other characters came running out of the doorway,

flashing glances behind them. Several of the sentries had tumbled down from the turret stairs in terror.

Parts of the frozen courtyard slumped. Snow melted in puddles as cracks opened in the ground and hot steam pushed out. Delrael planted his feet to keep his balance. He took a deep breath. The rest of his soldiers milled around in confusion. Too much was happening all at once.

Delrael felt the anger bubbling within him again. "I'm supposed to be in command of this army! Why does every character do whatever he pleases without telling me?"

Then the first ranks of old Sorcerers marched out of the fortress.

Delrael stared, speechless. Hundreds of powerful characters shuffled ahead, but he recognized none of them. They wore ancient robes and jewels and had long hair styled in the manner of Sorcerer lords and ladies whom he had seen on paintings and mosaics. He recalled all the frozen bodies that had been under the fortress.

The old Sorcerers marched out as if directed by something else. The *dayid*? Or Enrod? Delrael's own soldiers hurried out of the way as the resurrected characters moved toward the wall of ice.

A faint, pearly glow surrounded the Sorcerers. They carried their ancient swords; some bore shields, others had taken the weapons Siya stockpiled within the fortress. Several went toward the older characters from the Stronghold village, the ones who would not fight, and commandeered their swords. Shocked, the villagers did not resist.

One Sorcerer woman, tall and thin with an angular face and unblinking, vacant eyes, walked over to where Siya still lay only half conscious. The Sorcerer woman picked up Siya's sword and walked back to join the ranks.

They lined up and pushed forward, more than a

hundred of them, five across and more than twenty
deep. The first rank stood with their faces only inches
from the tall fortress wall.

The ice rippled, clarified, and then crawled away
from them, opening up a broad gate, a portal for the
old Sorcerer army. At an unheard signal, they all
moved forward, raising their swords to an attack position. They trotted out to meet Siryyk's army, without
a battle cry, without a sound.

Before Delrael could call after them and before
some of his own fighters could think to run and
join in the battle, the ice wall bunched and rose,
sealing them again within the protection of the ice
fortress.

Outside, the monsters howled and charged forward,
seeing an enemy out to face them at last.

The old Sorcerer army marched out to meet them.

INTERLUDE: OUTSIDE

David stared at the hexagons on the map. The black lines reminded him of an intricate net designed to trap him.

Outside, the wind from the storm sounded like the flapping fabric of a tent. Visions of the manticore flickered behind his mind. He sat cross-legged, as he had for the past hour, and ignored his aching knees. His cheek still stung from his injury, much as Siryyk's face must have felt.

A sharp thunder of pain went through his head—sympathetic hurt from the manticore? He squeezed his eyes shut.

"I've got an idea," Tyrone said. "And it's my turn."

David looked up at Tyrone. Scott went to try the phone again, but he heard nothing this time, not a dial tone, not Lellyn's voice. Melanie smiled at Tyrone, encouraging him.

She had lost the gargoyle and her Rognoth character —who had originally been played by David, back when he introduced Gairoth the ogre—but she had also saved Siya, and had now launched an entirely unexpected fighting force against David's manticore. Pleased with the game, she continued to flash defiant glances at him.

"I know you guys don't think I know what's going on," Tyrone said. "But I *do*! I'm just so amazed, that's all. I mean, who will ever believe us anyway?

Rule #1, always have fun. Isn't that what we said when we started this?" He looked at them.

"This is all straight out of the Twilight Zone. But think about it: if the Game can come out here and lock our doors and mess with the TV and the phone, and if it can blow up my mom's kitchen table, and draw its blue line on the map, and if Lellyn's ghost or whatever can come to talk to us . . . well, hey, what's to stop *us* from going *in*?"

"It can't work that way," Scott said.

Tyrone turned on Scott. He had been pouting ever since Scott had shouted at him before. "Listen, Mr. Science, you don't know how it works any more than the rest of us. Why should it be any different? We're the ones who came up with the rules in the first place. If I roll . . ." He grabbed the transparent twenty-sided die from beside the splintered edge of Melanie's map. "Say, a seventeen or better, what's to stop me from going *inside* Gamearth?"

"Tyrone, don't you dare," David said.

Melanie stared down at the white hexagons of frozen wasteland. "There's a battle going on down there. Are you sure you want—"

"A battle is the most exciting place! David plays Siryyk, but I'm handling the rest of the monsters. I handled the Black Falcon troops and all the other fighters. I can certainly handle this."

David grabbed his arm. "You don't know what you're doing."

Tyrone jerked away. "Quit telling me what to do! It's my turn, and I'm rolling."

"Don't!" Scott shouted.

Tyrone tossed the crystalline die on the carpet. It came to rest by the edge of the map, showing a perfect "20". Gamearth definitely wanted him in.

Tyrone vanished.

Scott stood with his mouth wide and gaping. Melanie let out a gasp, choking in a quick breath. David hung his head.

"What do we do now?" Scott whispered.

The snow under his feet felt real and wet and cold. Tyrone wore only his socks.

The air smelled different, biting and clean. The afternoon sun shone brightly in his eyes after the artificial light of the fireplace and the lamps in David's family room.

"Wow!" he said, looking up into the sky with astonishment. He didn't even notice the wind through his thin shirt. "It worked!"

He turned and saw the magnificent ice fortress, glinting like something out of Disneyland. Tyrone kept making sounds of disbelief.

He saw the marching ranks of old Sorcerers coming toward him, exactly as he had pictured them in his mind. All four of the players must have had the same visions to create something as real as this. "Wait'll I get back and tell them about this!"

Then he heard the shouting and the din of drawn weapons. He whirled to see the monster horde charging at him.

His nightmarish visions of reptilian monsters and sharp teeth and pointed blades had been only pale outlines of what he saw now. Even the most spectacular movie special effects had never been able to hint at the hideousness of these alien creatures.

They saw Tyrone and surged in his direction.

But he had created them. The monster horde with all its evil fighters were his own characters. He had moved them about, played them, used them to strike on the campaign. "Stop!" he said. But none of them noticed.

Tyrone realized too late that he should run.

*   *   *

The air in the family room made a wet, hissing sound, like rain falling on hot metal. Then Tyrone's body reappeared.

He sprawled on the carpet, not moving. Blood oozed from a hundred separate stab wounds. His battered face and open, staring eyes held an expression of profound disbelief.

Melanie screamed and shrank away.

Scott grabbed some old newspapers in a useless gesture to protect the floor as he vomited. His glasses fell off as he stumbled to the kitchen. David heard the water running.

He knelt down beside Tyrone and rolled him over to expose the horrible gashes that tore open his chest and abdomen. He saw no use in checking for a pulse, but he did anyway. "He's dead."

Scott stood by the entrance to the family room, shaking. Without his glasses he appeared strangely vulnerable. "It's just a game! It's just a *game*, dammit!" His voice had a thin, whining tone. "What are we going to do? We can't keep playing this stupid game! Tyrone's dead!"

Melanie looked at David, and he felt a kind of communion between them. She glared at the map of Gamearth as if it had betrayed her. "We can't stop," she said. "The doors are locked. We're cut off. The Game is never going to let us leave . . . until it's finished."

"It's not a game," David said. He held one of the crystalline dice in his hand. Tyrone's blood still clung to his fingers and smeared on the transparent facets of the die.

"It's war. And I'm going to put an end to it all."

24

WEREM GROTTO

> *"Characters must never give up. That is not one of our options. We have a responsibility to the Game that goes beyond our tendency to despair."*
> —Enrod, on the second rebuilding of Tairé

Vailret felt trapped in a cell darker than the darkest night imaginable. The packed dirt was gritty and damp against his skin, caked in his hair. His fingers throbbed and stung from trying to claw out of the grave. The air grew thick and stifling, liquid with dust and dampness from their own respiration.

He had too little room to move. Next to him, Bryl had given up in despair. "We have lost the Stones!" Bryl moaned. "All three of them. Everything's useless now."

"We have utterly failed," Vailret muttered.

After the werem had packed the walls down tight, the invisible force had abandoned Vailret and Bryl, leaving them free to move, but with nowhere to go.

"They're going to come back and plant their larvae in us," Bryl said in the total darkness. "I just know it."

Vailret could hear the half-Sorcerer's teeth chattering together. "Or they'll just leave us here to suffocate," he said. He kept trying to scrape at the wall, but the werem had done something to the dirt so that it seemed hard as dried mortar.

295

"If I still had the Fire Stone, I could blast us out of here," Bryl said.

"You'd probably burn us, too."

Vailret knew that Bryl had few other spells on his own without the help of the Stones. He tried to remember which ones Bryl knew. He could keep blades sharp or make them dull, or make flowers open prematurely. Neither of those seemed particularly useful at the moment.

Vailret stopped digging at the hard wall. He turned toward Bryl in the darkness. "You can still use your spell to replenish supplies, right?"

"Yes," Bryl replied, "but we're going to run out of air long before we starve to death."

"No!" Vailret felt excitement rising within him again. "Create water *within* the dirt wall. You can make the whole wall like soup, and we can just crawl through the mud."

From Bryl's silence, Vailret could tell he was thinking about the possibility. "I don't see why not," he said. "Any other time, I can direct the water into casks and bottles. I should be able to direct it into the middle of this wall."

"Then do it, Bryl!"

Bryl squirmed, jabbing Vailret with his elbow. Vailret tried to push his chest against the packed dirt, giving the half-Sorcerer as much room as he could. Bryl mumbled something and flailed his hands. "Well, I just rolled one of my dice, but I can't see what number I got."

But Vailret heard water trickling and running. His hands and chest suddenly felt drenched.

"It worked!" Bryl said. "See if you can push through."

Vailret extended his hands. The earth turned soft, into muck, and gave way. Vailret strained and moved forward.

Bryl shoved at his back. "Go on!"

Vailret scooped with his hands, swimming through mud like cold, sticky gravy as he clawed onward. He thrust his head into the opening, still tunneling. He held his breath, puffing his cheeks out and trying to clench his nostrils shut. Then, with a cough and a gasp, he burst through the wall as it slumped away, falling into a puddle on the floor.

He splashed and rolled out, falling to his knees on the floor, sucking in great gasps of breath. Cold, brown slime covered his hands and hair and face and clothes. He choked and then started laughing.

Bryl stumbled out and fell beside him. Everything remained dark and dank. He heard only the dripping slump of the waterlogged mud.

"Good job, Bryl," Vailret said.

Bryl muttered beside him, a disembodied voice in the blackness. "So now what do we do?"

Vailret sat against a firm portion of the opposite wall. The question had not occurred to him, but the only answer seemed obvious. "We go ahead with our plan."

"But we're defenseless! The werem took our Stones."

Vailret scowled at Bryl, who could not see his expression anyway, but he thought the cool tone in his voice would get the point across. "So? They can't use the Stones. *I* can't even use them. You need Sorcerer blood. You saw how the werem took the gems from Tryos's treasure. They must be just keeping them somewhere. We need to get them back."

"Are you sure that's all they're doing with them?"

"No," Vailret answered. "But we don't have any choice." His voice became hard-edged, and he thought Delrael would have been proud at his commanding tone. "If you and I fail to get those Stones back, and if we can't succeed in making the Allspirit, then Gamearth is doomed. We don't have any right to give up, whether we want to or not. Now make some light for us and let's go on."

Bryl used another minor spell to conjure up a small glow that lit their way. Vailret and Bryl stared at each other, shocked at their wide-eyed, mud-spattered appearance, and tried to refrain from laughing or sobbing at how pitiful they looked.

"Remember," Vailret said, "this is all supposed to be fun."

They traveled for days, it seemed. The werem tunnel continued under the earth, wide and straight; occasionally they found unused side passages. They had been so long out of natural light and away from landmarks that Vailret had no idea which direction they headed.

Around a sharp bend, they found another alcove scraped out of the side wall. As the bobbing, insubstantial light cast shadows on the sloping walls, Vailret at first thought three enemies lay waiting to spring on them. But as the glow fell on the figures, Vailret saw that these characters, sprawled in an uncovered grave, would never move again.

Bryl shuddered. Vailret leaned forward to see the horrifying corpses dressed in what appeared to be Sitnaltan clothes. They looked mummified, drained, and somehow broken, as if they had been devoured from the inside out. Their eye sockets were gaping, jagged holes in empty skulls where something had burst through the sockets. The joints looked broken; the chests had cracked outward.

Bryl turned sick and gray. "The larvae got them. That's what werem do. They plant their grubs on humans so they can eat their way out." He let the silence hang for a moment. "They're probably going to do that to us."

"*If* they catch us again." Vailret felt queasy. "But they only seemed interested in the Stones."

He put a finger to his lip, grimaced, then spat dried mud out of his mouth. "The invisible force in Sitnalta always seemed to be after us: when it made Dirac come with the car and when we tried to get away in Frankenstein's balloon. I wonder if this werem Master was trying to take our Stones from the start."

"Well, it got what it wanted," Bryl said.

"So we have to take the Stones back."

The side tunnels branched out more and more as they continued, until the hexagon seemed honeycombed with passages. Bryl's light illuminated only a small area around them, and they could see nothing but blackness ahead and behind. Vailret began to wonder what exactly they would do when they came upon the werem.

The passage widened, and Vailret could hear clicking and trickling sounds. A diffuse glow flickered ahead beyond the range of Bryl's light.

"Walk slower, Bryl," he whispered. "We don't know what this might be."

But before the half-Sorcerer could respond, two werem slithered out of side passages behind them. Bryl bit back a gasp, letting only a small whimper escape.

A shadow appeared in the glow ahead, the silhouette of a burly werem, nearly half again as large as any they had seen. Vailret felt afraid to move. "Nothing we can do," he said to Bryl.

"We can be captured," Bryl said.

"Besides that."

The large werem came toward them. In the uncertain glow, Vailret saw complicated insignia tattooed on his chest and shoulders. Gashes of ornamental scars stood out on his cheeks below staring, white eyes.

The werem spoke with a hollow, inhuman voice. "Master has been waiting for you."

The worm-man turned around at his waist and flowed back the way he had come. His long segmented body looped around and trailed after, dripping lubricating slime. The two werem behind them extended their

clawed hands and prodded the mud-spattered backs of
Vailret and Bryl.

The confining passage dropped away as they stepped
into a huge grotto with wide, echoing walls. Scores of
the werem dug down into warrens that housed their
swarming nest.

Thick, cement-hard support columns rose like sta-
lagmites from floor to ceiling, propping up the grotto.
Sharp, bright clusters of crystals, clear, pink, and pale
blue, protruded like ornaments from the walls. Gems
studded other sections of the dirt, glinting and half-
hidden as if the werem had planted them there. The
chamber carried a crystalline sheen, a glow sparkling
off everything, which the blind werem could never
see.

In the center of the grotto floor stood the sculpture
of a gigantic outstretched hand, fingers extended and
palm upward. Fashioned out of mud the same color as
the walls and floor, it was as large as a banquet table,
perhaps an altar of some kind. In the middle of the
cupped palm, Vailret saw the sparkling colors of the
four-sided diamond Air Stone, the eight-sided ruby
Fire Stone, and a perfect egg-sized ten-sided emerald—
the Earth Stone.

"There they are!" Bryl said.

Vailret flicked his glance around, checking the positions of the other werem in the grotto. The guardians
behind him had halted at the entrance to the grotto.
He wondered if he could rush forward and snatch the
Stones and toss them to Bryl, so that he could blast
their way out with the Fire Stone. He tensed. They
didn't seem to have any other choice. Vailret just
hoped that Bryl could react fast enough.

Then the fingers of the giant clay hand trembled,
as if loosening up. They curled together into a fist,
closing down and covering the three Stones.

The far wall of the grotto wavered and shifted. The
dirt and mud and clay became liquid, reforming as if

something behind the wall were pushing its way to the surface.

Then a huge human head emerged, made of mud and protruding through the membrane of the wall. Vailret saw the eyes, the forehead, nose and chin emerge to make a face as large as a Sitnaltan building.

The worm-men in the grotto focused their attention on the moving face. Gems and crystals popped out of the wall as the dirt convulsed. The werem hissed and swayed. They muttered the same word over and over again: "Master! Master!"

The clay smoothed, and distinctive features appeared on the cheeks, the eyelids and the lips. Vailret even noticed faint tracings of hair on the eyebrows, forehead, and beside the ears. It was a young face, a male face, and it seemed angry.

He had glimpsed this face long ago as just a distorted image when he had looked through the scattered lenses from Paenar's eye-staff and caught a distant reflection of the Outside Players.

This was the visage of the Outsider David.

"Master!" the werem whispered.

"You're not my master!" Vailret said. He stood defiant. Bryl looked at him in astonishment.

The enormous earthen face scowled at them, then the flexible lips curled up in a smile as wide as a fissure in the earth. "The one you called the 'Stranger Unlooked-For' was Melanie's 'Apprentice.' Her 'Journeyman' succeeded in destroying Scartaris.

"But I am *Master*. I have the Stones." The clay hand in the middle of the floor pushed up and opened again to display them.

"You can't win against the Outside. You're just characters in a Game. *Our* Game. We created you. You can't fight us."

The face pushed farther out of the wall. Vailret resisted his impulse to cringe.

"I ruined Sitnalta so they could find no solution. My manticore holds Verne's ultimate weapon."

The clay face let the smile broaden. "Delrael's troops are trapped in the ice fortress and can't do anything but annoy my monster army." He paused, and the echoes of his last words rumbled in the grotto. The worm-men stared with rapt attention.

"And you are here," David said. "In my grasp."

Another huge clay hand formed out of the side grotto wall and thrust toward them with blinding speed, knocking werem out of the way as it snatched both Vailret and Bryl in clay fingers.

The massive arm lifted them off the ground. Vailret's arms and legs were pinned in the powerful grip. The fist pulled them across the grotto, sliding without a ripple through the dirt floor. It held them directly in front of the enormous, frightening face.

As the David visage opened its mouth to shout, his gullet seemed to go straight through the bottom of the map. "You killed Tyrone! You've given me nightmares! You've ruined my life!"

The crushing fist pulled them between the towering eyes that flicked and moved in sockets made of wet dirt. The hand squeezed.

Vailret felt his bones about to crack. Black spots swirled in front of his eyes, and he could not breathe or even gasp.

"The Game is over!" David shouted. "And you have lost!"

25

BACKFIRE

"Desperate measures—how the Outsiders enjoy them."

—the Sentinel Oldahn,
before destroying a Slac citadel,
and himself, to rescue Doril

The old Sorcerers battled with no finesse, no imagination, simply with brutal persistence. But they attacked, and kept attacking, even after they received mortal injuries.

Siryyk's monster fighters fell by the score; many gave up and fled back toward the mountain terrain. The special Slac troops tried a different tactic, with five of them converging on a single Sorcerer, hacking the nondead body to pieces, then moving to the next opponent. The snow had been churned into mud and blood.

The monsters howled, snarled, and clanged their weapons as they battled; but the old Sorcerers spoke no word, indeed gave no cry of triumph, pain, or anger. They merely fought in silence with a deliberate and ponderous ferocity.

Siryyk stood by the carcass of the dragon and felt agony in his body. His scorpion tail remained drained of power. He felt cracked bones in his chest and hot blood in his mouth from Arken's attack; the wounds inflicted by Rognoth scored his hide. He had never come so close to defeat before.

When he had seen that the fighters marching out of

the ice fortress were yet another wild card Delrael's army was playing on him, he had felt his fury rise to its highest pitch.

With a sudden snap in his mind, he also sensed a greater freedom of his thoughts, as if the Outsider David had diverted his attentions elsewhere. Siryyk knew this would be his final chance to gain victory.

"I want those Stones now!" he snarled to himself, and then bellowed in a voice that crackled over the battlefield. "Korux!"

General Korux rode away from the fighting in the steam-engine car. Bound in the back, Professor Verne lay struggling. Korux enjoyed taunting the prisoner and trying to frighten him, but Siryyk had no more patience for that.

"Prepare the cannon!" the manticore said. "I want those fortress walls down immediately. Delrael is inside. These . . ." He glared at the attacking old Sorcerers. Blood-flecked saliva came down his black lips. "These are just diversions."

Siryyk turned his squarish head and looked around the battlefield, seeing how many of his monster fighters lay slaughtered. It angered him that his own troops were such pathetic fighters.

Throughout this entire march, the humans had defeated him again and again. Siryyk's horde had once outnumbered the humans five to one, but now the forces seemed equal.

"Hurry!" he snapped at Korux.

The Slac general leaped out of the steam-engine car and ran to the black cannon. Its surface gleamed in patches from where the goblins had scoured it that morning, but their work had been interrupted by the appearance of Arken.

As the old Sorcerers continued to fight, and as wounded monsters kept screaming and snarling, Korux and several Slac assistants aimed the cannon barrel at the thick ice walls.

Siryyk drew himself up. In a moment, the fortress would crumble. He would march in triumph and snatch the Stones out of Delrael's dying hand.

In the steam-engine car, Professor Verne squirmed and managed to get himself into a sitting position with his elbows propped behind him. He coughed. His eyes looked wide and bloodshot, his appearance haggard, like a character at the end of his play.

Korux and the Slac loaded the cannon with one of the last casks of firepowder, then they rolled the heavy cannonball down the gullet of the weapon.

"Wait!" Verne said. His voice was weak, but desperate. "Please wait. I know how to make it better."

The manticore turned to him. "I am quite satisfied with the performance of your cannon as it is."

"You don't understand," Verne sounded too tired to shout. "You saw the avalanche you created when you fired it before. Do you want to destroy the entire ice fortress? Please, I can adjust the detonation, so that the impact is less *brisant*. It will merely shatter the walls and open a way for you to get in."

"It is a trick," Korux said to Siryyk. The other Slac finished aiming the cannon and locked down the gears. They placed rocks behind the wheels to stop the recoil from hurling it backward.

"No trick. Let me save those characters. If I show you a clean way to break in, you can take what you want from them. There's no need to slaughter the entire army."

"Why should I bother?" Siryyk said.

Verne's haggard face grew hard, and he snapped, "What if your unnecessary destruction ruins the Stones? How long is it going to take you to dig through a mound of rubble and dead characters just to find a few tiny gems?"

"All right," Siryyk said. "But hurry." The possibility of tedious sifting through the wreckage had not occurred to him. If they could overwhelm the human forces and take Delrael prisoner, Siryyk would enjoy drawing claws across the human commander's throat. It would be much more satisfying than just blowing up the place.

"Korux, watch him!"

Siryyk yanked the professor out of the steam-engine car and used his claws to rip free the bindings on Verne's wrists and ankles. The professor cried out as the ropes snapped, and the manticore wondered if he had sprained the man's wrists, then decided it didn't matter.

Verne stumbled to the cannon, as if on the verge of breaking into sobs. He adjusted parts of the back end of the cannon, moving the bronze support struts that Siryyk had always suspected served no purpose. Verne seemed to know exactly what he was doing.

Korux stood beside Verne with a short sword poised against his ribs. The professor turned to the Slac general and sneered. "I am incredibly weary of your bullying. I have nothing left to fear, so you're wasting your energy."

Korux hissed, but Verne ignored him and finished with the cannon. He glared at Siryyk. "It's done. You may fire it—and the rest of your efforts be damned!"

Siryyk knocked Verne sprawling toward the steam-engine car and then took up his position behind the cannon. "Korux, bring me a torch! Prepare the entire army for a charge into the fortress when we blast the walls down. Have them ignore these other fighters."

Korux bellowed to all the monsters who could hear him. One of the other Slac handed Siryyk a burning stick from a scattered campfire.

The manticore, holding the torch in his huge paw, stepped behind the cannon.

Verne crawled to his knees and watched the end of his work. He had lived in such terror for so long that his emotions were scoured down into apathy. Tears seemed to freeze across his eyes.

Siryyk took his position directly behind the cannon, as he had done before, and raised his flame to the touchhole. The fuse hissed. The other Slac backed away, covering their ears.

The entire cannon exploded.

The back end of the barrel blew out in a tremendous burst of flame and shrapnel. The iron cylinder blasted apart.

Verne rolled behind the steam-engine car for shelter. As the smoke and flames cleared, he saw the twisted wreckage of his cannon tilted onto one side on a broken wheel. With a groan, it slumped and collapsed to the ground.

Behind it, thrown backward five feet from the concussion, the bulk of Siryyk lay in a mess of blood and mangled tissue. His face and broad chest had been blown away. His neck had been snapped backward, his spine turned inside out. A hiss like a leaking Sitnaltan air pump wheezed through the holes in the manticore's punctured lungs. With a crackle of sparks and a dying blue glow, the deadly scorpion tail twitched once and then lay still.

The other monsters howled and shouted. Several ran to Siryyk's body like flies settling on a fresh kill.

With a cry of triumph, Verne leaped to his feet and felt the raw edge of joy fill him again. In one blow he had destroyed the deadly cannon and killed the powerful commander of the horde—perhaps he had even saved Gamearth.

A sharp reptilian hand grabbed the hair behind Verne's head and dug claws into his scalp, tilting his face up. Korux, two feet taller than the professor, glared down with sizzling, slitted eyes.

"Now it's time for my fun, Professor. And no one is going to stop me." He put the point of his short sword against Verne's abdomen.

Verne could not summon the energy even to struggle. Unlike when he had tried to throw himself into the void of broken hexes, this time his self-preservation drive did not try to assert itself.

"You have begged for this a long time," Korux said.

Slowly, an inch at a time, he pushed the blade deep into Verne's stomach until the bloody point came out his back.

The professor's last thought was to wonder if he and Frankenstein had ever patented a sword-proof vest.

In disgust, Korux tossed Verne's body down to the ground. Many of the monsters had stopped fighting. But the remaining old Sorcerer forces continued to drive forward and attack.

Korux immediately took charge. "We will destroy them all now!" he shouted. His own Slac came to him, adding their instant support. He spoke to them.

"We will use a tactic Siryyk himself feared. The professor created an ultimate weapon—and after we detonate it, we will be the victors. Gamearth will be ours!"

With one hand, Korux snatched Verne's bloody body up from the ground and dumped him into the back seat of the still-chugging steam-engine car. "It's time for you to take a message to Delrael, Professor."

Korux set the Sitnaltan weapon upright on the seat. It looked so much smaller and less threatening than the cannon. However, Korux knew clearly the fear it inspired in Verne, and the hesitation that the manticore had felt when thinking about it.

Korux pushed the arming button and then set the newly repaired timer. He had watched the professor fix the device, and as he held a knife to Verne's scrawny throat and hissed in his ear, he had forced the man to tell him how to use the weapon for just such an occasion as this.

Now, when he released the timer and it began to

tick like the rattling of a viper, Korux adjusted the steering levers and disengaged the braking lock. He jumped out of the car as it rolled forward.

The Slac general signaled his own fighters to back away and to be prepared to shield their eyes. "This will be spectacular!" he said.

The Sitnaltan weapon continued to tick as the vehicle drove straight toward the ice fortress.

26

UNDERGROUND

"Since all characters are different, with different skills, we should have many solutions to any problem. What reason is there for us to worry?"
—the Sentinel Arken,
in the debates on the Scouring

Frankenstein's Drone clanked and thudded as it continued along the streets of Sitnalta. The attack from the invisible force had stopped, and the giant mechanical man moved without hindrance.

When Tareah pressed Frankenstein about possible damage to Drone, he just shrugged. "A few dings and dents perhaps. I took special care to develop adequate armor. I wasn't sure what it might be required to do."

Drone walked into the center of a broad square and then stopped among large hexagonal tiles. A water clock spilled thin silver streams into a transparent receptacle etched with precise lines.

The professor looked at the bank of dials and gauges in front of him, adjusted one, and tapped the glass surface until he saw a needle bouncing and moving.

"Ah!" he said. "This is probably the best place."

Frankenstein pulled a wide belt across his chest and buckled himself into the seat. "You'd better brace yourself. I have installed gyros to stabilize this control compartment, but . . ." He shrugged in his chair. "I didn't have time to test them."

He grabbed another switch and flicked it upward. A

hiss of steam shot from the boiler, and Drone sagged on its joints, bending into a crouch.

"But first," the professor said, "tell me about this Earth Stone. What are we fighting? Bryl mentioned something about his spells and the gems he carried."

As Tareah answered him, she remembered how her father had told the tale over and over again. She purposely altered some of the words and changed the phrasing so that the tale became her own.

"The four Stones together contain all the remaining magic of the old Sorcerers. Each Stone has power over one of the four elements. The Fire Stone controls fire, the Water Stone controls water and the weather, the Air Stone creates illusions out of the air—Bryl probably told you all that. The Air Stone and the Earth Stone had been lost since the Scouring, but Gairoth the ogre found the Air Stone and used it. The Earth Stone lay buried in Tryos's treasure pile, until Vailret and Bryl went to get it."

"But what does it *do*?" Frankenstein adjusted his lead helmet, cocking it sideways so he could hear her better. He seemed impatient with the history lesson, preferring practical information instead.

"Well, the Earth Stone controls living things. Whoever uses it can manipulate characters just like one of the Outside Players."

"Ah, another Game-master inside the Game itself."

Frankenstein's eyebrows raised. "So at last we have a rational explanation for what has happened to my city." He paused, then pursed his lips. "I'm not sure magic counts as part of a 'rational' explanation, though." He appeared puzzled.

"No matter. According to these readings, the controller—the character who holds the Earth Stone and now, from what you say, also the Air and Fire Stones—is directly below us, deep in the earth.

"With Drone, we will go down and attack. Between the technology of this mechanical fighter and your magical abilities, we should deal with every circumstance."

Frankenstein powered up the engine, and Drone settled against the tiles. Then the professor thrust the entire steering mechanism forward. Drone bowed down into a kneeling position, squeaking and groaning on its huge joints and gears. The control compartment tilted along its stabilizers, partially righting itself.

Tareah pushed her body against the side of Frankenstein's seat and a bare section of the control panel. She placed one hand against the far wall, but pulled it back from the hot metal.

Frankenstein narrowed his eyes and moved feverishly. Drone's hands spread out. The metal fingers twitched.

Tareah watched through the eye-windows as the powerful claws scraped at the tiles. Drone pawed away the hexagons and exposed the raw dirt underneath.

Its hands moved rapidly, shoveling out enormous handfuls of dirt with each scooping motion. It jerked out a long metal conduit buried under the ground, snapping the pipe and hauling it up. Frankenstein stopped the automaton's work and stared out the magnifying eye-window to see the broken metal end and the thin cables dangling inside.

"So much for the new street lighting system," Frankenstein said. "Too ambitious a project anyway."

Drone leaned forward as it continued to scrape, and dig into the earth. When its head pushed into the dark opening, all light blotted out from the eye-windows. In a distracted motion, Frankenstein flipped a small switch; a powerful light blazed out from the metal man's forehead. All Tareah could see, though, was the dirt and mud falling as Drone continued to tunnel deeper.

The control chamber tilted again as the automaton plunged at a steeper angle, tunneling like a gigantic rodent, scooping the dirt behind as it continued to plow ahead.

Frankenstein kept monitoring his gauges. "Yes, getting closer, getting closer."

Tareah's eyes stung from not blinking often enough. She felt her anxiety growing, and she gripped the Water Stone with her sweaty palm. She would get to the other three Stones soon. She had the last one in her hand. She could put an end to all this.

But she dreaded most of all that something terrible had happened to Vailret and Bryl.

The two had taken a balloon and gone off to Rokanun days before . . . but they had not returned. Somehow the Stones had come back here under Sitnalta.

The professor hunched forward to stare at one gauge that spun wildly. "Hang on! There's something unusual ahead, a lack of resis—"

Suddenly Drone broke through the dirt wall and nearly pitched forward into a gigantic underground grotto. Frankenstein yanked back on the steering yoke to steady the automaton.

The spotlight stabbed into a chamber filled with writhing worm-men, with gray bodies, wet-looking skins, and staring blind white eyes. They squirmed and covered their faces from the burning light. Tareah saw more gems and crystals than even Tryos had kept in his treasure horde.

Frankenstein moved Drone forward into the chamber. The spotlight fell on the far wall. Tareah froze. "Look, it's Bryl and Vailret! And the Stones!"

But the words seemed ridiculous to her as soon as she said them. The most awesome sight was the terrifying clay face taking up nearly one entire wall and the colossal hand that held Vailret and Bryl in a crushing grip.

"Great Maxwell!" Frankenstein said.

"There's your controller," Tareah said. "There's the thing that's been destroying Sitnalta."

The professor looked at the titanic clay face that scowled at them, and his own expression filled with fury. He slammed his activation levers forward, and Drone strode into the chamber.

Tareah peered through the eye-windows and saw the metal feet squashing werem that could not wriggle out of the way fast enough. Some worm-men threw clods of dirt and gems, which did nothing to the automaton.

Frankenstein gave a sidelong glance at the werem. "What sort of evolutionary process could have made *that* a viable survival trait?" He snorted. "Professor Darwin has some explaining to do." He yanked another lever that extended Drone's dirt-spattered metal hands forward, as if he wanted to strangle the immense earthen face.

Drone towered halfway to the ceiling of the grotto. As it stomped across the floor, Frankenstein had to step sideways to avoid the thick support columns in the center.

The Master's vast clay hands cast Vailret and Bryl carelessly to the floor. The hands extended from the wall, palms outward, and grew larger as they pulled more dirt and mud. Tareah watched the three tiny Stones patter to the ground.

Frankenstein made Drone's hands form two fists as the automaton steamed forward.

The right clay hand swelled larger and struck across, swatting Drone. The giant mechanical man reeled sideways and staggered to the far wall of the grotto. The left eye-window cracked and splintered; two of the smaller panes popped out and tinkled on the grotto floor.

Drouels control chamber rocked and tilted as the gyros tried to stabilize it against the violent motion. The professor grabbed at an emergency handle to regain control.

Below them, in the bobbing, glaring spotlight, the

werem continued to move and hiss, surrounding Drone's feet. But they could do nothing. They were soft.

Frankenstein checked his control panel. "Some damage, but not serious. It'll be harder to walk. One leg joint doesn't seem to respond properly."

"I have the Water Stone," Tareah said. "I could roll it in here and strike out at that thing."

"No," the professor said without hesitating. "Wouldn't work. We're shielded in here. If the Earth Stone magic can't get in to manipulate us, then yours can't get out. Complementarity principle, or something like that. It only makes sense."

"Then I have to get out of Drone! How will I make it past the worm-men down there? If I can just take my Stone to the other four . . ." She looked through the shattered eye-window and saw Vailret and Bryl both scurrying toward the other gems. "If I can bring all four together, then we'll be done! We'll have the Allspirit. We'll have won."

Frankenstein kept his jaw clenched tightly, and his voice sounded strange. Tareah wondered if he had ever been battered by an opponent before.

"I'm going to charge forward, straight into that face and poke its big mud eyes out. When I start moving, undog the hatch and climb out. If you land right, you won't hurt yourself. We're not that high up. Help me out with your Water Stone if you can."

"All right," Tareah said. She braced herself as Frankenstein jammed his motion levers all the way forward.

Drone lurched ahead, steaming and hissing. She heard an abrasive clanking, and knew that one of the gears in the automaton's knee must have been broken.

Tareah moved aside the locking levers in the hatch. She popped open the heavy metal door in Drone's back and hung onto the edge. She shouted at the professor in the clanking roar of Drone's charge. "Luck!"

"I don't believe in Luck," Frankenstein said without turning away from his controls. "It's just a matter of probabilities."

Tareah swung out from the hatch, tried to grab several of the handholds and footholds on Drone's side, but the automaton lurched too much. The robot had stomped away from most of the werem, and she let go.

The heavy hatch on Drone's back clanged shut but did not lock. It wobbled open and banged down each time the automaton took a step. Wet mud caked the Sitnaltan automaton, and a geyser of steam came from the exhaust vent on its shoulders. The steam grew black as Drone chugged toward the scowling visage on the wall.

The colossal clay hands extended out, reaching for the automaton. Drone held out its own metal hands and charged at its top speed into the clay.

Tareah rolled, got to her knees, and scrambled away. The werem, intent on their Master's battle, didn't notice her. She grabbed the six-sided Water Stone and made ready to roll it, to call up some kind of spell to help Frankenstein.

But it was too late. Drone jammed its splayed metal claws with an explosive thud into the towering eye sockets.

The huge face let out a howl of pain. The clay hands folded over Drone, and the face melted back into the wall, like a man sinking deep in a dark pool of water. The hands cupped around Drone, growing larger to cover the struggling automaton. The hands pulled back into the earthen wall as well, dragging Drone down with them into an abyss of solid earth.

After the wall swallowed Drone's spotlight, Tareah was blind until she grew accustomed to a dim glow. She felt sick. The worm-men stirred.

"Vailret!" she called.

"I'm here," he gasped. He sounded hurt.

She saw Bryl scrambling across the grotto floor, looking for the scattered Stones. He held the Air Stone in one hand and, as she watched, he grabbed the brilliant emerald Earth Stone.

"Bryl! I have the Water Stone," she said.

"Yes, for the Allspirit!" he answered, wheezing. He crawled about, searching for the Fire Stone.

Tareah moved toward him. The werem hissed, and she saw them rising up. Scores of them lay dead and squashed, oozing a thick, mudlike blood. Their broken segments and severed bodies continued to squirm in opposite directions.

With a *smack*, the far wall split open and Drone came flying out, stumbling backward, as if the jaws of the earth had spat out their morsel. Both eye-windows gaped, shattered, and she could dimly see Frankenstein moving sluggishly inside, as if injured. He tried to regain control of his machine. The spotlight danced around like a glowing whip on the grotto walls, and then it flickered and went out.

Drone whirled out of control. One leg didn't move and, as it tried to take too many steps forward, the automaton tottered, staggered, and then tipped over. Professor Frankenstein used the metal arms to try and stabilize it, but Drone toppled like a prodigious tree.

The automaton crashed into one of the thick support pillars. Dirt and chunks of cement-hard rock tumbled down. The ceiling groaned and split as a great fissure opened up.

Bryl cried out, sprawling toward the gleaming Fire Stone he had found among the debris on the floor. Drone had kicked it out of the way. "I've found the last one!" He scurried across the floor.

Frankenstein crawled out of Drone's smashed left eye-window, heaving himself out and looking dazed. Blood smeared his forehead, and he staggered down, picking his way along the metal chest and shoulders of his automaton. He stared up at the behemoth he had built, now smashed and battered beyond all hope of repair. He blinked in shock and sorrow.

Bryl's hand closed around the ruby Fire Stone. He sat up. His face gleamed in a rictus of triumph. "We have won!"

"Look out!" Vailret croaked.

Then an entire section of ceiling broke free and crushed down on top of Bryl.

27

ALLSPIRIT

*"Never bring all four Stones together unless
you are prepared for what will happen. It's like
magical synergy. More power resides in the combined Stones than even the six Spirits possess
... The Transition was an awesome enough
thing to do once in the Game."*
—the Sentinel Arken

Delrael watched the manticore die in the cannon
explosion.

He saw the havoc caused by the old Sorcerer troops
as they slaughtered the monster army.

"All fighters, get ready!" he shouted to his own
troops. "We're going to march out and end this. Siryyk
is dead. The monsters are on the run. We will win this
Game!"

His army cheered and raised their weapons, eager
to attack. But as soon as his army stood lined up and
ready to charge, Delrael realized he didn't know how
to lower the ice wall.

Instead, one by one, the fighters had to push through
the low doorways Enrod had left in the wall. A constant stream spilled outside of the ice walls, waiting
and regrouping.

Inside the fortress, Siya blinked her eyes, still groggy.
She looked completely exhausted, burned out from
the inside. But she managed a thin smile. "Was I
brave, Delrael?" she asked in a small voice.

"You were stupid!" Delrael said, but the harshness in his voice did not sound genuine.

"I was brave," Siya said and nodded. "That's enough for now, I think. But you don't have an excuse, Delrael. Go lead your army!"

When he passed under the low frozen arch, Delrael saw that most of his army had already gathered together and charged forward with no plan, just a frenzy of attack. Delrael drew his own sword and moved after them in disgust. "Thanks for waiting," he muttered.

He'd never had trouble managing his companions on a simple quest. They had all acted as a team with the same goal, each knowing his own responsibilities. But he did not think of himself as a domineering commander, and this army was too much for Delrael to hold under rigid control.

These characters had come to the Stronghold to meet and gain some training before they went off to face their common foe. They had been fidgeting inside the ice walls for days, with their enemy in sight. They had been stirred by the duels of Arken and Rognoth against Siryyk, even by Siya's bravery. Now they had no patience for waiting or listening to Delrael.

But they were going to win the battle anyway.

He saw that the monster army already appeared to be backing away, leaving behind the manticore's bloody carcass and the ruins of the giant cannon. The remaining old Sorcerers followed, leaving chopped enemy corpses in their wake.

Then Delrael noticed the empty steam-engine car chugging directly toward his army. He recognized it as a Sitnaltan vehicle.

Finally, something else made sense to him. He thought of the manticore's cannon and how improbable it had seemed that the monsters could have developed such an incredible weapon. He wondered with a shudder if Siryyk had somehow captured one of the Sitnaltan professors.

What if the monsters were even now retreating from some new weapon, something planted in the steam-engine car that would cause even more destruction? Why else would they be running away?

Most of Delrael's army veered to the left to engage the surviving monsters. Delrael planted his feet and waited for the steam-engine car to approach. It frightened him; the vehicle did not belong here. The monsters would not have given up such a prize so easily.

Someone had sent it on a mission.

He could see no driver. The steering levers had been tied down. A polished cylinder sat upright on the front seat, and a bloody human hand was draped over the back, trying to reach the device.

Delrael sprinted to meet the oncoming vehicle. He heard its chugging grow louder as the shouts from his army, the clash of weapons, and the roars of monsters echoed across the cold, still sky.

Far ahead, Delrael saw Ydaim Trailwalker and Tayron Tribeleader loping faster than any of the other fighters toward the front line of creatures. A tall Slac general stood directing the troops and trying to exert control.

Both Tayron and Ydaim attacked the Slac general at the same time, swinging down with their wooden swords, putting all the strength of their broad shoulders behind the blow. Delrael could see the muscles rippling in their backs. They reared up and raked sideways with their curved panther claws. The Slac general tumbled backward and flailed in his own defense, but the two khelebar struck him down.

Delrael tensed as the Sitnaltan car reached him. He dropped his sword in the snow, freeing his hands. He would not need the blade now, but his dexterity and his mind. Somehow, he would have to understand and outwit a Sitnaltan invention.

His boots kicked up wet, blood-spattered snow from the retreating monsters. He ran and grabbed the battered red vehicle, letting his feet skip on the ground.

Delrael dragged himself into the moving car, knocked the cylindrical device aside to make room for himself, and turned to the back seat. He looked with sick astonishment at the gaunt figure lying bloody in the back.

He barely recognized Professor Verne. The man appeared too thin and haggard, with great bags under his eyes, his bushy gray beard torn and unkempt. Blood soaked his torn shirt, and drying red spots stained his hands. With his last gasps of life, he must have tried to haul himself over the seat toward the device.

A ticking sound came from it. Whatever this weapon was, it seemed far more sinister than the cannon.

"Professor, can you hear me? Speak to me!"

Delrael reached over the seat and tried to haul him erect, but Verne's body felt stiff and cold. His jaws hung together by dead muscles. Delrael let the professor fall back.

He looked up and saw the car chugging straight for the wall of the ice fortress. He remembered how Mayer had pulled and yanked at the levers to steer her car. Delrael unlashed the ropes that someone had tied around the levers.

He pulled at one, and the car lurched to the side, veering away from the ice fortress. When he pushed another, the steam increased and the vehicle picked up speed. Delrael needed to get away from his troops and the fortress if he couldn't somehow learn what to do with this weapon of Verne's.

The steam-engine car ground past the ice-fortress walls, spinning deep ruts into the snow and ice, bouncing on barely covered rocks beneath the frozen desolation. They sped onward.

Verne had been trying to do something to the Sitnaltan device when he died. Delrael looked at the invention, but it made no sense to him: a cylinder of bright metal with red fins sticking out from the side; a trembling gauge indicating some quantity, its needle approaching a red area on the dial. On the back he found scrawled numbers, "17/2," but these meant nothing to him.

Then he located where the ticking came from—a large knob with painted numbers that descended toward a red line marked on the device. Smears of blood ran down the metal, long fat fingerprints like the trails of infernal slugs. Verne had been trying to do something to this knob.

Delrael didn't know what the knob did; he didn't know what the entire device did. But some intuition—based on what little he remembered from Sitnalta and the gadgets Mayer had explained—told him that this knob had something to do with activating the device.

If so, then the numbers on the side showed exactly how to stop it. He gripped the knob with both hands, using all his strength to turn it clockwise toward zero; then it would be shut off.

The clicking increased to a rapid rattle, and the red line moved quickly around.

Verne must have been clawing at the tight knob to do the same thing. Dying, the professor would never have been able to do it for himself.

Delrael twisted with his wrist. The zero approached, and he pushed harder. He would shut it off in just a moment.

Then his eyes flicked down, and he saw the curved smear of blood on the side of the knob. He stopped Now it seemed clear that Verne had been trying to rotate the knob the *other* way.

Delrael squeezed the knob with all his fingers to arrest its motion. The clicking slowed, but continued as the slippery knob kept turning.

He turned the knob the other way, but it seemed locked, able to progress in only one direction. He bashed at it with his fist. Finally, he jerked the dagger from his belt and used the blade to pry off the knob. The tip of the blade snapped, but the knob turned inside the device, and the clicking continued.

Delrael sagged back in the seat in despair. "Now what am I supposed to do?"

Tareah scrambled among the broken chunks of rock and earth. Dust and pebbles were still raining down, but she had reached the pile of debris that covered Bryl. She could see only deep shadows and jagged edges. The werem writhed in confusion; many had vanished into other catacombs.

"Bryl!" Tareah called. "Bryl!"

Vailret scrambled up to her and helped pull the rocks aside. Bryl had been kneeling there just a moment ago. "It's not fair! Not now—we're too close to the end," he said. Dirt and terror were smeared across his face.

With a grunt, he and Tareah rolled a large boulder away. She saw Bryl's bloodied hand looking pale and fragile. "There he is!" Tareah said. She worked harder. Vailret reached down to grasp the half-Sorcerer's hand and wrist. The thin fingers clenched in a weak but desperate response.

"Hurry!" Vailret said.

Together they uncovered most of Bryl's body. The avalanche had crushed and broken him. Blood streamed out of his mouth, but somehow his head had escaped severe injury. The rock fragments had smashed his rib cage as well as his legs. One arm was pulverized.

Bryl would not live much longer. His eyes were glazed and squeezed shut in pain, but he gasped out a single word, forming it around a scarlet bubble of blood. "Stones!" he said.

In his intact hand he still held the three Stones. Tareah knelt beside him, holding her Water Stone.

"Isn't he too weak to become the Allspirit?" Vailret said. "There's nothing we can do."

"He's still alive," Tareah said. "He could summon the magic. But you're right—he is too weak."

She stared down at the frail form of the old half-Sorcerer. Enrod's disjointed words came back to her. "Not even a pure Sorcerer. What kind of Allspirit would he make? Tainted! Tainted!"

Sardun had always insisted that Tareah represented a great hope for the future, because she, as the last of the old Sorcerer race, would undertake some important mission.

She saw very clearly what she would have to do, how she could serve the destiny that her father had claimed for her.

"I'll have to go with him. We can be the Allspirit together." She looked down at the dying half-Sorcerer. "My knowledge combined with his experience, my enthusiasm and fascination with his age and understanding of power."

Vailret looked at her in horror. "Are you crazy, Tareah? You have to stay here, stay here with me!"

Tareah felt a longing in her heart when she looked at him. It was the first time he had said something like that to her. She understood her attraction now; Delrael was the man she most admired, but Vailret the one to whom she felt the closest kinship.

Even so, she felt the greater calling of her Sorcerer blood.

Tareah had worked so hard to fit in with the human characters, playing her role but never feeling comfortable with it. She had spent three decades isolated, immersing herself in the study of the history of the Game, of the Rules, and of what characters must do. She had admired them all, studied the legends in an academic fashion, but now the choice weighed directly upon her.

She had to decide between remaining with Vailret,

which she would enjoy greatly, or taking on this responsibility as a Sorcerer. Her decision was as consequential as the old Sorcerers' choice to take the Transition in the first place.

"No," Tareah said. "This is what I need to do, and you know it as well as I do."

Vailret stared at her with his eyes wide, terribly hurt at seeing his friend Bryl near death and knowing that she was about to depart as well. He moved his lips several times, but could say nothing. Tareah turned away from him; she couldn't face any doubts.

She took out her Water Stone and bent down to lift the three Stones from Bryl's bloody hand. She took his slick hand in her own. He lay shuddering and dying, with only a moment left.

"We'll go together, Bryl."

She held the gems in her hand, feeling their heat, feeling their magic blinding her from the inside. Still grasping Bryl's wrist, she rolled all four Stones.

Vailret stumbled backward, shielding his eyes as light greater than an exploding star crackled out of the gems, white, blue, red, and green, soaring up to engulf both Tareah and Bryl, settling around them like incandescent snowflakes. Vailret couldn't tell exactly at what point he stopped seeing Tareah at all, when she and Bryl became indistinguishable from the glare. The pinpoints of sorcery spread and grew and swelled into a blaze unrivaled since the Transition.

The remaining worm-men, with their thin gray skin unaccustomed to any sort of light, shriveled backward as their bodies blackened. Those that did not die instantly fled deep into the earthen walls.

Vailret turned away from the brilliance, feeling a devastating sense of loss. He realized that he and Bryl had gone on their long quest for the sole purpose of bringing this about. But as he stared at the inferno of magic, he knew that Bryl was now as dead to him as if he had simply bled out his life on the grotto floor; and this way, Vailret lost Tareah as well.

But if this act had gained a future for Gamearth and all its characters, a future for them to forge their own lives without the Outsiders, then perhaps, in a way that his mind understood but his heart did not, the sacrifice was justified.

When he looked up again, blinking colored spots from his eyes, the titanic Allspirit filled the grotto.

The Allspirit towered gray-white and hooded, bearing no resemblance whatever to Bryl or Tareah. Its features were hidden: the cloak seemed merely a metaphor, a symbolic boundary that defined the limits of its tangible existence. The form stood so immense that it seemed to fold in upon itself to fit within the walls, like infinity wrapped in a shroud.

Vailret couldn't speak or move. He held his breath.

The Allspirit stretched out its silently flapping sleeves. It paid no attention to Vailret or to anything else in the ruins of the chamber.

Frankenstein peeped up over the edge of Drone and stared.

Vailret did not dare to make any noise. The Allspirit grew brighter with a wind of power, energy draining through the fabric of the map and into the Allspirit's body. Vailret wondered if it had drained the *dayid* from Rokanun . . . or even the other *dayids* as well. It seemed to reel with its own new power.

"NOW WE ARE MASTERS OF THE GAME." The sexless voice boomed out from the cavernous hollow in the hood. More stones and dust pattered down from the broken ceiling.

Vailret felt a surge of enthusiasm, then a chill as he realized that the Allspirit's "we" did not mean the characters on Gamearth, but only the plural identity of what had been Tareah and Bryl.

"LET US PLAY WITH NEW CHARACTERS."

With a wave of the flapping empty sleeves, another part of the wall cracked. But it wasn't so much a crack as a dark seam opening to somewhere else. More wind came out, this time with a silent roar that Vailret could neither hear nor feel, but which buffeted him backward nevertheless.

Streaming out from other parts of the map, other parts of the universe perhaps, came the original six Spirits, three white and three black. Vailret remembered seeing the Earthspirits as they emerged, immense and awesome from Delrael's silver belt on the threshold of Scartaris. He remembered the black Deathspirits, who had cursed Enrod, rising up from the broken hex-line, also to destroy Scartaris.

Now, though, the Earthspirits and Deathspirits appeared much diminished. Colossal as they had been before, they now looked weaker, even insubstantial in front of the dominating Allspirit. The Deathspirits and the Earthspirits remained silent, as if cowering.

Beside Vailret, Frankenstein stumbled over the motionless wreckage of Drone and stood gaping, his eyes bulging, at the Spirits.

"This is impossible! This is astonishing," he mumbled to himself. Vailret glared at him.

The Allspirit spoke to the six other hooded forms. "NOW WE CAN PLAY. NOW WE CAN HAVE FUN."

The air sang with power. The Earthspirits and Deathspirits flickered and struggled, but eventually buckled, crouching down in a symbolic bow to the Allspirit.

Vailret finally closed his eyes because he could not take in the immensity of the spectral shapes. The Allspirit's words sounded nothing like either Bryl's or Tareah's. The thoughts could not be theirs, but some sort of manifestation of the power in the Stones themselves, some reflection of the old Sorcerers who had created them, and who, dissatisfied with being manipulated by the Outsiders, had taken the extreme step of the Transition in an effort to escape.

"Tareah, listen to me!" Vailret shouted. His voice sounded like a ridiculous squeak. He kept his eyes squeezed shut, expecting to be wiped out of existence in a moment. The invisible weight of the Allspirit's attention felt like a building collapsing across his back.

Vailret had nothing to lose. If the Allspirit didn't do what the characters needed it to do, then Gamearth was doomed, whether at the hands of the Outsiders or of the Allspirit itself.

"Remember why you're here! Tareah and Bryl, remember why you gave your lives to create this! You must save Gamearth."

"WE WILL DO WHAT WE WISH TO DO."

The scorn in the Allspirit's voice made Vailret want to wither and throw himself over a cliff. But he shouted his next words through a raw throat, battering back his own emotions. They had to remember. Vailret had to make them see.

"Bryl, listen to me! Remember when you linked with the *dayid* to stop the forest fire in Ledaygen. You felt the power then, you know how dangerous it could be.

"Tareah, remember how Scartaris destroyed the Stronghold while you fought to save it. Remember how the power corrupted Enrod and made him want to use the Fire Stone for destruction!"

The Allspirit remained unmoved. Vailret continued to speak as fast as the words could tumble from his mouth.

"You knew this might happen! Think of the duel of Entarr and Dythat, when two rival Sorcerers unleashed forces that swallowed both characters up! You know all these legends, Tareah! Remember the wedding celebration of Lord Armund and Lady Maire, and the disputed stone throw that sparked centuries of war?

"Bryl, think about how your parents were too weak

to bear the accusations against them, so they used the magic to destroy themselves. Remember it! The power that's working through you now is not a part of you. You can't let it control you—it has to be the other way around! *You* control the power."

The six Spirits remained silent, but the Allspirit spoke. This time the genderless echoing voice carried hints and undertones of Tareah or Bryl. "WE CANNOT FORGET. WE REMEMBER."

Vailret realized he had a new tactic. "Then remember how you took on this quest, to gather all four Stones together to become the Allspirit. The object of that quest was for you to hold Gamearth together by taking it away from the Outsiders. *That* was your quest—remember Rule #2! 'Once characters undertake a quest, *they must see it through to completion!*' "

He stood tall and opened his eyes again. "To complete your quest, you must save Gamearth. You're still bound by the Rules."

"THE RULES ARE BREAKING," the Allspirit said. But despite the power behind the words, they seemed to lack conviction.

Vailret replied, "Your true opponents are the Outsiders. You saw the clay face of the Outsider David. You know about the Rulewoman Melanie, and the Outsiders Scott and Tyrone. You must confront them."

He let an excited smile flicker across his face, then lowered his voice. "If you play with us to exercise your power, you won't have much of a challenge. But if you confront a *real* opponent, imagine how much more fun it will be." Vailret paused for just a moment, then shouted, "Remember Rule #1! 'Always have fun!' "

The Allspirit shimmered. "Yes, Vailret. We remember." The voices were more subdued now, a clear duet of Bryl and Tareah. "Our focus lies Outside."

The Allspirit expanded and drew out its great cloaked form, as if unfolding from other dimensions. The smaller

Earthspirits and Deathspirits rose up as well; they all seemed to know what to do. The three black Deathspirits, the three white Earthspirits, and the single gray, overarching Allspirit broke down the boundaries between themselves, coalescing into one omnipotent being incalculably more powerful than any of the individual Spirits.

It was a kind of super-Transition that made the initial one seem like a half-hearted opening move.

Neither the grotto, nor the hexagon, nor the entire map of Gamearth could contain such a Spirit. Vailret fell to his knees, blinking and stunned as the being rose—and kept rising, streaming upward, pulling with it all the magic and all the knowledge that it had gathered from Gamearth.

Then it plunged outward into *reality*, leaving only silence roaring in its wake.

"Great Maxwell!" Frankenstein said.

Epilogue

GAME'S END

David felt pain exploding inside his head, in fact his whole body. Parts of him, characters that lived within him, were being murdered one by one. He tried to cry out but couldn't. His cheekbones felt as if they had been crushed like eggshells.

Tyrone's blood-soaked corpse lay wide-eyed and mangled on the living room carpet, growing cold.

Melanie kept screaming down at the map.

Scott appeared broken, as if he had not the slightest idea what to do and couldn't understand how it had happened this way.

David forced his eyes open through a red haze of pain.

With a crackling sound, the Allspirit streamed up out of the painted wooden map like some specter rising from a fire. The gray form spilled out of the hexagons, growing larger and larger until it towered to the ceiling.

David scrambled backward. Melanie gaped at it. Scott closed his eyes and shook his head.

The Allspirit surveyed them with its cavernous hood. The air sizzled with its buildup of power. "Your Game is over now," it said. The words echoed around the walls of the house. The wind outside seemed to have stopped. "We will take Gamearth away from you. We want nothing more to do with the Outside."

"And we want nothing more to do with you!" David shouted. His words snapped in his swollen throat.

Beneath the Allspirit, the map shimmered. The spidery black hexagon lines flowed like molten oil.

The Allspirit drew back, engulfing the map in its translucent form. The hexagons of Gamearth splintered and expanded, flying apart like pieces in a puzzle. Brilliant points of light spun like a galaxy around the form of the Allspirit. Even the tiny broken pieces by the fireplace lifted up and swirled into the cluster.

The Allspirit grew taller. "I leave only what is yours," it said, then vanished with an audible *pop*. A few remaining bright hexagons flashed once, then winked out.

Only the Sitnaltan weapon remained behind, canted on the living room carpet, as its timer ticked the last two seconds to detonation.

"Well, Overlord Migan, this is most enjoyable. Shall we let the weapon detonate?"

Comtar Durat stared down at the maps spread before him, the detailed sketches of the characters' houses, the careful drawing of the living room. Next to them rested crystalline chits showing statistics for the characters David, Melanie, and Scott; the chit for Tyrone had been removed from play.

Overlord Migan picked up the dice scattered on the playing surface. "I think we should roll for it."

He tossed the dice.

About the Author
Kevin J. Anderson

RULE #6. Authors born in Wisconsin and transplanted to California to work as technical writers for research laboratories must have eclectic interests, such as astronomy, Russian history, hiking, and brewing beer.

RULE #7. Readers who enjoy the Gamearth trilogy may also be interested in *Resurrection, Inc.* by the same author.

RULE #12. Authors who set out to write a quest/adventure fantasy trilogy should make every attempt to add new twists to the genre, while following the established form.

RULE #14. The three books in a trilogy should be considered a unit, plotted together, with the second and third volumes building upon the preceding story. This is much more effective than one novel and two sequels added as an afterthought.

RULE #15. Every RULE must be mentioned somewhere in the trilogy, even if only in the "About the Author" note at the end of the last volume. Otherwise readers will think you are holding out for a sequel.

RULE #16. There is no Rule #16.

RULE #17. The author, like the characters in his books, is himself bound by Rule #1.

RULE #1. Always have fun!

—from *The Book of Rules* (author's copy)